PRAISE FOR MONARCH SASSAFRAS 1

"Ever clear is the narrator in this wonderfully written debut novel by Lillah Lawson. You get swept up almost instantly by the sweet Southern charm of its characters and it gently nudges you forward. The movement and flow of the book feel very organic. It's not every day you get to peer into the intricate, complicated, and deep set bonds between family and friendship. Lawson poured her heart, soul, and lived experiences into this novel and it shows in the multifaceted and fully developed characters she created."

-Pascale Lemire, NYT Bestselling author of *Dogshaming*

"Lillah Lawson spins a yarn that's wonderful in its knottiness. *Monarchs Under the Sassafras Tree* is a historical Southern fable about butterflies, biscuits and the healing power of family, both biological and chosen. The images are evocative, the dialogue rough and realistic, the emotions achingly real. A must-read."

– Lauren Emily Whalen, author of *Satellite*

"A hauntingly beautiful story, full of twists and tragedy, rich in detail and told with gorgeous lyrical flair… A deeply moving, unforgettable read."

– Alice Hayes, author of *The Thread that Binds*

"An exquisite read, with the tender yet gritty undertones of Steinback, *Monarchs Under the Sassafras Tree* is a solemn walk through the deep south during one of the most difficult eras in American history: the early twentieth century. Lawson captures the southern gothic through the often fragile, yet always hopeful hearts of her characters as they try to cope with the hard knocks of life. This book will touch your heart in the beautifully tragic way that only southern gothic can, slowly at first, and then all at once."

-Melanie Cossey, author of *A Peculiar Curiosity*

Monarchs Under the Sassafras Tree

Lillah Lawson

Regal House Publishing

Published by
Regal House Publishing, LLC
Raleigh, NC 27612
All rights reserved

ISBN -13 (paperback): 9781947548282
ISBN -13 (epub): 9781947548299
ISBN -13 (mobi): 9781947548893
Library of Congress Control Number: 2019931667

Interior and cover design by Lafayette & Greene
lafayetteandgreene.com
Cover images © by Milosz_G/Shutterstock

Regal House Publishing, LLC
https://regalhousepublishing.com

"Fall On Me". Words and Music by William Berry, Peter Buck, Michael Mills and Michael Stipe Copyright (c) 1986 NIGHT GARDEN MUSIC All Rights Controlled and Administered by SONGS OF UNIVERSAL, INC. All Rights Reserved. Reprinted with Permission of Hal Leonard LLC

"Malt Liquor." Written by Claire Campbell of the band Hope For Agoldensummer (adapted from a letter by Ben Roth) Reprinted with permission.

Author photography by Caitlin E. Photography

Printed in the United States of America by McNaughton & Gunn

To Robbie (1976-2016),
our own "singing cook."
We miss you.

and

To Julia Ann (1940-2019),
my biggest cheerleader and critic, confidant, teacher,
and inspiration, but most importantly: my Grandma.
This book is for you.

PART 1

And if you sit here long enough,
on this root under this tree,
I swear, I will sneak up right beside you,
Unlock your heart and set you free.

-Hope For Agoldensummer

CHAPTER ONE

August, 1916
Five Forks, Georgia

Two monarch butterflies were dancing on the mid-afternoon breeze as O.T. Lawrence and his brother, Walt, sweated in the field. One butterfly was orange, the other blue. O.T. paid them no mind, but Walt stood up from his work for a minute, watching the two insects air-dance, a blade of grass jutting from between his lips. He chewed on blades of grass pretty much round the clock, especially when he felt a nervous spell coming on or if he was concentrating hard. He stared at the butterflies so long that finally O.T. stopped too, leaning on his hoe, looking at his brother with exasperation.

"If'n you don't hop to it, we ain't gon' be done in time for the tent revival," he reminded Walt, but his tone was gentle. "What you lookin' at, anyhow?"

"Them butterflies," Walt replied. "One of 'em is orange, and one blue. Ain't that something?"

"Not partic-ly." O.T. went back to his work. The ground was harder than it should have been this time of year. The drought had just about ruined the dirt—it had no nutrients, no moisture. How anything could grow in it was beyond him. What else could they do, though? Cotton farmers was what they *were*, and planting seed was what folks *did*. He wished Walt would just hop to it. O.T. was itching to get done, to get in the house for a bath, and to spruce up before the revival tonight. Betty Lou Pittman was going to be there. At this rate, by the time they got in the house the water in the wash tub would be ice cold. *He* wasn't studying on butterflies.

"It is, though," Walt insisted, still chewing on the blade of grass. He reminded O.T. of a calf chewing its cud. His mouth worked side to side, the blade of grass now a lime-green pulp. "You rarely see the two together. Orange and blue, I mean."

"They's both monarchs, ain't they?"

"Yeah, but the two colors don't usually mix comp'ny."

"Like people, I reckon," O.T. said, with a smirk.

"What you mean?" Walt asked, the joke sailing past him.

"Nothin'. Last I checked, you wadn't no butterfly expert." O.T. enjoyed teasing his brother, though Lord knew why, because most of the time Walt didn't even know when he was being teased. He just carried on in that far-off voice about whatever it was that had struck his fancy. Once he got on his prattling, there was no use in trying to pick at him or get a word in edgeways. If O.T. didn't respond, though, let Walt know he was listening, Walt'd get upset, and it was hard to bring him back down once he got that way. Because Walt was the sweetest, kindest boy you ever did meet, hurting Walt's feelings was like kicking a puppy dog—cruel. Walt was *smart*, O.T. knew; probably smarter than anybody O.T.'d ever met, but he was "off with the faeries," as their older sister, Hazel, always said. Hazel's husband, Tom, was less kind. "He's teched," he'd say with a smug smirk. Well, maybe Walt was touched, O.T. thought, but who cared, anyhow?

"No expert, naw," Walt replied, finally looking down at his hoe, as if considering it. He took things quite literally. "But I like t'observe things."

"Observe that cotton patch, then," O.T. barked. "I'd like to get finished 'fore next year, if'n you please." O.T. didn't want to look at the butterflies anyhow; they brought him bad feelings, dumb as that seemed.

Walt went back to work, and O.T. breathed a sigh of relief. Any other time he'd be glad to chew the fat with Walt about any old thing he wanted, because he loved his brother and indulged him, but not today. O.T. was positively twitterpated today. Everybody in Five Forks had been looking forward to the tent revival, and the fish fry afterward at Misrus Maybelle's, for a solid month. That would have been enough for O.T.—just the possibility of getting out of the house for an evening, out from under Hazel's stern, watchful eye—but adding to his excitement was the fact that Betty Lou was going to be there.

Betty Lou Pittman was O.T.'s sweetheart, but she didn't know it yet. O.T.'d decided he was just about ready to start courting her, if she'd have him. There was no other girl in all of Five Forks that he liked so well as Betty Lou. He wasn't really good enough for her;

he knew it, her parents knew it, but he sure hoped Betty Lou didn't know it. O.T. figured he had just enough charm and good looks to coast on, maybe. *If I could get into a not-cold washtub and scrub my behind, that is.*

O.T. was itching to get out from his sister and Tom's house and make it on his own. He wanted nothing more than to be a man, have a house and family to call his own. And Betty Lou was just as pretty as a speckled pup under a red wagon, as the old timers used to say. With her light blonde, almost white hair—he'd heard her pa affectionately call her "cotton top" while patting her on her delicate head, and he'd been jealous as hell—and cool blue eyes, she made his heart skip a beat. She always smelled like talcum powder and roses, and her sack dresses were the cleanest and best pressed in the county. Yeah, he reckoned he was in love with Betty Lou Pittman.

Walt, who often read his brother's thoughts, interrupted O.T.'s reverie. "You gonna borrow some of Tom's pomade tonight, you reckon? Did you ask Hazel to press yer good shirt? 'Cause y'know Betty Lou is going to be there." Walt stabbed his hoe into the ground and dragged it over the roots, cutting his eyes at O.T. in a mock-flirtatious fashion. Walt wasn't much for teasing, but it was different with O.T. Not only would Walt look his brother directly in the eye, but he'd mock him while doing it.

O.T. pretended not to notice. "Yeah, reckon she'll be there. Don't go giving me hell about it, neither."

"I ain't," Walt said, still cutting his eyes at his brother. They had the same wide-set, light-gray eyes, and both were lean and wiry, just like their daddy had been. Walt and O.T. were identical twins, the only ones in Five Forks, or anywhere nearby, far as they knew. A birthmark below O.T.'s right ear was the only feature that distinguished them, and nobody had ever noticed that but Ma. They had the same dark-blond hair, fine and shaggy, which Walt wore in an unruly mop, with cowlicks and a mess of tangles down about his ears. O.T.—who was nothing if not in tune with his future lady's tastes—would neatly slick his hair back with pomade when he could get it. Their hair was how most folks told them apart. "I just got to figuring you gon' marry that girl and leave us. You gon' leave me, brother?"

Walt's voice was teasing, but O.T. could hear the worry in it. Walt wouldn't do well alone with Tom and Hazel. Tom was rough as a cob, didn't like boys to be soft, and was not inclined to spare the rod, not on the boys, and not on their sister, either.

"If'n me and Hazel ever have a son," Tom liked to boast to Walt and O.T. at the dinner table, "he wouldn't be soft. No sirree. You boys is raised soft as an ol' egg."

Every time Hazel's husband took a switch to Walt's tender skin—which was often, since Walt just couldn't help acting so funny—O.T. would dig his fingernails into his hands to keep from crying himself. Walt didn't like to be touched anyhow, but Tom had to go and *hurt* him.

"Don't worry 'bout that," O.T. said, gesturing at Walt to keep digging. "Anywhere I go, you go too. If'n you want to, that is."

"Really? You mean it? You'd let me live with you and yer ol' lady?"

"Why, sure."

"Even if'n you all have a bunch of young'uns?"

"'Specially then. You can watch after 'em while me and the missus go drink Co-Colas in town."

Walt didn't laugh. "I can really stay with y'all?"

"Accorse. Yer my twin brother, dummy. I ain't leaving you." O.T. grinned. "Unless you keep slacking on yer work, that is. Jee-ma-nee, Walt, could you hop to it?" O.T. could see Walt's relieved grin out of the corner of his eye, as he resumed his digging. "Anyhow, I figger you might up and leave *me* soon."

"How you figger that?" Walt asked, perplexed.

"I hear'd that there's a right purdy girl traveling with the tent revival. You remember that preacher man, that guy they call Billy Rev?"

"Yeah, I 'member. Tall man, real skinny. Like a string bean. Wears white suits and a big ol' hat, bigger'n his head," Walt replied. "What about 'im?"

"This year he's got a new apprentice, a gal. His niece, I heard tell. They say she's right purdy. And our age."

Walt shrugged. "What's that got to do with me?"

"Nothing atall, I don't reckon. Since you're too fool to go and talk to her."

"I ain't."

"You are."

"You calling me yaller?"

"Reckon so."

"I ain't."

"Prove it, then," O.T. said. "You go on up to her tonight, introduce yerself. Bet you cain't."

"I'll go right on up and say how-do," Walt said, still chewing. "That'll fix yer waggin'."

"Yep, that'll fix me but good," O.T. said, turning his head to hide his smile.

The two butterflies were still flitting over their heads, orange and blue, light and dark. As the midday sun crept through the sky toward dusk, one twin dug his hoe into the unforgiving soil, while the other chewed a fresh blade of grass, turning his lips green.

Walt pushed his hair down nervously, licking at his green-tinged mouth. "Hand me that comb," he said to O.T., holding out his hand. "I'm going to go get some water from the kitchen and wet it down good. It won't stay for nothin'."

"If you'd get you a proper haircut and comb that rat's nest from time to time," O.T. said with a grin, "you wouldn't be havin' this problem."

"You just hush, brother," Walt replied, with a nervous smile. "I don't like haircuts. You knowed that."

"What's so skeery about a haircut, anyhow?" O.T. asked, tucking in his good shirt and buckling his brown belt. The right leg of his best pants was mud-stained, and nothing he or Hazel might do now could get it out. O.T. was mightily embarrassed about it. "Hazel's good at cuttin' hair. She ain't never nicked my ears, not once. Not like that fool barber."

One of O.T.'s earliest memories was of Ma, having saved her pennies, taking him and Walt for their first *real* haircuts in town. The barber had onion breath, rusty scissors, and no patience for Walt's nervous squirming. He'd shoved a towel around Walt's neck and started anyway. The end result had been a chopped-up mess and a bleeding ear. Walt hadn't let a barber near his head since.

"I just don't like 'em." Walt disappeared into the kitchen with the comb. O.T. wished he'd hurry up; he needed to use the comb himself. He'd managed to filch himself a dab of Tom's pomade without him noticing, and he wanted to slick back his own hair just before they left for Misrus Maybelle's. He was itching to go. Hazel and Tom wouldn't appear till sometime later, after supper, but most of the young folks went down early to help set up. He knew his friends were already there, and Betty Lou and her sisters were likely to show up before long. Unless they came down with their ma and daddy in the motorcar, which was possible. Betty Lou's daddy loved to be seen with his family in the motorcar, a black '16 Model T Touring with high-back seats, the only one of its kind anybody had ever seen in these parts. He'd bought it right off the lot, people said. The Pittmans all looked pretty as pictures, sitting up in the thing, just as nice as you please. Betty Lou's pa, Mr. Pittman, was what Hazel called "right hoity toity." He owned a whole bunch of land all over Madison County, farming a few acres himself and sharecropping the rest. He'd even hired workers. Mr. Pittman had made Hazel and Tom several offers on their property—willed to Hazel when their parents had died—but so far she'd held out. O.T. didn't hate Mr. Pittman like his sister did, though. He figured that if he were a successful businessman with a comely, respectable wife and a bunch of pretty white-headed daughters, he'd put on an air or two himself. And he was mighty jealous of that car. O.T. aimed to buy an even better one for Betty Lou one day, after she was his bride.

"Bring that dang comb back here, would ya?"

"Keep yer hat on," Walt said, returning to the bedroom the two of them shared. The light was dim, and without a mirror they had to rely on each other. Walt looked his brother up and down, still chewing his blade of grass. "You got a mud stain on yer good britches there," he pointed out.

"Yeah, I knowed that, dummy," O.T. scowled. If Walt had noticed the stain, as off with the faeries as he was, Betty Lou was sure to notice, too. "And *you* got a big green stain on yer face. Oh wait, that's yer dang mouth."

"I think I got my hair to lay down some," Walt said, shoving his hands in and out of his pants pockets. "Does it look like yers, brother?"

8

"Purdy much," O.T. answered, glancing at Walt distractedly. His twin looked as presentable as he had in a long spell—probably since Ma's funeral five years before. Both brothers had dressed in their very best that morning; Hazel made sure of it. That might have been the last time, before tonight, that they'd looked downright identical.

O.T. didn't want to get to thinking about Ma. It led to other thoughts—Pa falling down the well and dying in pain; Ma losing the baby she'd been carrying; Hazel leaving off with Tom—"I don't like a daughter of mine to git married at fourteen," Ma had said, her eyes red-rimmed, "but the Good Lord knows Tom can afford to feed ya better than I can." Not to mention the drought and the boll weevil working in cahoots to destroy their cotton crop. Despite it all, Ma had tried to hold the farm and the house together on her own for the boys' sake, often going without meals so they could stay fed; but the pellagra claimed her in the end, after three years of fighting, just like it did everyone else.

Then, suddenly, the boys were thirteen and she was gone. O.T. didn't know if his ma had let herself starve and sicken from grief or from martyrdom. Maybe both. But he'd never forget the look of her—the odd, almost beautiful butterfly-shaped rash that had appeared on her cheeks and the bridge of her nose when she'd first taken ill. It would come and go every few months, redder and redder on her sunken cheeks as she was dying. The telltale sign of pellagra, the butterfly rash. He hoped never to see it on another body again.

"O.T," Walt's reedy voice shook him from his thoughts. "I said is you ready to go, brother?"

"Yeah, yeah," O.T. said, wishing he had the use of a mirror and that he and his brother didn't have on the exact same white shirt and dark slacks. "Does it look okay?"

"You look right handsome," Walt said, with a smile. "Like you on the way to Bible Study."

O.T. groaned. "Don't say that." The last thing he wanted was to look like some daggum preacher boy in front of Betty Lou. He would rather look older, handsome, a little bit dangerous. He knew that was the kind of boys teenage girls liked. He'd seen Betty Lou cutting her eyes at Hank Scarborough more than once, a much older guy who hung around the school.

"Well, it *is* a revival we're going to, ain't it?" Walt asked.

O.T. grabbed the comb and put it in his pocket as they walked out of the bedroom, their hard-soled black shoes clacking against the wooden floor. Neither of them wore shoes most days, preferring to work the farm barefoot. Shoes were hard to come by, expensive, and easily ruined in the red Georgia clay.

"Yeah, I reckon so. If I recall correck-ly, that Billy Rev is going to preach a sermon, and there will be some sangin' and dancin', like they done last year. People will stand up and give their test'mony, and when that's done the fish fry'll start." O.T.'s mouth watered, thinking of Misrus Maybelle's hush puppies. He hadn't had a taste of fried fish in well over a year. All the boys and a few of the girls had been fishing themselves silly in the creeks around Five Forks all week long, getting up enough fish to fry. Misrus Maybelle always sprang for a big ice block to keep them all cool. Everyone looked more forward to the fish fry than they did the revival, but of course nobody would admit it, especially not to Billy Rev, who had traveled so far to give them the Word of the Lord. "Got to run by the barn affore we leave, and git my banjo. They ast me to play."

"That reverend gon' do the baptisms again this year?" Walt asked as they stepped off the porch and began the walk into town. The sun had receded into the west, leaving just the faintest orange glimmer on the horizon. Hazel and Tom must have been out back, still taking their baths in the wash tub, O.T. thought to himself. They'd never admit it, but they were probably just as excited at the prospect of a night off as the young folks.

"Yeah, I reckon so," O.T. replied, retrieving a tin of snuff from his pocket. "He'll probably stay on a spell with folks' that'll show him hospitality. And then, after church on Sundy, he'll do all the savin' and baptisin'."

"You gon' get saved?"

"Hell no." O.T. grinned with pleasure at the look of pious shock on Walt's face. "I'm just pullin' yer string, brother. You know I'm already baptized. Both of us, when we was babies."

"You could get saved again."

"Ha! I'm surprised the church didn't bust into flame when they did it the first time."

"You shouldn't joke, O.T." Walt's eyes were serious. "Ain't none of us knowin' when the Holy Spirit might come and—" Walt was obsessed with the thought of dying young and going to hell. The young deaths of both their parents had molded Walt's innocent mind—he couldn't bear the thought of Ma and Pa being anywhere but heaven.

"Don't you start that nonsense," O.T. interjected, putting a hand on his brother's shoulder, giving him a little shove. "Jee-man-ee, can't you enjoy yerself for one night? Cain't you walk faster? Hurry up, affore we're late."

Misrus Maybelle had an enormous barn in back of her house that was rarely used for anything but community gatherings. Her husband had died years before, leaving her with enough money that she'd never have to farm cotton. Despite her good fortune, which many less blessed might have begrudged her, Maybelle was well loved due to her quiet determination to share and share alike. There wasn't a baby for miles around that didn't have a hand-crocheted blanket, just as soft as a cloud, made by Misrus Maybelle's own hands. And boy howdy, could she cook, thought O.T.

And if these were not virtues enough, Maybelle was also a handsome woman, with curly dark hair, plump cheeks, and violet eyes that sparkled with mirth. She could have her pick of eligible older widowers, O.T. reckoned, but it seemed she didn't want them. She was a god-fearing woman, but she wasn't heavy-handed with the fire and brimstone; she preferred the golden rule, of treating others as she wished to be treated.

The same could not be said for the visiting Billy Rev. O.T. didn't know the man's policy on the Golden Rule, but he definitely didn't have any problems with fire and brimstone. It was the main part of his act—O.T. recognized that he ought to be careful calling it an "act" in certain company, lest he get his hide painted with a hickory switch—and everyone in the town lapped it up like cats with sweetmilk.

O.T. could hear Billy Rev inside the barn as they approached, his booming, guttural voice carrying out over the windless night in a song. The barn was lit up with soft yellow candles, the dirt floor freshly swept, and crude wooden tables laid out with refreshments. In a fervor of excitement, Walt grabbed his brother's arm, but O.T. barely noticed; he was busy scanning the people milling about the barn for a glimpse of Betty Lou.

"She ain't here yet." Standing behind them, with his usual crooked-toothed grin, was Hosey Brown, O.T.'s best friend and next-door neighbor. He hadn't bothered to spiff himself up for the revival; his tattered denim overalls were covered in streaks of dirt, and his feet were bare and dirtier than his overalls. With his ash-blond hair, serious brown eyes, and cheeks covered in boyish freckles, Hosey remained one of the most handsome young men in the county, unwashed and wild though he was. More than once O.T. had heard the local girls cooing over his good looks and had burned with jealousy. He tried to ignore it as best he could, because Hosey's heart was every bit as pure and sweet as Walt's, and he was charming and cunning to boot. Hosey had gotten the twins out of more than one tight spot.

"Who ain't?"

"Don't he ever get tired of playing dumb about that gal?" Hosey asked Walt, clapping him on the back. Walt flushed with pleasure. He, too, loved Hosey, and didn't even mind if he touched him.

"Naw, reckon he don't," Walt answered, mesmerized by the candles' soft twinkling light. "Sure is pretty here tonight, ain't it, Hosey?"

"Yeah, sure is, Walt," Hosey agreed good-naturedly. "Reckon I might have to steal one of them fried pies. Might get my hide tanned, but I'm like to starve if I don't eat soon."

"All you ever think about is food," O.T. teased. "Like yer mama don't feed you at home."

"She don't," Hosey replied, laughing. "One more marble and the sack's empty. Only woman I know who can burn cornbread on the edge and still have raw dough in the middle."

"You shouldn't talk about yer ma like that," Walt said, scandalized. Walt was a firm believer in respecting your elders, especially if the elder was a woman and your own ma. He never understood that Hosey didn't mean nothin' by it, that he loved his ma more than anything on earth. O.T. had tried to explain to Walt that Hosey's jokes were a way of hiding his pain, but Walt didn't understand things like that. Either things *were* or they *weren't*. If you were hurt, you cried or got mad. What did a joke have to do with it? "If he loves his ma so much," Walt would say, his cheeks pink, "why does he taunt her so?" To Walt, having lost his own mother at thirteen, the word "mother" truly did mean "God."

"He don't mean it," O.T. would explain for the hundredth time. "His deddy dyin' like he did, and his ma not right in the head"— O.T. always felt a little guilty when he'd say this to Walt, it didn't seem right somehow—"it's hard on Hosey. It's just his way of copin', that's all."

"The Bible says to honor thy father and mother," Walt would answer primly, his lips pursing into a thin line.

"So it does, brother." At this point, O.T. usually gave up arguing; Walt saw things in black and white and was color-blind to shades of gray.

Hosey's story was sadder than most, but you wouldn't know it to look at him. He went about his days with that same old crooked smile of his, always laughing and cutting up. And while everybody in town knew that his dad had taken his own life with a sawed-off shotgun and his ma had lost what was left of her sanity as a result, they all guarded Hosey's secret as if it were a well-loved family heirloom. Hosey was everybody's favorite orphan. The girls all had crushes on him, the wives all wanted to mother him, and the fathers all wanted to give him a job. O.T. was right proud of his friend and would have given him the shirt off his back before anyone else had a chance. It was only when the day's work was done and the night was quiet enough to think that O.T. would see the deep sadness settle in the creases and shadows of Hosey's face.

To make it in this world, a man got to be strong, O.T. thought to himself grimly, or at least make a pretense of it. Wasn't fair, but nothing was, not in Five Forks, or anywhere else.

O.T. watched as his best friend's filthy, suntanned hand darted across one of the picnic tables and grabbed an apple-fried pie right in front of Misrus Maybelle's eyes. It was polite—and *expected*—to wait until after the reverend had spoken before eating. The fish hadn't even been dropped into the cornmeal yet. But Maybelle just playfully wagged a gloved finger at Hosey, and he gave her a sheepish grin.

"You could charm the devil himself," O.T. acknowledged with a smile.

"Speakin' of the devil," Hosey said, biting into the pie. "Where is Tom anyhow?"

O.T. grinned. "Better shush that talk. Hazel catches you sayin' it and you'll never pass another night at our house again."

"One of these days I'm gonna get Hazel alone and make love to her," Hosey declared, popping the last crust of pie into his mouth. "She'll throw Tom right out with the bathwater, she will, after she's spent an evenin' with me."

O.T. and Walt didn't bat an eye—long past were the days when they might've taken offense and felt the need to defend their sister with their fists. Hosey had been in love with Hazel-Jo Hawkins née Lawrence since he was just out of short overalls. And he'd been saying he was gonna marry her right up until she'd gone off and married Tom instead. Now, he just talked about stealing her away. He didn't care a whit that she was eight years older than him, saddled with a heavy-handed husband, or that, to her, Hosey was nothing more than another wayward little brother.

"Good luck with that, dressed like you are," Walt said. "You look like a ruffian."

"He's right," O.T, laughed, cuffing Hosey good-naturedly. "Ain't you met Hazel, you dumb lout? She don't let us leave for church on Sundy without pressed pants and scrubbed ears. When she sees the likes of you in yer dirty coveralls and no shoes she'll probably blush to her hair with the scandal of it." Hazel was a firm believer in cleanliness-next-to-godliness. She let Walt get away without brushing his hair, but that was *all*, and she'd only given up on that because of the sheer force of his will and her desire to avoid one of his fits. If she caught sight of the stain on O.T's pants, he'd be in for it. The whole town might think it a reflection on her housekeeping, and he'd catch mighty hell.

"I'll scrub up first then," Hosey said, wiping his knuckles prissily against his coveralls then inspecting his dirty nails. "Before I get in her bed." He leered.

This was usually the time O.T. told Hosey to shut his trap, but he didn't even hear his friend, for walking up to the barn with her sisters was Betty Lou Pittman.

O.T. watched her glance around the room, her white-gloved hands resting lightly just above her waist in a show of ladylike propriety. She—like all her sisters, her mother, and every other woman in the poor-and-getting-poorer county—wore a sack dress. Betty Lou's, however, was covered with little red flowers and had been done up fancy with puckering around the waist, from beneath which delicate red buttons trailed to her neckline. She wore polished black shoes that buttoned up to the ankle with a slight heel, and her cotton-white hair was swept back into a style O.T. had never seen on any girl; when she turned to say hello to Misrus Maybelle—a sweet little laugh on her flushed face—he saw that her hair was woven into an intricately pinned braid.

"Gosh," O.T. said to his companions, unaware if they were even standing beside him still. "Gosh amighty, y'all. Would y'all just *look*."

"She's right pretty, O.T.," Walt said, ever agreeable. "Right pretty as always."

"Yeah, yeah, so she's a looker," Hosey said, returning the playful cuff to O.T.'s head. "But dang, O.T., it ain't like she's Mary Pickford. You been knowin' Betty Lou since we was all swimming nekkit in the creek. You act like she's the queen of damn—"

"Hesh up," Walt said, his tone uncharacteristically firm. "Don't be teasing my brother. He's in love." Without a blade of grass to chew on, his eyes cut to the side, shifting back and forth like a mustache-twirling heel in a silent movie.

Hosey snorted, but O.T. was already making his way toward Betty Lou. He figured he'd talk to her now before he lost his nerve.

Betty Lou was shadowed by her mama, whose sour expression made her look like she'd just eaten a bitter grapefruit. Her pursed lips, coated in an orange-red lipstick, were thick as wax and twice as shiny. Mrs. Pittman had the same white, feathery hair as her daughters, but hers was always yanked into a tight bun. O.T. wondered if Mr. Pittman called her "cotton top," too, when she let her hair down. What might it look like out of that bun, falling around her white shoulders? he wondered. O.T. couldn't imagine Mr. and Mrs. Pittman alone, much less without clothes—they were both buttoned up right to their very souls. The closest Mr. Pittman had ever come to cracking a smile was when he was driving around in that flashy motorcar, and even then his knuckles gripped the steering wheel so hard they were bone-white.

"Hoity toity. Uppity and partic-lar. Just so," Hazel would proclaim as the Pittmans roared past in their fancy motorcar.

It was true, the Pittmans seemed to have the best of everything—a large house, a thriving farm, four beautiful blonde-haired daughters and a son away at college, a nice shiny motorcar—and they accepted it all with tight-lipped, exasperated smiles. They were too busy studying on what they might lose to enjoy what they had. It didn't seem fair, O.T. thought, that they had been so blessed and couldn't even smile about it. Betty Lou, however, though as prim as her parents, had her moments; moments where O.T. caught glimpses of her dancing or giggling with her sisters, when she would flash those icy blue eyes in a wild, secret way. Life brimmed below the surface of her coolness, and he wanted to dive in and swim around in it. He was more than happy to accept the cold Pittmans as his in-laws, and it wasn't because they came with a lot of nice things and a high-falutin' reputation around Five Forks. He just wanted Betty Lou.

As he approached, Betty Lou turned to him and smiled. "Hey, O.T.," she said in her soft, low voice; a voice that seemed older than her years. Sometimes when he talked to her, O.T. felt like a small scolded child. "How're you?"

Mrs. Jean Pittman also managed a small, tight smile. "Hello, Owen."

O.T. went to tip his hat and immediately felt stupid because he hadn't worn one that evening. He dropped his hand stiffly to his side, hoping he hadn't inadvertently drawn attention to his stained slacks. "Miss Betty Lou. How y'all tonight?"

"Jes' fine," Betty Lou replied with a polite nod as she scanned the barn, taking inventory of who else was present. Her heart, O.T. thought with some dismay, didn't seem to be beating as fast as his. She had to know that he was nuts for her—it was plain to God and everybody—but she was too polite to let it show. "I see Hosey and yer brother are here."

"Yes." He scratched his face, not sure what to say. "And yer sisters, too."

"Yes." She smiled at him patiently.

Mrs. Pittman patted at her bun. "Where is *your* sister, Owen? And Mr. Hawkins?"

"Hazel and Tom will be along any minute now," O.T. answered, wondering just what *was* keeping his sister. Everyone else, it seemed, had arrived already, and Hazel set a store by being punctual. She had them all—Tom, O.T., and Walt—in the church pews every Sunday a good ten minutes before services began, without fail. A faint glimmer of worry began in his chest, the thought that maybe Tom had got all worked up again…Well, he couldn't worry about it now, not with Betty Lou as pretty as a picture in front of him.

"How is your brother doing, Owen?" Mrs. Pittman always asked just that way—"How is he *doing?*"—as if his brother's oddness were an illness to be gotten over; as if the answer might change one of these days. This ritual annoyed O.T.—Walt wasn't sick, and he wasn't going to get any "better" neither. But for the love of Betty Lou, he smiled anyway, a picture of politeness.

"I'm doing good, ma'am." Walt was suddenly beside O.T., taking Mrs. Pittman's extended gloved hand. He had noticed nothing amiss; his obliviousness was, at times, a blessing. "And yer family and yerself?"

"Just fine, hon. Just fine. I was just telling your brother that I'd love to say hello to Hazel, but she doesn't appear to be here yet." Mrs. Pittman was fishing. Everybody in town knew that sometimes Hazel and Tom had "troubles," and Mrs. Pittman was as nosy as a crow.

"She and Tom just pulled up in the car," Walt replied, oblivious to Mrs. Pittman's pressing. "She'll be in direckly."

"Ah, well, good. I'm going to mosey on over and say how-do to some folks. You boys have fun tonight." Mrs. Pittman patted Walt's shoulder with her gloved hand, not noticing him tense as she did so, and was gone. Walt was far too polite to voice his discomfort, but Betty Lou had noticed his flinch. Meeting O.T.'s eyes, she mouthed *sorry*. He shook his head, an unspoken, *that's okay*. O.T. wished she'd keep looking in his eyes forever.

"Did y'all come in yer motorcar?" Walt asked Betty Lou. While O.T. might be in love with Betty Lou, Walt was in love with her pa's car. Tom had a car, but it was a beat-up Model T monstrosity that would likely die an agonizing death any day. For all his boasting about being a man's man, Tom was a lousy mechanic. The Pittmans' Ford was brand new, shiny as spit, and *fancy*. Whenever the Pittman family showed up, Walt was bound to be found outside, staring spellbound at their car, memorizing its lines, its logos, its mechanisms.

"Yeah, we did." Betty Lou nodded. "Daddy's finally learned to drive the thing. For a while, we was afraid that he'd sling one of us clear out the back, the way he drove." Her laugh was like tinkling glass.

"I'd love to drive a car, myself," Walt said, puffing up his shoulders. "Shore would. I aim to learn one day and get me my own car."

"You should," Betty Lou said. "I've driven ours once't or twice't. It's fun. Nice to have an automobile." She paused for a moment, thoughtful, then her blue eyes lit up. "Say, Walt. How would you like to take a ride?"

"Why," Walt exclaimed, his face lighting up in a grin, "I reckon I'd just about *love* it! You mean it, Miss Betty Lou?"

"Sure do. I can't say that Daddy would let you *drive* it, accorse," she said quickly, and flashed an apologetic smile O.T.'s way. "But I'm sure he'd be right glad to let the both of you take a ride in it." Her cheeks flushed a little, and she lowered her voice. "He's so proud of that dang car. I think he loves it more than us and Mama put together." She laughed again, silk and glass mixed together.

"I'm much obliged, Miss Betty Lou," Walt said, his face bright red with excitement. "Much obliged. You just say when, and I'm there, yes sirree!"

"Let me just go and talk to Pa about it."

O.T.'s heart surged with pride—he'd have been jealous of any young man that Betty Lou had offered to take out in her car, but not Walt. He'd give anything at all to Walt, even Betty Lou's attention. O.T. smiled, though, because he wouldn't have to—Betty Lou had invited him, too.

❧

The smell of fried cornmeal, briny fish, grease, and woodsmoke drifted to the little wagon parked outside the grove of trees.

Harvey was whittling again. Some type of gadget—a whistling toy, maybe? Or perhaps a smoking pipe for Uncle Billy—known in these parts as Billy Rev. Every time he starts in with that "yes, boss, no boss," all I hear is "yes, master, no master," Sivvy thought, biting into the side of her cheek, hard enough to draw blood. Billy Rev's company these past weeks had turned her mean and ugly. What would Mama say if she knew Sivvy was thinking such things? Mama and her lectures about how all kinds was the same, in their hearts; Mama, who was quick to remind them that even if they did "pass," they weren't white as milk, and don't they dare forget it.

Oh, who cared what Mama would say, Sivvy thought crossly to herself. Mama was good as dead to her now, and Deddy too, and her brothers and sister. She hated all of 'em.

Uncle Billy said neither her nor Harvey could come to the fish fry. It was obvious why Harvey couldn't—he was colored, after all—but Sivvy had expected to go. She was dang hungry; all other reasons a teenage girl might want to go to the social event of the year in a little town like this paled in comparison to that. Her empty, gnawing belly protested loudly under her shift.

"You ain't memorized the song," Billy had told her as he prepared to leave. "It's yer own sorry fault, and don't be lookin' at me thataway. I cain't do nothin' for it. Shoulda memorized it before now. I'll try to bring y'all a hush puppy or two if they's any left." Sivvy felt her face redden in angry protest; she knew a lie when she heard one.

He had been gone a long time. The only sounds in the looming dusk were the sounds of the birds, an errant frog or two, and Harvey's knife as it whittled the wood.

Sivvy turned her attention to the song lyrics, even though she'd had them down pat for three days, and her eyes were crossed with exhaustion. If she was lucky, she might get a few winks of sleep tonight on the cool, dewy grass before Uncle Billy's rough voice woke her up and the whole thing started over.

CHAPTER TWO

"Brothers and Sisters, I beg of ALL y'all, to repent yer backslidin' ways and bathe yerself in the blood of the LAMB!"

Faint whispers and murmurs of "amen" and "hallelujah" rang out among the crowd gathered in the tent beside Misrus Maybelle's barn.

The Reverend Billy Hargrove—who, in the year since the last revival, had begun styling himself "Billy Rev"—paced animatedly on a makeshift stage composed of wooden pallets. His small, dark eyes scanned the crowd, picking out sinners amid the huddled flock, each face appropriately chastened. Billy Rev was dressed smartly in a crisp white suit with wide lapels, large black buttons, and pants that skimmed the top of heavy black shoes, polished to gleaming. His face was flushed and sweaty, and he licked at his thin lips with a furtive tongue. He looks like he's fixin' to have a stroke, O.T. thought.

He wondered if the small stage would even hold the man up for the duration of the sermon, the way he was carrying on. Billy Rev might be skinny as a stork, but his presence was *heavy*. Every time he crouched, jumped, shifted, and spun on the little pallets in his shiny black boots, the wooden boards creaked and groaned. Nobody could claim he hadn't given them a show. He was practically dancing up there, bellowing all the while.

"I KNOW you, brothers and sisters! I see and hear your 'hallelujahs' and can see the earnestness on yer faces! GOOD people, GOD FEARING people in the town of Five Forks! You SEEN the error of your ways, and you mean to follow the path of Jesus! Ain't it so?" There was a faint murmur of agreement. "But I tell ya, BACKSLIDIN' is easy as pie! Easy. As. Pie. Folks. No sooner'n I finish up my preachin', and y'all'll head on down yonder and have you some supper and some good comp'ny"—he lowered his voice to a theatrical, exaggerated whisper—"and git you to DRANKIN' and LUSTIN' and affore you know what happent, YER BACKSLID!" He wiped at his face with the handkerchief and continued. "And ya wake up tomorr-y with every thought of the LORD slid right outta yer heads. Continue on in yer ways of sinfulness. Excusin' yourself from the LORD's mighty word. Because the DEVIL—oh, he's a slippery one, a wily one!—aims to work in us all, ever chance he gets! *Ain't it so?*"

O.T. hid his smile and looked around. The blue-haired ladies murmured a few "amens"; they could always be relied upon for moral superiority. The rest of Five Forks folks had gone silent, though, affronted but duty-bound to take the licking. O.T. never could understand the Christian way of enjoying a brow-beating. Folks just love to be told how bad they are, he thought to himself. Makes 'em feel so good. Walt was watching with rapt attention, sharing none of his brother's cynicism.

Billy Rev's face was coated with a sheen of thick sweat as he took a glass of water from the pulpit with a shaking hand, his chest heaving, his face beet red. The air under the tent was muggy and stale, and the excited fervor had worn off, folks slumping in their chairs, fanning their faces, bored. The tent was clogged with the smell of armpit. Billy Rev had prattled on for a good forty-five minutes already and showed no sign of stopping.

"I say, 'tis a right SHAME that OUR FATHER WHO ART IN HEAV'N don't just come on down and smite us all in one quick swoop. For I say unto y'all, afflictions are the judgment of the LORD GOD! Smallpox, the typhus, and pellagra, those are BLESSINGS from our Lord, meant to wipe the earth clean of backslidin' sin!"

O.T. dug his fingernails into his hand, his teeth clenched in anger.

"SINS, I say, sins of the body, of the mind, of the soul! Fornicatin' and takin' to drink, gossipin', gamblin', gluttony"—*God, would the man ever shut up?*—"smokin' and covetin' they neighbor's wife and—"

O.T. looked over at Hosey, who was stifling laughter, and caught the gaze of Betty Lou. Her mouth held a hint of a smirk, and O.T. felt his heart swell, his anger lifting. Feeling brazen, he winked at her. Then he looked down at his lap, immediately horrified at what he had done. Not that he cared, and he reckoned Betty Lou didn't either, but other folks might. It wasn't proper at all in any time or place, but *especially* not at revival. If Hazel saw, she'd clean his clock.

"So I say to ask yerself, friends, neighbors. Are you on the RIGHTEOUS path? The path of our Lord God and our precious Christ Jesus? Or is you BACKSLIDIN' into the very flames of hell? Mayhap we don't even KNOW when we're backslidin', such is the cunning ways of that devil! Search your hearts, friends—"

The air was muggy, and O.T.'s eyelids mirrored the slow droop of his head toward his brother's shoulder. Walt, however, wasn't paying him any mind—he was staring at the girl who had quietly appeared on the stage, holding a tattered leather-bound notebook. The infamous niece, O.T. reckoned. She gingerly held the notebook out to her uncle, wary of his sweeping arm movements—which reminded O.T. of a giant wind turbine in a thunderstorm—but he took no notice of her. Billy Rev would clearly finish his *entire* rant before he'd even acknowledge her presence. O.T. was no stranger to that kind of attitude in the menfolk around town, but watching the Rev's niece, his heart burned with anger at the blatant and very public disrespect.

"Get you home tonight and on your knees! Never misremember the commandments the Lord gave you! Christ Jesus died on the CROSS to absolve you of sin; see that you sin no more!" His booming voice almost sang as it echoed through the tent, and he raised his arms high into the air, invoking the Holy Spirit. Finally taking notice of the girl, the reverend whirled to seize the notebook from her hands, narrowly missing hitting her in the face. She ducked, her face burning as she exited the stage.

"Nay, niece. Stay fer a spell," Billy Rev commanded, smiling at the congregation. "This here's my kin, Miss Savilia Hargrove. I'm right proud to say this girl's aiming to inherit the Gospel and preach the word of God alongside her uncle!"

Savilia smiled wanly at the crowd. There was a smattering of reluctant applause—Billy Rev had scared the gaiety right out of the place. O.T. glanced over at his brother, who wore an expression of slack-jawed awe.

"Goshamighty," Walt murmured, shaking his head, his teeth chewing on his lower lip. "Goshamighty."

O.T. was astounded, unable to recall a single instance of Walt's ever having cursed before, and certainly never in a house of the Lord.

Billy Rev's niece was around their age, he'd heard. She was short, waifish, and skinny as a rail, with angular elbows and legs, and a sharply pointed chin and nose. It seemed a stiff breeze might blow her right away, except for her shoulders, which anchored her in place, jaunty and proud. Savilia's face was thin and delicate, her skin smooth and browned from the late September sun. Her lips, the only plump thing about her, were as red as cranberries. Most of the women in Five Forks braided their hair, pulled it back in a bun, or tucked it beneath a bonnet or kerchief, but Savilia Hargrove's black hair was long and free, like a girl's. She stood ramrod straight, looking mightily uncomfortable, but still somehow dignified, as if she were a real lady and not a girl in the middle of a sweaty tent revival in Five Forks, Georgia. She held herself like royalty. A monarch, O.T. thought, whose expression was one of dignified patience, as though this charade had been enacted a thousand times before and would be again a thousand times hence.

Savilia's gaze landed briefly on Walt and O.T.; she glanced from one to the other in the span of a second, a flash of surprise crossing her face, the way it always did when people saw identical twins. Walt let his breath out in a loud whoosh, and O.T. suddenly regretted teasing him about the girl, certain that the likes of Savilia would eat Walt alive and play with the carcass afterward, woman of the Lord or not.

"Now, ladies and gents, if you please, and since she's already standin' here"—Billy Rev chuckled magnanimously—"I'll have my goodly niece carry the sermon out with a hymn. Our kind sister Maybelle has offered to play the pia-ner."

Seating herself at the piano, Misrus Maybelle struck up a jaunty tune, her face rosy, her dark curls bobbing on her shoulders as she tickled the keys. Stepping to the center of the stage, Savilia shook her head slightly, black hair rippling down her back, her dark eyes flashing. She began to sing in a reedy but melodic voice:

"Lord Jesus came a walkin' along one day,
with a crowd all gathered around.
He cast his eyes in a syc-more tree,
and what d'ya think he found?
He found a man a lookin' for him,
way up in a syc-more tree.
He said, 'Zaccaheus, you come down,

today I must abide with thee.
Well, all you people with your proud little hearts,
this is what you are to me.
You're just another Zaccahaeus,
When th'Lord come to bless you,
too high in the syc-more tree,
too high in the syc-more tree."

The young woman's face was flushed by the time she was done, her hair clinging to her skin in damp tendrils. The hymn she was sang was one O.T. had never heard. More verses followed—about women who wore too-tight dresses and men who were too proud to say they loved the Lord. O.T. vaguely remembered the biblical story of Zaccaheus, a tax collector who climbed a tree to get a better look at the Messiah; Jesus shocked the crowd by telling the man to come down and visit with him—his good will extended even to money grabbers, at least in this story. O.T. could see why Billy Rev was fond of it.

Finally, the performance was over and Savilia made her way off the stage, stopping unsmilingly at the edge to give a brief half-bow-half-curtsy.

"Savilia Hargrove, good women and men!" Billy Rev announced, sweeping his arm in her direction. "Say thank you!"

"Thank you!" the sweaty crowd replied obediently.

O.T. hoped the sermon portion of the evening was over. Miss Savilia was right pretty and a fair singer, but he was bored and starving. He could see Betty Lou in his peripheral vision, fanning her face with a flier. He ached to look over at her, but he was too scared she might look back.

"What say you, folks?" Billy Rev thundered, his wide, toothy grin pushing apples into his thin cheeks. "Should we head on over to the barn, say grace and have us a goodly Christian feast?"

There were murmurs of agreement, and O.T. sighed with relief. He wasn't the only one fit to eat a horse. Billy Rev would undoubtedly prattle on throughout the meal and then treat them to another stern sermon after they ate, not to mention how many other lectures before he packed up for good, but O.T. would mind a lot less on a full stomach.

ॐ

O.T. stood awkwardly in the church courtyard with Walt, Hosey, Betty Lou, and her younger sister Lila, who was eleven and still wearing pigtails. After an hour of hellfire, it was time for baptising. Harvey, the reverend's helper—a young, dark-skinned boy, who O.T. figured was about his age—sat by the door, kicking at rocks with his scuffed black shoes, looking bored as the dickens. Since they were all saved already, Mr. Pittman and Hazel said the kids could go for a short ride down Main Street, so long as they came right back. "Y'all don't be gone longer than thirty minutes," Mr. Pittman warned, wagging a finger at the girls. He had pushed Lila into going along; sending his oldest and prettiest daughter off with a bunch of teenage boys unchaperoned was unthinkable. O.T. felt embarrassed. He'd never dream of getting forward with Betty Lou, chaperoned or not. Betty Lou was a lady, and O.T.'s ma had raised him better than that.

"If I have to come out lookin' fer ya, someone's like to get a hiding," Mr. Pittman declared, glaring pointedly at the young men.

"Yes, sir, Pa," his daughters replied dutifully. Their pa gave them another long look, before shuffling off in the direction of the church.

"I'll drive," Betty Lou proclaimed, once the church doors had swung shut behind him. "I promised I wouldn't let nobody else behind the wheel."

"Sure thing, darlin'," Hosey said, reaching out to pat the car.

Betty Lou gave him a sharp look. "Beg pardon, Hosey Brown?"

"I just said, yes, please, ma'am. Miss Pittman."

Betty Lou smiled, mollified. "Well, let's get on in, then. Time's a'wastin'."

O.T. offered her his hand and she held it gratefully, climbing up behind the driver's seat. He shut her door, then walked briskly round to the passenger side, not giving anyone else a chance to call shotgun. Lila clambered in over him, and he felt a flicker of irritation, but dutifully allowed her to settle on his lap, giving Betty Lou an unruffled smile. Hosey sat in the back—Walt beside him—and put his feet up on the seat, kicking O.T. playfully behind the ear.

"Feet down, if you please, Mr. Brown," Betty Lou said with mock sternness as she started up the car. The engine roared to life like a feisty toddler having a tantrum, the exhaust sputtering, the fierce rumbling shaking the ground and vibrating loudly in their ears. Betty Lou fiddled with the gears, a lock of blonde hair falling into her eyes. O.T. stared at her, his stomach doing flip-flops. "Let's hope it don't rain!" she yelled over the engine, her cool blue eyes looking up at the sky.

"Hey, wait!" Running up to the driver's side was a red-faced, petite girl with streaming black hair.

"What is it, Miss Savilia?" asked Hosey good-naturedly, as though they were old pals. "Cain't you see we's trying to make a getaway?"

"I don't aim to stop you," said the dark-haired girl pertly, with a sly smile. "I was just hoping to join you, if Miss Betty Lou don't mind." She extended a hand to Betty Lou. "We ain't met proper. I'm Savilia Hargrove—Sivvy, if you please. Billy Rev's niece."

"I know who you are," Betty Lou replied. "Yer uncle don't mind if you join us?"

"Oh naw, he don't."

"There's an extra seat in the back, then," Betty Lou said politely. "If one of these hooligans will let you sit down."

Walt scrambled out of the car quicker than lightning and offered Sivvy his arm. Grinning like a cat who'd gotten the cream, she stepped up into the back and slid in beside Hosey. Walt sat beside Savilia, staring straight ahead, his ears bright red. O.T. wanted to ask Miss Sivvy how she'd managed to get out of an afternoon of saving folks, but the engine was too loud. If she minded being sandwiched between two stinking boys, she did not show it.

"Let's roll, y'all," Betty Lou shouted with a giggle, shifting the car into gear. They took off with a jolt, dust flying through the church parking lot. She laughed again, hollering over the rumble of the engine. "I'm going to catch heck for that one with my pa, just you wait." In the side mirror, O.T. could see the figure of Harvey, watching them depart, his face a blank.

They drove in silence for a while. O.T. was content just sitting beside Betty Lou, sneaking sideways glances, watching the way her hair fell out of her pins and onto her creamy, long neck. Occasionally, he managed to tear his eyes away to look out over the road at the trees, which were beginning to turn. It was still Indian summer, but the beginnings of fall weren't far away. Leaves were beginning to drift from the trees in hues of tell-tale Georgia red, russet, orange, and bright yellow. It wouldn't be long, O.T. knew, before the leaves would crunch underfoot, and a hint of smoke from folks' chimneys would scent the breeze. Fall was O.T.'s favorite time of year because it reminded him of his ma before she'd gotten sick. She'd always made a big to-do of "apple time" and would whip up apple cake, apple jelly, fried apple pies, dried apples, and everything in between. Every year, once the leaves began to turn and the sweet tang of cinnamon and cloves filled the ladies' kitchens, O.T. would think of his ma. It had been a long time since he'd had apple cake.

Walt gave him a nudge from behind, and O.T. wondered if he, too, was thinking of Ma and the apples, or if he was just excited to be in a new motorcar with two pretty girls.

"Just up ahead, around the corner," O.T. hollered over the roaring car, resting his hand on Betty Lou's shoulder, "is the purdiest tree in all 'o Five Forks."

"You mean in front of old Mr. and Mrs. Hawkins' place?" Betty Lou asked, looking over at O.T.

"That's the one. They won't mind if we wanted to stop and look." Mr. and Mrs. Hawkins were Tom's folks and the closest to grandparents he and Walt had. O.T. had spent much of his youth sitting in their little parlor, eating homemade peach ice cream and watching Walt play gin rummy with Pap. The twins loved to hear Pap's stories of how he had run away from home when he was thirteen years old to join the Confederate Army. The gaining of Granny and Pap had been the only good thing to have come out of Hazel's unhappy marriage.

"All right," Betty Lou said smoothly. "If y'all want to."

"Yeah, let's," Hosey called from the back. "They got a nice creek off to the side of their place, and they let us fish there all th'time. I'll show y'all where I slipped and busted my tail last week. Still got a bruise on my ass—"

"Language!" Walt exclaimed loudly, and O.T. busted out laughing.

❧

27

Around the curve, Betty Lou veered slowly off the road and pulled into Mr. and Mrs. Hawkins' yard. There was twice as much dirt as grass, and what little grew there was ratty and sparse—little tufts of sharp blades, more yellowed than green. Mr. and Mrs. Hawkins were too old to do much yard work, and Tom seldom ventured over to help his parents with the farm—he had more important things to do. Like runnin' off ever chance he gets to tomcat around on my sister, O.T. thought bitterly. O.T. and Walt had helped Granny and Pap whenever they could, as did Hosey from time to time, but their own chores often kept them too busy. Both sets of his and Walt's biological grandparents—Ma's folks as well as Deddy's family—were long dead. While O.T. and Walt came from a long line of folks who had lived in Five Forks for generations, none of them lived very long. O.T. had grown up hearing about their "rich fambly history," but it was a poor substitute for a ma to tuck you in the bed at night and a daddy to toss a baseball around with you. This lack of immediate family made O.T. feel ashamed and detached, as if he didn't come from anybody and didn't belong anywhere, no matter what other folks said.

Betty Lou shut off the car, and before she or Sivvy could so much as shift in their seats, all three young men had clambered out, ready to open a door or offer an elbow. Nobody can say we ain't gentlemen, poor or not, O.T. thought with a smile. Little Lila didn't want to get out of the car; she folded her arms over her skinny chest and said she'd rather sit up and read, so they left her to her book. O.T. tipped his imaginary hat at Betty Lou as she took his arm, and she giggled. He hoped it was because she found him charming and not a plum fool. He'd been inwardly cringing these two nights since, when he'd gone to tip his hat at her, only to discover he wasn't wearing one. Walt suggested he just "make it part of yer how-de-do." Relieved, O.T. decided he'd tip his lack of hat at Betty Lou every chance he got. Walt had good ideas sometimes. For a boy off with the faeries, he sure had the sight.

Sivvy stepped out of the car, oblivious to both Walt and Hosey, both of whom were waiting on her. She stared off into the trees, her eyes wide and strangely sad. "What a beaut this place is," she whispered, almost reverently. The entire afternoon had taken on the feel of an elaborate, genteel country date, and O.T. wanted to laugh. They were all standing around in a dust bowl full of dry, red clay, putting on such airs.

Farce or not, O.T. couldn't help the grin on his face. The Hawkins place was tiny, just a shack—a stiff wind from even the smallest spring storm would probably knock it over—and the yard was covered in junk: old car parts and farming equipment, all coated in the dry red dirt that seemed to get most everywhere. O.T. was right glad to be wearing shoes; whenever he and Walt left the Hawkins place their feet were as orange as a pumpkin shell. But Sivvy was right—there was something about this land, always had been, something that just made you want to take in a deep breath.

It was a sight that warmed O.T.'s heart. The trees were mostly pine with a few dogwoods and oaks. Wildflowers grew in bunches of purple, red, and pink down by the creek. Rugged outcrops of shale, granite, and ocher dotted the fields, along with the chalky kaolin or "white dirt" that folks ate when times were bad. Winding through the property was the creek, with its surprisingly clear water for all the red Georgia mud in it. O.T. had discovered so many arrowheads on the Hawkinses' land that Hazel had had to sew him a pouch to hold them all. Even the unruly pokeberry bushes, with their unfurling, fast-growing purplish-pink stalks, were beautiful here. O.T. loved this land more even than his own family's property and dreamed that one day the Hawkins lot might be his; but he'd never told anyone, not even Walt.

"Let's see the tree," O.T. said with a grin, momentarily forgetting that Betty Lou was holding his arm. "Then we'll go say how-do to the folks." Mr. and Mrs. Hawkins had both come out at the sound of the car and stood on the porch with eager, welcoming smiles.

"I reckon it's sweet that you call 'em yer folks," Betty Lou said, patting her hair and brushing off her dress. Did she give his arm a little squeeze? Her blue eyes flashed, and O.T. felt his heart beat faster.

Walt called out, "Hey, Granny and Pap! We're here to see the tree and the creek, if'n y'all don't mind!"

"Y'all gon' ahead!" Mrs. Hawkins yelled. "Come on in fer a glass a'tea when yer done!"

"Ain't she sweet?" Betty Lou murmured. "We'd best remember not to be longer than a half hour, though, or my pa will send out the sheriff looking for us."

"Or the goodly Billy Rev!" Hosey guffawed, then choked it off with a gulp, remembering Sivvy.

"It's just around the corner here," O.T. said, leading the little group into the edge of the woods.

"Speaking of the reverend, Miss Savilia," Walt said, his tone deferential. "Are you right sure he didn't mind you leaving the baptisms to come with us?"

"Naw," Sivvy said. "Call me Sivvy. I think he druther I be far from him when he's pouring water. I git in the way. He druther git Harvey to help him when he does the baptisin'."

"If he's training *you*," Betty Lou remarked, "it seems that he would want you to know all about the business of baptisms."

Two spots of color appeared on Sivilia's olive-tinted cheeks. "He says it's not fit for a woman to do baptisin'. It's not a woman's callin', he says." Sivvy smiled. "Accorse, when it's my turn to take over, I'll do as I please." She squared her shoulders. "Including baptisms."

"Good for you," Betty Lou said, with a smile.

"So he's aimin' to let you take over one day?" Walt asked.

"He says he is," Sivvy answered. "He don't mean it. Just says it. But it don't matter, because I aim to anyway." She looked at O.T. with a smile, her green eyes flashing. So lovely they were, he mused, with her tanned skin and dark hair. "I'll keep Harvey on to help, and we'll put a sight more joy into the whole thing, I reckon. Play instruments, and tell Bible stories, and all."

O.T.'s tree was old, with a gray mottled trunk that was a good twenty feet around, and branches that twisted to the left. Someone had explained once why the branches were bent, but O.T. hadn't paid much attention—he was too busy being charmed by the tree's beauty to worry about its reasons. He didn't like to study too much on a thing; that was more Walt.

Over the years, O.T. had spent many a fall afternoon sitting under the bright orange leaves, which somehow seemed both red and yellow at the same time. Hazel called it "day-glow," and O.T. reckoned she was right. Some days the leaves glowed so orange that the tree seemed to be on fire; and on others, as winter approached, the colors would deepen to a pinkish orange, and then a blood-red rust before falling to the ground. O.T. had climbed the tree, perched on every branch, and hung from every limb. Together with Walt and Hosey, he'd passed his boyhood under it, reading, whittling, and dipping stolen snuff. He loved it like Walt loved his dang butterflies, and it felt grand to show it off to two pretty girls.

"This here's a sassafras tree," Sivvy said, running her hand over the mottled bark. "They grow all over where I'm from. These trees just love the mountains."

Hosey seized a branch and hauled himself up into the tree, bare legs and feet dangling. "That so?"

"Ayuh. You can tell by how crookit it is. Mountain trees is like that. Have to lean to get at the sun. Sassafras leaves makes mighty fine tea, too. And candy and tonics and all," Sivvy declared sagely. "My mama kin tell you allerbout what they's used fer. Sassafras is good trees. Purdy, too, like." She nodded at O.T. with a smile. "I kin very well yer feelin', Mr. Lawrence. I could pass a lifetime under this here tree."

O.T. waved Sivvy away, embarrassed. He suddenly felt like he might cry, which horrified him. Sivvy stared at him with those keen green eyes. It was unnerving but not wholly unpleasant. Something in her gaze seemed to strip him bare, and he felt like a little boy again, vulnerable and shy.

"Please, O.T.'ll do jus' fine," he muttered. Then, as an afterthought: "And this accorse is my twin brother, Walt, but you knowed that, I reckon." O.T. pushed Walt forward, reluctant to be the center of attention anymore.

Betty Lou, arm entwined with his, led him off toward the creek, just the two of them, and O.T. couldn't believe his luck. Evidently she didn't want him to be the center of attention, either, save for her own.

O.T. and Betty Lou sat on a large flat rock next to the creek. Betty Lou kicked off her shoes, dipping her feet in and out of the cold water. O.T., feeling light-headed, tried not to stare at her smooth, bare legs. Neither of them said much, but he felt giddy with happiness. Something had shifted; somehow in the span of an afternoon, Betty

Lou had gone from being a friend he'd loved from afar, to being *his girl*. He wasn't quite sure how he knew it, what had changed, when or why, but something in Betty Lou's body language, the way she kept looking at him out of the corner of her eyes, a sideways glance, told him that he was right.

They sat without talking for a while, the only sound the trickling of the creek water over the stones, until Betty Lou finally broke the silence, asking quietly, "Is yer sister Hazel awright?"

When O.T. had finally caught sight of his sister at the revival two days before, she and Tom straggling in late, Hazel's face had been streaked and sad, her efforts to conceal blotchy tear stains with cheap rouge and powder unsuccessful. Of course Betty Lou had noticed; everyone had. Hazel had laughed it off with stories about how the hay and fall blooms always got her sniffling; nobody had bought it, though Hazel could count on their willful ignorance. She was assuredly out of earshot before the whispered *bless her heart*s of powdery-haired old ladies began. Tongues would wag, but not out in the open, not to her face.

"It's fine, boys," she'd said to them after—a familiar refrain— when O.T. had confronted her, demanding to know what Tom had done this time. Hazel had sighed with exasperation, drawing a brush through her long, honey-colored hair. "Just a little dust up. I was being right silly. It were my fault. I don't want to get into it now; it's done with. Awright?"

"Then where'd he go?" Tom had dropped them all off home and gone out again, slamming the screen door behind him. O.T. knew good and well where Tom had gone and didn't know why he continued to ask her, to force her to make up excuses.

"He had some business in Commerce," Hazel lied absently, too tired even to try to sound convincing. "He'll be back tomorrow, or th'day after, I reckon."

Probably more like a week, O.T. had thought bitterly. Hazel had given up the last years of her childhood to marry Tom, for the sake of her twin brothers. Tom treated her awful, and the whole town knew it, but what could Hazel do about it? She was stuck in it but good.

"Y'all go on to bed now," Hazel had said softly. "I'm fine. And anyhow, y'all ain't to meddle in grown affairs. I done told you that."

Walt had snagged a blade of grass from the yard and had already gnawed it down to a pulpy mess. His eyes cut nervously to the side.

O.T. had propelled Walt out of Hazel's room and into their own, before one of his panic fits could set in. The eye thing was the first sign, then he would wring his hands and pull on his thumbs, and his color would go gray. He might start humming, or crying. The crying was the worst. But O.T. could stave off a fit if he acted quick. He helped Walt undress and tucked him into the little cot, tightening the covers around Walt's sides into a snug cocoon, the way he liked it. O.T. sat on the bed beside his brother, who rolled over with a sigh.

"Rub my back, brother?"

After sixteen years, Walt knew he did not have to ask, but he always did anyhow.

"Okay." O.T. pulled up his brother's nightshirt and began rubbing his pale skin in concentric circles, which he would do until his arm cramped or he fell asleep himself. Thankfully Walt fell asleep almost immediately, arms tucked under his chin, legs curled up to his chest, like a child. O.T. kept rubbing his back until his arm was wore out. Finally, dog tired, he climbed into his own bed, not bothering with nightclothes or fixing the covers.

As O.T. turned off the torch lamp, he heard Hazel's voice in the doorway. "Love you, boys." He knew she'd been standing there for a while, that watching him put Walt to sleep comforted her, too, in some little way.

"Hazel's awright," he answered Betty Lou finally, deciding not to tell her too much. He'd spare his sister the indignity—and the hiding he'd get if she knew he had been gossiping about her. "She's had a cold. Certain weeds grow this time a'year makes her sick."

"I mean her and Tom," Betty Lou insisted firmly. "And you know it." Gosh, but she was lovely, O.T. mused. Her ice-blue eyes flashed, and the crisp fall weather had brightened her cheeks to a rosy pink. "It's all right, Owen, really. I won't say nothin' to my folks or my sisters. It's only—she looks so sad all the time. I feel right bad for her."

O.T. was touched. He figured it might be all right to confide in Betty Lou, whose concern seemed genuine. "I reckon she is. Unhappy, I mean. Not all the time. But often enough. And yeah, Tom's got the blame of it all."

"She's so sweet," Betty Lou said. "I remember yer mama from church, how she'd dress up in those pretty, clean dresses and that nice purple hat she had. Velveteen, like. And I just smile every time I see Hazel in church in the same hat. But she seems so sad, married to that old galoot." Betty Lou sniffed. "If you had a wife as lovely as Hazel, what reason would you have to go round with someone else?"

O.T. made to reply, but thought the better of it. It wasn't fittin' conversation to be having with a young unmarried woman, even if Betty Lou had started it.

"Oh, I ain't stupid, Owen." O.T had to smile at the way she kept calling him Owen. "I know men will get down in the dirt every chance they get, for *that.*" She stared down at the water. "But it just ain't fair. Hazel as sweet and pretty as she is. If she can't keep her man, what chance do the rest of us have?"

"We ain't all like Tom," O.T. said firmly, taking the chance to put his hand over hers. Her skin was cool and light under his own, and to his delight, she didn't pull away.

Betty Lou shook her head fiercely, a white curl coming loose. "I won't settle for no man like that. I won't."

O.T. felt ashamed, chastised, though he'd done nothing wrong. "You won't have to, Betty Lou."

"They all say they ain't like that, I bet. Till they get what they want, then they're bored." She shook her head fiercely. "I'm telling you right now, Owen Lawrence, I won't settle for no man that runs around on me and talks with his fists and makes me cry and lose face in front of my friends and family. No sirree. I want a man who loves me like my daddy loves my mama." Betty Lou looked at him right in the eye. "He might be an uptight old codger, and I know you all think he's a showoff, my pa. But he loves my mama. He'd do anything in the world to make her happy. She—and us kids—we're his world, you know?"

"Yeah," O.T. said sadly. "My pa and ma—from what I remember before he died—they was like that, too."

Betty Lou smiled. "That's nice. I don't remember much of yer daddy, but I remember he was nice."

"That's awright," O.T. said uneasily. "He died a lot of years ago."

"I'm sorry for it," Betty Lou said. "Right sorry. That ain't fair, to lose both yer parents so young."

"It's awright," he repeated, feeling a little uncomfortable.

Betty Lou laid her head on his shoulder.

"You ain't got to settle for nobody who don't love you," O.T. said quietly, his heart beating fast. "The man you marry will love you his whole life."

"Will he now?" He could feel her cheek curling into a smile against his shoulder.

Somehow she had managed to get the upper hand on him and, boy, was he in big trouble. O.T. was desperately trying to decide if he should kiss Betty Lou or not, when a noise startled them.

Walt stood behind them, shifting his weight from one foot to the other. "We ought to head back, brother," he said. "Miss Lila's gripin' about how long she been in the car."

O.T. wanted to groan in frustration, but he nodded at his twin. "Okay." The two of them stood, brushing off their clothes. He blushed, wondering how much Walt had seen and heard. Though it didn't matter—if there was anyone he could trust with a secret, it was Walt.

O.T. held out his arm to her, and Betty Lou took it, a faint blush on her own cheeks. "You just remember what I said, Owen Lawrence," she said in her smooth voice, low enough for only him to hear. "And heed it before you go…asking nothin'."

O.T. smiled back at her and winked. "You heard what I said, too."

"So long as it's true." Her lips curled into a sweet smile.

"Accorse it's true." His boy's heart meant it. If he had Betty Lou, there'd never be a need for any other woman as long as he lived. They could all go hang.

CHAPTER THREE

The kitchen was filled with apples. They were all over the counters, two buckets full on the floor, and a huge pile of them tumbling off the kitchen table, where Walt and O.T. sat, peeling and chopping. Hazel must have read O.T.'s mind, because when he'd woken up that morning, she'd beamed at him from the skillet where she was frying eggs and announced that it was apple day. For the first time in what seemed like a coon's age, the trees outside had actually bore fruit—edible fruit, not ruined by worms or rot, and they'd picked themselves half to death. Misrus Maybelle had also sent over several buckets of apples from her own trees, too. Apples were drying on tinfoil sheets out in the morning sun, and Hazel was working lard into flour for the pie crust out on the porch. O.T. hoped she'd make an apple cake, too. His mouth was watering, just thinking about it. He peeled another rosy apple and sliced off a chunk, popping it into his mouth.

"Quit eating them apples," Walt said irritably, glaring at him. "We ain't never gonna get done if you don't quit stuffing yer face."

"I cain't help it. They're so good."

"When yer stuck in the outhouse all af'ernoon, don't be callin' to me to bring you no corn cobs," Walt said crossly. O.T. laughed, but Walt didn't return the smile. He had been in a mood all morning. He stared at the pink-and-yellow apples, peeling them mechanically, the blade of grass between his lips bobbing up and down furiously. For every apple O.T. peeled, Walt peeled four.

"What's got yer goat this morning, brother?" O.T. asked him, biting into another chunk of the juicy, sour apple. It wasn't like Walt to get cross with him, or anybody, for that matter.

"Nothin'," Walt muttered sullenly.

"Go on and tell me."

"Naw." Walt grabbed another apple and peeled it quickly. O.T. reckoned he had a decent chance of slicing off his thumb. "You'll jes' laugh at me."

"I won't. What's got you madder than a settin' hen?"

"I ain't mad," Walt said with a sigh, setting down the half-peeled apple. "I'm…dunno…worrit, I reckon."

"Worrit about what?"

Walt looked glanced furtively around the kitchen.

"Hazel's outside mixing the dough. You know she likes workin' her bowl out on the porch, where she can set in the rockin' chair," O.T. said. "Now tell me." He was dying to know what kind of secret his straight-laced brother could have that wasn't fitting for Hazel's ears.

"Awright. Well, the thang is—" Walt swallowed nervously, the blade of grass bobbing up and down, "I kinda got me a…a date, I reckon." His ears turned bright red.

"Do you now?" O.T. was shocked. His face broke into a grin. Well, if that didn't beat all! "With Miss Sivvy?"

"Yes." Walt did not look up.

"I cain't believe you got up the guts to ask her," O.T. said with a proud grin.

"Didn't." Walt resumed peeling the apple, his face flushed with embarrassment. "She ast me." He chewed on the blade of grass. "I like to died. When you was down at the creek with Miss Betty Lou, and Hosey went in to say how-do to Pap and Granny. Miss Lila, she was sittin' in the car. We got left all alone." He shook his head, embarrassed. "I din't know what to say to her, but she was nice. She just ast me if later I wanted to meet her at the tree and look up at the stars. Shocked me to death. I said accorse I would—even if she warn't so purdy I would've, just for politeness sake, but accorse she *is* purdy…."

O.T. was a little astounded at the little lady named Sivvy, the niece of the big and bold Billy Rev, who seemed to have her own ideas about things. He wondered what the good reverend would say if he knew she'd asked a young man to meet her in the evening under a tree. He felt a sudden wariness, then, that it was all a joke, that she was having Walt on; it wouldn't have been the first time. But he shook the feeling off, remembering how the dark-haired girl had cut her eyes at the both of them, almost like a drowning woman staring at a pitcher full of water. How those green eyes had flashed when she was at Granny and Pap's, staring at that tree. That girl was lonely.

And she couldn't find a nicer—or safer—person to pal around with than Walt, that was for sure. He supposed he didn't even mind that she'd picked *his* tree for their rendezvous.

"What time you suppost to go?" O.T. asked.

"Just after seb'n, she said," Walt replied, swallowing. "Thang is… O.T., I don't think I kin go after all."

"The heck you say, brother," O.T. protested. "If you done made the plan, you can't stand her up! That's not proper atall!"

"I cain't," Walt insisted, his face turning redder. "My stomach… it's all knotted up. Ever time I think about meeting her under that tree I get all to tremblin' and my heart just a'flutters. What if it's some kinda joke, or I show up there and Billy Rev is waitin'…what if it ain't proper? To be meetin' her?" He swallowed again. "If I knew for sure that she really did like me, then that'd be awright, but I cain't be sure. I ain't confident like you, brother." Walt seldom, if ever, talked about his feelings.

He really was tore up, O.T. reckoned with a sigh. "Hesh that up, now," he said good-naturedly. "And just stop that frettin'. You go on tonight and meet Miss Sivvy tonight like you done said you would. It will be awright. Yer gettin' yerself worked up for nuthin'."

"But I—"

"You just go on and do it," O.T. assured him firmly.

"I cain't." Walt shook his head furiously, looking pained. "I jes' cain't, O.T."

"So you just gon' stand her up then? With her and Billy Rev leavin' tomorry?"

"Naw…" Walt's face underwent a transformation, from worried and pained to somehow sly. "I reckoned that you might…brother.…" He swallowed. "Will you go in my place?"

"Jee-ma-nee!" O.T. bellowed.

"Shhhh!" Walt hushed him, eyes wide.

"Go on yer date *for* ya? Shoot, you crazier than a shithouse rat." O.T. shook his head in disbelief at Walt's gall.

"Language," Walt said primly, rolling the peeled apple back and forth in his hands.

"I cain't go on yer date for you, ya galoot. For one thang, I got me a gal now." O.T.'s chest puffed with pride. "And she done warned me about steppin' out on her. I ain't doin' *nuthin'* to mess things up with Betty Lou. And anyhow, it's *yer* date. You should go. You like her, don't you?"

"Accorse I do. That's why I cain't go." Walt was about to cry. "Please, brother. I beg of ya. Just go meet her under the tree and see if she really likes me. I cain't stand her up, but I cain't go, neither. I'm scairt. If she do—if she really likes me—then maybe she'll write to me. Y'know, while she's on her travels. Writin' is easy, I kin do that. Even *I* cain't mess that up. And then maybe next year, if'n they come back this way...." Walt looked down, embarrassed.

O.T. felt a pang of tenderness toward his brother, knowing that if he did not agree, Walt would let Sivvy pass him by. But this was dishonest, and not just to Sivvy, either. What would Betty Lou say if she knew O.T.'d been out with another girl, innocent or not, after that speech of hers? He'd never seen her angry, but he could imagine it would be something fierce. She might even stop going with him.

"Walt—" he started, but the desperate look in his brother's eyes stopped him.

There was one person he loved even more than Betty Lou.

"Awright," he said finally. "I'll go on yer date, you dern bumbling idiot. But you got to peel the rest of these apples by yer dang self."

Sivvy pulled a cardigan over her thin white dress and pushed a brush through her dark hair. The mirror in the guestroom was grimy and gummy with age. She could barely see her own reflection, but it was still a sight better than nothing—which was the typical state of things. Often days went by before she had a chance to wash up. She had been wearing the same dress for so long she barely noticed the discoloration in the armpits or the threadbare spots in the knees anymore. It didn't matter none. She'd got to where she looked at herself through other folks' eyes anyhow, and found she could see herself pretty clear thataway, if she knew how to look. Billy Rev had got her started. Go into town, she'd been told, and pick out the man that looks at you from the side of his eyes, the one who gets away with it because his wife is oblivious or too tired to care. The one who pretends he isn't looking, his Adam's apple bobbing nervously in his throat, who looks down when you meet his eyes. Those are always the ones. The ones who see you back.

It was a good thing Maybelle seemed content to make cow eyes at Billy Rev all afternoon, and Sivvy hoped the sad spectacle would continue on through supper and into the night. Those cow eyes were the only thing keeping her uncle from busting up on her and discovering her not where she was supposed to be. He kept his eyes on her, his prize pony. The risk of getting caught was big—she knew it was—but the thrill outweighed the risk, and by God she was *going*.

It had just about taken an act of God to convince Harvey, though, and she didn't blame him. The young black man nearabout jumped out of his skin every time a white person walked opposite him on the street, and he was frightful terrified of Billy Rev. Sivvy knew full well the only reason Harvey had agreed was because she was sweet and pretty and she'd flitted her eyelashes. She supposed she should feel some shame about using Harvey so, but she didn't feel too bad about it. Harvey didn't know about the men she flirted with and the extra income Billy Rev got out of the bargain, and that was good enough. This one time, mayhaps, a little flirtation might benefit *her* rather than Billy Rev.

Billy Rev thought she was meeting the dark-haired man with the hard eyes, with whom she'd brushed shoulders after church, the one whose wife had dishwater-colored hair in a braid down her back. She hadn't had to make eyes at him; he'd approached her the minute he'd seen her step off alone. She'd told him, glancing sideways from under hooded eyes, that she'd meet him in the park for a stroll after supper, but she had no intention of doing so. The man had raised a little fear in her—he was used to getting what he wanted, and he might use violence to get it, she reckoned. She'd lie to Billy Rev, Sivvy decided, and say the man had failed to show. Besides, he had enough to blackmail the man already. Just approaching Sivvy for a tryst was enough.

While Sivvy felt a pang of remorse for involving Harvey, she didn't let herself dwell on that overlong.

Everybody got to look out for their own self, she thought as she shoved the brush into her pocket. "It ain't none of my affair if some folks don't watch their own back," she murmured to herself.

No, she wouldn't be seeing the hard-eyed man under cover of darkness tonight, but rather his nephew, a boy with pretty gray eyes every bit as soft as his uncle's were hard. A lovely boy, to be sure. She bit her cheek again, tasting the warm salt of her own blood, and glanced one more time at her reflection. Pretty as a picture.

O.T. stood under the sassafras tree, leaning up against the great gray trunk, listening to the sounds of the coming night. It was too late in the year for crickets, but he could hear the rustling birds in the branches, and the occasional faint song of their feathered brethren. The sky was blue-melting-into-gray, inching toward black, and he counted two stars, silver pinpricks overhead. Five honking geese flew by in a V, and he smiled, pulling his snuff out of his pocket. He'd messed up his hair and was wearing his brother's clothes, and if anybody knew Walt well enough to copy his mannerisms and speech, it was O.T. Hell, Sivvy barely knew either of them anyway, so she wasn't like to notice. He still felt guilty, though, and sad for his brother, that he should miss out on his own first date. Part of him hoped that Sivvy would back out, not come at all.

"Walt?" O.T. turned, momentarily startled. Sivvy stood behind him, dressed in the white lacy dress she'd worn at revival. A pink cardigan, buttoned all the way up, covered her dress, and a jaunty black hat with a lace veil perched atop her dark hair. Her arms were crossed tightly over her chest; whether she was cold or nervous, O.T. couldn't tell.

"Thought fer a minute you warn't comin'," he said, mimicking Walt's fast-paced, slightly monotone twang. "How do, Missus Sivvy?"

"I'm good, I rankin," she said, and it took O.T. a moment to decipher that *rankin* might mean *reckon*. "Yerself?"

"Mighty good, Miss Sivvy." He smiled down at her, marveling at how jet-black her hair looked in the dim light of dusk. Being from the mountains, perhaps she was part Creek or Cherokee. Wouldn't be polite to ask, though.

They stood awkwardly for a few moments. Walt, O.T. knew, would have stood around tittering nervously, waiting for Sivvy's cues. So that's just what O.T. did. Finally, she reached out and grabbed his arm.

"Shall we go fer a walk, Walt?"

"I s'pose," O.T. said, feeling a trifle nervous. If anybody saw them walking alone together at dusk, tongues might wag. He hadn't told Pap and Granny that he would be here tonight, meeting a girl in their yard. They turned in for bed right after supper and slept like the dead, so there was little chance of encountering them. It did seem a strange request, Sivvy asking Walt to meet here. Hardly the actions of a respectable young lady, particularly one under the stern eye of a reverend. "I know a little path off in the woods where we can walk. It's almost dark so we'll have to watch our step, but if you trust me—"

"I trust you," she said in a quiet voice that seemed to have a little laughter in it.

"You don't want yer uncle knowin' you're out with me, huh?" O.T. blurted out. "That why you wanted to meet here? At night time?"

"Part of it," she answered dreamily, reaching out to caress a pine tree, her fingers grazing the bark as though it were an old friend. "The other part, I rankin, is that I just really like this piece o'land. I wanted to come back and see it one more time."

O.T. smiled at that. He really liked this piece of land, too. He could imagine him and Betty Lou raising a bunch of kids, with cottony white hair and icy blue eyes, who would play in these woods while he played them ditties on his banjo. He could see Betty Lou standing on the front porch, welcoming company, and himself growing old beneath the day-glow leaves of that sassafras tree. He could imagine all of that just fine.

"Y'all leaving tomorry, then?" he asked, aware of the weight of her arm in his own.

"Ayuh," she answered. "After supper. We'll stay most of the day, let Billy Rev congregate with folks. He just likes to stay on so he can get him breakfast and lunch. He's so tight he'll squeeze two pennies till juice runs out of 'em," Sivvy confided, looking up at O.T. "But rankin we'll leave jest after supper. Mosey on to the next town, do it all over again. Me, him, and Harvey."

"D'ya like learning the Gospel?" O.T. asked. Walt would want to know all about her work for the Lord. He'd probably recite Bible verses and ask her interpretation of scripture. "Have you learned much from yer uncle? I reckon you'll be giving sermons yerself soon enough."

Sivvy made a noise in her throat. "He ain't ever gon' let me preach, Walt. Anythin' I learned about sermons and the Gospels I learned mahself from readin' the good book, or at school." She pronounced "book" like "buk," and the word "school" rolled off her lips in a whispery, dreamy fashion, like a woman talking about a lover. "And from listenin' to him preach, though the good Lord knows I heard enough a'his sermons to last me all my days."

O.T. was faintly scandalized but delighted. Perhaps it hadn't been such a bad thing that Walt hadn't come tonight. "Y'all don't get along, you and your uncle?"

O.T. felt the sudden tension in Sivvy's arm as she rushed to reply, "Aye? Accorse we do! Uncle Billy has been so *good* to me. I owe him so much I kin never repay. Why, he's shown me such Christian kindness…"

"I didn't mean to make you upset," he said quietly. "If I was astin' too much, bein' nosy—"

"Nay, it's nothin' to me," Sivvy said airily. "Sometimes I get ahead of myself, is all. I gotta learn how to stop talkin' affore I git in treble." She stared up at his face for a moment, her eyes dark and stormy. "But I trust you, Walt. I rankin I do."

Sivvy had no reason to trust him. She didn't even know him, didn't know either of them. It seemed to O.T. that this girl was playing with fire, deliberately. He felt faintly uneasy, as if he were a pawn in some kind of game, but a little thrilled, too. He'd never been out at night with a pretty girl before, and his heart beat fast in his chest.

They came upon the clearing O.T. and Walt called the "butterfly spot"—a secluded grove with room enough to stand, a heap of slowly rotting logs off to the side where a person could sit if they weren't afraid of fire ants, and a lean-to woodshed. Fragrant blossoms never bloomed here, but the butterflies came all the same, flitting by the dozen. The twins came here often—O.T. sitting under his beloved sassafras tree, and Walt watching for his butterflies—separate, but always together, the two of them. "This is the butterfly spot," O.T. told her. "I come out here a lot to be on my own."

"And you showed it to me." Sivvy smiled. "I'm right touched, so I am." The top of her head barely reached his chin, she was so short, but when she tilted her head back, her bright eyes looking into his, O.T. felt his insides turn to liquid, and he couldn't look away.

"Walt," she whispered.

"Yes'm?"

Sivvy raised herself up on tiptoe and pressed her mouth to his. For a moment O.T. hesitated, unsure what to do, but then madness kicked in and he wrapped his own arms around her waist and pulled her close. She smelled good, like biscuit dough, warm vanilla, cinnamon and lilac. O.T. could feel her heart beating against his chest, her slim fingers digging lightly into his shoulders. He pulled her closer, feeling her plump red lips working over his, her tongue probing his mouth, tasting of sweet tea and honey. He kissed her back, losing himself, his mouth and body and brain all responding to her touch, her taste, her smell. His arms tightened around her and he picked her up, swung her around a little, still kissing, still tasting her. She was light as a feather and her black hair tickled his face.

When they finally broke apart, it was Sivvy who pulled away, her bottom lip grazing his chin. She looked up at him, her glittering green eyes searching his own. Her mouth, plump and red after the kiss, bloomed into a slow smile.

O.T., breathing hard, felt a cascade of guilt. A small voice inside said, *That was yer first kiss, you dummy. You stupid dummy.* An even smaller voice: *If that's what kissin' feels like, I don't ever want to stop.*

The smallest voice, so quiet and buried that he almost didn't hear it: *pick her up and do it again.*

It was as if Sivvy, too, had heard that smallest voice. "That was right forward of me, I rankin…" she murmured, resting a hand on his chest, her glittery dark eyes starting into his. "I hope you don't think I'm a lowly gal—some Jezebel—"

"Hush," O.T. heard himself saying, his voice husky. "I don't think nothin', Miss Sivvy. Nothin' atall." That was the opposite of true. His thoughts were a-tumbling around like monkeys in a barrel; he couldn't grasp ahold of them, they were running to and fro so fast his blood felt hot, and he was uncomfortable all over. He fought the urge to grab her up again, after which the good Lord only *knew* what would've happened. Even now, with her touching his chest, he was almost desperate to—O.T. shook his head, clearing the cobwebs, and stepped back.

"Rankin we oughter head back?" Sivvy said resignedly. "I s'pose it ain't proper, us bein' here alone."

He nodded gratefully. "Reckon' we oughter." He offered her his arm, ignoring the goosebumps that prickled where her skin brushed his, and they started walking back down the path. He prayed nobody would drive by, prayed that Granny and Pap would stay snoring, prayed that he could escort her home safely without a body knowing that he'd been out with her alone.

"You don't have to escort me back," she said quietly.

"I shore do, Miss Sivvy," he said firmly. "I cain't let you go off in the night by yerself. Why, you don't even know this town. I'll see you at least back to Main Street. It ain't far. We'll walk off to the side, near the trees. With a bit a luck nobody'll happen upon us. And if they do, we'll make up some story."

"Thank you, Walt," Sivvy said, squeezing his arm.

They walked the two miles back to town without speaking much, both lost in their thoughts. O.T. glanced up at the stars and wondered what the hell had happened between them. They didn't meet a soul on the way back to town—he was grateful for that.

Upon reaching Main Street, O.T. ducked behind the post office, pulling her with him. Two street lights lit the main stretch of Five Forks, and this side of town was shrouded in darkness. "You can make it back to where yer stayin' the rest of the way on yer own?" he asked hopefully.

Sivvy nodded, her eyes liquid pools in the darkness. Was she crying? O.T. wondered with a pang of guilt. She bit her bottom lip, and his eyes fell to it, remembering the plumpness of it against his own. He flushed, glad she couldn't see the heat in his cheeks.

"Yes'r, I kin make it back on my own."

"You ain't gonna catch no trouble for bein' out?"

"I'll sneak back in," she said, blinking rapidly.

"Well…Miss Sivvy…" O.T. suddenly remembered Walt's request. "Say, would you care to write to me? Once yer gone from town?"

"Well, I s'pose," Sivvy said, with a startled smile, brightening. "Might help pass the time. I will if I can."

"Well, awright then. Good." O.T. patted his pockets for a pencil and cursed himself for having nothing.

"It's okay." Sivvy smiled. "I right enjoyed tonight, Mr. Lawrence. Walt," she said formally, reaching out to shake his hand, a gesture that made him grin. He took her hand, shook it firmly, and they both laughed. "Say, will ya be around tomorry?" Sivvy asked. "Could ya get away right aft' lunch fer a spell? I'll bring something to write down yer address. So we can write."

"I reckon so," O.T. said, thinking. Walt could go himself, which would give him a chance to see Sivvy and say farewell. It was no good, him being out on his brother's date. He was so guilty his stomach was doing somersaults.

"Meet me out by the diner then," she said, dropping his hand and looking suddenly shy. "If yer agreeable?"

"Yes'm, I'll be glad to." O.T. tipped an imaginary hat at her, and she giggled softly. For a moment they swayed toward each other, and then each pulled back. He dismissed the brief disappointment that she didn't lean up to kiss him goodnight. Instead she smiled at him one more time, before disappearing into the darkness, her footsteps quiet on the gravel. O.T. turned in the opposite direction to walk home.

Walt appeared at a dead run, moving so fast he practically ran into the door in his rush to get out of it. One hand was grasping a cup of lukewarm coffee, which he usually didn't drink, and the other was trying to comb the snarl of hair that stuck up on the back of his head. "I'm gonna be late, O.T.," Walt cried. "She'll see I ain't there and leave."

"She won't," O.T. said firmly. Sivvy would wait as long as she was able, he knew, thinking of the fierce dermination in her eyes. "Stop frettin' and just get yerself out the door. You look fine. Put down that cup of coffee before you spill it on yer pants."

"Awright then," Walt said nervously, handing his brother the half-full cup. "I'm gone, then, brother. Wish me luck."

"Luck," O.T. said, before burying his nose in his newspaper. Walt hadn't asked too many questions about what had happened on his date with Sivvy, and O.T. reckoned it was better that way.

O.T. had lain awake a full hour the night before, recalling the way Sivvy's lips had felt on his. Betty Lou's beautiful face swam through his mind like an accusation. He loved Betty Lou, had loved her forever, and he was going to make her his if it were the last thing he ever did. He didn't care a whit for the little girl with the dark straight hair and oddly disquiet eyes. She wasn't worth betraying his brother and his sweetheart for, no chance. So why had he kissed her? He didn't have an answer. He'd fallen asleep, finally, tossing and turning the entire night in soundless guilt, still feeling the weight of Sivvy's body pressed against his.

When he'd awoken the next morning he'd let Walt grill him over breakfast, and Walt accepted his recounting without question: They'd met under the tree; they'd talked a little; they'd walked to the butterfly spot. Then he'd walked her back to town, and at the post office he'd asked her if she wanted to write. She'd said sure, and to meet her the next day. Walt had brightened at that.

"You asked her to write in front of the *post office?*" He'd exclaimed gleefully. "Don't that beat all! Did you plan it that way?"

"Naw," O.T. had answered, biting into a piece of bacon. "Didn't think nuthin' of it."

"Golly," Walt had said, slapping the table. "And she wants to see me again. Golly!"

"Yeah," O.T. had answered. "And *yer* going this time, not me. I'm not gonna be yer fill-in no more. Grow a pair of—" Hazel had walked in, cutting off his vulgarity with a pointed look. Both O.T. and Walt had flushed and finished the breakfast in silence, the matter settled.

And now Walt had gone off to meet his girl, and O.T. was glad to be shut of the whole business. He attributed the faint twinge in his gut to guilt and not jealousy. After all, Betty Lou was the prettiest girl in town and she had all but told him yesterday that he was her guy. He would put the business with Sivvy out of his head. As far as Sivvy Hargrove was concerned, the outing had technically happened to Walt, and that was the end of it.

Two hours later, O.T. was sweating in the field, cussing up a storm and wishing Walt would get back to help him. How long did it take to exchange addresses? They hadn't had any rain in two months at least, and the dirt was rock solid. Hazel kept coming out to the edge of the field and yelling at him for something or another. It had been almost a week since they had seen Tom. Maybe the fool would never come back, save them all a heap of trouble.

O.T. heard a car coming down the road and stopped for a minute, wiping the sweat off his brow, leaving a streak of red dust in its place. It was the Pittmans' car. O.T. groaned. He wasn't fittin' to see Betty Lou, not dressed in his coveralls and naught else, no shoes and caked with red mud head to toe. O.T. resignedly dropped the hoe and walked up to the house to greet whoever it was, wishing to hell he weren't so filthy.

Mrs. Pittman sat in the driver's seat, her dainty white gloves gripping the wheel, her mouth pursed grimly. Betty Lou sat in the passenger seat, her own face flushed and distressed. O.T. glanced in the back of the cab and instantly forgot his embarrassment at looking so bedraggled. Walt was sitting in the backseat, leaning on Hosey Brown, his face streaked with tears.

O.T. ran to the car, to his brother, forgetting all about Betty Lou. "What's happened?" he asked. "What in the hell has happened?"

"Let's get us inside and we'll tell you, son," Mrs. Pittman said, her mouth still pursed. O.T. began to panic—had he been found out, somehow? Had Walt had come clean and told everyone that it had been O.T. with Sivvy after all? Had Betty Lou and her mother driven here to give him the hosing down he deserved? Betty Lou's face was grim. Even Hosey, usually a blabbermouth, was quiet and gray-faced. O.T. had no choice but to lead them all inside, his insides quivering, as Walt trailed behind him, sniffling.

Inside, Hazel set out coffee, teacakes, and dried apples. O.T. furiously wiped his dirty hands on his coveralls and threw on his old pair of shoes, inwardly cussing at how filthy he looked. Mrs. Pittman bit daintily into a teacake and accepted a cup of coffee silently.

"Walter, hon, tell us what's happened," Hazel said finally, placing a gentle hand over Walt's.

"I didn't do what he said I did," Walt protested sullenly.

Dropping his head into his hands, Walt started to beat at his face. "I. Did. Not. Do. It."

"He's doing it again," Mrs. Pittman said helplessly to Betty Lou, who looked stricken. "He was doing that in the car."

"He's awright," Hosey said, gently guiding Walt's hands back down to his lap.

"Would somebody tell me what in the sam hell has got my brother so worked up!" O.T. interjected impatiently.

"O.T., calm down. I'll tell you," Betty Lou said quickly, touching his hand. "We were leavin' the diner after lunch, and we happened upon Walt and Billy Rev. Walt was crying and carrying on. Doing like he's doing now, with his hands. Billy Rev was screamin' at him."

"He shore was," Mrs. Pittman agreed. "Bellowin' like a bull, right in that poor boy's face. And to think—a man of the Lord!"

O.T.'s heart begin to sink. "Sivvy warn't there?"

"No, she wasn't," Betty Lou replied, "just Billy Rev. And he was yelling to beat the band. Sayin' all kinds of things, and Walt just standing there, crying, saying he didn't do it. We thought we might be of help, so we went up to 'em, asked if everything was awright. Billy Rev took no notice of us. He was plum red in the face. Yellin' at Walt, accusing him of things."

"What things?" Hazel's face had gone a little white.

There was a long silence. "Of...of tarnishing his niece," Mrs. Pittman said, after a pause. "Accused him of meeting her in secret last night. Said he'd taken her girlhood from right under his nose. Accused him of being a—" She blushed, her cheeks turning a pretty pink. "Of...meddling with her." She looked down at her lap, her lips pressed together so tight they all but disappeared.

"But Walt wasn't even out last night!" Hazel exclaimed. "O.T. was out with Hosey, but Walt was here!" Hosey looked at O.T. sharply, and O.T. thanked the good Lord that Hosey was the best friend he had in the world, knowing that Hosey would die before exposing O.T.'s lie.

"That's just what we told him," Mrs. Pittman said firmly. "We told the reverend that he *must* be mistaken. That Walt's the sweetest, most God-fearing boy in town and that he'd never, ever—"

"I told him," Walt interjected, his face ashen. "I told him I never."

"We all told him," Betty Lou said angrily. "But he was raving like the dickens and wouldn't listen. That skinny, chicken-necked old codger."

"Betty Lou!" Mrs. Pittman exclaimed, feigning shock.

"The reverend talked like he was going to get the sheriff have Walt locked up," Betty Lou went on. "We told him no he *wasn't*. And we wanted to know where he'd even got such an idea that Walt had taken advantage of his niece."

"What did he say?" O.T. asked, straining to keep his face calm.

"Said he just knew. Said a little bird told him. I like to spit in his face."

"*Betty Lou,*" Mrs. Pittman warned again, but with a smile.

"That's when Hosey come up, and by then there was a crowd of folks watchin' us. A couple spoke up for Walt. And then Miss Sivvy come out herself. She'd been cryin', too, poor thing. You could tell. She told the Rev that Walt had never laid a finger on her, had never even clapped eyes on her more'n twice. I felt right bad for her."

"So what happened?"

"Oh, he puffed and ranted a little bit more, and then put his big ol' fat finger in Walt's face and told him to stay the devil away from his niece. Said he'd lock him up if he so much as looked in her direction. A bunch of dumb threats," Hosey said with a grin. "Said he'd never come back to this one-horse town to spread the word of the Lord again. He was gon' leave us to our sin. Then he stomped his ass back down to the motel, 'bout wrenchin' that poor girl's arm out of the socket the whole way. Her just a cryin'. That sumbitch."

"Language," Hazel warned, before Walt had a chance, and Hosey winked at her. She pretended not to notice.

"He hurt Miss Sivvy," Walt moaned, dropping his head into his hands again. "She was crying so hard!"

"It's okay," O.T. said softly, placing a protective arm around his brother's shoulders.

"No, it ain't," Walt cried, his voice muffled. "I never did give her my address. How we gon' write to each other now?"

O.T couldn't answer, the shame bubbling up deep in his belly. Somehow the reverend had found out what had happened. He thought Walt had ruined his niece, but it had been O.T. all along.

The road was in ill repair. Every time the wagon hit a bump or a pothole, Sivvy was thrown into Harvey's shoulder, rigid and tense beside her. She could feel the fear and anger coming off him in waves, but his face, when she caught a glimpse of it, was blank.

Billy Rev drove erratically down Highway 29, out of Five Forks, and toward Athens. The moon was visible from Sivvy's window, high in the sky and round and as white as a breast. Sivvy thought of her mother, whom she missed but would never admit it. She and her mother had never really found each other's threads. Sivvy's six brothers and sister, who came before her, had sapped up the best parts of Mama before Sivvy had had a chance. Even after all this time, she could not bring herself to forgive her parents; the door to her heart was shut to them, even though she knew it wasn't fair.

But there was no use dwelling on that now.

Her face felt crusty and tight with her tears dried on her cheeks, tears she hadn't bothered to wipe away. She had wanted Billy Rev to see those tears and feel bad, unaware, then, that it would only spur him on, that any evidence of her pain was a thrill to him.

Hours before, Sivvy had been giddy with excitement at the thought of meeting the boy. She'd wanted only to feel young, free—just for a minute. How could she ever have thought she could get away with it? And she'd gone and gotten that sweet boy in a heap of trouble.

For a brief moment, as she gazed at the moon, Sivvy wished she were lying with her head on her mama's chest, a child again, warm and safe in the grove of crooked trees back on the ridge. She dropped her eyes to her lap, to her hands, which were streaked with grime, the skin around her fingernails ragged, ugly, and torn. They trembled a little as she brought them up to her face and wiped off the old salt of her tears.

Harvey's shoulder twitched beside her, then was still. The wagon rumbled on.

PART II

Buy the sky and sell the sky, and lift your arms up to the sky
And tell the sky and tell the sky, don't fall on me

-R.E.M.

CHAPTER FOUR

September 8, 1929
Five Forks, Georgia

O.T. dipped his makeshift paintbrush into the foul black mixture, ran it carefully over the sides of the tin can, then gently painted the new growth at the top of the cotton plant. The tender little blooms could take a soaking of arsenic and molasses and still live to tell the tale, so long as you didn't overdo it. O.T. had spilled so much of the stuff on himself over the years that he reckoned he had a permanent sticky sheen.

Leaning back for a moment, O.T. wiped the sweat from his eyes and surveyed the field. Between him, Walt, and Hosey, they'd just about finished the job, but the task had taken the entire day. He hadn't clapped eyes on Betty Lou or the children since breakfast, choosing to skip lunch and finish up his work, something he did quite often. His stomach was rumbling to beat the band, and he could feel the beginnings of a late-summer sunburn on his upper arms and the back of his neck. Just a couple more rows and they'd be done.

"Y'all go on and finish up fer the day," he called to his helpers, feeling magnanimous. "Betty Lou's prob'ly got supper fixed. Go get it while it's hot. I'll be on in direckly."

"We's almost done," Walt argued good-naturedly, dipping his own cotton paintbrush in the poison syrup. "Might as well stay on and help ya."

"Shoot, Walt," Hosey laughed from his own side of the field. "When a man tells you it's quittin' time, you oughter listen to 'im." But he was still working steadily along himself.

"Suit yerselves, ya galoots." O.T. went back to his work with a happy grin. Tending cotton fields was backbreaking, tiring work, but having his brother and best friend around to help him sure did help pass the job away easy. The three of them together could lick just about any job, and quick. Were it not for the boll weevil—which in the course of a few short years had gone from being an annoying pest to a terrifying scourge—and the never-ending drought, he reckoned he'd have a huge cotton crop this time around, a real fortune. As it was, though, he was hoping for a crop sufficient to pay the bills and keep a little food on Betty Lou's table.

As he leaned down to dip his paintbrush—a stick whittled to straightness, topped with a bushy piece of cotton pulled out at the ends to form a brush—into the molasses and arsenic, he heard Betty Lou calling from the house: "O.T.! Y'all! Supper's on!"

"Almost done, sweetness!" he hollered back. Betty Lou hated when he was late for supper. He'd told her time and again to go on and serve herself and the kids, but she just had to hold the table for him, and she'd sit there sighing ever louder every second it took him to get inside, wash up, and finally sit down to say grace. Then the moment the "amen" was out of his mouth, she'd tell him it was all cold, thanks to him. "Y'all go on ahead!" O.T. yelled.

"We certainly will not, Owen Lawrence! Y'all come on! 'Fore it ain't hot no more!"

"Five minutes!" he called back with a chuckle, his stomach growling painfully. The larders were almost bare; they'd been scrimping their pennies for a few weeks, hoping to make them last as long as possible before having to go to the store to buy what staples they couldn't grow. Betty Lou kept a careful budget, and she hadn't raised it a penny the past year, despite the dismal cotton crop, and the disappearance of their laying hen (which had wandered into the woods, they assumed; but it was just as possible a hungry neighbor had snatched it for eggs or meat). The vegetable garden had just about dried up. O.T. had had enough of sun-scorched, dry banana peppers and withered, rubbery crooknecks to last him a lifetime. He hoped Betty Lou had managed to rustle up some meat today.

The three of them finished their work in the five minutes he'd allotted and trudged back to the house, holding their pails of godawful poison molasses and their dirty, homemade brushes out to the side, careful not to slosh. They rinsed everything out in the tin bucket by the barn, and washed their hands with strong lye soap. O.T. pulled out his packet of Beech-Nut tobacco, tearing off a chew for each of them. The Beech Nut would be the next luxury to go, if things didn't pick up soon.

"Crop ain't gon' amount to much'a nuthin' this year," O.T. warned as the three of them walked up to the house. As they passed the sassafras tree, he reached out and grazed his knuckles across the bark the way he always did. It wasn't quite late enough in the year for the leaves to turn orange, but he was waiting for it. "But with a lil' bit'a luck, we might scrape by just enough to make our payments and buy some groceries."

"Why'nt you just hit up Melvin Brooks's store and git what you need on credit?" Hosey asked, not for the first time. "He does it fer everybody in town."

"Well, I ain't everybody in town," O.T. said, chewing on his plug. He leaned down to spit.

"That's sure," Hosey replied, cuffing him on the shoulder. "Yer ten times more proud than the rest of us put together. Too good for dang credit. You'd rather starve to death."

Walt was silent. His lip puffed out on the left side, where the plug of tobacco lodged; on the right, his usual blade of grass hung out of his mouth, fluttering a little in the breeze. O.T. wondered what was on his mind. Walt hadn't said much the past few days; he seemed to be studying on something. With Walt, it was best to wait until he was ready to give over—pestering only made him clam up more.

"You okay, brother?" O.T. asked.

"Ayuh," Walt replied, his voice far off. "Jes' hongry."

"You and me both," O.T. replied. Betty Lou stood barefoot on the porch, hands on her shapely hips. O.T. looked up at his wife approvingly. Even with her tattered old apron and a crocheted cloth over her light-blonde hair, she looked fresh as morning. Her red dress, crisply neat from the hem at her ankles to the high round collar at her neck, was hand-sewn and taken in at her waist. The early-evening sun lit across her head, casting her aglow.

Betty Lou couldn't maintain her annoyance for long. "You boys look like hell," she said with a laugh, reaching out and tousling her husband's hair. "And if it ain't my forever houseguest." She eyed Hosey. "You stayin' for supper, I reckon?"

"Aw, shoot, Betty Lou," Hosey said with a bashful leer. "I reckon I am."

"Good thing I set another place, then," she said, turning on her heel, her red dress swishing behind her. "But yer all three gonna wash yer hands again before you set at my table. Ain't none of you done a good enough job."

O.T. watched her backside as it disappeared inside the house. God, he loved that woman.

❧

O.T. sighed with audible relief when he saw the fried pork and potatoes, alongside the usual cornbread, sorghum syrup, and turnip greens. It wasn't much meat, but enough for everybody to have a taste. How that woman managed to rustle up food from nothing never ceased to amaze him.

He clasped his hands together and said a quick grace—"thank'ya, Father, who art in heaven for this thy bounty, amen"—and Betty Lou passed the plates around. Beside her was their littlest, Isabelle, who at three years old had the same white cottony hair and attitude as her mama; beside Belle was Owen Jr., eight, who was already digging into the skillet for the crispiest piece of cornbread. Betty Lou smacked his hand, not hard enough to hurt, but he sucked in his breath and his lip trembled, as if he might cry.

"Don't you even think about it," Betty Lou fixed Owen with a stern eye, then winked at him. He brightened as she put the cornbread on his plate. O.T. shook his head. Spoiled kids. Genevieve, their eldest, known to the family as Ginny, sat across from him. At thirteen, she was starting to grow faster than Betty Lou could take out her dresses, and while she was a durn good helper in the fields *and* the kitchen, she'd been sullen just lately. O.T. often wondered where his sweet, smiling little girl, who had once loved ponies and hydrangeas, had gone.

Maybe I oughter have Walt talk to her, O.T. mused, watching his twin brother place a tiny piece of cornbread on his plate and cover it with sorghum syrup. The two were close.

"Get you some meat and some greens," O.T. told his brother firmly. Walt would eat just enough to make somebody mad: a piece of cornbread or one lousy biscuit dipped in apple jelly, or the world's smallest bowl of grits. He claimed he hadn't much appetite, but O.T. knew that he was forgoing his own portion so that the kids could eat more. And he aimed to put a stop to it, one way or another. He might not have two pennies to rub together, but his brother worked like a dog to help around the farm and by God, he would feed *all* his family till they were full. "I done told you I ain't gon' sit by and watch you live off cornbread and syrup. A man's gotta eat, Walt."

"You done shriveled up to a string bean, Uncle Walt," Owen Jr. said, with a mouth full of potatoes.

Betty Lou grabbed the serving spoon and dished some pork onto Walt's plate. He raised a hand in protest. "Naw, naw. I'm not very hungry, sister. I couldn't eat it. Naw."

"You'll eat at least that, Walt, and another helping if I have my say," Betty Lou replied in the tone that nobody dared argue with.

"I really couldn't," Walt protested weakly, then gave up and raised the fork to his mouth. He did look a little peaked, O.T. thought, watching his brother, hoping Walt was not working himself into a fit; it had been almost two years since Walt had had one, and O.T. hoped they were now behind him.

"So, dear wife, where did you happen to get this fine pork and these here taters?" he asked Betty Lou with a wide smile. "What'd ya trade this time? My car? Yer garters?"

"Har har," Betty Lou replied, pouring herself a glass of tea and passing the pitcher down the line. "As a matter of fact, I traded a jar of persimmon wine for the pork, and I got the taters as a payment for watching Misrus Maybelle's grand-young'un yesterday. She had an aching head and could hardly get outta bed, so I kep' him here at the house to play with the kids."

"You ain't traded *all* the persimmon wine, did you?" O.T. teased. "What's Hosey gon' get drunk on?"

"Oh, hush up," Hosey said, his mouth full. "That was one time, what, five year ago? And you ain't ever gon' let up. Anyhow, I get my own hooch these days." He winked at Walt, who didn't seem to take notice.

"Let's not discuss this at the supper table," Betty Lou said smoothly, even though she'd been the one to bring it up. She looked at O.T. with bright eyes—the devil in 'em, looked like—and wiped at her lip with her napkin. O.T. knew that look well. Good enough for him. Suddenly he couldn't wait for bedtime. He felt Betty Lou's foot find his under the table and he nudged her back, letting his foot trail up her ankle and under her red dress. The angelic smile never left her face.

"Gon' head out fer a spell after supper," Walt said.

"What fer?" O.T. asked, tearing into a piece of cornbread. "You need a ride? I kin take you in the car."

"Naw," Walt said. "I reckon I'll catch a ride with Hosey. You headin' into town later?" Walt asked Hosey, avoiding O.T.'s eyes.

"Yeah, I reckon I'll mosey on home after I done et," Hosey said, with a sigh. He lived alone, and had done since his ma had died twelve years past. O.T. knew that just as he needed Hosey's help on the farm, so did Hosey need the company; that, and he would've long since starved to death out there by himself, with barely enough money to buy food and no sense in the kitchen. "At least fer a bit," Hosey said with a widening grin. "I got me a date tonight."

"Who with?" Betty Lou asked.

"*Pshaw*, ain't nobody. Just Miss Ella Hardman," Hosey said, waving a hand dismissively.

"Why, Ella Hardman's a lovely gal!" Betty Lou exclaimed, her face lighting up. "She taught Sunday school with me. Pretty, and young and sweet! She'll make you a wonderful—"

"Don't even say it, Betty Lou," Hosey wagged a finger at her. "I ain't got no designs on gittin' marrit, so don't even—"

"Hosey Brown, you hear what I say. You're dang near thirty and it's high time you—"

"I ain't gon' marry nobody," he proclaimed, snatching a sliced banana pepper from the cold plate and popping it into his mouth. "'Less it's one woman in partic-lar. And only one woman."

O.T. and Walt shared a smile. "Jee-ma-nee, Hosey, ain't you ever gon' let it go? Hazel's done been marrit to Tom for goin' on twenty years—"

"And I'll wait twenty more. Heck, forty, if I have to."

"You's a damn fool," O.T. groaned. But so is Hazel, he thought to himself. At church Sunday past, Hazel had deftly avoided O.T.'s question about how long Tom had been gone. He reckoned it had been near a month this time, maybe longer. Tom—interested only in cash, booze, and tail—had sold his land to sharecroppers years ago, and the family homestead to O.T. the second he'd made an offer. While these transactions had eased his expenses, they left a mighty burden on Hazel. With her husband's frequent absences, she was the one left to meet the obligations. O.T. and Walt stepped in whenever they could to help her, but O.T. had his own farm and family to attend to. He made a mental note to set a few coins by. It'd put his family in hardship, but he wasn't going to let his sister starve.

O.T. still couldn't believe he'd got his place so easy. Tom was a cad, but his folks had willed it to him, their only son. "Place always meant more to y'all than it did me," Tom had told O.T. with a shrug. So O.T. had groveled and got a small loan from Mr. Pittman, and had saved up the rest doing side jobs, working himself near to death. Finally the place was his. Tom didn't so much as bat an eye signing the papers. It made O.T. guilty, to think of Hazel having to work like a dog when he had this place. He'd offered more than once to let her come stay, but Hazel was a Lawrence through and through—stubborn as the dickens and full of pride. O.T. had bought his patch of land and house from Tom fair and square. It held a place of honor in his heart, just below that of his wife, children, and siblings.

Betty Lou came into the bedroom, kicking off her shoes and sinking onto the bed, which creaked under her weight.

"Lord, I'm tired," she groaned, rolling onto him and throwing an arm over his chest.

"You don't look it." And she didn't. Betty Lou had the knack for looking fresh-faced and smooth no matter what. He'd seen her covered in the kids' sick, out in the fields digging with the hoe, chasing the hen through the dirty yard, cooking fatback over a hot stove, and always just as pretty as on her wedding day.

Betty Lou propped her head on his belly, staring at him. "Well, you sure do, hon." She traced circles on his stomach with her finger. "Y'all worked yerselves damn near to death today. Please tell me yer done."

"All done," he said with a smile. "All the cotton's painted, and tomorry I'm all yers."

"All mine?"

"Yes, ma'am," he replied, leaning on his arms to look at her. "I ain't forgot about that plank on the porch you need fixed. And I reckon I'll take Owen Jr. out to the vegetable patch and see what I can't teach him. See if we can't get a mess of greens for our supper." He grinned at her slyly. "And I might even get around to fixin' that chiffarobe of yers that's been laying out in the barn broke for the past year. So you can put up yer delicate lacy things and stop storin' 'em in the suitcase."

"I've been beggin' you to fix that chiffarobe for a coon's age," Betty Lou said, laughing, still tracing circles on his skin. O.T. closed his eyes, enjoying the feel of her hands on him. Even after all this time, she drove him nuts. "I just cain't believe yer suddenly aimin' to do it now."

"Just you wait, woman," he said, leaning back on the pillows with a sigh. "I'm gonna do it. If I'm not too wore out."

"Wore out from what?"

"Let's see, darlin'." He reached for her, and as she rose up to meet him, she blew out the bedside candles. After all this time, they could see each other just fine in the dark.

CHAPTER FIVE

Milledgeville, GA

The sun had finally crept up the sky far enough to stream through the small thick-paned window in the corner of the room, splintering into dots of sunlight that danced upon her face as she slept. Sivvy threw an arm over her eyes, re-positioned herself on the narrow, hard mattress, and groaned. It had to be past seven already if the sun was streaming through so brightly, but the nurse hadn't been round.

Sivvy sat up in the small bed, not sure if the creaking was from the rusty bed frame or her own back. She rubbed at her eyes, the awful coating on her tongue leaving a foul metallic taste in her mouth, a side effect of her many medications. Her throat felt parched, and she yearned for a glass of water, but the water on the third floor wasn't fit to drink—it tasted like dirt—and would involve a walk through areas she didn't want to venture into.

Sivvy shivered in her thin nightshirt, which clung damply to her skin. She had been dreaming. She didn't remember it, but it must have been about *him,* because she always woke up in a sweat from those dreams. Her cell was cold as usual—always cold, no matter the season. The glass, while thick, provided no insulation, and the walls were damp and slick with moisture. Even in the dead of summer her room had a chill to it, and it always the smell of mold.

She threw her legs over the side of the bed, allowing herself a momentary daydream. She would wake to the smell of fresh-brewed coffee. She would pull on a soft, warm housecoat and venture out into the hall, brightly lit from the morning sun. Her dream house was full of windows—large windows that opened, with clear, clean panes, and framed with blue gingham curtains she'd made herself. She would walk into the parlor where her girls would be playing with their dolls, her boys playing checkers, and her man—who was faceless, but had a head full of peppery dark blond hair—would be reading the newspaper. She'd say, "Who's hungry?" and their eyes would light up. She would then whip up a platter of hoecakes, sausages, over-hard eggs, fried potatoes, and apple cake.

Sivvy's bare feet poked at the cold floor, but there were no soft house slippers. There was no house coat to throw around her narrow shoulders, and while chaotic sounds came from the hall, it wasn't a passel of fresh-cheeked young'uns, but her fellow inmates. "Guests," as the superintendent, Dr. Swint, preferred to call them. She could hear Laney, the woman who occasionally shared her room, outside her door yelling that she needed a bandage for her finger. The nurse hollered back that she'd already had two yesterday, and bandages were dear. She'd have to re-use one or find a bit of cloth. Laney called back that all her cloth had been confiscated because she'd tried to tie a noose. "I wasn't going to try and strangle one of the *guests*," she cried. "Just lil' ol' myself."

Savilia Marie Tryphena Shelnutt née Hargrove—or Miss Sivvy as they all called her—sighed and forced herself to stand. She might as well get dressed before the nurses came in and gave her a hiding. While they might have forgotten her this morning, she still had her duties. There was no man or young'uns to cook for, but in less than fifteen minutes there would be a dining area full of mental patients waiting for their cornmeal porridge and turnips.

She hoped—as she pulled on the starched kitchen dress and pushed her feet into the heavy shoes that pinched her feet—that the other cooks had left her a sip of something hot. She knew, even as she wished it, that they hadn't.

Sivvy opened the door, freshly dressed, her uniform clean but worn and faded, and stood in the hallway, waiting for Nurse Jennings. Patients were not allowed to take the elevator unattended, and Sivvy had no desire to wear the strong dress or be stuck scrubbing toilets in the privy, even though she would be late to the kitchens and that would hold its own punishment.

"Nurse Jennings?" Sivvy called. "I need to git downstairs." Other than an ancient gray-haired woman attempting to remove her nightshirt—her knobby, pale knees drawn together in what was unmistakably a gesture of going to the toilet—and from whom Sivvy hastily averted her eyes, the hallway was deserted. Most everyone had already been shuffled down to the dining room, or were confined to their rooms, awaiting attendants to bathe and dress them. Some able-bodied patients, like Sivvy, had earned the privilege of being allowed to dress themselves and come and go with reasonable freedom.

"I'm here, I'm here." Nurse Jennings appeared, shutting and locking a patient's door behind her and slipping the key into her frock. "Let's get you downstairs. Why aren't you already down, Sivvy? It's ten past seven."

"Apologies, marm," Sivvy answered, looking down at her feet. She did not point out that nobody had been in to wake her, even though the nurses were supposed to come in every morning at half past six. To draw attention to the misdeeds of the staff was to invite trouble. "I overslept."

"Perhaps you're getting sick," Nurse Jennings said finally, peering at Sivvy. "Shall we ask the doctor to take your temperature? We don't want you catching a cold."

Sivvy shuddered. Dr. Lowell—young and entitled, fresh out of college—had a habit of pressing his groin against her hip, and enjoyed putting his hands in unwelcome places, among other proclivities. At her last visit, two months ago, the doctor had extolled the virtues of more extreme forms of treatment. "I tell ya, I cain't wait for this place to git with the times, and get electroshock therapy," he'd told Sivvy eagerly, pressing his head against her chest, his greasy black hair leaving a smudge of pomade on her apron. He had insisted upon listening to her heartbeat, even though she'd been in for a kitchen burn. "Keep all these folks in line, a little jolt to the system. Patients here git too many freedoms." He was scarcely a day over twenty-three, she figured, but already he was an "adult," a young man who took old-man liberties.

"Thank you kindly, marm," Sivvy said anxiously. "But I feel all right. Perhaps it's just my monthly." It was due any day—or so she hoped. "I won't oversleep again. I promise."

"Yes, well. Let's get you downstairs. They'll be hungry."

Wordlessly, Sivvy followed Nurse Jennings down the carpeted hall to the ancient, creaking lift, and down several floors to what the staff liked to call "the largest kitchen in the world." Knotting her apron around her waist, Sivvy approached the central counter where the head cook, May, was chopping onions.

"You're late, Ms. Shelnutt," was the only greeting she was to receive. May always insisted on calling her "girls" by their surnames, even though all the employed cooks were referred to on a first-name basis, as was May herself. Her propriety felt less like reverence and more like mockery.

"I'm sorry, marm," Sivvy replied, washing her hands at the sink and pulling a chopping board from the cupboards. She set herself up beside one of the new girls—a pretty young thing with blonde pigtails, who could not be more than nineteen. Sivvy did not bother to defend herself—May was not interested in why she had been late. Nor did she exchange pleasantries with the girl. She grabbed an onion and began to chop.

"No, leave the onions. They're for stew at lunchtime, and I need you frying bacon for this morning's breakfast," May advised, looking up from her work. "Dr. Heath van Dyck is touring the hospital today, and him and some of the staff are planning to eat breakfast with the patients this morning, so I need extra. Don't burn it, mind."

"Yes'm." Sivvy was one of a few that were allowed to fry bacon, though she was careful not to smile about it in front of May, who, taking offense at her haughtiness, might take the privilege away.

"I've set the bacon out. Just over there," May gestured with a glove-covered finger. She was the type of woman who thought bacon a luxury, and Sivvy supposed it was, though she couldn't muster up any joy over it. It was a point of pride for May—even though she didn't own the hospital, and didn't pay for the groceries—that Milledgeville Asylum had bacon. She was a straight-faced woman with iron-gray hair, yanked back in a severe bun, and cold blue eyes with faint lashes that were almost invisible. "Fry the lot of it. Hope it's enough, because I haven't got any more meat to be delivered until Wednesday next."

"Yes, marm," Sivvy said. Bacon, along with the cornmeal mush and plain drop biscuits, was the highlight of the morning for most of the patients. Breakfast would be grim through Wednesday, with only turnips to serve. Perhaps May would allow her to make something special for Saturday's breakfast. Times were hard, but the asylum had a communal garden and an orchard brimming with apples and pecans, where Sivvy liked to walk on afternoons when she was allowed out. Perhaps May would let her make pralines. Or, lacking for sugar, she could parch them in a little oil and serve them salted. She would offer to gather the pecans herself.

Sivvy fried the bacon, lost in her own thoughts, absently turning the pieces with the large silver fork. As a child she hadn't given a fig for cooking, to her ma's chagrin, and yet here she was now, fifteen years later, preparing meals for thousands of patients and planning special little treats to brighten their days. Julie-Anne Hargrove might've even been proud of her daughter.

Dr. Russell, who saw her for therapy once a month, had encouraged Sivvy to write to her ma, but her words dried up every time she tried. *My family probably think I'm dead and maybe that's better than them knowing the truth*, she thought.

It had been a long while since Uncle Billy had last visited, and she allowed herself to hope he'd stay away for good. She'd begged the staff at the asylum not to allow his visits, but the superintendent had insisted that as her closest relation—her husband now being dead—he had a right.

"But he's a danger to me," Sivvy had protested hotly. "What about *my* rights?" She knew good and well that she had none. "Just ast that therapist you all force me to talk to about the things he done. Just ast!"

"You're perfectly safe here," the superintendent had assured her. "Within these walls, with all the security and nurses a few steps away, you can't come to any harm."

Tell that to all the inmates who die here every week, Sivvy thought to herself bitterly. In the fifteen years she'd been here, she'd seen more suicides and pellagra deaths than she could count, and other deaths, too—complications from medical procedures, starvation, accidents, and even a murder or two. She glanced over at the large metal mixing bowls, filled to the brim with cornmeal and flour for biscuits and cornbread. Years ago, a young male kitchen hand had climbed into one of those mixing bowls and drowned in the soup. *Patients drowning in soup, and they dared to tell her that she was safe here.*

There was nowhere in the world safe—especially not from *that* man.

It was true that Uncle Billy had made no move to harm her since she'd been here. She didn't suppose he'd even try, not in front of the prying eyes of the superintendent and staff. Still, she dreaded his visits—the way he'd sit across from her in the parlor, his small white teeth set in a grin, his eyes dancing. She was here, most likely for life, her entire existence crumbled to ash, and here he came, to leer. She had been captured, like a lightning bug in a dusty jar, the light gone out forever, and he'd come, like a grubby-faced kid, to poke at her with cruel, entitled fingers.

Sivvy finished frying the bacon and put two thick cloth napkins down over the giant platter, blotting gently to remove a little of the excess grease but not too much; little luxuries like slightly greasy bacon were not to be underestimated, in these times and this place.

"Ma'am? Can I do anything else?" Sivvy asked May, already imagining her walk among the pecan groves. Few of the patients were allowed the liberty to stroll, and those that did tended to avoid the pecan grove, which had served as a burial ground for pellagra victims after the graveyard had been filled to bursting.

"Yes, Ms. Shelnutt, if you please." Sivvy hated when the cook called her that. She'd repeatedly asked May to call her "Miss Sivvy," or even "Triphy," which is what Clay had called her, but May had refused to oblige her. "Take up a paddle and stir up the cornmeal. Add a little oil to it; we don't want it stickin' to the pans."

"Yes, marm."

Sivvy dipped a long wooden paddle into the metal bowl and swirled the cornmeal and water around, adding a cup of oil to each one.

"When you've finished the batter you may be dismissed."

"Thank you, marm. Can I pick some pecans in the grove, ma'am? For a dish?"

"I reckon you can. Take an extra apron out there with you. I ain't got no spare pails to loan you."

"Yes'm."

❧

Sivvy strolled through the pecan grove, relishing the soft squish of the damp green grass under her boots. She needed a new pair, but she would have to wait at least a month, maybe more, as the cobbler went in strict order and supplies were scarce. Nobody would make new shoes a priority here; what for? The wetness of the grass crept into a small hole in the heel and dampened her stocking, but she scarcely noticed. It had rained the day before, and everything had a wet, musty smell, but the world seemed fresh and clean, which made Sivvy smile. She recalled the mountain rains of her childhood, always cold, trickling down the path beside her as she walked home from school. She used to deliberately dawdle, careful not to be really late, but just enough to get well and truly soaked.

Sivvy walked past a gravedigger at his work and tipped her black felt hat to him. He glanced up, his gaze lingering overlong on her face. Sivvy had lost most of her looks, she knew—at least what little she'd had—in the years she'd been in the asylum. Her slanted green eyes were now embellished with crow's feet and her dark hair had a few threads of gray. But there was something about her face, apparently, that gave people pause. "I must have a crazy look," she'd confided once to Nurse Aycock, with a light laugh.

"No, Miss Sivvy," Nurse Aycock had replied, "it isn't because you look crazy."

"It ain't?" she'd asked curiously. "Then what it is, you rankin?"

"You have a sad look about you," the nurse had said. "Haunted, like. Your eyes are like a shadow on your face."

Sivvy had fallen quiet, not sure if the nurse had intended a compliment or an insult, and decided it didn't really matter. She supposed her looks, or lack of them, didn't matter; she had little interest in a passing fancy. It had been fifteen years since she had felt the touch of a man, and while she did get lonely sometimes, aching for a little human contact, nothing good could come of such a dalliance. It was strictly forbidden, for one, and while plenty of female patients got around it in clever ways, Sivvy had no interest in taking the risk. She'd gotten herself into enough trouble before she'd ever come to the asylum, allowed her loneliness to risk more necks than her own. Denying herself physical pleasure was the least she deserved after what had happened to Harvey.

Sivvy shook her head, banishing the thought. She untied her apron and fanned it out on the ground. Kneeling in the damp grass, she collected the sturdy brown nuts, feeling the weight of them, the coarse roughness of their shells, their sharply pointed edges. Back home, the ridge had been covered in wild walnuts and pecans, and Sivvy used to collect them for Ma, who would grind them into flour. On cool days, just before winter set in, they used to rack nuts over the fire, roasting and parching them, and then eating them with a sprinkle of coarse salt. She and her brothers had harvested blackberries and wild strawberries for wine and cobblers, and the tender green leaves of poke sallet for the fried greens that her daddy had loved so much. A briny, pungent smell would fill the house as Mama cooked the leaves, which had to be triple-washed and simmered to remove all the bitter poison. She recalled the tang of home brew, acrid and bitter on her tongue—secreted to her by older siblings who weren't supposed to let her have a taste—and the vinegar and honey of the summer switchell. She remembered pulling sassafras leaves until her fingers were sore, and helping Mama with the washing on blueing day—how fast Mama had worked!

Wafting from the asylum's kitchen window, behind the pecan grove, came the smell of baking cornbread and drop biscuits for the day's lunch, but it didn't hold a candle to the way her mother's kitchen had smelled when Sivvy was a child. Her ma's hands remained vivid in her recollections—her worn sun-freckled hands spreading lard into the pan before the spooning of batter for cornbread; her gentle hands brewing sassafras tea, pouring the steaming hot water into cracked ceramic mugs; and the aniseed-like smell that would waft through the house—such a comfort it had been on cold winter days. The children had left mugs of sassafras tea out with tea cakes for Santy Claus. So many memories interwoven with food, lovingly prepared, lovingly served. Mama had always believed that you showed people you loved them with food. Sivvy wished she'd learned more from her ma, before they'd become dead to one another.

Sivvy tied up her collection of nuts in her apron and rose to her feet. It would soon be time to peel and wash the potatoes, a mindless task in which Sivvy found some comfort. The scalding water stopped her hands from trembling for a spell.

Walking back toward the women's building, she noticed that the male farm helpers—also patients—were already sweating in the fields. The asylum was, for the most part, self-sustaining and fed patients and staff through the efforts of the inmates, who broke their backs trying to get in a record amount of fruits and vegetables every harvest. Sivvy had heard the staff joke that Milledgeville State Asylum was a city unto itself, and it seemed to be true. Other than the odd therapist or lawyer or patient's relative who came into the common room, she couldn't remember the last time she'd seen a stranger face to face. As for herself, the only visitor she'd had these ten years was Uncle Billy. Damn his eyes.

CHAPTER SIX

It was almost one in the morning, and Betty Lou still hadn't come to bed. She was still tending to Walt, and O.T. was tempted to go fetch her; she needed her rest, but he heard her stern instruction in his head every time he moved to rise from the bed. "Don't you dare come out there," she had said in a steely voice. "I'm not sure if he's contagious."

O.T. knew she was fibbing—of course it was contagious. She had been wearing that mask for days, and every time she came home she scrubbed her hands on the back porch with water near to scalding, until her hands were raw and welted.

O.T. pounded the pillow and stared out the window, watching the sliver of moonlight move higher and higher into the sky. The house was so quiet without the sounds of Owen Jr.'s snoring and Belle's teeth grinding. The kids had been staying with Hazel and Tom for the past week—"Just in case," Betty Lou had insisted—and O.T. wasn't sure what to do with the silence. He and Betty Lou had never had the house to themselves before, not been completely alone, since they'd first gotten married fourteen years ago. Betty Lou was consumed by a blind determination to bring Walt back around, and O.T. threw himself into his work, staying out until dark every night taking care of the cotton. The physical exertion was needful, distracting him from his growing fear and dread.

O.T. wished Betty Lou would come on home. He ached for her, wanted to feel her hands on him, even if it was just to wrap them in his own and go to sleep. The silence in the house was crippling. He felt himself suspended in place, unable to close his eyes, unable to look at anything, simply frozen with worry.

It had been a week since Walt had fallen ill. He had come home from town looking green around the gills, and the next day, the telltale red spots brightened his cheeks and faded into his collar—scarlet fever.

O.T. had been dipping the cotton plants with poison syrup, cursing all the while.

"My throat's got pins in it," Walt had moaned, "and I'm like to freeze."

O.T. had helped him into his room above the barn, Walt barely able to climb the ladder. Betty Lou, after a quick look at Walt, had started packing the children's clothes.

"Just in case," she'd said to O.T. "I can tend him better if they aren't underfoot, is all. Go wash yer hands."

Betty Lou had given him a sunny smile, but the way she'd scrambled the children out within ten short minutes told him all he needed to know. The rash appeared a day later, and the day after that the fever worsened, but O.T. had known the worst that first day, by the calm, smooth tone of her voice.

O.T. heard the back porch door bang shut, and the sound of water being poured. Betty Lou was back. He sighed, sinking down further into the pillow, ashamed at the relief he felt knowing she was home. The moon shone through the bedroom window and lit her face clearly as she came through the door. Her hair was pulled up neatly, and the smell of powder and roses followed in behind her. He watched silently from the bed as she pulled the pins out of her hair and let it fall to her shoulders, then stepped out of her clean pink dress, her slip, and her stockings. Only when she was sitting on the bed in her slip did he speak.

"Hey, purdy lady."

Betty Lou jumped a little, then turned around and smiled, seeing him lying there.

"Heavens, Owen. I thought you were asleep." She paused, let her shoulders slump a little. "Hoped you were."

"I've been in bed for two hours now," he confessed. "Couldn't sleep without ya."

"That's a lie," she said, smiling, rubbing her arms, as if she were cold. "I've seen you doze off in the middle of the field. In church. Just about anywhere. You don't need me layin' beside you to catch a few Zs."

O.T. reached out and caressed her shoulder, feeling the softness of her skin, remembering how, at sixteen, he had dreamed of seeing her hair down, of touching her. He wondered how it was that he had been so lucky.

"How's Walt doing?" O.T. asked tentatively.

"Fair," she answered, after a pause. "No real change. But that ain't bad, mind."

"I reckon." O.T. sensed she was attempting to spare him, and he wasn't sure if he was grateful or ashamed. Perhaps both.

"The thing that kills me," she said finally, looking out the window at the moon-grazed fields, "is how sorry he is. Like it's his fault. Every time I go in there, Owen, he says sorry. Sorry to be puttin' me out, sorry the kids had to go to Hazel's, sorry he can't be helpin' you in the field—"

"That's just his way," O.T. said quietly, grazing her shoulder with his fingertips. "He's always been thataway." He felt a lump in his throat. "He's been apologizin' since the day he was born, just about."

Betty Lou pulled away with a sigh. "Sorry," she murmured. "I ain't tryin' to be cold, Owen. It's just been a long night."

"I know it has, honey," he said, quietly.

"I don't like to see nobody hurtin', nobody. But *him*—" her voice caught. "I cain't stand to see Walt hurtin', Owen. I just want to kiss every boo-boo like he's a little bitty child. Ain't that silly?"

"No, it ain't silly, darlin'. I felt the same way about him my whole life," he answered, touching her arm. "Won't you come on to bed, though? I ain't gonna try nothin'. I swear on yer family Bible."

Betty Lou laughed quietly. "I reckon you think you's a saint," she said with a smile, finally turning around and crawling under the covers. "Kids been gone all week and you ain't put one move on me. Suppose you'll be wantin' yer award for best-behaved husband."

"No award," he said. "I ain't aimin' to seduce no woman don't want to be seduced."

Betty Lou drifted into his arms with a sigh. Her skin was a little cold, and her hair tickled his face. He could smell the lye soap from her hands as she put her arms around his neck. "Well go on, then," she murmured into his ear. "Love me."

He did.

❧

O.T. woke the next morning before the sun was up, and sat up, stretching to get the kinks out of his back. It seemed as if every day he felt his age creeping up on him more. At his next birthday he'd be thirty, but he felt forty-five already.

He glanced behind him, startled to see Betty Lou still abed, curled in a ball, a pillow over her head. Usually, she rose well before O.T. to get breakfast going.

His heart began to thud in alarm. She'd been so careful to wash her hands and wear a mask....

Stirring, Betty Lou shifted the pillow and sat up, rubbing her eyes, her hair a tousled halo around her head. "Mornin', stranger," she said with a sleepy smile.

"Darlin'." He put a hand to her forehead, and she leaned into it, closing her eyes with pleasure. "You feelin' all right?"

"Fine," she said, and relief rushed over him so fast he audibly sighed. "Why?"

"You ain't never in bed when I get up," he said. "Not once in, what, fourteen years?"

"That's an exaggeration," she laughed, throwing off the covers. "I've slept in once or twice. Say, can't a woman have a lie-in now and again? I worked hard yesterday, and the kids ain't here, and besides, you kept me up half the night—"

"Now, now," O.T. said, throwing his hands up in mock surrender. "Don't go getting sore. I wasn't criticizin', was just worrit, is all. You can sleep half the day, if'n you want to."

"Reckon I'll get up and cook yer dang breakfast, affore you start gripin' about that—" Betty Lou rose to her feet.

"Naw you don't, purdy lady," O.T. said, tugging her back down to the bed. He gently smoothed her hair out of her eyes, then kissed her mouth softly. "Since we're both still here—"

"What about yer breakfast?" Betty Lou asked, giggling, moving her hips against his in a way that made his brain short-circuit.

"I ain't hungry no damn way," O.T. said, pushing himself into her. "Not for food, anyhow." Her laughter was like music.

❧

Three hours later, he was out in the field, the afterglow of the morning activities and the hearty breakfast he'd enjoyed afterward both wearing off. After the cotton plants had been painted, he'd pick what little greens were ready from the vegetable garden and do some weeding. Then, he meant to fix Betty Lou's chiffarobe, which had been sitting in the barn for a year. She'd been working herself near to death trying to take care of his brother; it was the least O.T. could do.

He painted the last of the cotton, cussing as he dribbled some of the foul syrup on his pant leg. Betty Lou would raise hell. He thought of how they'd carried on the night before, and that morning, and he grinned. His wife had been unexpectedly fiery. He wasn't sure if her passion had been stoked by stress or the fact that the kids weren't around, but she'd been on fire for him, and O.T. felt like a new man because of it. He wondered briefly if they'd made a baby, and felt guilty for hoping not. Three was enough; adding a fourth would just about break them, not to mention drive poor Betty Lou's sanity to the brink. She already took care of too much.

"Deddy?" O.T. turned, startled. Ginny, his eldest, stood by the fence, digging a bare foot into the moist soil. She wore her old patched dress, the one she kept for tending the fields. "You need some help?"

"Genevieve Lawrence, what the devil are ya doin' here?" O.T. demanded, setting the paintbrush in the poison molasses and putting his hands on his hips. "Does yer Aunt Hazel know yer here? Never mind that—does yer *ma* know yer here?"

"Naw sir," Ginny replied, pushing her hair back from her face in a charmingly defiant gesture. Sometimes she looked so much like her uncle Walt that it made O.T. smile. Now, he was just annoyed. "I was so bored over there. Hazel's makin' divinity candy, and she wants to teach me…but I just ain't got the head for it. Belle's the cook of the fambly, not me." She smiled slyly. "And I know you need help over here, what with Uncle Walt—"

"There's a reason yer ma sent you over to Hazel's, you dang headstrong gal," O.T. said, glaring at her. "Yer uncle might well be contagious and she wants to make sure you ain't gonna catch nothin'. Now git yer hind end on back over to Hazel's. I'm awright here— almost done, in fact. Thank ya, but go on now."

"Yer here, ain't ya?" Ginny argued. "You could catch whatever he's got, too."

"I'm grown," he said. "I got responsibilities here cain't be put off. It's fine for me to take the risk. As for you, you need to do what yer ma tells ya."

"I don't want to go back there," Ginny said petulantly.

O.T.'s eyes narrowed. "Ginny, gal…somethin' happen over there? At Hazel's?"

"Like what?" she asked, staring at the ground.

"Somebody mess with you?" O.T. asked, wishing he didn't have to. "Maybe…yer Uncle Tom?"

"Jee-ma-nee, Deddy, no!" Ginny exclaimed, two bright red dots appearing on her cheeks. "He left yester-dy. Went into town."

"Oh, he did, did he?" O.T. resumed painting the cotton, relieved. "Git on back over there, gal. I promise as soon as Uncle Walt's mending up, we'll come and fetch y'all."

"But I'm afraid Uncle Walt might die," Ginny said, piteously. "And if he got to die, I want to be here fer him."

"That's what you studyin' on?" O.T.'s stomach lurched painfully.

Ginny nodded slowly, pulling nervously on her hair. "Can Mama make him better?"

"I don' t know, honey. She's tryin' hard as she can," O.T. sighed. "But it just ain't safe to be here right now. Uncle Walt would be right heartened to know you came, though. That yer worrit about him. I'll see that yer ma tells him, awright? But git on back with ya and see that yer brother and sister stay away, too."

Ginny lingered around the fence a moment more, then ran off down the driveway and around to the front of the house. O.T. hoped she'd mind him. Hazel lived just around the corner, but if it provided Betty Lou with peace of mind that her babies were safe, it was only to the good.

O.T. finished up the last cotton plant and grabbed the bucket, walking back toward the house. The day was gray, drab, and cool. The summer had been unseasonably warm, sweltering and muggy, and the cool of fall was a blessed relief. O.T.'s long jacket had finally bit the dust last season, and he hated to ask Betty Lou to mend it, busy as she'd been. He couldn't bear the thought of taking money out of his emergency funds to buy one, neither. He'd go another week or two without the coat. It wasn't quite cold yet.

O.T. washed out his paintbrush in the tin basin on the porch, scrubbed his hands, and set the bucket in the corner of the barn. He started out of the barn, aiming to go to the kitchen to grab a piece of cold cornbread and buttermilk. Just as he was leaving the barn, he heard a low moan coming from Walt's room and stopped, his blood going cold.

Walking to the stairs, he called up. "Betty Lou? Walt?"

Betty Lou appeared at the top of the steps, her eyes dark with weariness. "What is it, hon?"

"I was puttin' up the bucket, and I heard Walt. He sounded right upset. He awright?"

"Walt, I'll be back in a jiffy," Betty Lou said, turning her head. "I'm comin' down, Owen. Go over to the corner and get one of those masks that's hangin'. Put it on."

O.T. did as he was told. Betty Lou came from a tendin' family, with generations of nurses, midwives, and healers. Just about every woman in her family, including all her sisters, had delivered at least one baby in their time. She knew how to tend a person. When she said to do something, you did it.

A few moments later, she stepped down onto the hay of the barn floor. "It's colder down here than it is upstairs," she said, looking out toward the house. "Winter's on the way."

He nodded. "Walt awright?"

She sighed. "O.T.," Betty Lou sighed. O.T. felt his pulse begin to race—she always called him Owen. "He's took a turn. His fever's up. I've been trying all morning to break it, but it's got a hold on him."

O.T. nodded.

"He's askin' for you to rub his back."

O.T. didn't realize he was crying until he felt the tears on his cheeks.

Betty Lou tenderly touched his face, wiping away his tears with a brush of her thumb. "I don't like to let ya up there, hon, to tell the truth. Scarlet fever's highly contagious. But he's yer brother, and I know...I know it's important to both of y'all. That you be able to see him." She did not say "one more time," but it was there all the same.

O.T. felt like he'd been punched in the gut, and a sudden spasm of rage came over him. "Are you tellin' me that my brother might *die*? And I been out in the field when I coulda been there with him?"

"I told you…." She trailed off, and he realized her eyes were full of tears, too. "I was worried you might catch it, Owen. I couldn't bear the thought of you or the kids—"

"You kept me from him."

"I was just tryin' to keep you safe."

"Well, I'm going up now," O.T. said, pushing past her. "I'll wear yer dang mask, but I swear to the good Lord, woman, I couldn't give a rat's ass if I catch it, too." He didn't mean it, and he expected her to snap back with a retort of her own, but she didn't. He turned to look at her before he ascended up the steps. She was crying silently, staring out the barn window.

The nurse tapped lightly with her knuckles on the heavy wooden door. Sivvy could see her white cap through the small window in the door; she would stand there and watch to see that Sivvy got up. If she didn't, the nurse would knock again and wait. If Sivvy still didn't rouse herself, the nurse would enter, and depending on which nurse it was, she might get a smack.

Sivvy wasn't going to be any trouble. She rose to her feet and pulled on the thin housecoat, tying it around her waist. Sivvy waited by the door until the nurse pulled it open—a new girl, barely out of her teens, with the prim, pinched mouth of someone trying to mask terror with sternness. "Patient Shelnutt," the nurse said flatly, "I am Nurse Burns. Please visit the lavatory, do your business, then I will escort you back here to dress. You are expected in the kitchens in ten minutes."

It was probably Nurse Burns's first day, Sivvy mused, as she padded wordlessly down the cold floor of the hall into the shared bathrooms. After a while the nurses seldom bothered barking commands; everyone on this floor had been here long enough to know the drill. The nurses, Sivvy had found, could usually be divided into two groups—the bored ones, who were sick of their job and ambivalent toward their patients, who paid just enough attention to keep their "guests" from harm; and the uppity ones, who loved their jobs, who carefully ticked every box on their list, who greeted the patients with bright, fake smiles and insisted upon exchanging forced pleasantries during unpleasant tasks. There was, however, a third category of nurses, more rarely found, but of the kind that made the hairs on the back of Sivvy's neck stand up. These nurses sought to inflict pain and suffering, by which they could assert control and manage their own fear. Nurse Burns, with her tight, wary expression, seemed to Sivvy a nurse of the third kind, and of whom patients should steer well clear.

Sivvy used the toilet, wincing at the stink of the communal bathroom, and washed her hands. The water was cold, but at least there was soap. The rear wall held rows upon rows of pegs, each containing a toothbrush. Someone—either bored or a lunatic, probably both—liked to come in after breakfast and rearrange the toothbrushes. Sivvy stood on tiptoe and scanned the tip of each one until she finally found the tan colored brush labeled Shelnutt. Even after all these years, she didn't think of herself as a Shelnutt. When May or Dr. Swint called for Ms. Shelnutt, oftentimes she didn't respond, not out of obstinacy, but because she forgot.

Sivvy ran her toothbrush under the water at the second sink, wishing for tooth powder. A back tooth was giving her an awful pain, but she hadn't mentioned it. The dentist, with his dirty, rusted instruments, was another Dr. Lowell, and judging by the rotting and discolored teeth of the women around her, Sivvy's aversion was a shared one.

Rinsing her brush, she stuck it back on a different peg this time and wondered where she would find it tomorrow. She hoped the woman who rearranged the toothbrushes didn't scrub the floors with them when nobody was around, but Sivvy wouldn't blame her if she did. Sometimes, it was these little acts of defiance that kept them alive.

Nurse Burns stood in the doorway, and Sivvy silently waited for her next command. She didn't need to be told her schedule, but felt instinctively that this nurse would not take kindly to initiative. You learned these things as you went along, Sivvy reflected, how to handle the nurses by letting them handle you. Patient or staff, lower or upper class, it seemed to Sivvy that all women were the same, clinging to little acts of control, and taking ownership of their lives in whatever way they could.

"Back to your room, patient Shelnutt, and dress for the kitchens."

"Yes, marm." Sivvy returned to her room,

Sivvy pulled her white uniform from the drawer beside her bed and slipped it over her head, buttoning it soundlessly. Tying the apron strings tightly about her waist, Sivvy was reminded of a corset she had worn in a school Nativity play when she was eleven or so. Misrus Shunt had loaned her the costume—an ethereal, flowing angel's dress in shimmering white and sapphire blue—with a partial corset that had taken forever to tie. She remembered Misrus Shunt's gentle fingers as she threaded and tied it. Mama and Daddy and all her siblings had come to see her in the play; Sivvy had been so proud. Tears filled her eyes, and Sivvy beat them back by blinking furiously. She had made it a point never to cry in this place. Sivvy tied up her black shoes, then straightened, resisting the urge to curtsy. In her heart, she was as full of sass as ever.

"Let's go." Nurse Burns opened the door and ushered Sivvy out, following two paces behind. The corridor was full of other patients, rushing back and forth from the communal bathroom, getting ready for their own days ahead. They passed the heavy wooden doors where the violent patients were held—twice as thick as the doors in Sivvy's own wing, with revolving windows for dinner trays and heavy metal deadbolts. She felt she understood the violent inmates—the ones who cut up and down their arms with whatever sharp thing they could get; the ones who lashed out and pummeled the faces of the nurses who tried to hold them down; the ones who smashed the windows and tried to climb out; the ones who pinched pens from clipboards and butter knives from the kitchens and hid them in their thin mattresses, waiting for an opportunity; the ones who beat their heads on the wooden floors, over and over again, until they had to be transported to the Jones building. Sivvy understood them, understood that all that stood between civilized behavior and madness was the will to please others. Once you succumbed to being well and truly alone, without a care for how others perceived you, once you'd been shown enough times that you did not matter, the will to please disappeared, and the descent into madness began.

They entered the elevator and the doors shut behind them. The loud whir as they descended was a comfort to Sivvy, who did not like silence. Things lurked in silence.

"Patient Shelnutt," Nurse Burns asked, "do you know when this hospital was built?"

"Why," Sivvy said, surprised. "If I recall correct, marm, it was in er…1842? Yes, I believe it was."

"I'm surprised you know that," the nurse said flatly. "Do you have lessons here?"

"No'm," Sivvy said. "But I do read to pass the time. When I'm allowed."

"I see," the nurse replied. "So the place is quite old. Was built even before the war. Did it have slaves?"

"I cain't say I know the answer to that, marm," Sivvy replied. "Pretty likely, I 'spect."

"I'll have to find out." The nurse gave her a chilling smile. "I can tell you for certain, though, it does have ghosts. I've seen them. There's one in your room." The elevator doors opened, and without another word, Nurse Burns strode down the hallway.

Sivvy stared after her a moment, then forced her legs to move, walking toward the kitchens. She had been mistaken, putting the woman in category three. No, Nurse Burns was in a category all her own.

Sivvy didn't know if Nurse Burns was insane, deranged, or just plain out mean—maybe all three—but there *were* ghosts. Sivvy had seen them, too. Some she knew—Nona Leigh, her boy, Clay, Harvey—those were the worst ones.

Then there were the spirits of people who had died in this place, who had never gotten out, to whom the cold, damp walls of Milledgeville Asylum had become *home*; those who had merged with the place, who had become the bones and brick and mortar of Milledgeville Asylum. The old asylum reminded Sivvy of a skull—dirty windows, overgrown with ivy, peering at passersby like lidded eyes; straight, narrow steps like crooked teeth, the wide door a gaping mouth ready to swallow a person whole. While the dead slept beneath the stately pecan trees, they also, Sivvy knew, lingered within the asylum walls. The chapel was gloomily ominous, the kitchen full of eerie metal clangs, and the hospital a clinical, detached study in terror.

Sivvy often saw the ghosts while in solitary, fitted out in the strong dress, the sleeves tied behind her, unable to use her arms and unwilling to use her legs. She'd lie down, playing possum, afraid to move, afraid to breathe. The dead were rarely fooled; they crept into her head, and in sweet, coaxing voices told her things, reminded her of memories she'd rather forget. Folks on the outside might be surprised at just how many patients had managed to shift off the mortal coil while wearing a strong dress. It did not surprise Sivvy. She'd tried it herself once. She shuddered, recalling one occasion when she'd managed to loop both arms of the strong dress around her neck, dislocating her shoulder in the process.

"Well, you've got yourself into a right mess," the nurse had scolded her, drawn finally by the sounds of her screams. "But since you're just fine, perhaps you ought to stay that way for a spell. Teach you a lesson." The nurse had turned out all the lights and locked her in. Several hours in solitary, in so much pain she'd screamed till her throat was raw, rats scrambling across the floor beside her.

In recent years Sivvy had reached a shaky kind of peace with the asylum, a sort of willing blindness. She threw herself into work and became adept at the art of willful ignorance. *I see nothing. I hear nothing. I am nothing.*

Whenever the light started to creep into the windows of her mind—the faint tendrils of hope, emerging from a long, joyless winter—she'd shut the sashes tight and block it out. Sivvy found that if she steeled herself rigorously enough, she could block out all manner of hope, and all manner of evil.

A lot of the time it worked, except for when it didn't.

CHAPTER SEVEN

Walt's lips were dry and cracked, and O.T. poured a little water into a clay cup and lifted it to his brother's lips. Walt shook his head, his face clammy, pink and swollen, his eyes barely open, but focused on O.T. with a desperate urgency.

"Brother—" Walt rasped, and stopped, closing his eyes in a grimace.

"Save yer strength, Walt," O.T. said gently. "You don't gotta talk. Just rest. I'm here."

"How's the cotton gittin' on?" Walt asked hoarsely, pushing himself up on the pillows with some effort, his face a sheen of sweat. It was a good sign, O.T. reckoned; his fever was breaking. How ludicrous that Walt would ask about cotton at a time like this, burning with fever and sweating like a pig.

"Fine. I finished paintin' the plants again yester-dy. Better've got them weevils this time," O.T. replied. "How ya feelin' today?"

"Comes and goes," Walt managed. "I'll feel better for a spell, then it's ten times worse."

"Betty Lou's gonna tend you up good," O.T. assured him. "She can heal anybody. You know that."

"Not me," Walt said, meeting O.T.'s gaze; his eyes clear, and focused. "Not this time."

"Shoot, Walt, that's crazy talk. Betty Lou said you was gettin' better—"

"Well, she was either lyin' or she cain't see, then," Walt said. "O.T., I'm pretty sure it's my time. Like the preacher talks about in church… God's callin' me home. No, don't try to argue. 'Cause yer just wastin' what little time I *do* have. I need to tell you somethin'."

Panic rose in O.T.'s chest. He didn't like Walt talking this way, not a bit. He was a firm believer that people could make themselves sick, could talk themselves right into dying. "I ain't gonna hear none of that talk, Walter Lawrence. You ain't dyin'. You always think the worst. But if you wanna tell me somethin', go on ahead. I'm listenin'."

"You remember back when the tent revivals came to town? When we was boys?" Walt asked, licking at his dry lips. His voice was so low and quiet O.T. had to strain to hear him. "I think it were 1914, 1915?"

"The last one came through in 1916. We was barely still boys—almost growed up," O.T. answered. "The year Betty Lou and me got engaged. And that ol' reverend and his niece came to town."

"Them, yeah," Walt answered.

"They never came back after that year," O.T. said. "I was sorry fer it. I didn't care much for the revival part but I shore did like those fish fries at Misrus Maybelle's." He smiled.

"They never came back because of…that *b-business*…that Billy Rev thinking I'd…s-soiled his niece. Sivvy, her name was."

"I remember. Sivvy. Skinny little gal with the black hair."

"She was right purdy, and so sweet. I liked her," Walt muttered, wistfully.

"I know you did," O.T. replied. "Too bad her uncle was a dang charlatan and a devil and a cad."

"O.T., you shouldn't talk like that 'bout a man o' God," Walt protested weakly. He lacked the energy to scold his brother, which made O.T. nervous. "Anyhow, he was wrong. I ain't never…I didn't even touch the girl, never offered her so much as my arm. Why, the one 'date' we had, you had to go on for me."

The memory of that night suddenly rushed back to O.T.—the kiss he'd shared with the black-haired girl beneath the sassafras tree, and all that had followed—and he felt the heat rise in his cheeks.

"Why you bringin' that up now, Walt?" O.T. asked. "That's been the better part of fifteen years ago."

"That gal Sivvy," Walt said, wiping the sweat from his face with a shaking hand. "I heard tell of her when I was in town last. Heard some news 'bout her."

"Is that a fact?"

"Hosey tol' me. He ran into some of her folks up in the mountains. And he tol' me—he figured I'd want to know."

"What about her?" O.T. asked, trying to hide the impatience in his voice. He had no hankering to talk about some skinny little girl from a lifetime ago, or Hosey for that matter, when his brother was ailing and like to die.

"It's jes' terrible, O.T.," Walt said, his voice quiet but filled with a grief that tore at O.T.'s heart. "The poor, poor girl. Brother, she's at Milledgeville."

"She lives in Milledgeville?" O.T. shrugged. "So?"

"No, she don't jes' live there," Walt replied. "I mean, she lives there, but—she—she's *at* Milledgeville. At the—" he took a sip of water and grimaced "—the asylum."

"*Oh,*" O.T. said, realizing. "I see. Well, shoot." Milledgeville was so infamous that he'd never really thought of it as *real.*

"He said she'd been there ten year—at *least,*" Walt moaned, his eyes red and glazed; perhaps from tears, fever, or both.

"Well, that's a right shame, Walt," O.T. said finally, not sure what to say. "I hate to hear it." And he did. But he still didn't know what it had to do with Walt.

"Sweet girl like her in that place," Walt shuddered. "I cain't bear it, brother."

"Walt," O.T. touched his brother's arm gently. "There ain't nothin' you could do to help her. And you don't know why she—I mean, you ain't clapped an eye on her in fifteen years. That place supposed to help folks, ain't it? She might be better for it, you reckon?" He tried for a joke, to make Walt smile. "Might be a sight better than livin' with that uncle of hers."

Walt didn't smile. "There was a time when…"—he caught his breath a moment, his face drawn in sorrow, his voice a whisper—"… when I thought *I* might get sent off to Milledgeville."

"Walt, no," O.T. breathed. "Never think it. We'd *never.*" He squeezed his brother's arm again. "Not in a million, billion years. Anyhow, you ain't…like *them* people."

Walt looked at O.T. silently, his face unreadable and suddenly very pale. "Yes, I am."

"You ain't," O.T. shook his head. "Not atall."

"I ain't ashamed to say so," Walt said weakly. "I ain't like a—like normal folks. I always knowed that and so have you. You think I don't know that I'm different, that I always been different? It's the truth. Wasn't for Hazel, I mighta ended up at that place."

O.T. wanted to argue, but his brother wasn't wrong. He and Walt had grown up just like every other kid in Georgia. If you were misbehaving or just plain getting on your folks' nerves, the first thing you'd hear was, "You better act right or I'll send you off to Milledgeville!" It was the stuff of young'uns' nightmares. O.T. supposed—now that he was an adult, and less scared of boogers and haints—that the asylum was just like any other place where sick people went; it was just a sickness of the head rather than of the body. While O.T. could tell himself that a gal like Sivvy would be faring just fine there, happy as you please, the thought of Walt in the asylum gave him the horrors, and wasn't it true that people just like Walt got sent there every day? Every town had at least one person whom the rumors seemed to follow like a shadow; one person who had lost their mind after childbirth, or who had succumbed to fits, or who had been too slow to take care of themselves, or whose mind had started to sleep when they got old, or who had never been quite right after an illness. Folks like that existed all over, and they got sent to asylums like the one in Milledgeville. The family would hush it up best as they could, and that was that. It was the way things were. But Walt was his *twin*. And he didn't have violent outbursts, or delusions, or talk to imaginary folks. It was true that he was a little different— he didn't like to be touched, he didn't like looking in folks' eyes, and he had more of a head for facts and figures than women and marryin', but what of it? He wasn't the first kooky bachelor around these parts. He was certain Hazel, and Ma before her, had never considered sending Walt to Milledgeville. Still, it nagged at him: what if Walt had never had a twin to see after him?

"I hate to hear it," O.T. said again. "But jes' because this gal is there, don't mean you should be studyin' on yerself going there. Ain't nobody sendin' you to Milledgeville, Walt. We need you here." He smiled at Walt, trying to ignore the sweat that beaded on his brother's forehead and the glassy look of his eyes. "When was the last time you ate?"

"Betty Lou got some broth down me yesterd-y evenin'," Walt said softly. "I wrote to her, O.T."

"Wrote to who?"

"To Miss Sivvy," Walt rasped. "'Member how we said we'd write? Then her uncle carried her off and I never heard nuthin'. Which warn't no surprise because I never gave her my address. But now…"

His voice trailed off into a cough. "I figger what do I got to lose? Her wastin' away in a place like that, and me here sick...." A tired smile crept onto his face. "I figger if I didn't write to her now, I'd lose the chance."

"Well, then I'm glad," O.T. said sincerely. "I'm glad you did it. But you ought to be restin', Walt, and not writin' letters and tirin' yerself out. And quit yer yappin' about dyin'."

"Will you send my letter, O.T.?" Walt asked, his face deathly pale. His hands gripped at the sheets, and he shivered. "If I give you the keepin' of it, kin you take it to the post office and put it in the mail fer me?"

"Accorse I will," O.T. replied immediately.

"I'll give you the postage—" Walt coughed. "Look in the drawer over there, I got—"

"No you won't, you dummy," O.T. said. "I'll take care of it. I'll go this afternoon." He paused, then smiled. "But on'y if you promise me you'll get well. You got to git better so you kin read her reply, don't you reckon? I don't want to hear no more of this dyin' nonsense. We square?"

Walt looked at O.T. for a few moments, then he smiled. "Yeah, okay, brother. We square."

"I mean it, Walt," O.T. said firmly.

"I know."

"How did Hosey hear, anyway?" O.T. asked, curious. "How does he know her fambly? I didn't know he even went to the mountains recently."

Walt was silent a moment. "Ask him, I reckon," he said finally.

"Awright, baby brother," O.T. said, not wanting to distress Walt any further. "I'll mail yer letter."

Walt seemed finally satisfied. "Well," he said. "I reckon I ought to sleep some. Betty Lou said rest is the best medicine, though I wish I could git outer this bed. I ain't never laid still for so long in my life."

"Just the same, you keep on layin' there and sleep," O.T. advised.

"I will. I couldn't git up if I wanted to," Walt answered, another coughing spasm rolling through him. "I ache all over, and my head's all swimmy. And this rash itches the daylights outer me. Hot, then cold. I ain't never seen nothin' to beat it."

"Yer on the way to gettin' well," O.T. said. "Yer on the mend."

Walt reached out and seized O.T.'s hand. "Just in case, though, O.T. I've had a mighty fine time here with you all these years. You lettin' me stay with y'all, lettin' me live here, bein' part of yer fambly."

"Yer my brother, you dang dummy. Wherever you go, I go. And wherever I go, you go," O.T. said. "Ain't it always been thataway?"

"I reckon, until it's time for one of us to go where the other cain't follow," Walt said, licking his lips.

"If you don't stop talking thataway, I'm leavin'," O.T. said with a hollow laugh, a sharp pain lancing through his belly.

"You've always been that way, brother," Walt said, letting go of O.T.'s hand. "You don't like to face nothin'. Folks act like it's me the one that's soft, and I reckon that's true where it counts, but…I think when it comes to the business of reality, getting down to the hard stuff, it's you that's the weak one." Walt smiled weakly. "I mean no offense, brother. I reckon it's a good thing. Life don't make you hard."

"That ain't true, not even a little bit," O.T. protested crossly. "I can face anything, can *lick* anything—"

"Most of the time," Walt interjected. "But you cain't cheat death. The good book says—"

"Oh, shuddup, you big lug." O.T. wiped at his eyes. Walt was scaring him. He pulled out his packet of tobacco from his pocket.

"Don't you dare take off that mask to put that plug in yer lip, not till you're safe downstairs and got yer hands washed," Walt said hurriedly. "Don't you dare. This is catchin'."

"I know that," O.T. said irritably, but secretly horrified, because he'd momentarily forgotten. "Let's get you some sleep now," he said with forced cheer. "And I'll git to town and mail yer letter. I'll come back and see you again tonight."

"Might not oughter, O.T.," Walt protested weakly. "Don't take the risk."

"I said I'll be back later and I will, dammit," O.T. said, and patted his brother on the arm. "Now you sleep." He gently helped Walt turn over onto his side. Gingerly, he reached under the covers and below his brother's shirt, which was soaked through with sticky sweat. O.T. rubbed his brother's damp back in concentric circles, over and over, listening to his ragged, shallow breaths, until Walt was finally asleep.

He sat for a long time, rubbing Walt's back, staring at the side of his brother's sleeping face, and wishing they could trade places.

❧

O.T. scrubbed his hands until the skin damn near came off, and pressed them, red and throbbing, on his coveralls to dry. Sitting on the top step of the porch, he yanked his mask away and took out the packet of Beech Nut.

"That you, Owen?" Betty Lou's voice came through the screen door.

"Yeah," he said, rocking. "What you doin', gal?"

Betty Lou appeared at the door, a hand pressed to her brow. "I was gonna make a bit of broth, and maybe put a sweet potato or two in the coals. Walt needs food in him. He always loved sweet potatoes. But I'm so dang tired I don't know if I can stay on my feet long enough to do it."

"Come sit down a spell with me," O.T. said, patting the step beside him. "Walt's nappin' anyhow. He'll be out a while, I reckon. You can make him some chow later."

"I doubt he'll be able to eat it anyway," Betty Lou admitted, sitting beside him. She pulled her feet up and off to the side, like a little girl. Her white blonde hair was pulled up in its usual neat bun. She wrapped her arms around her knees. "He ain't doin' good, Owen. I don't think—"

"Let's talk 'bout somethin' else," O.T. pleaded quietly. "Jes' fer a spell."

"Awright, then," she agreed. But his request was met with silence. They couldn't think of a thing to say. O.T. could hear birds chirping their sweet songs in the trees.

After a time, O.T. forced himself to talk. "Walt had an interestin' thing to tell me. About a gal." Betty Lou perked up with interest. O.T. told her about Miss Sivvy and what Walt had told him.

Betty Lou made a face. "I knowed he was writin' something a day or two ago," she said, "because I saw his scratch paper out on the nightstand. Figurin' he was writin' some poetry or somethin'. I'm glad he was occupyin' his mind, but I tell ya, Owen, I ain't so sure he should be writin' to that gal."

"Why, you reckon?"

"She's tucked away in that place, livin' like the Lord only knows what. You know what they say about invitin' trouble. Don't go doin' that unless you want it on yer own doorstep. What if they get to writin' and she wants to come here—"

"Aw, shoot," O.T. said good-naturedly. "It ain't like Walt can go fetch her from the asylum, Betty Lou. Not sick as he is, not without a car or no money, and he ain't her fambly." He started to say more but suddenly couldn't bear to.

Betty Lou put her arm around him. "Yeah, I know. I'm not being fair. I didn't like that gal all those years ago, but it was just me bein' a silly teenage girl. I oughter be over that nonsense by now. Begrudging some poor gal who is stuck in an asylum, livin' no kind of life." She looked embarrassed. "And anyhow, I owe her a debt, I suppose. She's the reason you and I are together."

"How's that?" O.T. was baffled. "What's she got to do with it?"

"Yer kiddin' me," Betty Lou said with a smile. "You dumber'n a box of rocks if you don't know."

"Guess I'm dumb, then." He couldn't see what one woman had to do with the other.

"Don't you remember the revival, that Indian Summer we was sixteen? Goin' for the ride in the motorcar—me, you, Walt, Hosey, Lila, and *her*?"

"Yeah, I remember, but what's that got to do with—?"

"She was passing cow eyes over you all the time. I seen her. In the rearview mirror when I was drivin' down the road, I saw her sittin' behind you just a'lookin'. Like she was memorizing every hair on yer head. In a swoon, just about," Betty Lou smirked, remembering. "Then we got to that tree that you love so much"—she gestured out to O.T's tree, at the edge of the yard—"and she about fell over herself tellin' you how much she loved it. She might as well have fell over kissin' you right there in the leaves, in front of all of us."

"That ain't quite how I remember it," O.T. protested with a laugh. But he recalled their kiss the following night, he and Miss Sivvy, and his belly flopped a little. But of course she'd thought he was Walt.

"I always knowed you liked me," Betty Lou went on, her voice wistful. "Wasn't like you kept it a secret. But I didn't reckon I liked you the same…didn't like any boy, really. You were cute, and sweet, but I didn't study on marryin' you or nuthin…" Her voice had taken on a dreamy quality. "Till I saw that gal droolin' over you. And then suddenly I was fierce jealous. I couldn't *stand* the thought of you goin' off with that gal. That you might like her better. I just knew right then I had to cinch you in."

O.T. flushed then laughed out loud. He was too old to be so tickled, but he couldn't help it. Had he known about all this when he was sixteen, his head would have swelled up like the moon. "Dang, Betty Lou, you always knew I had eyes only fer you. That gal didn't mean nothin' to me, and anyhow, it was Walt she was crazy for."

"Naw, she liked *you*," Betty insisted. "Or maybe both a'y'all, I dunno…twins and everything. But it was you she wanted." She pursed her mouth, looking like her mother. "I was so jealous of her. So mysterious, she was, from up in them mountains, with her dark black hair and those eyes of hers. Green like jewels, they were. She was everything I wasn't."

"Yer bein' ridiculous, woman," O.T. said, pulling her close to him and placing a kiss on the top of her blonde head. "She was pretty, I reckon, but yer beautiful. The most beautiful woman I ever seen in real life. And I ain't never had an eye for any gal but you. You been knowin' that since we was in clouts. And I ain't never gon' have an eye for nobody else, neither."

Betty Lou settled her head under O.T.'s chin and sighed contentedly. "Oh, stop with yer declarations, Owen. I ain't still jealous of her. I feel right sorry for her. That uncle of hers was awful, and he treated her bad, you could tell. I cain't imagine what her life must have been like to get sent off to Milledgeville. What it must be like now." She sighed again. "She was real pretty, she was. She had a sparkle in her eye."

They were silent for a few minutes, both lost in their thoughts. The wind had picked up a little, whipping the damp clothes on the clothesline.

"Gettin' cold now," O.T. said, changing the subject. "Finally. We'll have to pull out our winter clothes, and I need to git us some firewood chopped."

"Yeah," Betty Lou agreed. "When the kids get back thisaway, I reckon I'll need to measure their arm lengths and let out their coats. Ever one of 'em has growed a foot since last winter."

"Kids'll do that," he agreed, with a smile that didn't quite reach his eyes.

O.T. couldn't remember the last time they'd sat and passed the time of day just talkin' about folks they knew, firewood, and coats—the mundane details of their everyday lives. They just quietly got on with daily chores and duties, working together like a well-oiled machine, taking care of things as they needed to be taken care of. When he was with Betty Lou, O.T. felt as if they could be anywhere, on any adventure. Sitting on the porch with her now, watching her cradle her arms around her knees like a shy child, and talking of boring wintertime chores, filled his heart with dread. It seemed a clear indicator that something was very wrong. He felt his brain finally start to give, to wonder. If it could be possible that Walt....

O.T. pulled away from her, standing up a little too quickly. He got a head rush and leaned against the banister for support. He spit his tobacco into the bushes, and put his hands in his coverall pockets, suddenly freezing.

"You awright, doll?" Betty Lou asked, her smooth, low voice bone-weary. She started to rise, but he waved her back.

"Fine," he answered. "You just set awhile. You look tired."

"Bring some firewood in later, would ya? That chill in the air is gettin' fierce." Betty Lou wrapped her shawl around her shoulders and went inside.

O.T. hoped she would lie down and take some rest, but he knew she wouldn't. She'd finish her cooking and then head right back out to tend Walt. Betty Lou was nothing if not *herself*, after all. You couldn't tell her nothin'. It was what he loved about her most.

The least he could do was chop her some firewood. He trudged out to the woodpile, axe in hand, wishing he were more of a praying man. He felt the urge, but he'd never really prayed before, so he wasn't sure he could find the words. *Just...please*—was all he could muster up in his mind. The words ran through his mind, over and over as he chopped, scattering a frenzy of wood chunks in all directions. *Just. Please.*

CHAPTER EIGHT

"O.T."

O.T. woke up from where he'd been dozing on the couch with a start. A trickle of drool had dribbled from his mouth onto his white undershirt. He hadn't meant to fall asleep, only to sit down and rest for a minute before he went back out for more wood. He'd sat down, taken out a plug of tobacco, and then somehow nodded off. Glancing at his pocket watch, he saw he had been asleep for almost two hours.

"What is it, Betty Lou?" he asked, groggily. "I brought the firewood in. Just got to git the last pile from the—"

"It ain't about the firewood," she said sharply, urgently. She stood in the doorway, a cardigan pulled tightly around her torso, her face grim. "It's Walt."

O.T. nodded, his mouth dry as sawdust. Some part of him had known ever since he'd left Walt's room that his brother was not going to recover; had known all the while he was reassuring him and telling him to stop talking about dyin'; had known while he was chopping firewood.

"What?" he croaked, feeling suddenly light-headed. "Is he dead?"

Betty Lou shook her head, tendrils of blonde hair coming loose from her bun and lying in wisps about her face, shining in the dim room like candy floss. "No, hon. He ain't dead…but…it ain't gonna be long. If you want to say yer—"

O.T. brushed past her, out into the cool evening, before she could finish her sentence. It wasn't full dark yet, and the sky was a slate blue color, with one or two stars twinkling overhead. The screen door slammed behind him as he rushed toward the barn. He heard it slam again and Betty Lou's footsteps following.

O.T. went into the barn and started up the steps, then turned back, remembering the mask, the damned mask. Betty Lou held it out to him. He took it and put it on, then took a deep breath, seeking strength, because he felt like a piteous child. "You comin'?" he asked Betty Lou.

93

"No," she replied softly, squeezing his arm and kissing his forehead. "I'll be down here, though, if'n you need me. Or if he does." Her voice was scarcely a whisper, roughened by unshed tears. "I don't think he's got no more need of me, though."

Walt seemed to have shrunken to half his size in the two or three hours since O.T. had seen him last. He seemed shriveled and gray, like a sliver of person in a sea of white linen. Walt opened his eyes—bright, shiny with fever, and red-rimmed—as O.T. climbed the last step and approached the bed. If his brother weren't on his deathbed, O.T. could have mistaken him for an eager little boy on Christmas morning, so bright were his eyes. Walt's gaze fixed unerringly on his brother, his chest barely moving.

"Walt," O.T. cried in helpless despair. He reached out a hand to touch his brother, then drew it back. He couldn't do it—what if he touched him, and it was the last time?

"O....T...." Walt wheezed. "D'ya...remem...ber...."

"Remember what, brother?" His brother was going to ask if he sent the letter. The damned letter he'd forgotten to send, because he'd fallen asleep after chopping wood. Christ almighty, couldn't he do anything right?

But Walt wasn't asking about the letter. "...day in the field..."

"There's been a lot'a those." O.T. tried to crack a smile, but he gave way to tears instead.

"...member...the...butter..."

Butter? O.T. didn't remember anything about the field and butter. Was he losing his senses? O.T. wiped furiously at his eyes. It wouldn't do for his brother to see him cry. It would make it worse. He wanted Walt to feel at peace, if it was possible.

"...butterflies." Walt finished his sentence, his voice full of gravel, his eyes streaming with tears, his face a deathly white. He looked like he might laugh, if he'd had sufficient strength.

Walt closed his eyes, and for a moment O.T. imagined he had stopped breathing, but then his chest moved slightly. "D'ya remember...bro...ther...?"

O.T. wasn't sure he remembered any particular butterflies. They reminded him of the pellagra rash that had killed their mama, and as such he didn't like the damn things. Not like Walt, who loved them.

"You talkin' about yer path in the woods, Walt? Near my tree? The butterfly spot?"

Walt smiled slightly. "Yeah…reckon…I…shore…love…that… place. But…not…that…" He licked his dry lips. Even his tongue looked pale. "…member…day in the fiel'…'fore the…revival?… them…butterfl…" His voice trailed off, and his eyes drooped closed.

"I remember," O.T. said, hoarsely. "I remember now, you dummy. You stopped workin' to talk about how pretty they was. Blue and orange. One of each. Right?" Walt did not respond. "Chewing on that blade a'grass, talkin' about how you almost never see the two colors together. You was studyin' on butterflies that day."

Walt opened one eye and looked at him, as if opening both was too much effort. "S'right," he whispered. "S'right, O.T."

O.T. laid his head down on the bed beside his brother's frail form and cried. He didn't want Walt to see him, but he could restrain himself no longer. He thought his heart might break. *Please, God, if you even exist, don't take him away from me. He's the person I love most in this world.* O.T. felt Walt's thin hand rest lightly on his head, a hand with nails and lines just like his own, down to his very fingerprints.

"You gotta be both now," Walt said, his voice suddenly loud and clear as a bell.

"Both?" O.T. cried. "What do you mean, Walt?"

"Both, brother," Walt rasped. "Orange and blue. Got to be both." Walt's eyes, mirrors of his own, slowly cut to the left, sightless, and the mouth that looked just like O.T.'s bit down, searching for a blade of grass that was not there. With a gasp, Walt uttered his last sentence on earth: "Don't fret, brother, because I ain't dead. You're both of us now."

O.T. closed his eyes against the terrible pain that grew in his chest, shaking his head furiously. "You cannot leave me, Walt," he cried hoarsely. "You cannot, do you hear me?" With tears streaming unchecked down his cheeks, O.T. opened his eyes to find that Walt had already gone.

❧

Some hours after Walt had passed, when O.T. was finally able to wrench himself from his brother's side—after the crying, screaming, pleading with God, and cussing him too—he staggered down the stairs, expecting to fall into Betty Lou's arms, but she was nowhere to be seen. The barn was dark save for the glow of a single lantern. It was odd, O.T. noticed fleetingly, that Betty Lou had left the lantern unattended. The barn was stacked with bales of hay, and with the constant drought in these parts, it was the type of thing they never, ever did—you ran a farm, you just knew things like that.

He grabbed the lantern and lurched unsteadily toward the house, his body numb and boneless. Every room within was dark and cold. Betty Lou had left the screen open, and the hearth was cold and empty. He'd piled the wood up earlier, but she hadn't so much as touched it. In her grief, he supposed. O.T. leaned against the kitchen table, holding his head in his hands. He felt a rising, whirling storm within his skull, and a scream that if released would have no end. It was physically painful to move, to breathe, to *exist* in a world where his brother did not. Even taking one step forward was a physical pain.

But he needed to let Betty Lou know. He forced himself toward their bedroom. Betty Lou lay on the bed, her bare legs exposed to the cold night air. He would find a blanket to cover her, and let her sleep awhile before he told her. But as he approached the bed he realized she wasn't asleep at all.

"Hon." That one word, half a word, really—spoken in the voice of a woman he did not recognize. Betty Lou's smooth, low voice, that cinnamon-and-honey voice he loved so, now had the same gravel in it that Walt's had done. "You gotta get on out of here," she said calmly. With horror, O.T. realized that her dress clung damply to her narrow frame and her hair fell in sweaty tangles about her flushed cheeks. She struggled for breath, and an ugly red rash descended from the neckline of her dress.

"Betty Lou?" O.T. breathed in stunned disbelief. "What the—? I don't understand, darlin'. You was fine not an hour ago—"

She shook her head, her eyes bright and glittering. "No, hon. I could feel it comin'—to tell true, I felt off last night, but hoped maybe—" she grimaced in sudden pain. "I thought I had a fever when I was cookin' broth for Walt, but I was tryin' so hard to make him well…I shoulda *never* sat with you, touched you…but I just wanted to be close to you, it's been so hard…that was so dang *stupid*…" she trailed off, then seemed to collect her senses, her eyes widening. "You gotta git outta here, hon," she said, her voice sharpened by fear. "This hits quick. You need to get on down to Hazel's—scrub yerself head to toe first, hard as you can stand it, then git outta here. Maybe you oughta go to Hosey's instead, not risk exposin' the kids—"

"I ain't gonna leave you," O.T. said fiercely. "You need tendin'." He moved toward the bed, to lie beside her. He couldn't bear to leave. He'd rather lie right here and both of them die, than lose her and be alone. Couldn't she understand that?

"No!" She stopped him before he could move closer. "O.T., no. It's catchin'."

"I don't care—"

She didn't seem to hear him. "Send Hazel," Betty Lou said, coughing. "No, not her. You need her. Send Misrus Maybelle. Or go fetch my sisters. Someone without kids. Lila, I reckon. Someone who can risk—"

"Betty Lou, I ain't leavin'—"

"*Yes. You. ARE!*" she roared, almost coming off the bed with the ferocity of her voice. "'Cause if you die and leave our kids all alone, I will never forgive you, Owen, ya hear?"

O.T. caressed her hair and leaned down to kiss her forehead. "I will do this for you, darlin', but…only if you promise you'll get well. You're stronger than Walt…you can mend. Cain't you? Say you can, Betty Lou."

"I'll try my best, dear heart," Betty Lou said with a weary smile. "Send someone soon'us you can. Please."

"I swear it. I'll fetch somebody right away."

"I love you, Owen," she said. "I love you somethin' terrible."

"I love you too," he replied softly, pulling a strand of her white blonde hair between his fingers. "Walt's gone, Betty Lou."

"I know it," she said, her eyes bright in the dim room. "I felt him go."

"I'll get help." O.T. took one last searching, terrified look at his wife and went for the door.

Chapter Nine

Dr. Russell had suggested Sivvy write letters to someone, anyone. She'd refused at first, giving the excuse that she didn't write well. "Well, most folks don't read well, so it scarcely matters," he'd replied.

"I wouldn't know what to say," she'd argued.

"Write of the weather, or the kitchens. Write about whatever you like. The point is to just start writing."

She'd argued that too much time had passed to write to her family and disrupt their lives now. They likely thought she was dead. It would be a terrible shock to tell them otherwise, and then break the awful news that she was in the asylum on top of it. Better that they thought her dead.

"I imagine they would be heartened to hear from you no matter the circumstances," Dr. Russell had replied in his calm voice. "But if you won't write to them, why not write to someone else? A friend, an acquaintance, someone from church whom you admired?"

His mention of church irritated her; he'd read her file, didn't he know better? To hell with Dr. Russell's stupid letters. She wouldn't write one.

But, as time passed, the thought of writing to somebody started to seem appealing. But who? Then, the letter had arrived, out of nowhere, from a boy she'd known years and years ago, from Five Forks. Walter Lawrence—Walt, a skinny, nervous boy with bedraggled dark blond hair. A twin, Sivvy recalled. Cute as a button. His brother had been sweet, too. Sivvy had a sudden, vivid image of him leaning his young body against a sassafras tree, as if it were part of himself. She remembered his startling gray eyes, intent upon her own, and the moment that had marked the beginning of a series of bad decisions. It was after that town, those eyes, and the subsequent hiding, when she first realized she was *not free* and she would never be so.

At her next session, she told Dr. Russell that she would write a letter to Walt Lawrence. He provided her with papers and a quill pen, and she spent the afternoon writing her letter, fretting over her poor penmanship and spelling. She sent it off before she had a chance to talk herself out of it. She hoped Walt wouldn't think poorly of her after reading it.

∝

"You eat anything today?" Hazel asked, looming over O.T. with a wet dish rag in her hand. She'd been scrubbing the kitchen half the morning.

"Yeah," O.T. muttered, and went back to strumming his banjo.

"Ever' single casserole been brought over in the past two days is untouched on that table," Hazel scolded, her mouth pursed. "You ain't touched nary a one, and didn't even have the sense to cover them with a tea towel. They's flies in the kitchen. All of 'em rurnt."

Hazel was a firm believer that waste was a sin, and normally O.T. would agree with her. There were so few resources, so little food, in Five Forks, that those casseroles in his kitchen were a sign of real love and regard. But he just didn't give a damn right now.

O.T. adjusted the strings. One of them was out of tune and had a flat sound to it. He leaned around, past Hazel's legs, and spat a mouthful of tobacco juice off the porch.

"That kitchen was a right mess, let me just tell you. But I've got it licked now," Hazel said, waiting for O.T.'s acknowledgment. When he did not look up from the banjo, she grunted in frustration. "You ain't cleaned a dish in a week, from the looks of it. Milk spoiled on the counter, all Betty Lou's—" she hesitated a moment before forging on "—all the skillets an inch thick in grease. Had to pull the flies off 'em. That ain't sanitry, O.T."

He leaned around her and spat again.

"I ain't sayin' you got it easy, O.T.," she said, gentler now. "I know you's hurtin', but—"

"I'm fine," O.T. interrupted. "Just feel like playin' my banjo, is all."

"I reckon it's all that makes ya feel better just now, is it?" Her voice had gone soft, all the stern nagging gone right out of it. Hazel crouched down, looking her brother in the face. He refused to meet her eyes but he could feel the force of her gaze, willing him to. "O.T."

"What, woman?" He was just strumming random chords now, and not very well.

"I know it's hard, but you got to get up and outta this chair. You got to get up and eat a bite." When he did not respond, she added, "For the young'uns, O.T. Not fer yerself, but fer the young'uns."

The truth, which O.T. could never reveal to her or anybody else, was that he didn't give a rat's ass for the young'uns or her or anyone else. Right now, the only thing keeping him tethered to God's green—no, red and dusty and ugly besides—earth was the damn banjo, which was out of tune no matter how many times he'd tried to tune it. The thought of eating disgusted him, like a foreign thing that he did not do, had never done. He thought if he tried even a bite, he'd be out in the yard, bringing up his guts. It was all he could do to manage even a few sips of water here and there, and a plug of tobacco. None of life's pleasures or necessities—food, drink, family—could be tolerated right now, not when Betty Lou and Walt were both newly buried under the sassafras tree.

The day-glow orange tree had been his favorite ever since he was a boy. And it was just the right time of year; those deeply orange leaves—almost red, almost pink in some places, curled and pointed at the ends—had started falling off the branches, blanketing the bodies of his beloved wife and twin in a lovely rosy warm pile. Anybody with any sense of God or spirit might have said that was a beautiful thing, poignant somehow. O.T. did not. He had realized, staring out at the tree as the leaves fluttered down to cover the freshly dug graves, that he would never be able to stand under that tree again. The bodies of those he loved more than anything now nourished that tree, and O.T. could not bear it. He *hated* that fucking tree.

"Tom tol' undertakers you'd want 'em buried there," Hazel said, clearing her throat. "I didn't think you'd want 'em buried with Ma and Pa, since they's on our property…I knew you'd want 'em both close to you. Figgered we'd start a little fambly cemetery, right here under yer favorite tree." She waited for him to agree, to say a word of thanks. He said nothing. What could he say? He stood on shaking legs and walked inside the house without a word, hearing her call after him, her voice a little shaky, "That was the right thing, weren't it, O.T.? That's where you wanted 'em?" As the door slammed behind him, her voice, faintly, "Well, it ain't like we can change it now."

In his room, he lay on the bed sideways, trying to fall asleep.

Sleeping and absently strumming his banjo was all he'd done for days, not for lack of Hazel's nagging.

O.T. had his .38 tucked away in a box in the shed, and plenty of rat poison, too. He hadn't seriously entertained the notion of the rat poison, because he reckoned poison was a woman's way to go, and it wasn't dignified for a man, especially one with children who would forever judge him. But the .38—he'd thought about that long and hard, and plenty. He had imagined scrawling a note to the young'uns, walking down to the creek (in the past he might've considered the tree, but the tree was ruined for all things now), putting the gun to his head and just ending it.

Hosey's voice was in his head sometimes, when things were real bad. *Don't be a goddang coward, O.T.* Hosey, whose dad had blown off his head with a shotgun. O.T. wondered if the voice would fade, if he stopped listening to it.

"O.T." Hazel stood in the doorway. It would do no good to pretend he was asleep.

"What?"

"Git on back up, and come git you a bite."

O.T. groaned. After a moment, he wrenched himself from the bed and made his way into the kitchen, grumbling under his breath. Forget any drastic measures—Hazel's nagging would kill him for sure.

Hazel stood over him, arms folded, until he took a plate down from the cupboard. The kitchen was now spotless and smelled faintly of bleach. His stomach churned. "Thank ya for the kitchen," he mumbled.

She gestured toward the dishes on the table. "Maybelle sent over chicken mull, and you know how good her mull is." She pulled the tea towel off the deep bowl, and O.T. thought he'd gag. Chicken mull was usually a favorite, but the pieces of greasy chicken swimming in the thick, peppery broth made his stomach lurch. "They's also greens, spoonbread, zucchini bread, sausage and bean casserole, and cake." O.T. swayed in the doorway. "Two kinds. Chiffon cake and sour cream chocolate. Which slice d'ya want?"

"No cake," he croaked. "Give it to the young'uns. Jes'…uh… gimme a piece of that zucchini bread, and a little of the beans."

"They's also baked sweet taters, that Betty Lou's sister Lila sent, sorghum syrup, and I have some side meat—"

The mention of Betty Lou's name gave him a low, dull pain in his belly. "Naw, Hazel. I don't want naught else, just that fer now. My guts are gripin' and I ain't got no appetite."

Hazel heaped a plate with the zucchini bread and beans, spooning a little chicken mull on the side. "I know you ain't," she said softly with an apologetic smile. "But it's my job to make sure you eat anyway. For the young'uns."

"Yeah, yeah." O.T. wished folks would quit reminding him of the young'uns, as if he could forget. He took the plate from her and ventured into the living room, sitting down on the couch. He expected her to gripe after him that the couch was no place to eat, and that he wasn't to start living like a hobo in the woods just because *she* was gone, but Hazel was blessedly silent. She was choosing her battles.

He dug his fork into the beans and held a bite to his mouth, forcing himself to chew. He couldn't taste anything; the food felt thick and strange on his tongue and teeth. The front door slammed—Hazel had gone outside, likely to hang up his washing. She'd been a busy bee for days, and O.T. knew he ought to have been more grateful. It wasn't her job to take care of his house, and he knew she was tired and grieving herself. But he couldn't find room in his heart for gratitude or for shame, only for grief.

He dug his fork in again and raised a bite of beans to his mouth, but feeling his gorge rise, he leapt up. Heading for the sink, he managed to get halfway there before his stomach emptied itself all over the gleaming kitchen floor.

He cleaned up the mess the best he could with a dish towel, grateful that Hazel was outside. Not just because he didn't feel like hearing her nag him, but because he didn't want her to have to deal with another mess. Not after she'd spent so much time cleaning his kitchen. Scraping his leftovers into the trash bin, he hoped she wouldn't notice. He rinsed his plate in the sink and washed his mouth out with water. His head was buzzing, as if a million little bees were flying around between his ears.

O.T. walked back out onto the porch, listening to the buzzing in his head, feeling his blood getting thicker. He grabbed his banjo, strumming at the strings as he walked down the steps and out to the barn where the chiffarobe gathered dust. He had told Betty Lou how he was gonna finally fix it up, after a year of promising, and he'd been so proud of himself, expecting her to fall over herself in thanks. She had only laughed, knowing he was full of mess, that he never got around to half the things he meant to start. And she'd been right this time, too. She had died with her special undergarments stored in boxes because her no-good, lazy husband couldn't find an afternoon to fix her damn chiffarobe.

Later, he would have no recollection of walking into the barn or of raising up his banjo. It was as if his brain suddenly *split* and he was in the corner, by the pile of hay, watching himself as he slammed the banjo against the chiffarobe, splintering the instrument into large, jagged pieces. The chiffarobe had been her mother's. Well, he'd fix it, all right. He'd fix it good. He reared back and slammed the shredded remnants of the banjo into the chiffarobe's mirror, watching the glass splinter and crack, needlelike shards glittering in the hay at his feet. A banjo string popped and broke as he laid siege to a remaining drawer that refused to break.

Finally, he was spent. Panting and paying no mind to the blood running from his fingers, O.T. stared out the window of the barn at the land he had loved. The place that had been his dream, the tree he'd adored, now his nightmare.

He crossed the yard in a daze and stood beneath the tree for a few minutes, staring up at the leaves. The graves had no headstones yet; he would have to save his money, as headstones were dear. How many times had he stood beneath this tree, hoping and dreaming, marveling at its simple beauty?

O.T. had dreamed of Betty Lou here as a boy; it had been here that he'd made plans to marry her, to start a family. He thought of Sivvy, the traveling preacher-in-training with the dark hair and glittering green eyes. She had loved this tree, too. He remembered the reverence on her face as she had touched it. It seemed that those who loved this tree were doomed.

O.T. reared back and smashed the remnants of the banjo into the tree with all his might, until nothing remained but the instrument's slender neck, which he threw in the dirt. O.T. leaned up against the tree, pressing his face against the bark, and cried.

O.T. tore into the house, nearly ripping the screen door off the hinges, and pounded down the hallway to his bedroom—he no longer thought of it as *their* bedroom; he had banished the thought from his mind almost as soon as she'd died, because it would be unbearable to even enter the room otherwise. The bed was unmade, his meager clothes spread all over the floor. O.T. flung the doors of the wardrobe open, looking past the hanging row of Betty Lou's crisp, bright dresses, all of them tailored and embellished with her own hands, all of them as unique and clean and sweet-smelling as she had been. He rummaged past scarves, winter gloves, scraps of cloth, things she had collected in life as the years had crept on, and found the bottle he had stashed there two days previous. He had protested angrily when Hosey had put it into his hand with a knowing look, after the funerals, had insisted he didn't want no dad-blasted hooch in his house, but Hosey had said to take it "jes' in case of emergency." Well, the emergency had arrived.

O.T. twisted off the cap and tilted his head back, pouring the contents in his mouth. He took a second long swig, ignoring the burning feeling in his tongue and throat, the hot feeling that immediately took root in his chest. He paused for a breath, then took another deep swig. The hooch was foul, and it only confirmed his opinion that people who wasted their hard-earned dollars on this stuff, risked going to jail for it, were crazier than shithouse rats. But he drank it anyway, waiting for the numb forgetfulness that he hoped would come. Even if it was just for an hour, even if it was just till he passed out with his head in a ditch or with Hazel throwing him into an icy cold washtub. He didn't care. He just wanted to be numb for a little while.

Two more swigs and O.T. fell to the bed, burying his head in a thin pillow, the bottle sloshing beside him. Already the liquor was working him over. Neither he nor Walt had ever thought much of folks who drank, who dealt in 'shine—dealing with Tom had ruined them on it—but damn if the warm lull in his belly didn't feel good. He closed his eyes, imagining Betty Lou beside him, in the crook of his arm, her head up under his chin, or with her back to him, the warmth of her pressed up against him as he held her.

O.T.'s thoughts drifted to the day his life had changed, how he had broke the news of Walt's death to Hazel. She carried on, clutching him and wailing; she had broken a butter dish in her grief. The children had gathered around and she had told them, between sobs, "Yer Uncle Walt, rest his sweet, sweet soul, has gone on to the Lord Jesus." Even Tom, the bastard, had wiped at a tear and said, "Amen." The two younger children had been ashen and silent but not shocked. In these parts, poor as everybody was, illness and death were familiar things. Only Ginny had taken it bad, running barefoot from the house, sobs trailing behind her. O.T. had followed, bringing her a sweater, because the night was cold, but she'd refused it and pushed at him, yelling at him blindly through her tears. "You promised me he'd git better. You made me leave! I wanted to see him!"

O.T.'s thoughts kept returning to that fateful morning when he had first learned of Betty Lou's passing. He had wanted to return to Betty Lou after summoning her sisters, Lila and Isabella, but Hazel had urged him to stay the night. "Her fambly is good at tendin'," Hazel assured him. "They'll set her to rights. You kin go see her in the mornin'. Yer young'uns need you here." O.T. was anxious and uneasy but complied. Ginny had finally returned to the house after an hour, her nose red with the cold and from crying. She had not spoken, but curled up on the couch, trying to make herself as small as possible, staring out the window. Hazel threw a crocheted afghan over Ginny's huddled form, her feet sticking out from under it— looking eerily like her own mama, O.T. thought. He thought, too, of Walt, who lay cold and alone in the barn, untended to. O.T. could imagine Walt, with a chuckle, saying, "I'll keep." But it wasn't fitting, to leave his brother alone that way.

O.T. pounded the pillow, angry. He knew it was possible that he could still sicken, but he felt fine. Why should the two people he loved most in the world sicken and one of them die, and he stay well? A cruel joke if ever there was one. He drifted off into a fitful sleep somewhere around the witching hour, and slept for an hour—

violent, sad dreams peppering his sleep—then wakened when he heard Hazel padding around the kitchen.

O.T. drove into town early, before the rest of the world was awake, forgoing breakfast or coffee, since his stomach lurched with nerves. He parked in front of the post office, Walt's letter in his pocket. He fished it out, looking at the handwriting, not wanting to let go this piece of his brother. Finally, with a jagged sigh, he pulled open the mail slot and pushed the letter in. He had fulfilled his promise. The coroner wasn't in yet, so O.T. took a brisk walk down Main Street, hoping to work out some of his rising anxiety.

Five Forks had once been a quaint little town, with a population of three hundred folks or so, mostly cotton and tobacco farmers. Most got by well enough with a bit of land to support their wives and children. The yards and cotton fields all looked much the same, with hard-packed, dusty red dirt. Beyond the town, thin streams with muddy red banks wound their way through forested groves of dogwood, oak, and sassafras. Black crows and buzzards circled the sky, waiting for sick cows and goats to die. Life was tough, but got on the same way it had for generations.

O.T. strode past Main Street's shops and storefronts, lined up like toy boxes, each painted a different color, a pattern of red, green, blue, and brown that went on for half a mile or so. There was a law office, where Mister Lark was in two days a week, dividing his time between offices in Dogsborough and Comer, and a dusty little post office that didn't do much trade, manned by a single half-blind mailman, who was a godawful driver—he'd crashed the mail truck twice last year alone. Five Forks had no eye doctor to fit him for glasses, just Dr. Kidd, the on-call doc who shuttled back and forth through Madison County, serving as pediatrician, midwife, dentist, and surgeon besides. The small diner, previously a barbecue shack, now served only hamburgers because pork was dear. A soda shop occupied the corner, but it had been a long time since they'd served root beers. You'd be lucky to get a scoop of butter pecan or peach ice cream, and you could forget the cone. Times were hard—the boll weevil and the drought had worked in tandem these past years, squeezing working folks till they were all out of juice.

It was a quaint little town, marked in the center of town with a big red boxcar, a relic from an old train that had long since ceased to run. Every year town folks re-painted it, so it remained that same candy apple color, bright and shiny and somehow hopeful. Hope, though, was fading fast for everybody, and not just in Five Forks.

By the time the coroner, Bill Overton, arrived at his office, O.T. had circled Main Street four times and was out of his mind with anxiety. Bill kept a respectful silence as O.T. drove him to the farm. Once there, O.T. left the man, running to the house to check on Betty Lou, his heart pounding with fear. He held a mask in his hand and secured it across his face quickly, knowing Betty Lou would insist. He'd expected opposition the moment he got to the front door, but while Betty Lou's sisters, Isabella and Lila stood to meet him, they offered none.

"O.T.," Lila said, from the other side of the screen door, dark circles pouched beneath her eyes. "Was that Bill Overton I saw?"

"Yeah," O.T. said, shifting his weight from one foot to the other. "He went on up…to see to Walt. How's—"

His hand was on the screen door, ready to open it, when Lila spoke, cutting him off, "Better tell him when he's done with Walt to come on in here." She turned and went back into the house.

O.T. looked at her retreating back, uncomprehending.

Isabella opened the screen door, came out onto the porch, and laid a hand on O.T.'s arm. Her face was splotchy and red, and her eyes, the same light blue as Betty Lou's, were bloodshot. "I'm awful sorry, hon," she said, dazed. "We did what we could, but the fever had took hold of her like I ain't never seen. Lord, it was fast—not two hours after you left. Betty Lou is with the angels now."

Evidently O.T. had screamed, loud and shrill like a woman, but he didn't remember that, either. Nor did he remember the coroner and Isabella having to hold him down, to keep him from tearing into the house and seizing Betty Lou from her deathbed.

A day passed, maybe two. He'd lost track of time. There had been a funeral; two of them. He'd been encouraged to have a joint funeral for Betty Lou and Walt, for the sake of cost and expediency, but O.T. insisted that they each deserved their own separate service. Walt's service was Sunday morning, right after church services— which O.T. skipped and didn't give a damn who judged him for it—in the reception hall that doubled as the Sunday school room, and Betty Lou's began two hours after Walt's. Reverend Hill presided over both services, tears streaming down his cheeks as he asked the congregation to pray for O.T. and his children. People milled past, paying their last respects, touching O.T. on the knee or shoulder and hugging the children. Hosey, who knew loss better than most, put the bottle in his hand, and gave him a fierce, bone-crushing hug. Later, Misrus Maybelle held a separate reception in her barn, with refreshments and music and people sharing memories of Walt and Betty Lou. O.T. had not gone.

The next morning, Betty Lou and Walt were placed in their respective coffins, holes were dug, and they were lowered into the ground. Later, O.T. supposed it did not matter that Betty Lou and Walt had been buried beneath his favorite tree, because he was certain he would never find joy in anything again anyway.

Chapter Ten

O.T. woke with a start, his mouth tasting like burnt rubber, feeling disconcerted. Sitting up, he winced at the knife-like pain in his temple and the foul-tasting substance that coated his tongue. His wife and brother were dead, and he was hungover for the first time in his life. He smelled an astringent, sour odor, realizing with dull horror that he had vomited on himself in his sleep. He needed to get his sheets and clothes into the washtub before Hazel had to deal with it, but he couldn't seem to move.

"Deddy," Ginny said from the doorway, startling him. She had a newspaper tucked under her arm and a cup of coffee in her hand. Her face, so like her mother's, was full of quiet judgment. In one short week, she'd endured so much more than a girl her age should have to, and he had made it no better.

"Since when do you drink coffee?" he asked, with an attempt at levity.

She didn't smile. "You need a bath."

"Reckon I do," O.T. said, embarrassed and ashamed. "I'm sorry, gal. I'm 'bout to git up and tend myself. I don't want you to see me like this."

Ginny shrugged. "Aunt Hazel ast me to check on ya. Wanted to make sure you got up."

"Don't tell me she wants me to eat," he sighed.

"Naw. Not this time, but I'm sure she'll start in 'fore long," Ginny answered. "She's got other things on her mind just now." She gave him a pointed look. He had apparently missed something important while he'd been passed out. The sun was high in the sky, and he reckoned it was at least lunch time. He had never slept so late a day in his life.

Ginny leaned against the doorway, appraising him. "It's Hallowe'en," she said.

"So it is." O.T. put a hand to his temple. There were plenty of boogers and haints in there, it felt like. "I'm gittin' up. I'll be out in a minute."

"I won't tell Aunt Hazel that you got sick," Ginny said. "If you promise you'll clean it up yerself."

"I will," O.T. promised, managing a tender smile for his eldest daughter despite his deep shame and self-disgust. "Yer a good girl."

She gave another careless shrug, then tossed the newspaper she'd had under her arm onto the foot of the bed. "Might want to give that a read, affore you come out," she said, not unkindly. "Catch up on the news." With that, she left the room.

O.T. stood slowly on shaking legs, his head burning and pounding, his arms trembling. Yanking his bedsheets off the mattress, he balled them up on the floor and stepped gingerly out of his reeking clothes. He dressed slowly, painfully, in a clean white undershirt and coveralls, wiped at his face with a handkerchief, and spit on his comb, smoothing back his tangled hair. Finally, he sat on the bare mattress and opened up the newspaper, wondering what was going on. Nobody bought the newspaper except on the weekends, and Hazel *never* did. He noted the date in the top corner. Wait, he thought. Had Ginny said it was Hallowe'en? That meant it was Thursday. Had he really slept through Wednesday?

O.T. stared at the page for a while, waiting for his vision to clear, then read the headline, not sure what to make of it. He sat there gaping, reading it over and over again, not understanding.

WALL STREET CRASH!
NEW YORK STOCK EXCHANGE IN PANIC!
BANKERS SCRAMBLE AS BILLIONS LOST ON "BLACK
TUESDAY"!

It was quiet and cool under the pecan trees. The slight rustle of branches felt wistful, and a little ominous, perhaps because it was Hallows Eve, Sivvy figured, spreading her apron over the lush grass, or Hallowe'en, as the young folks called it. The day didn't mean much to her; her family had never been big on tricks or treats, partly owing to their Christian nature, but also because it was hard to go from house to house begging for sweets when you lived on the side of a mountain. Still, you marked the day. Hallowe'en—the day the dead came back to the land of the living to say how-do—if you invited them, that is.

Sivvy reckoned she invited her dead daily. Her brain persisted in conjuring them up, despite her best efforts to keep them buried.

"There are ghosts, though. There's one in your room," Nurse Burns had said.

It was dusk; the macabre night was brewing. There were few people about in the pecan grove—a nurse lingering nearby; a gravedigger, bringing up soft dirt; one of the evening doctors, standing outside for a smoke; another patient, a young man, pacing back and forth in front of the men's building. They were all silent as ghosts themselves.

Usually Sivvy was allowed to visit the pecan grove only in the hour after breakfast, but Dr. Russell had recommended the late-afternoon excursion; perhaps he sensed something desperate in her, something fraught. "I think it would be fine to go for a stroll after supper," he'd told her during therapy. "Just for ten minutes or so, mind. I'll tell your nurse."

Dr. Russell and the rest of the asylum staff had been distracted these past two days. Sivvy had heard rumors of some doings in the city, something to do with banks and the stock market. May, already scaling back breakfast rations, told Sivvy to make a dozen fewer biscuits that morning.

Sivvy didn't know what any of it meant, and she didn't really care one way or the other. Just getting through the days was hard enough without politickin'. If there was food, they ate; if there wasn't, they wouldn't. The asylum had suffered famine before; the lush, well-nourished grass under her feet told that tale. Whatever would happen would happen; that was the way it always had, the way it always would. Most people didn't have any power over their own lives and what little power they had was pretense. Milledgeville inmates had even less power than everyone else. What good would it do to fret over it?

Ultimately, they were all destined for the earth anyway, she thought, thinking of the pellagra victims. Folks were afraid to walk among the pecan groves, either reluctant to walk over the graves of the dead, or afraid of ghosts, or both. Sivvy had no time for such superstitions; there were ghosts and ghouls enough in her own head, and she felt a kinship with those buried under her feet, whose bones now fed the trees and helped them bear fruit. She had mentioned this to Dr. Russell once, and he had dismissed the thought as morbid. "Best not to dwell on such things," he had said. "Dwelling on the negative only leads to sorrow."

But Sivvy could not understand why healthy, sane persons insisted that death was something negative, something to be feared. The inmates at Milledgeville, living lives of hardship and privation, were close to death always; perhaps this was the reason they saw Death as someone they would one day clasp by the hands and welcome as a friend. The insane accepted their unavoidable fate much more readily than the sane, who kicked and twisted in denial, Sivvy thought.

Brushing off her apron, Sivvy stood and tied it around her waist. The nurse stepped out of the shadows and extended an arm to lead Sivvy back to the Powell Building and upstairs to bed. As they walked up the cold granite steps, heading back into confinement, Sivvy opened her mouth to tell the nurse, "Happy Hallows Eve," but changed her mind at the last minute and coughed quietly into her hand.

CHAPTER ELEVEN

"You look rode hard and put up wet."

O.T. didn't answer, still out of breath, as he put his hoe away in the barn. Hosey Brown followed, trying like the dickens to pull him into conversation. O.T. brushed past Hosey and back out into the yard. When he finished with the cotton, he had to tend the vegetable garden, if they expected a summer crop to eat. And they needed one. He couldn't keep feeding the children nothing but cornmeal mush and molasses. They needed greens, they needed meat, lest they get pellagra, and he'd die himself before he let that happen. He grabbed the pail of seeds and slipped the handle over his arm.

"Owen Tolbert Lawrence, when you gon' tire of this mess?" Hosey followed him through the yard, past the chicken coop where one sad, withered old hen still lived, past the empty hog pen, and into the shed, where O.T. kept his smaller digging tools.

"Never," O.T. replied out of the corner of his mouth, grabbing the hand shovel. "Ain't you got a liquor run to make?"

"I ain't seen nothin' to beat it," Hosey exclaimed. "You gon' sit there on yer high horse judgin' me for running a little liquor, tryin' to make a livin', and you done turned into a daytime drunk in less than six months?"

"Git on outta here," O.T. scowled, brushing past, deliberately ramming into Hosey's shoulder. "I cain't sit around and pass the time a'day with you. Some of us got actual jobs."

Hosey sighed. "You got more pride than you got sense, and more work than you got time or hands for. If you'd just let me help—"

"I said git on outta here!" O.T. thundered, his expression fierce. "Go on and git!" He was a little ashamed, yelling at his best friend as if he were a mangy dog begging for scraps on the porch, but he didn't want to see Hosey. Not now, not ever. He could come around every day for another six months for all O.T. cared, but it wouldn't amount to a hill of beans.

"Suit yerself, you dumb ol' lout," Hosey retorted, unruffled, which just made O.T. madder. Nothing ever made Hosey mad, which drove O.T. crazy. "I got to run to Dogsborough anyhow. See ya tomorry." O.T. did not turn as Hosey walked out to the driveway, climbed into his motorcar, and left.

He heard a rustling behind him and turned to find Ginny standing at the barn doorway, tugging on her honey-blonde hair. "Was that Uncle Hosey?" she asked, peering at the car backing out of the driveway.

"He ain't yer uncle," O.T. said irritably, before smiling at his daughter. "You come out to help yer old man?" He held out the bucket of seeds. "Lotta plantin' to do. Last frost is done, so we better git on it, if we want to have a decent crop this year." He tried to sound optimistic, but he doubted very much that they'd have a decent crop, if they had a crop at all. His efforts to paint the plants last year had done little to dissuade the weevils and the drought had killed what little had survived the insects. The bills were mounting, and now, for the first time, he had sharecroppers to pay, too.

"I reckon," Ginny said, squaring her shoulders. "I was gon' meet Bessy Childs tonight just after supper, if'n it's awright with you. She got a trade fer me."

"What she tradin'?"

"Dozen eggs for a quart of sorghum syrup and some tomatoes."

O.T. sighed. There was only one tomato plant in the garden that was bearing fruit, and they were tiny and mealy and half of them had worms. There were at least two, though, that were good enough to serve up with the night's dinner, and he had been looking forward to them. But he knew the children needed eggs more. "Awright," he said. "Have at 'em, but Lord knows they ain't fittin' to eat."

"She won't notice," Ginny said with a giggle. "She ain't got no sense."

"You ought not talk about yer friends thataway," O.T. said, concealing his smile.

"Why not?" she asked, returning his grin. "You talk to Hosey like he's a cow got loose in the pasture."

"That's different," O.T. said, defensively. "That's man's business, you just see that you keep yer nose right on out of it."

"Oh, Deddy," Ginny retorted with a mock sigh. "Man's business is understood least of all by men." She smiled at him. "Mama told me that." She dug into the pail of seeds.

Dusk was just starting to creep in when O.T. and Ginny made their way back to the house. As he washed his hands in the wash pail, he noticed a cloying, bitter smell wafting from the screen door.

"Yer lil' sister cookin' supper again?" he asked Ginny as they ascended the stairs. "You know she ain't supposed to cook unattended. I can smell burnt syrup." Belle liked her syrup warm, but she didn't know when to stop heating. Ginny had had to scrub the toffee-like glue off the skillets more than once.

"Aunt Hazel couldn't come today, and I had to help you in the field, so—" Ginny gave O.T. a look, as if daring him to complain. She was looking, and acting, more like her mama every day. "I tol' Junior to watch her." O.T. grinned.

"I ain't sayin' a word," he said. And he wouldn't, but he felt a pang of guilt nonetheless. Belle was barely four; she ought not have to help at all, and neither should his son. They were just kids, they should be out playing.

O.T. splashed his face with cold water, slicking a palm-full through his hair, which had grown long in recent months. Ginny washed up next and they went inside to the kitchen, where Belle, standing on a step stool at the stove, was dishing out cornmeal mush into bowls and topping it with the scorched, sticky syrup. Owen Jr. stood in the corner, arms crossed over his chest.

"Looks good enough to eat," O.T. proclaimed, winking at his youngest daughter. "You got us some nice ribeyes to go with that?"

"Har," Belle muttered sarcastically as she handed her father his bowl. "This all we got, Deddy. Oh, wait!" she exclaimed, the pink in her cheeks deepening. "I almost fergot!" She leapt from the step stool, disappeared into the day room, and returned triumphantly, with a foil-covered tray. "Aunt Hazel sent me home with these yest-dy. They wasn't ready yet then, but they is now!" Belle peeled off the foil to reveal a tray filled with dried apples.

Ginny smiled, took a handful, and popped them in her mouth. "Yum."

"I'm gon' save some fer fried pies," Belle boasted proudly. "I'm gon' make those tomorry."

"You ain't old enough to make fried pies," Owen Jr. said petulantly. "You'll catch yerself on fire."

Belle's lip protruded, and O.T. gave his son a look. "Brother's right that you ain't old enough to fry 'em yerself," he said to Belle, tucking a finger under her chin. "But I'm sure that sister Ginny can find the time to help you with the fryin' part. You can do all the rest, awright? Will that do ya?"

"Okay, Deddy." Belle brightened and went back to dishing out the mush, sticking her tongue out at her brother. O.T. didn't have much appetite—particularly for rubbery dried apples, scorched sorghum syrup, and the same old cornmeal mush he'd been eating every day for God knew how long. But he had to make an effort to eat for the sake of the children, who would notice. They had been watching him like hawks ever since Black Tuesday, watching for signs of him puking on himself, or passing out in a ditch, or blowing his damn head off. The kids knew he drank, but he hoped they could at least see that he was hanging on. Hanging on just long enough to tend the farm, pay the sharecroppers, and see the kids raised, and then who knew.

Who knew.

O.T. sure as hell didn't, and worse, he didn't care. A wave of apathy had fallen over him the week of Black Tuesday, when he'd well and truly known that all was lost. When the markets fell, he knew it was only a matter of time before he lost the house. Seeing it go back to the bank had been hard enough. He was months behind on his payments, but the bank hadn't turned them out yet. The thought of losing the land where Ma and Pap had built a home, where his children had been born, where his brother and wife were now buried—well, he couldn't even begin to think about that.

Not to mention, he'd lost Hosey.

Well, he hadn't really *lost* Hosey. He'd put him aside. Hosey hadn't accepted it yet, but he'd have to eventually. O.T. was better off alone, and it suited him just fine. Seemed better to him to lose everyone in one fell swoop than stand around waiting for them to drop like birds from a tree branch.

❧

Several months before, O.T. had been tinkering with the truck, attempting to change the oil. Just as he cranked the jack all the way up—which held the truck half a foot above the ground—it busted and the truck fell back down with a loud clank, O.T. just barely scampering out of the way.

"God, motherfuckin' damn it!" he roared, not giving a flip who heard him—though he heard Walt's prim voice in his head say, "Language!" The truck hit the dirt so hard it knocked his rearview mirror loose, and now he'd have to repair that, too. His tools had needed replacing for a coon's age, and O.T. had no money for it and no time anyhow. Now his jack was busted on top of everything else.

"Well, at least your reflexes are still good," a familiar voice declared behind him.

O.T. turned and scowled to see Hosey, with a shit-eating grin on his face. He was decked out like a dandy in a new jacket, gleaming black shoes, and pomade-shiny hair.

"It ain't funny, you sumbitch," O.T. spat into the dirt, pulling out his rag and wiping grease off his hands. "All I got to do 'round here, and I cain't even get the daggum oil changed in my truck! No, not a damn thing can just be *easy*. Every single thing's got to be as hard as—"

"Oh, rub some dirt in it."

O.T. scowled, but he could already feel himself softening. It wasn't just the pack of Beech-Nut that Hosey held out to him—O.T.'s tobacco pouch had been empty going on two days, with no prospect of filling it anytime soon—but the easygoing, playful grin on his friend's face that always had the ability to calm him. O.T. felt his shoulders relaxing. "My jack's busted," he acknowledged with a rueful grin. "Don't that beat all?"

"Hop on in my car. Let's go," Hosey said.

"I cain't go nowhere. I got a day's work ahead of me in the—"

"Won't be but an hour. Just ridin' into Carlton for a minute. We'll stop by my place on the way back and grab my jack. I'll change yer oil for ya while you go do the garden."

"I ain't got nothin' to pay ya."

"Shut the hell up."

O.T. knew better than to argue. He followed his friend to the car—a gleaming Studebaker—and slid into the passenger seat. The car was sleek and slick with chrome, the paint a glossy gray-green, the interior roomy, the seats made of supple leather, emitting that gorgeous smell that O.T. couldn't help but breathe in. He figured Hosey wouldn't have the car long—who could make payments on a car like this, in times like these?—but why not enjoy it while it lasted? After all, O.T. doubted he'd have a new car for many a long year, if ever again.

"I oughter wring yer neck for buyin' this car," O.T. said, rolling the window down and letting his hand ride on the breeze. As Hosey drove down Main Street, O.T. noticed more than one head turn to admire the car as it passed. How Hosey must love that! "Didn't you ever learn not to buy expensive things on credit? The payments are like to kill you. Ain't you noticed we in the middle of a drought? And them folks up north, the fi-nance experts, say we're about to be in a depression, whatever that is."

"I know."

"That's probly why they sold it to ya. Knowin' they'd get it back from ya in short order."

"O.T., I didn't buy the car on credit."

"You musta. How else you got the dough for a beaut like this?" Hosey had never had two nickels to rub together.

"Paid cash."

"Shoot. You a lie." Hosey was putting him on. A car like this, right off the lot, had to cost close to a thousand buckaroos, O.T. guessed.

"I did, too."

"How?" O.T. demanded as they turned onto Highway 72.

"You got to be the dumbest son of a gun on this earth, or either blind one," Hosey said with a laugh. "Why you think we're going to Carlton? Ain't you noticed I'm always headin' somewheres? Day before yest'dy I was up at Mule Camp Springs; day before that I was up in Licklog, in the mountains. I got to spell it out for ya? Ain't you never thought what I been doing, goin' to all those places?"

"I don't pay no attention to what you do. Figgered you was seein' some gal. I been right distracted, or ain't you noticed?" O.T. retorted. Then it dawned on him. "You mean to tell me you—?"

Hosey gestured to the backseat of the car, and O.T. twisted in his seat to look. Beneath a tarp, on the floorboard, was a crate of glass bottles.

"Yer runnin' 'shine?" O.T. demanded, furious at himself for not having figured it out sooner.

Hosey grinned. "I know you used to be right judgy about folks who drank, but you're lit more often than not these days, so I figger we can be honest about it now." He looked over at O.T. "It's long past time I cut you in. Good money in it, and you got mouths to feed."

"Say what?"

"Money's scarce and gettin' scarcer. What they say up in New York is true. Good money. I could use a hand, O.T., now that..." he trailed off.

"Now that *what?*"

"Forget it. You want in or not?" Hosey rolled down his window and spit out tobacco juice; a little got on the window, and he wiped it off with his sleeve, carefully. "I don't wanna hear nothin' about how it ain't Christian, neither. Mouths got to be fed, and since when did you or I give a damn about all that anyhow?"

"Who was helpin' you before?" O.T. demanded.

"Just workin' by myself, mainly," Hosey replied, smoothly.

"You a lie," O.T. retorted. "Walt was with you more than he was with me there at the end. Hosey Brown, if you—"

"O.T., I only needed help every now and again—"

"My brother." O.T.'s ears were hot, and his temple pounded. "You got my brother—innocent Walt—into this shit? You had him breakin' the law, runnin' 'shine?"

"No, he wasn't runnin' nothin'. He rode along, helped me with deliveries from time to time, but only when I had a big order—"

"Him not even right in the head, probably not even fully understandin' what y'all was doin'—"

"You always said not to treat him no different. And now listen at you, talkin' about him like he was a—"

"He *trusted* you, Hosey. Like you were his own brother! And you got him into this...this... You coulda got him put in jail!"

"Oh, come off it, O.T.! I never woulda let nothin' happen to Walt—"

"'Cept catch scarlet fever! Goddamnit! Where did y'all go? I reckon you dragged him all over tarnation, exposin' him to God knows what, and he got sick and he *died*."

"Now that's a road too far, O.T.," Hosey protested. "We never went around nobody who was sick. He only helped out a little. Just over at Harmony Grove, and once or twice at Ila... He wanted a little pocket money, wanted to help you and Betty Lou put food on the table. I was tryin' to help—"

"Tryin' to help *yerself*," O.T. spat. "Usin' my brother as yer mule. And now you want to use me for the same."

"You got a gall, sittin' on yer high horse over there, knowin' good and well you put a bottle of this stuff away every night," Hosey said, finally losing a little of his own cool. "Cain't even feed yer kids; yer lettin' 'em roam all over town, dirty and hungry, and you at the house drunk, layin' under the bed. I'm tryin' to give you a leg up, see. If we work together we can branch out, make more money—"

"I don't want to hear no more."

"O.T., just listen for a minute—"

"No."

They had arrived in Carlton. If Five Forks was a one-horse town, then Carlton didn't have a horse at all. It was a blink-and-you-miss-it kind of place, home to a mule trading post and a general store—a drafty, white-planked building built over a stream.

"Stop here," O.T. commanded. Hosey stopped the car, and O.T. got out.

"You goin' in for a drink or to use the john?" Hosey asked affably, his expression hopeful.

"Neither. I'm gettin' out and goin' home."

"What, you gonna walk?" Hosey laughed incredulously.

"I'll hitch a ride from somebody."

"O.T., quit actin' like a damn fool. Get back in the car."

"Go to hell." O.T. leaned forward, looking through the window of the shiny new Studebaker. "Yer ma would be ashamed of you,

Hosey. And so am I. I'll never forgive you for what you done to my brother. I don't ever want to see yer sorry face again, you hear? Now get the hell out of here." O.T. turned on his heel and walked into the general store, letting the door slam behind him. He heard the roar of the Studebaker's engine starting up, and when he came back outside a few minutes later, Hosey was gone.

❧

That trip to Carlton had been the last time O.T. talked to Hosey, though it wasn't for Hosey's lack of trying. O.T. sat down at the kitchen table and dug into his mush with his spoon, wishing he were drunker so he wouldn't remember all this mess. "Sister's trading for some eggs tonight," he said to Belle. "So you can have a fry up tomorrow if you want to."

"Oh, goody," Belle beamed. She was going to turn into a swell cook, even with her skillet mishaps. She seemed to like nothing more than to tinker in the kitchen, young as she was, but Ginny had to teach her not to burn any more syrup. It was wasteful and tasted like tar, besides.

"We got any milk?" Owen Jr. asked, hopefully.

"Just about a cup's worth of sweetmilk in the well," Ginny said, to everyone's surprise. "Hazel sent it. Ain't enough for much of anything, but it's somethin'. You want to split it with Belle?" Owen Jr. nodded eagerly, and Ginny went out to fetch it.

O.T. could cry. He didn't take up enough time with the boy, with any of them. Hosey was right—the kids were neglected, dirty, hungry as hell—and O.T. couldn't do a damn thing about it. Owen Jr. would soon be a man, and he'd want nothing to do with his pitiful mess of a daddy. And Hazel, sending things she didn't have to spare; if Tom caught her giving away milk and apples, he'd rough her up.

"You got to be both of us now," Walt had told him. What the hell was O.T. supposed to do? Even if he quit drinkin'—hell, smokin' too—they would still be on the brink of starvation; he would still be a widower with no help around the farm, forced to use his children as pack mules, living on borrowed time. What difference did it make if he was drunk or not?

At least he got the liquor on trade—not from Hosey; he'd never, ever do business with Hosey—he had at least that much dignity left.

121

O.T. did the odd job for Melvin Brooks, or traded him for seeds or a little sorghum syrup, and even the odd bit of cornmeal or flour when he had extra, which was hardly ever. Melvin's wife had died the year before, and now he did nothing but run shine. Eventually the time would come when nobody had anything to trade—O.T. could see that well enough—and poor Melvin would be flush in liquor and starving to death.

O.T. spooned cornmeal into his mouth, wishing he had a piece of fatback or some turnip greens to cut the blandness, and listened to the kids as they prattled on. He couldn't wait for supper to end, for them all to go to bed, when he could grab the old familiar bottle from the wardrobe and let it sing him to sleep—just enough to ease the pain and soften the edges so he could close his eyes and get a few winks in. And he'd learned to manage the headaches that came after.

"Want me to get it?" Owen Jr. asked.

"Huh?"

"I said, 'Do you want me to get the letter, Deddy?'" Owen's scowl was back, his default expression nowadays.

"What letter?" O.T. asked, wiping his mouth with a napkin, pushing his bowl aside with only two bites gone. "Sorry, son, I was off with the crows. Thinkin' about work," he lied.

"You got a letter today. When you and Ginny was out plantin', the mail man come by. You want me to git it?"

"Oh. Yeah. I reckon," O.T. sighed. Likely a bill, he thought.

Owen Jr. pushed his own plate away and retreated into the hall. He came back holding a large white envelope with several stamps on it. He handed it to O.T. "Wonder if it's from Santy Clause," he said with a grin.

"Santy Clause don't send folks letters, you dummy," Belle said primly. "He just brings the presents. We send *him* the letters."

O.T. stared at the envelope. *Mr. Walter Lawrence* was written across the front in an unfamiliar, slanted script. Nobody had ever called his brother "Walter." There was no return address, but he could just make out the faded gray letters on the postmark: Baldwin County.

O.T. stared at the envelope for a few minutes, then got up from his chair, deciding to read it later, when he had a drink in him. For now, it was time to get the kids cleaned up and in bed.

"Y'all goin' to school tomorry?" he asked his kids.

All three nodded eagerly. O.T. smiled, wanting to be encouraging, even though he could really use Ginny's help at the house.

After the kids had been tucked into their beds for the night, O.T. changed into his nightshirt and sat on his bed, cradling the bottle of shine in one hand and the letter in the other. He took a swig, then lay back on the pillows on what used to be Betty Lou's side of the bed.

Ripping open the envelope, he pulled out a thin sheet of brown paper. The script was slanted and tight on the page, as though someone had written it very carefully, someone who didn't write often and was trying to remember how. He propped himself up on the pillows and took one more swig, letting it warm his gut as he began to read.

Dearest Walter,

I could scarce believe you remembered me, as it's been yars since we met. I was ever surprised to git your letter but right tuched at how sweet and kind you was to ast after my health and see bout me. It had been a coon's age sinse I had heared from a soul.

You may be wondrin why I took so long a time to writ to you, when I had your letter so many months, and the anser is that I have deep shame. You ast in the letter to know my story. We'll just say that life got me sick. I had a bad run of luck due to my Uncle and some unfortunate sircumstance. I fell ill after the death of my boy and culd not get rite agin. I have been here at the asylum for over ten year, and even though it is my shame I admit that it has holped me. But I do not want nobody to fret for me none or to think I am soft haided or ravin. I have made my pease. I thought to rite to my folks once too but I cain't never tell them my shame. And I don't want to see them anyhow. Druther they think I'm dead. I once considert throwin' myself off the old steel bridge behind our house, into the Toccoa River rather than them know my shame and I have had plenty more shame to add to it in the yars sinse then.

Please Walt, dont think ill of me or think me a loon of some kind and I will be happy to write to you agin. If you will send me another letter to say so.

Tis been such a long spell sinse I heared from another soul that I dont rankin this letter even makes a lick of sinse but my therpist wants me to write and the nurses says they will mail it for me so I am sending it along anyhow.

Thank you for yer time and I hope you and your fambly are doing gud. You ast if I would even remember you. Accorse I remember you and your kind heart, and your brother too. Sweeter boys never lived. And I want to say sorry for the way my Uncle yelled at you. I have deep shame over that, too. That your brother is marrit to the purdy blond gal from the car ride and has a bunch of young'uns and a big farm is not a surprise atall. Some folks got a clear path, and dont we jus' envy them, Walt?

I take your meanin' plain, Mr. Lawrence, and no, I ain't offended. Perhaps I'll hear from you agin should you take a notion.

Yours Ev'r
Savilia Marie Tryphena Hargrove Shelnutt

O.T. read it once then read it again. Sivvy—or Savilia Marie Tryphena Hargrove Shelnutt, which was way too long a name for the petite girl he remembered—had managed to write an entire page and not say much of anything. It was obvious from her name that she had married, and she'd had a child who'd died. Beyond that, he knew nothing.

O.T. supposed none of it really mattered now, seeing as Walt was dead and gone and would never know. But her letter had all but begged for a reply. O.T. sighed. She would expect to hear from Walt and might fall into despair if he didn't write. O.T. felt a pang in his stomach and thought sadly that Walt would have been right glad to hear from her. He never would have judged her. He never would have dreamed of it. Everything Sivvy had said about his sweetness, his tender heart, had been true.

But Walt had died and O.T. had not. O.T., who was drunk yet again this night, who was failing miserably at running the farm and raising the kids, and who was going to have to write this woman back—for Walt's sake, if nothing else—and he had no idea what on earth to say.

O.T. studied Sivvy's handwriting: its tiny cursive letters, and the way she signed her name. He wondered what it was like to live in Milledgeville Asylum. Where did she sit to write such a letter? Did she have her own room? Likely she shared space with women who were violent, who were dangerously crazy. Was she crazy, too? Did she want out? Or was she content where she was?

What had she done to get sent off to Milledgeville?

O.T. put the letter on the nightstand and raised the glass bottle to his trembling lips. It was time for bed.

≈

All was darkness, except for a tiny beam of moonlight that came through the square window. Sivvy tossed in her bed, grimacing at the sharp pains in her hips as she tossed and turned on the thin mattress. They were supposed to report these aches and pains, even the littlest ones, to the nurses, but Sivvy was staying clear of the Jones building. Just the sight of that doctor or the mere mention of his name sent her into shaking fits.

Sivvy could not sleep. Tomorrow was Saturday. She would be expected to bust tail in the kitchens, not only preparing extra food and punch for the Saturday dance, but prepping for breakfast the following morning. Milledgeville Asylum set a store by doing "nice" things for their patients—throwing dances, serving a big fry-up after chapel on Sunday—to keep them happy. Did it work? Sivvy thought not, but what did she know? She only knew she felt as wound up as a fiddle string. The fact that the late-October chill was turning into a more frigid November didn't help.

She had no right to be unhappy. She had a place to sleep, a roof over her head, three square meals a day, and good steady work, a therapist to talk to when her thoughts got out of control and a chapel for her spiritual needs. Sivvy had learned how to avoid trouble, and how to shut off her brain when trouble found her nonetheless. Considering how far she'd fallen, Sivvy supposed she ought not to want for much else. She'd made it through these past ten years resigned to her lot. After all that had happened, she didn't have any dreams left anyhow.

Losing her boy had been the final straw. Her only regret was that she had not died, too. Instead, her life had been saved, but that saving of a life had also robbed her of one—the asylum had seen to that.

A thump sounded from out in the hall, followed by a wail. Then, the sound of running footsteps and hushed whispers. Some poor soul would be given an injection, hauled back to her bed, and locked in tight. And the night would carry on, until the next incident.

Sivvy knew she would never get to sleep now. She rose from her bed and walked over to the dresser where she fished around under her uniform, retrieving a small piece of paper, folded and re-folded so many times it was soft as cloth. She had long since memorized the contents of the letter but still loved to cast her eyes over the loopy scrawl. The room was dark, but a pale thread of moonlight shone enough to read line by meticulous line:

Dearest Savilia,

I am Walter Lawrence. I met you fifteen years past, and I do not know if you will remember me. The only thing particularly memorable about me is that I'm a twin, and you met my brother and me at a revival in my town of Five Forks back in 1916. I live with him and his wife Betty Lou and their children in the very same town. I have remembered you all of these years, not just because of the unpleasant business where your Uncle thought I had tarnished your reputation.

I have thought of you many a time since then, and wondered how you are faring. By chance, I happened to hear that you were in Milledgeville, and have thought of nothing else since. I wonder if there is anything I might do to help you. If there is, would you please write to me and say? I will help in any way I can. I would like very much to know that you are well.

You may not know that I study on butterflies—my brother hates it. But I want to tell you, Sivvy, that butterflies have two lives. As a caterpillar, they have more limitations. They are ground-bound, wingless. When they go into the cocoon to shed their body and become something else, they welcome the transition. When they emerge a butterfly, they have all the same memories and feelings, but there are no limitations. Because then they can fly. I think people can be like butterflies that way. Leastways I like to hope that's true.

I have never been married. Sometimes it makes me sad and right lonely. I wonder if you, too, are sad? And if my sadness could somehow help with yours. If mayhap it's time for the both of us to shed the cocoon.

If you take my meaning, and I pray to the good Lord above you aren't offended, please respond to this letter straight away.

Yours Ever,

Walter Lawrence

Sivvy refolded the note, placed it back in the drawer, and returned to bed. Her room was icy, the windows cinched tightly shut, foggy condensation forming on the panes. A trickle of dew ran down, leaving a B-shaped rivulet on the wet glass. An old water stain covered one corner of the ceiling, and Sivvy stared at it, imagining it growing bigger and bigger, until it swallowed her and her bed whole.

CHAPTER TWELVE

"That'll be ten cent."

O.T. dug the change out of his coveralls and slapped it on the counter before he had a chance to change his mind. It was damn near the last of his money, but it couldn't be helped. He'd been in town since dinner time and had bought the children penny candy, oranges, and a blank book of white pages to write in, and now he was buying the newspaper to wrap it all up with. And his tobacco, of course. Hazel had made dolls for the girls and O.T. had whittled a few cars for Owen Jr. He hoped the meager gifts would bring them some happiness.

Christmas with Betty Lou had always been a big affair. She'd start weeks ahead of time with her baking—she always managed to trade for the sugar and fruit she needed for her cakes and cookies—and her decorating. She would sew new dresses for the girls and a suit for Owen Jr. Walt could usually be counted on to make the kids some elaborate board game or a spinning top or something fun to occupy the entire day.

Ginny, Belle, and Owen Jr. knew Christmas would be lean; kids all over Five Forks and the entire country, O.T. imagined, knew things were going to be lean this Christmas. Nobody had anything at all; they could barely afford to eat, much less buy presents. Many families in Five Forks were not bothering with Christmas at all. But O.T. had been determined to do *something*. The kids had been through hell. They'd lost their ma and their uncle, and had been near working themselves to death on a farm they didn't even own anymore. And if that weren't bad enough, their pa had turned himself into a drunk. O.T. had more guilt than he knew what to do with. He was going to give the kids a little bit of Christmas, even if it was sorry as hell, by God. After all, little Belle still believed in Santy Clause, least he hoped she did.

Evan Brown, Hosey's cousin, was behind the counter today— Melvin Brooks must be home sleeping off another drunk. He pushed the newspaper and tobacco toward O.T. "Got a big Christmas supper planned?" Evan asked pleasantly.

"Shoot. Naw," O.T. answered, tucking the newspaper under his arm. He already had the other bundle, his earlier business with Evan under his other arm. He and Hazel had scraped together a small meal for both their families, and while it was nothing fancy—just a little side meat, potatoes and greens, and a tiny cornmeal cake—it was a lot more than many families had. A lot more than what they themselves usually had. O.T. wasn't sure if he stayed quiet about his supper plans because he didn't want to boast, or because he was afraid somebody might relieve him of his food. Such things had happened. Everybody in Five Forks was good folks, but when people got hungry something came over a body. "You?"

Evan shook his head. "Naw. Have to git me a wife and a fambly first. And that ain't bound to happen with the whole country starvin' near to death."

"Ain't that the truth."

"Article I read in the *Statesman* says we got to stop lettin' our jobs go to the Negroes," Evan said, pushing his glasses—broken in the middle and taped back together—up on his nose. "They willin' to work for cheaper than we is, and they's snappin' up our jobs lef' and right."

"Yeah, I reckon so," O.T. replied. He wished he had enough coins to rub together to hire somebody to help him around the farm. "Cain't blame a man for takin' work where he can git it, though."

"Yeah, but we oughter be hirin' our own, first and foremost," Evan argued. "Takin' care of our white babies first."

"Reckon white and black folks got the same hunger pains," O.T. said quietly.

"Aw, hell. You turnin' soft, O.T.?" Evan teased. "Gonna start takin' up collections for the N double A-cap?"

"Ain't a soft spot anywhere on this body," O.T. responded, patting his stomach, which was rock hard and concave. "Ain't nobody in town got any soft spots left, I reckon."

"Ain't that the truth," Evan agreed. His expression suggested he knew he had lost the thread of the conversation in some way, but he was too dumb to bother with the when or how. "You jus' soundin' a lot like yer brother, rest his soul. He went in for all that ni—"

O.T. had neither the time nor the patience. He gave Evan a polite smile. "That'll do it, then?"

"Oh. Oh, yeah. You need a bag?"

"Naw."

"Well, I hope you and yer fambly have you a right nice Christmas."

"We gon' try," O.T. said, and tipped his hat. "And a good'un to you as well, Evan."

He took his newspaper and tobacco and exited the store. The air was cold and had a crispness to it; it was going to snow. The kids would go into fits over a white Christmas. He smiled, picturing them out in the snow, making a snowman and throwing snowballs at each other. For himself, O.T. dreaded the thought of snow, which would put him far behind in his work, and he barely had enough wood to heat the house as it was. The kids would have to huddle in his bed the next few nights, which meant he couldn't drink.

O.T. hadn't had money to put gas in the car in months, and it needed oil, too, so he'd walked into town to do his shopping. He set off at a brisk pace, hoping the snowfall would hold off until he made it the three miles home.

"Need a ride, fella?"

O.T. turned, scowling. Hosey sat behind the wheel of his pale green Studebaker, the window rolled down a crack. His dark hair was hidden under a woolen cap, and his eyes were tired but sparkling.

"Naw. Thanks," O.T. said stiffly, and resumed walking.

"Cold as a witch's tit out here," Hosey said, coaxing. That old familiar phrase used to make O.T. laugh, but now he was in no mood. "Sure you don't want a lift? I don't mind—hey, in the spirit of Christmas?"

"No." O.T. kept walking, and eventually he heard Hosey put the car into gear and drive off.

O.T. knew through the grapevine that Hosey was still running 'shine from here to the mountains and, from the looks of it, he was one of the few people who were actually making a decent living. He was still starving like the rest of them, of course, but just a little more slowly. As long as that Studebaker held out, he might just make it through the worst of it, O.T. thought to himself bitterly.

O.T. knew he was being a hypocritical bastard and he didn't care. He didn't buy his liquor from Hosey; he bought it from Melvin Brooks or Evan Brown, who was, of course, getting it from his cousin. A man could do just about any amount of justifying if it suited his purposes.

The snow started when O.T. was about fifteen yards from the driveway. His initial urge was to pull his coat over his head and book it to the house, but he found himself looking up instead. While gray snow clouds covered half the sky, the rest gave way to inky black with a dotting of stars. They twinkled benignly down, unaware of him, this irrelevant human being on some blue planet who was falling apart. The icy snowflakes fell on his face, freezing on his skin. O.T.'s relationship with the good Lord, never strong to begin with, had broken irrevocably in the past twelve months. Fervor and faith had been more a passion of Walt's. O.T. was not a praying man, was like to nod off in church, and had never put too much stock in some higher power saving him. He had little belief and no reverence. Was there really some benevolent God with white hair lookin' down on him and his? If there were, what kind of God could sit idly by and watch folks starve and die? O.T. wasn't so sure that he wanted anything to do with a Lord like that, anyway. And no amount of pretty snowflakes would make up for it.

I ain't got no time for the Good Lord, if he's even there, O.T. thought, staring up. *But maybe Betty Lou and Walt might be lookin' down on us. Tonight, at least, on Christmas Eve.*

O.T. resolved not to drink this night. He could scarcely recall the kids' first Christmas without their mother, and he felt he should be on good behavior for the second.

But as O.T. ascended the porch steps he felt the pangs of hunger, and knowing there wasn't enough food to fill all their bellies, he thought he might just have one warming nip to ease the hollowness, after the kids had all gone to bed. He was surprised to find that the kids had cut down a pine tree from the woods. Fortunately Ginny had done most of the work, because he didn't like to think of Owen Jr. with an ax. Ginny, Belle, and Owen had found a string of moth-eaten gold tinsel from the attic and strung it around the tree in a happy little spiral. They had fashioned a large star out of sticks and glue which perched crookedly at the top. All three children were beaming with pride as he came in and set his sacks at the door.

"Well now," he said with a smile. "I reckon y'all done Christmas up just right." And they all rushed into his arms.

Hazel arrived shortly after O.T., her arms weighed down with gifts. Tom followed, sullen and distracted—intent, O.T. supposed, on eating and raising hell. Under the guise of helping him (and Lord knew he needed the help, falling apart as he was), Hazel was avoiding home. O.T. suspected Tom would run off again before too long; he wished for Hazel's sake this time he'd stay gone. It was likely to happen sooner or later; some men had that yearning-to-be-gone look, and Tom was one of them.

"Funny lookin' star, ain't it?" Tom remarked, eyeing the tree with a laugh. "What'd y'all use, sticks?"

Owen Jr.'s face flushed red, and his chest puffed out. "We made it ourselves—"

"And it's just as purdy as a picture," Hazel finished with a bright smile as she kissed the children. Carrying her bags into the kitchen, she deposited them on the counter.

"Merry Christmas, sis," O.T. said, following her. "What can I help with?"

"Nothin'. It ain't much, and that's the truth," Hazel answered, unpacking dishes. "I've got the potatoes done already and the greens. The cake is done too, but I need a little of your syrup to go a'top. There ain't no cookies like Betty Lou used to make. Sorry. I couldn't get a lick of sugar. But if you got a little side meat I can fry that up."

"The meat's on the counter," O.T. said, gesturing. "I traded the last of the pecans for it. And don't worry about no cookies. I was able to get a few cents together and bought the young'uns some penny candy. They ain't gon' be hurtin' for sugar."

"Oh, that's wonderful, O.T.!" Hazel exclaimed. To think, O.T thought, with a pang of guilt, them all getting fit to be tied over penny candy and a sliver of side meat. And they had a damn sight more than most people.

Tom came into the kitchen. "So, penny candy for the kids, what you got for us grown-ups?"

O.T. forced a smile, for Hazel's sake. "Plug of tobaccy do you, Tom?"

Tom smirked, watching Hazel putting out the dishes, and twirled at his black mustache. "Reckon I'd rather have a drink of the good stuff, if you got it." He knew as well as everyone else that O.T. had it. As young'uns, O.T. and Walt had hated Tom for being a boozer. Now that O.T. had taken to drink, Tom couldn't stop smiling about it. *Smug bastard.*

O.T. intended to drink the little hooch he had left himself later that night, his own little Christmas present to himself, as it were. The bottle was only a quarter full, anyhow—about which O.T. was both relieved and dismayed. "I ain't got none, Tom. Not enough for all three of us, nohow. Not even enough for a toast."

"You a lie." Tom was smiling, but his eyes flashed. Tom did this every time, just about—beggin' for 'shine. O.T. gave it to him sometimes, just to keep the peace, but he knew Hazel hated it when Tom drank.

"Tell you what, though. There's just a nip or two of persimmon wine in the well house—Betty Lou made it two year ago or so, I reckon. She used to keep it to trade for thangs from time to time. It's mighty sweet, but it's good and tart, too. Ain't gon' get a man drunk, but it's a good toastin' drink. I'll pour you and Hazel both a nip of that."

Hazel shook her head. "Naw, thanks, brother."

"I ain't wantin' no persimmon wine," Tom sneered. "I ain't gon' sit here and drink with my pinky up like a got-dang woman."

"Language, Tom," Hazel said from the stove, sounding like Walt. "O.T., the side meat is about done. Would you get the young'uns to the table?"

O.T. complied, glad to be away from Tom's sneering face for a spell. He wished to the good Lord that Hazel had never married that joker. She'd spent half her life with him already, more tired and weary every damn day.

O.T. washed Belle and Owen Jr.'s dirt-streaked faces with a damp dish cloth. "Which one of y'all wants to say grace?" O.T. asked cheerfully, taking his own place at the head of the table.

"Uncle Walt always says grace." Belle stuck her lip out.

"That's true, he did," Ginny said gently. "But he's not here to say it no more."

"I don't want to say it," Owen Jr. said, his face flushed and red.

"Me neither," Belle muttered.

O.T. knew Ginny didn't want to. She'd never said so, but she didn't seem to be on the good Lord's side these days, either. She skipped church every chance she got. He reckoned she had lost her faith when she lost her mother. He knew just how she felt. "Aunt Hazel can say it," O.T. said brightly as his sister appeared in the dining room, plates in her hands. "She's always been real good at sayin' grace."

"But it's yer house, you're the head of the—"

"I want you to say it, sister," O.T. said firmly.

"Awright, then," Hazel said as she took her place at the table. They all bowed their heads dutifully. "Dear Lord, on this night before Christmas, yer beloved birthday, we say thanks for this food and thanks for our fambly. We ain't got much, but we know they's folks out in this very community that got even less than we do. Our every blessing is a reminder of yer good will and generosity. We thank you for yer bounty and in Jesus' name, amen."

"Amen," they all parroted.

O.T. looked up. Tom was already digging into the side meat, taking half the portion, and leaving scarcely enough for the children. O.T. was quick to grab the serving fork and dish the remainder onto the children's plates, giving the largest amount to Ginny. She shook her head at him, and scooped most of what he'd given her onto Belle and Owen Jr.'s plates.

O.T. took a small portion of potatoes and a smaller portion of greens for himself, before noticing the plate of biscuits. "Now where did these come from?"

"We made 'em!" Belle said proudly. "Me and Ginny did!"

"Where did you get flour?" Hazel asked. "I haven't had any in forty forevers."

"Earned it," Ginny said with a small smile. "Misrus Maybelle let me work in trade. I watched her grandson three times last week for a cup and a half of flour. I been saving it in my room so me and Belle could make some biscuits." She frowned. "Ain't no butter though."

"It'll do us just fine," Hazel said, getting up from the table. "I'll get some sorghum syrup."

O.T. doled out the biscuits, dividing his own in half. Ginny, who knew what he intended—to give half his portion to the children—shook her head. "No, Deddy. You keep that for yerself. You need to eat. You as skinny as a string bean. Hard as you work, you need the nourishment." With a pang, O.T. was reminded of the way Betty Lou used to scold Walt.

"He gets his nourishment liquid-like," Tom said with a laugh.

O.T. shot him a look of warning. *Let him make another remark like that in front of the kids. We'll take it outside and I'll wish the sumbitch a merry Christmas, awright.* Tom shut up and tore into his side meat.

Fortunately, the rest of the night Tom saw fit to keep his gob shut. They got through supper, and even though O.T.'s stomach still rumbled, he was happy that he'd been able to give the kids a decent Christmas Eve dinner.

After supper, and after the kids had drifted off to bed, Hazel kissed him on the cheek. "I'll be back in the mornin' to see 'em get their presents," she said. "And you behave yerself tonight, y'hear?"

"No shenanigans, big sister. I promise," O.T. smiled. "I'll send my lady date away."

Hazel rolled her eyes as she bundled her coat about herself. Then she set off into the night, following behind her husband, who was not even gentleman enough to wait and offer his wife his arm. In the quiet house, O.T. wrapped the presents and put them under the tree, cleaned up the kitchen, and prepared the fire for the next morning. He was just deciding to go to bed early, when he'd thought again of Tom's snide comment over dinner. Tense and irritable, he found himself taking a swig out of his bottle of 'shine, almost to spite Tom.

O.T. woke up earlier than usual the next morning with a pounding head and an uneasy stomach. Hiding the empty bottle under his pillow, O.T. yawned, smelling the liquor on his breath. He craned an ear toward the door, listening for the kids. Pulling on his housecoat, which was covered in holes and threadbare in the arms (Betty Lou had made it and there would be no more of them), he hunted for his slippers, which were equally worn out. He made his way to the door, wishing to hell there was coffee to be had.

"Merry Christmas!" O.T. called out in a jolly tone. He heard rustling on the other side of the kids' bedroom door. "Come on out, you lugheads," he said with a laugh, padding to the parlor to start up a fire. The door opened and the kids all came tumbling out and into the parlor, on each others' heels. O.T. was hunting for the matches, which he had apparently misplaced the night before, and turned to the kids, who stood watching him solemnly.

"What is it, young'uns?" he asked. "Ain't you interested in yer presents?"

Ginny spoke up. "It's just…without Ma here…it's sad."

"It is, yeah," O.T. agreed, sitting up and looking at them plain. "I ain't gonna pretend it ain't sad. I'm sad, too. But yer ma wouldn't want this to be a sad time. Just the thought of you all moping and not enjoying yer Christmas would have made her cry. You know it's true. So go on and lookit yer presents and paste on a smile for yer ma's sake, awright?" Then, after a pause, he added, "And for yer Uncle Walt's, too."

O.T. watched as the kids unwrapped their candies; the girls, their dolls; and Owen Jr., his whittled car. Hazel had knitted socks for each of them, and they got a handkerchief that O.T. had found among Betty Lou's things. Clearly, she'd meant to give them to the kids; each was embroidered with their initials. O.T. didn't know what she'd been saving them for, but he figured now was as good a time as any to dole them out.

"It's all just perfect, Deddy," Ginny said, clutching her handkerchief to her cheek. "Thank you." She was a bit too old for dolls, but she was a kind, sweet girl and would never say so.

"I got a stick of Beech-Nut gum," Owen Jr. said proudly, unwrapping the stick and popping it in his mouth.

"That was supposed to wait till after breakfast," O.T. said with a laugh. "And what'd you git, Miss Belle?"

"I got a dolly, and some candy. And this." She held out her own handkerchief. "It's a blanket for my dolly."

"It's a hankie," Owen Jr. corrected her.

"It ain't. It's a blanket for Lilly Mae. Ma made it. See, she used her pink thread, the one she always used for the roses on my dress. And now my doll has one on her blanket." Belle beamed proudly. Owen opened his mouth to argue, but was stopped by a look from O.T.

"Good morning! Merry Christmas!" Hazel called from the porch, shaking snow out of her hair. "I'd give y'all kisses but my lips are like icicles. It's snowin' up a storm out there! Sorry I'm late."

"Down to Tom, I reckon," O.T. began bitterly, but she cut him off.

"Owen," she said, a little desperately. "Let's don't."

"Deddy! Can we make a snowman?" Owen Jr. jumped up and ran to the window. O.T. nodded his assent.

"Did they like their presents?" Hazel asked.

"They did, I reckon," O.T. answered her, poking at the fire.

"And how are my two favorite nieces?" Hazel asked, turning to the girls. "Have you had breakfast yet?"

"No," Belle answered. "What we got, anyway? Cornmeal mush?"

"Yeah," O.T. answered. "And you each got an orange from Santy Clause. You can have that with yer porridge."

"I brought some apple jam," Hazel said. "I had a can put up way in the back that I found the other day. And a pear—last one off the tree. I don't know how it ain't rotten, but it looks ripe to me. We'll all have a piece."

"I ain't got no coffee," O.T. apologized. "I might could brew up some chicory coffee, there's a tad left in the can, but it's old and don't taste like much."

"Better than nothin'," Hazel said with a cheery smile. "We'll stir in some syrup and call it good."

❧

O.T. sat out on the porch, smoking his pipe and watching the kids build a snowman. Hazel's gift to him had been some pipe tobacco, and he had given her a housecoat that he'd found folded up among Betty Lou's things. Betty Lou had evidently been thinking ahead to the holidays when she'd died. He had also found a new man's shirt that was just his size. He planned to wear it to the next church service, even though every time he looked at it his head hurt.

"Ginny talked to you yet?" Hazel asked, stepping out on the porch. She was wrapped up in one of O.T.'s old coats.

"'Bout what?"

"She's nervous to talk to you about it," his sister replied, taking the pipe from his hand and puffing on it. "I wish to everything I had some snuff. She's had an offer."

"An offer?" O.T. was momentarily confused. "What kind of offer?" He shook his head. "You don't mean…who?"

"What do ya mean, who?" Hazel said with a sly smile. "Who else?"

"Grady Bridges, I reckon," O.T. said uneasily. "He's been sniffing around her since she wasn't more than eleven years old. I ain't liked it one bit."

"I know you ain't," Hazel said, shivering. "But he's been sweet on her for years, like you said, and he's what, seventeen? No older than you was when you married Betty Lou. You had to of knowed it was comin'."

"What kind of young man don't even come ast for her father's blessin'?"

"I reckon he aims to," Hazel replied, watching the kids hoist a huge snow head on the snowman's body. It was too heavy and toppled off. Ginny scrambled to put it back together, hoisting it up, with a shout of laughter. She's still a kid, for God's sake, O.T. thought. "He's scared to death of you. He ast Ginny first, and then he was going to come to you, I reckon, after he knew it was clear."

"Coward," O.T. spat. "That ain't the way it's done." He puffed on the pipe again. He had, of course, gone to Betty Lou's father first. He had known what was expected of him, and even if he'd been terrified, he'd done it proper. "So I reckon she said yes, then."

"I think she put him off for now, till she talks to you," Hazel replied. "But she's been sittin' on it for durn near a week already. I think she do aim to say yes to him, though. She ain't a fool."

"What you mean, she ain't a fool?" O.T. barked. "Don't let me hear tell you agree with this! She don't love that boy. She don't talk about him. She don't sneak away to clap eyes on him or write his name on her school books." He wasn't so old that he couldn't recall how it had been with Betty Lou. The way he'd thought about her constantly, had snuck glances at her, and had blushed any time he heard her name. O.T. had never seen Ginny so much as smile at Grady Bridges. "I ain't seen her give him no second glance. So why would she say yes to him?"

"Why wouldn't she?" Hazel said. "He comes from a decent family, they got a farm…I reckon she's thinking one less mouth to feed for you. And that he might be able to help you some in the fiel'." She looked at him with a shy smile. "Same thing I did."

"She ain't but fourteen years old. Just barely."

"That's how old I was, brother."

"Yeah, I know it," O.T. sighed. "And don't you wish someone had talked sense to you when you had the chance?"

"No," Hazel answered. "Wouldn't of made a bit of difference. Folks do what they got to."

"She don't love him."

"And what's that got to do with a hungry stomach?" Hazel asked pointedly. "Besides, how would you know? You don't pay attention to nothin' but that bottle. You don't see everything. Maybe she does love him."

"Well, I guess I'm just sorry as hell," O.T. spat, angry. "Just like yer fool husband. 'Cept I never cheated on *my* wife."

Hazel flushed hotly and looked away. O.T. was instantly sorry he'd said it, but the thought of Ginny marrying some fool-headed boy that she didn't even like made him furious. And he knew, even if Grady didn't come ask for his blessing, that Ginny would say yes to him and do it anyway, if she thought it would help their family. She was headstrong and, since she'd lost her ma and uncle, aimless and lost. O.T. was afraid of the decisions she might make in such a state.

"I'm sorry, sis," O.T. sighed. "That wasn't fair. But I cain't let her do it. If she loved the boy, that would be one thing. But she don't."

"Maybe she don't," Hazel said. "But he's a nice boy. Marriages can work—"

"No, they can't," O.T. said simply. "Not where it counts." He had been on fire for Betty Lou; just the sight of her cool blonde hair or her pursed lips, or the powder and roses smell of her had been enough to drive him into a frenzy; the flirty, silly way she'd cut her icy blue eyes at him; the way her touch had felt on his skin. He had loved her for so long, and she him. Their marriage had had its trials and tribulations like anyone's, but they'd always been on fire for each other when it mattered. He felt an ache in his gut.

"I'll talk to Ginny," he said. "Later on. I'll talk sense to her."

"Do as you want," Hazel replied. "But she's yer daughter, after all. You ain't gonna change her mind if'n it's already made up."

Sivvy was in isolation. The window had been bolted, and the serving chute in the door opened only once a day. She was allowed to use the bathroom once—provided she kept on good behavior—and she hoped to do so soon. While Sivvy was horrified at the prospect of relieving herself on the floor, it wouldn't be long now, from the way her guts were clenching.

Sivvy's unraveling had started two days before. It had been so long since she'd had a spell that she had missed the signs. She had been embroidering Christmas napkins with four other patients in the common room, humming a song to herself. She did not know who the Christmas napkins were for—the patients were never given cloth napkins, not even at the dances. Maybe they were gifts for the staff, she thought, still humming idly.

"You sing just like a pretty little bird," one of the women said, craning toward her. This woman, Faye, had been described by staff as "hysterical," a term used to diagnose women who had nothing wrong with them, as far as Sivvy could figure. "In all these years I ain't ever heard you sing before."

"I don't feel like it much," Sivvy answered. "The mood just struck me. Bein' Christmas and all."

"I hope it keeps up," Faye said with a kind smile as she added another neatly embroidered napkin to her own pile. "We could do with a bit of music around this haunted place. What I wouldn't give for a bit of fiddle music."

Sivvy didn't reply, feeling a rising anxiety; her blood felt sludgy in her veins, sick-feeling; the nerves beneath her skin rapid-firing, her breath a little gaspy in her throat. Despite the churning, Sivvy tried to maintain a calm decorum, gave Faye a small smile, and continued stabbing the needle into the cloth. It always happened this way. She could feel her nerves rise, the same as an old-timer might feel a thunderstorm looming on the horizon. They'd feel the rain in their bones before the sky even turned one shade, and could smell the coming thunder, and feel the lightning in their old, ticking hearts.

The embroidering staved off the trembling of her hands, for a time. If she could only keep the nerves at bay until she got to her room, the nurses would be none the wiser; she could avoid the extra dose of medication, the straps, Dr. Lowell.

The parlor door opened and one of the maids came in, holding a large stack of cloth. "Oh, Sivvy, Ms. May in the kitchen said she needs to see you, when you got you a spare minute."

"Thank you, marm," Sivvy said, taking a deep breath. "Is something the matter?"

The maid shrugged. "How should I know? She ain't discussed nothin' with me. Just said to pass along the message."

"Yes'm," Sivvy answered. Her right hand jerked wildly, and she stabbed her needle into the cloth at an angle, missing the flower and stabbing herself in her index finger. She cried out and Faye and the other women looked up in surprise.

Often, Sivvy could alert someone before the fit fully came upon her, before the screaming began. If she was *really* lucky, the nurses could get her to her room and calm her down before she ever opened her mouth. But other times....

Sivvy was screaming before her ears had a chance to catch up; she thought she was still humming, and it was only when she saw Faye cover her own ears and read her lips—"Oh no, oh no, she's doing it *again*!"—did she realize the fit had started.

So Sivvy was locked in her room, and the patients were downstairs enjoying sweet oranges, rolls, and fried eggs for their Christmas breakfasts, awaiting the attentions of Dr. Lowell who, administering his own brand of medicine, would be sure to wish her a *very* merry Christmas indeed.

At least she didn't have to wear the strong dress. They'd intended to put her in it, but some other poor nut had gotten it first. Thank God for small favors, for the meager Christmas present. She'd take whatever she could get.

❧

With Christmas over, it was back to the business of trying not to starve. The ground was coated with a thick blanket of crusty white snow, glinting like hardened sugar in the sun. O.T. stood on the front porch, surveying his—*their*—land. O.T. still couldn't believe that his house now belonged to the bank; it was a nightmare he couldn't wake up from.

There was little fieldwork that could be done in weather like this. For now, at least, O.T. could drum up some firewood. He worked quickly, his ax cutting through the logs with a loud *thwack* that reverberated through the barn, puffs of smoke filling the air as he exhaled. Gathering up the wood, he carried it inside, his boots leaving icy, muddy smears on the hall rug.

The kids were still in bed, as was Hazel. His sister had moved in when Tom had taken off—this time, apparently, for good. The rumor was that he had taken up with a widow who had come into some life insurance. A day or two after Christmas, he'd come home, packed up a few things, and told Hazel the marriage was over. Tom was too lazy and cheap to divorce her, so O.T. supposed they'd just carry on married, but Hazel was finally free. At least until Tom's latest la-di-da was over, but O.T. sure hoped that would be a good long while, for Hazel's sake.

O.T. and the children had been relieved to see the back of Tom, but Hazel had taken to her bed, crying over that lout. O.T. had pointed out that she was better off with him gone, after he'd beaten her and run around on her, but she'd just covered her face with a pillow and said, "You don't get nothin', O.T."

He didn't get it, that was sure; didn't get women at all.

O.T. noticed, as he deposited wood by the fireplace, that his sister was still in bed, which was a blessing—the woman never got enough sleep. Trudging back outside to get the next load, O.T. descended the porch steps as a car turned slowly into the driveway. The tires crunched across the snow, leaving muddy red tracks in their wake; two long, red lines in a sea of white. As the car rolled to a stop, he realized it was Rudesil Hardigree, the manager at Madison County Bank. The little man, who was no more than five foot six and as big around as he was tall, stepped out of his little Ford roadster, wrapped in two scarves and a heavy woolen hat. He threw up a hand in greeting, stepping gingerly over the thick snow in his shiny black shoes.

"Howdy-do, Mr. Lawrence," he said when he reached O.T. His black shoes sank into the snow, wetting the hem of his pants.

"Mornin', Mr. Hardigree," O.T. said, his mouth clamped in a thin smile. "Come on inside, git yerself outta the cold."

"Naw, naw, Mr. Lawrence, I cain't stay. Got more than one stop this morn," Rudesil objected, with a smile that was polite but all business. He had a packet of paperwork in his hands.

O.T. knew what was coming, but his ma had raised him to be polite. "Well, at least step up on the porch, get yer nice shoes out of the snow," he offered, and the little man agreed. O.T. followed him up the steps, dread sinking deeper in his shoulders with every step.

"I ain't gonna beat around the bush, Mr. Lawrence, and I hate to be the bearer of bad news just aft' Christmas," Rudesil said. He did look sorry, O.T. thought grimly, to his credit. "Your land—and several other homesteads in this part of town—are gonna be rented out to new tenants. As bank manager, it falls on me to go around and tell you all."

"They gon' rent out my house?" O.T. mused. "Why? Ain't nobody can work this land good as I can. It is *mine*, after all. Or was."

"I shore do know that, Mr. Lawrence. But, see, the bank gotta look aft' it's bottom line. And they got folks lined up that'll pay rent *and* work the land, for cheaper'n you can," Rudesil said, his voice lowering to a whisper, even though they were alone on the porch. "It's the name of the game, son. I don't like it no more than you do, but I'm just the bank manager. I got to do the dirty work."

"So what's it mean, then?"

"It means you're out, Mr. Lawrence. You all got to shift, move out."

"I know that. I mean, when. When do we gotta be out?"

"End of next month," Rudesil said. O.T. flinched. "Now, don't get upset, son. Compared to some, bank's bein' right generous in givin' you a whole month to vacate. It bein' the holidays and all, they insisted on givin' you all some time. Most folks get a week."

"Excuse me if I don't feel all that grateful," O.T. responded bitterly.

"I won't take it personal," Rudesil replied, handing O.T. the stack of papers. "That's the official paperwork, there. I'm right sorry to have to do it to ya, I know your family's been in hardship lately. But it's my job."

O.T. said nothing, just chewed the inside of his mouth thoughtfully. He would hold his tongue.

"Well, Happy New Year to you and yourn, Mr. Lawrence."

"Same."

Mr. Hardigree didn't linger. He had other people to evict, no time for empty pleasantries, and probably no heart for it, either. He shook O.T.'s shaking hand and was gone, back down into the snow, stumbling through the drifts back to his car, off to the next piece of business. O.T. didn't bother reading through the papers. He used them to light the fire instead.

O.T. sat at the little side table in his bedroom, staring at a blank white card, the letter from Sivvy in his lap. He had picked the pen up a dozen times and put it back down. He had no idea what to write to the girl. He needed a drink.

He had a month—just thirty days—to pack up his entire life, his kids, and his farm and get out. The past fourteen years' worth of memories, of *life,* were now cut loose from this place, adrift. It seemed a cruel joke, and he might even have laughed at the absurdity were he not so sick with fear. O.T. felt that he was well and truly Job now, tested and tested and ready to break. His beautiful house, the house he'd worked for, paid for—where his kids had been born, where his wife and brother were buried—yanked out from under his feet. It was too cruel to bear.

He and the children would have to move in with Hazel; five of them crowded into a two bedroom shack with peeling shingles and not a penny between them. At least Tom's trifling hide was gone, but would he stay gone? It was Tom's house, after all. O.T. wasn't sure if he could lower himself to such an indignity. But what other choice did he have? He had to think of the kids. A month. That was all he had to begin his life again. He didn't know if he had the strength.

Count yer blessings, you ungrateful fool, he told himself, chewing on the pen. *Quit feelin' sorry for yerself. There are worse things than living with Hazel. She's already raising yer kids any dang way. What would Walt say? He'd tell ya to think of poor Sivvy, wasting away in the asylum, where she'll likely spend the rest of her life.*

O.T. couldn't imagine life inside the asylum, though he'd tried several times, especially lately, sitting up by the cold, fogged-up windows nursing his bottle.

He'd seen a portrait of Milledgeville Asylum once—a large, looming brick building, stately but somehow haunted, with huge pillars, narrow brick steps stacked like teeth, and dozens of windows like spider eyes. He could imagine the rooms—cells, more like—with barred windows and slots in the doors, narrow beds and no curtains or carpets. He'd heard that the asylum had its own hospital, kitchens, and even a morgue. No need for folks to go in, or ever come out. He could conjure up a picture of the place well enough, but what was it like to truly be there?

Milledgeville Asylum was one of the few places in middle Georgia that had been spared by Sherman on his march to the sea. What about that terrifying monstrosity had the rough-necked William T. Sherman found worth saving, O.T. wondered. He chewed the pen absently before it suddenly dawned on him what Sivvy had meant when she'd written, *I take your meaning, and I ain't offended.* It was as though Walt had whispered in his ear. It was a fool-brained idea that would solve none of his current problems, yet he knew it must be done before he could pack up and move on from this place. For Walt.

O.T. went in search of his sister and found her plaiting Belle's hair in front of the fireplace, a damp log sputtering out orange sparks.

"Shouldn't put a wet log on a fire," he said absently.

"That's all that was out there," Hazel answered. She had braided Belle's hair into two neat pigtails that stuck out stiffly on either side of her head.

"Hazel," O.T. began. "If I were to go away for a spell…just for a couple weeks, probably…could the kids stay with you?"

She looked alarmed. "Where on earth you goin', O.T.?"

"I need to make a trip," O.T. replied. "Business, of a sort. But it requires goin' a few places. If I leave you by with a little money can you make do?"

"Can barely make do as it is," she said with a small sigh. "I guess it don't make no nevermind if you're here or not." O.T. shouldered aside this lackluster endorsement—he didn't have the right to be hurt by it.

"The kids will be here to help you," O.T. said. "I won't be gone too long. You don't reckon Tom'll come pull the house out from under you?"

"Like to see him try," Hazel said with a dry laugh. "After all the fool put me through, this time I'm like to blow his head off with the shotgun. Though Ginny'll probably make off with Grady affore you get back, that boy is in a screamin' hurry—"

"Ginny ain't goin' off with him," O.T. said. "She's goin' off with me. I need somebody to help me on the road, and it'll give her some time to think what she wants to do. If she's still aimin' to marry Grady Bridges when we get back, then I won't stand in the way."

"Well," Hazel said. "I guess you got it all figgered out then."

"First time for everything," he replied with a grin.

Hazel cracked a smile at that. O.T. reached out and tousled her golden blonde hair, feeling a sudden tenderness toward his big sister. "You'll be awright here on yer own?"

"Have been this long, ain't I?" Hazel shrugged and then looked up with sudden alarm. "So long as you *are* coming back! You ain't gon' run off like Tom and never—?"

"No, I ain't," O.T. assured her. "Yer the only fambly I got left. I might be a no-good drunk with nothin' to my name, but I ain't gon' run off on my family. I just have to take care of this business, is all."

"Awright, then," she said. "When you leavin'?"

"I was thinkin' the day after tomorry. I got to get packed."

"You'll need gas in the car. It ain't been turned over in months, and you'd better get the oil changed. Takin' you a little vacation," Hazel said with another hollow laugh. "Ain't you just Mr. Jim Dandy!"

"One of these days I'm gon' send you on a vacation of yer own," O.T. promised. "Just as soon as I can rub two nickels together. Might send you on a cruise to Hawaii or put you on one of them aeroplanes like Mr. Lindbergh."

"I ain't seen nothin' to beat it," Hazel said with petulant look. "The way you lie and carry on."

CHAPTER THIRTEEN

"Got it all in there?" O.T. hoisted the last suitcase into the back of the car and turned to Ginny.

"I ain't got much," she said with a shrug. "Not much that I need to bring, anyway."

"Well, awright then," O.T. said. "Let's say goodbye to the young'uns and hit the road."

Belle and Owen Jr. stood with Hazel, both upset that they couldn't go along. O.T. had told them that they needed to stay behind to help take care of Aunt Hazel and attend school.

"But Ginny ain't goin' to school," Owen Jr. argued. "And lots of my friends stopped going to school anyway to help their deddies tend the farm."

"We ain't goin' ta farm no more, lil' man," O.T. said, patting his head. "Or won't soon enough. And anyway, school's important, and yer good at it. Don't stop now. Mayhap it's yer ticket out of here."

Both of them wore their brave little faces and weren't crying, but O.T. could see the dejected expressions they tried to hide. "We ain't gon' be gone forever," O.T. assured them. "And we're gon' bring presents. I promise. I'm gon' find you both somethin' from the mountains that you'll go ape over, just you wait and see."

"Promise, Deddy?" Belle asked.

"I promise. I told you I promise."

"And I will too," Ginny said. "We'll both bring presents home. But only if yer real good for Aunt Hazel, and go to school, and wash up when she says to. Do you swear?"

"We swear," they both said in unison.

It took O.T. a few miles to get used to driving the car again. The day was cold, and the thin hat O.T. wore did little to curb the pain in his ears. He looked over to make sure Ginny had her scarf tied tight around her own ears. "Happy to be gon' on a trip?" he asked her with a smile.

"I reckon so," she answered, staring out the window. "I ain't never been to the mountains, have I?"

"Once't," he said, his hands resting lightly on the wheel as they passed Five Forks city limits. "You wasn't but a baby, though. Me and yer ma went up to Tallulah Gorge for the day. She wanted to see the falls. That was a long time ago. 1920, I reckon. You was still in clouts."

"Did Mama like it?" Ginny asked. "Tallulah Gorge and the falls?"

"Lord, she sure did," O.T. replied with a grin. "We went in the fall; best time to go. Both yer ma and me was crazy for the autumn colors, the way the trees turn gold and red and yellow. We spent dang near the whole day up there just lookin' at the leaves on the trees and smellin' the air. In the fall, folks start up their fires, start warmin' up the house again, and you can smell that sweet smoke fer miles. Puts you in a right holiday mood."

Ginny nodded, but he knew she wouldn't quite understand. The holidays didn't have quite the same meaning as they once did, not since times had turned hard. People still lit their fires, but there wasn't much to go around by way of comfort.

"We picked the wrong time to go on a road trip, to tell the truth," O.T. continued with forced brightness. "Snow still meltin' on the ground, and it's cold and gray out there. But the mountains is always purdy, no matter the time of year. You'll see."

"Do they know we're comin'?" Ginny asked.

"Naw, ain't got a clue," O.T. answered. He had considered sending a letter ahead of him, but he hadn't wanted to wait that long, and he wasn't sure of where to send it anyhow. He'd only mapped out his route the day before. Not only did Sivvy's family not know he was coming, but they didn't know he even existed. "But they'll be glad to see us all the same. Southern folks is always welcome to comp'ny."

O.T. and Ginny passed through Ila, a tiny hole-in-the-wall town with a little four-way stop, a few brick buildings, and not much else. The truck stalled out at the intersection, and O.T. cussed. Across from the stop sign was a little ramshackle junk store, piled high with odds and ends—clothing, busted furniture, tin cans, pictures, farm equipment, toys, and more. A wooden bin with the words PRODUCE—VEG & FRUITS burned in scrawling script stood empty. A little old woman or man—so small and shrunken that O.T. couldn't determine the gender—sat out in a rocking chair in front of the pile, rocking back and forth and spitting tobacco. She, or he, laughed at O.T. as he tried to get the truck started.

"Deddy, let's stop," Ginny pleaded. "I want to see what kind of junk they've got."

"Not today," O.T. said irritably. "We ain't got time. We need to book on up to the mountains if we want to get there affore dark." Finally the truck roared to life, emitting a fog of dark smoke from the exhaust. O.T. moseyed on through the stop sign, ignoring the cackling laughter from the oldie as they passed.

"Didja know that Ila means 'land of the dead'?" O.T. told her. "Funny, ain't it?"

"Not that much," Ginny answered. "That's right creepy. It does look dead out here. Nothin' around but that old junk store and a single stoplight out here on its lonesome. I bet at night this place is slap full of haints and boogers."

O.T. chuckled. "Mayhap so. But by then we'll be outta here. We'll keep on down Highway 98, and then up 441 all the way till we hit the mountains. Just gets prettier and prettier the whole way. You'll see the slopes from right far off and just watch 'em get closer and closer." O.T. hoped the snow would hold off, for he wanted Ginny to be able to see the view.

"This is a vacation for us," he said, glancing over at Ginny with a smile.

"Too bad Aunt Hazel and brother and sister couldn't come with us, though," Ginny replied.

"I know it, Gin. But the kids need to stay on in school as long as they can. And I couldn't afford to take us all, no way. I only brought you along because—"

"Because you wanted to get me away from Grady."

"Now—" he protested.

"Don't try to weasel yer way out of the truth, Deddy," Ginny said primly.

"Genevieve Lawrence, I'll tell you just like I tol' yer Aunt Hazel. You are far too young to be makin' a decision like that, and—"

"Deddy, it's okay," she interrupted him with a small smile. "I understand. And anyway—She dropped her voice conspiratorially, as if someone might be listening—"I was right glad. I mean…" She blushed. "Grady is a real nice boy, truly he is. Even if you don't like him, I do. But I don't want to marry him. Truth is, I don't want to marry anybody. At least, not yet."

"I'm right glad to hear you say it, gal," O.T. said sincerely. "Lots of gals get married when they're yer age, but I don't see no reason that you gotta hurry."

"The truth is," Ginny said, cutting her eyes to the side, regarding him, "I kinda had a plan affore Mama died, but now that she's gone I just don't know anymore."

"What was yer plan?" O.T. asked, curious.

"You won't approve."

"Let's hear."

"I want to be a teacher," Ginny said, her voice small and shy. "*Been* wantin' to for the longest. Ain't never tol' nobody but Mama. I swore her to secrecy. She said I could do it. Said lots of folks do it. Said I could even go to college if I wanted. She was gon' save up, do extry jobs to help me pay fer it." She bit her lip and looked down. "But I was being right foolish, I reckon. I don't know if Mama even meant to really help me or if she was just bein' nice. But it meant a lot to me all the same."

"I see." O.T. had a huge rock in his throat, it felt like. He had no doubt that Betty Lou had pledged her promise sincerely, but now it would be awfully hard to keep. "I'm right proud of that dream, Ginny. I reckon you should hold on to it. Yer young yet. Who knows what might happen?"

"But college is expensive," Ginny said. "And most gals don't go. Heck, most boys can't ever go, come to that."

"That's true," O.T. agreed. "College is like a fairy tale for folks like us. But that don't mean you can't be a teacher. Lots of teachers don't go to college. You don't have to have a degree—"

"But I *want* one," Ginny said fiercely. "I want one, or not at all. Don't you see? It's all or nothin'. I want to do it right."

O.T. said nothing, but was smiling proudly as he drove on.

After a time O.T. turned right onto highway 441, toward Banks County. The air had turned colder, and his ears ached.

Ginny, however, stared out the window with a big smile on her face, watching the side of the road, as if she'd never seen the outdoors before. It did his heart good to see her so.

Ginny asked, "Deddy, what do you think Mama would think of this? Us going to the mountains?"

"She'd say I was a dang fool and clap me over the head with the first thing she could get her hands on," O.T. said with a grin.

Ginny nodded and burst into laughter. "Just what I was thinkin'."

They passed into Banks County and as the road started to gain in altitude, the air got thinner and their ears popped. The treeline grew thicker and the sky was full of thick, milky fog. O.T. wanted to stop before long to get some gas—he had meant to fill up in Five Forks, but when he'd driven by the petrol station he'd seen Hosey outside, chewing the fat with Larry, the owner, and he hadn't felt like stopping.

O.T. suddenly found himself thinking of the afternoon they'd gotten Yappers, the golden retriever he and Walt had had when they were seven. Hosey's pa had come to visit with O.T.'s daddy and Hosey had accompanied him, pulling a little red wagon behind him—a Christmas present of which he was immensely proud, since no other kid in town had one, a grin as wide as the sun on his face. Inside the wagon, wrapped up in an old afghan, was a shaggy, dirty little puppy. O.T. and Walt had jumped up from the sandbox, where they'd been playing cars, and ran over with great excitement.

"Me and Daddy found him by the creek, whinin' and carryin' on," Hosey said, picking up the little puppy, who gave him a lick, right in the mouth. The boys all laughed. "Ain't he cute?"

O.T. reached out a hand to pet the little dog, whose fur was as soft as goose down, except for the matted parts, which looked to be dried red mud. "He needs him a bath."

"He's been out by his lonesome for a while, I reckon," Hosey replied, scratching the puppy under the chin. "He was howling to beat the band. Bet he misses his mama. Daddy said we can keep him if I do all the feedin' and takin' care of him." Hosey held the puppy out, its fat little legs dangling. "Want to hold him?"

Walt hadn't spoken a word, and O.T. turned to see his brother holding out his arms silently, an expression of awe on his face. Hosey put the wriggling puppy in Walt's waiting arms. The boy, sinking to the ground with the puppy nestled under his chin, closed his eyes, a blissful smile crossing his face.

"Shoot," Hosey said, as he and O.T. regarded the scene. "He acts like he ain't seen a puppy a day before in his life."

"Just look at him," O.T. agreed.

"I sure do love this puppy," Walt declared in a sure voice, his eyes still closed. "What's his name, Hosey?"

"We ain't named him yet," Hosey replied. "Although Daddy was callin' him Yappers, on account of how he was bellowin' down by the creek."

"Yappers," Walt murmured, stroking the puppy's fur, his eyes still closed. O.T. and Hosey, bored, played in the sandbox while Walt and the puppy napped in the dirt, which was pretty weird, but Walt was Walt.

After a time, Hosey's daddy said it was time to get going. Hosey nudged Walt awake with his bare foot. "Time to go. Can I have Yappers back?"

Walt sat up, pressed his face into the little dog's fur then handed him back to Hosey. "Bye, Yappers," he said in a clear, high voice. Hosey put the dog back in the little red wagon, wrapped him in the afghan, and took off for home.

After Hosey and his pa had disappeared around the curve of the driveway, Walt's face crumpled. He ran into the barn, where he cried for much of the night, and he didn't want to talk to O.T. or Ma about it.

The next day, before they'd finished breakfast, there came a knock at the door. O.T. got up to answer it.

Hosey stood in the doorway in his dirty overalls, barefoot as always, grinning from ear to ear. "Tell him I said happy early birthday." And he was gone, running down the driveway, leaving behind a little red wagon and the puppy, with a big red bow tied around both.

After an hour of driving, O.T. stopped for gas in Cornelia.

"I'm hungry, Deddy," Ginny said.

"Let's see what they got." O.T. went in to the general store pay for his gas and get a quart of oil. The man behind the counter wore coveralls so greasy and grimy that O.T. figured they hadn't been washed in ten years or more. He had hair as white as snow with a bald patch on the top of his head, with large, bushy eyebrows that looked like albino caterpillars.

"How do," the old man said simply, nodding at the oil. "How much gas?"

"Two dollars' worth," O.T. answered, glancing at the dusty counters. He didn't see anything too appetizing or edible in here.

"Where ya headed?"

"Rock Creek," O.T, said, handing him the money. "Or thereabouts."

"Visitin' fambly up thataways?"

"Yeah, of a sort." O.T. didn't feel like explaining to the old timer, though he seemed friendly enough.

"Where you from?"

"Five Forks."

"Ain't made it too far yet," the old man said through teethless gums. "Know a fella from Five Forks."

"Oh, do ya?" O.T. asked. "Who's that?"

"Name of Hosey," the old man said. "He passes through here a fair bit."

"Yeah, I know Hosey," O.T. replied stiffly.

"Nice fella."

"Sure."

"Snowstorm comin'," the old man said, handing O.T. his change. "Keep the rest o' that.The oil is free a'charge."

"Naw, I can't take—"

"Just take yer money on," the old man said with a genial smile. "You'uns look hongry. There's a stand up the road aways, not even a mile. Buy yerself some skrawberries or peanuts. And git you where you goin' affore that storm hits. I ain't a lie—it's comin' and soon."

"I thought the snow might hold off a day or two," O.T. said.

"Thought wrong, fella, it's on the way. Affore the day is out, I reckon. Now git you on and quick."

"I'm mighty obliged," O.T. answered. "Thank you."

"Tell Hosey, next time you see 'im, I said howdy," the old man called after him. "He ain't been through in near a month. He doin' awright?"

"Sure, fine," O.T. answered. This man didn't look like the type to buy hooch, but if he was friendly with Hosey, he must either sell or drink the stuff. O.T. was tempted to ask if the man had 'shine to sell, but that wouldn't be proper, not with Ginny hungry for something to eat. "Thank ya again, sir."

"Yeah."

O.T. walked back to the car and pumped the gas, the cold wind whipping past his ears. He could smell snow on the air, and the sky was getting dark. The old man was right—the snow was on its way. He could see Ginny through the window, shivering. He finished pumping the gas and jumped back in the car, swearing.

"Jee-ma-nee, it's cold!" He looked at Ginny. "The old timer didn't have no food decent to eat, but he said there's a stand just up the road a-ways where we can get somethin'."

She nodded. "Okay."

O.T. pulled out of the general store and headed back up 441, cursing the cold all the while. The sky was gray, and a thick fog had settled over the trees. It made a right pretty sight, or would have if he weren't so cold. The farther up the mountain they got, the colder it would be, O.T. knew, and there was a good chance of ice on the roads.

What had he been thinking to take this fool-headed trip?

"There's the stand, Deddy," Ginny said, pointing. A ramshackle fruit stand appeared on the left, with an old colored couple packing things up for the day.

O.T. pulled in, rolled down his window, and called out, "Y'all got anythin' left we could buy for dinner before you pack it in?"

"Ayuh, some," the old man called. "Come on out and have a look-see, but quick. Snow's comin'."

"So I hear." O.T. parked the car, and he and Ginny walked over to the stand. A few shriveled strawberries were all that remained.

"Got anything to warm us up on our travels, old timer?" O.T. asked in a friendly voice.

"Sho. Hope you like peanuts, though," the old man said with a cackle. "I got parched peanuts and boiled peanuts. And Lillie here might have some warm apple cider left, if she ain't poured it back in the jug yet."

"I got some," said the old lady, spitting snuff. "I ain't poured it back yet."

"Y'all gettin' ready to go on home?" O.T. asked.

"Yes'r," the old man answered. "Got to get back to the homestead and stoke the fires, reckon. Looks like a few inches headed this way at least. Bad time to be on the roads, 'specially if'n you headed north." He cast a judgmental eye toward O.T.'s car.

"Well, we won't keep y'all. I'll take a bag of the parched peanuts and some boiled peanuts, too. You want cider?" he asked Ginny. She nodded. "And a cup of cider too, if it ain't too dear."

"Naw, it ain't. Real fair," the old lady replied. With a shaking hand, she ladled cider into a cup. "Ten cents for the lot, mister. You all want skrawberries?"

"No'm." O.T. dug a ten-cent piece out of his coveralls and handed it over. "Thank ya kindly," he said, handing the bag of peanuts to Ginny. "Y'all mind if we set a bit over there and eat? I don't like to eat and drive, not when the sky's gettin' so dark."

"Free country," the old man replied. "But see that you be careful when you get back on the road. It's a doozy comin'."

"I thank ya." O.T. and Ginny sat in the car, splitting the peanuts between them. The hot peanuts were slick with oil, covered in coarse salt, and delicious. O.T. and Ginny scarfed them down with abandon.

"I reckon we better get back movin', if we're gon' reach the mountains affore nightfall," O.T. said. "Or before the snow comes."

"Ought we to stay somewhere for the night, you think?"

"Naw. Ain't nowhere to stay, I don't reckon," O.T. said, shaking his head. "Anyway we cain't really afford it. I got things budgeted out real careful."

Ginny looked worried for the first time. "Well, let's go then."

O.T. wiped his hands on his coveralls and started the truck. The old couple paused their packing to raise their hands in farewell as O.T. and Ginny pulled out.

The old man called out something. O.T. stopped and rolled down the window, putting a hand to his ear, gesturing for the old man to repeat himself.

Bellowing, the old man obliged. "I say, you white folks shore is crazy!"

O.T. laughed, a little nervously, waved at the old timer, and drove on, rolling his window back up, his breath a puff of smoke in the frosty car.

"They act like we're drivin' off to our death," he remarked with a tight smile.

"Probably don't see folks off joy-ridin' too much in the winter like this," Ginny answered. "You know how old folks is."

The sky was steadily darkening, and O.T. could smell ice in the air. But the visibility was good and the roads were clear. He reckoned if they made good time, they could be in the mountains before the snow really started to fall hard.

The next hour passed slowly. O.T. clutched the steering wheel, staring at the road, his muscles aching with cold. The sky had taken on a steely quality as the air grew thinner and thinner, and the truck's cab felt like an icebox. The view was something else; had it not been so cold O.T. would have pulled over so Ginny could have a look-see. Endless gray-brown pine trees on either side of the road stood up straight and leafless like soldiers at attention, and rock-hard brown dirt sloped into gorges and chasms that seemed to drop forever. Gone was the red clay of Five Forks; up here, the dirt was rich and brown, rocky and full of nutrients. The road was winding but smooth, like a large roller coaster, and O.T. felt it soothe him as he drove, his mind running clear and free.

"Passin' by Sautee-Nacoochee here in a minute," he said, after a time. "If the weather was a little nicer, we'd stop and look around."

"I like that word," Ginny said absently, staring out the window. "Sautee. It just sounds pretty. Is it Cherokee or Creek? I cain't ever remember which of 'em was where."

"It's Cherokee, hon," O.T. replied as tiny flutters of snow swirled across the windshield. "Sautee was a young Indian chief and Nacoochee was a princess." O.T.'s ma had told him that, when he was a boy. Or had it been Walt?

"Oh, really?" Ginny breathed. "I love that."

"Yeah. There's a legend about 'em."

"I want to hear it."

"I cain't remember right," O.T, said. "I ain't heard it in such a long time. Had to do with the burial mound up yonder, and some business between the chief's son from the Chicakasaw tribe and the princess from the Cherokee, I reckon. Nacooche and Hiawassee, their names was."

"That's where the town names come from?"

"Yeah." He wiped at the fogged glass in front of him. "Probably ain't a lick of truth to the story. Look it up in Uncle Walt's books when we get back, if you want to know."

"Can we stop at the burial mound, Deddy?"

"It's startin' to snow pretty hard, darlin'," O.T. answered. "And it'll be dark soon."

"Please. We're already here. Jes' for a moment?"

"Awright." O.T. turned the sputtering truck down the road, smiling despite himself. Ginny was so much like Walt.

Years before, Walt had given the kids a lesson about the Native Americans in Georgia and the treatment of Native people under President Andrew Jackson. He'd described how the Indians were run off the North Georgia mountains and how those who weren't able to hide or successfully integrate had been forced onto the Trail of Tears, where many had died and the few that did not were forced to resettle on government land thousands of miles away. In 1832 Indians sued the government, winning the right to their land, but President Andrew Jackson sent his men in to cast them out anyway. Now, you hardly ever saw a full-blooded Native person on the land in the foothills of Appalachia. Ginny had cried for weeks after that.

"This is where they were, isn't it?" she asked. "The Cherokee?"

"All around here, hon," O.T. said. "Cherokee, Chickasaw, Creek. Still are, too, some of 'em. The ones that were able to integrate."

"How'd they do that? Pass as white?"

"Some did, I reckon...they converted to Christian ways, and opened up schools to teach themselves English. Eventually, many of 'em married in with us white folks and integrated on in."

"Oh," Ginny said. "I cain't decide if that's good or bad."

"Ain't good or bad," O.T. said. "Just is. They fared a sight better than the ones who couldn't—or wouldn't—integrate."

"I don't see how," Ginny argued gloomily. "Seems to me like the difference between bad and worse."

"White man have done a lot of bad things to a lot of people over the years," O.T. said finally, clearing his throat. "Ain't gon' do nobody any good to deny it. And those things is still goin' on, too."

"Like lynching?"

O.T. looked at her sharply. "What you know about lynching?"

"There was a man lynched last summer over in Grove Hill," Ginny said. "Don't you remember?"

"Accorse I do. I just didn't know *you* knew about it."

"Doesn't seem right," she said finally, biting her lip. "Killin' a man like that. Seems like it's murder to me. No matter what he did."

O.T. waited a moment before he spoke. "I reckon I agree with you, hon."

"Most don't."

"No, they don't."

Father and daughter both fell silent as O.T. slowed the truck to a crawl. A general store with a slanted roof and a large white sign that read Old Sautee Store was situated beside the road. A large white, round thermometer, the hand stopped in its tracks, hung above the sign, and a flag, frozen stiff with ice, crackled in the wind. A candy-apple red sign hung on the side of the store. *Ice-cold Coca-Cola 5 cent.*

"Oh, Deddy, can we stop and get a co-cola?"

"They ain't open, hon," O.T. pointed out, relieved—he didn't want to spend money on a cola. "Maybe on our way back down?"

From there it was only a two-minute drive to the burial mound, and by the time they arrived, the snow was falling in thick sheets.

O.T. stopped the truck on the side of the road, hoping it would start back up again when they left.

"Let's get out, then," he said. They parked on a steep bank, and O.T. held tightly to Ginny's arm as they made their way down the hill toward the large snow-covered burial mound. The air was eerie and quiet, except for the gentle whoosh of snowflakes sweeping the ground.

"So this is where they're buried?" Ginny asked, holding her pa's arm. "Sautee and Nacoochee?"

"Accordin' to rumor," O.T. replied. "Though they ain't the only ones. They found more bodies than just them."

"Somebody went diggin' in there?" she asked, horrified.

"Yeah. Not too long past, some folks from the college came up here and did a dig."

"Why?" Ginny asked. "That seems disrespectful."

"I reckon it is, but you know what they say—can't know the future if you don't know the past."

"Still," she proclaimed haughtily. "I don't like it. What's that thing on the top?" She pointed toward the red-roofed gazebo that sat on the top of the mound, like a trinket on a wedding cake.

"It was built half a century ago, or thereabouts, by the same family that still owns this land, I reckon." He smiled. "Hope they don't shoot us as trespassers."

"Imagine, building a gazebo on top of a grave," Ginny said solemnly. "Like you gonna have people out there and serve 'em tea or somethin'."

"I don't know what he meant by it," O.T. said honestly. "Only that it's there."

"Folks do a lot of things," she said, staring out into the snow. "Just because they're there and they can."

"Reckon they do," he said softly, smiling at his daughter who was growing up too fast. She looked so much older than fourteen and so much like her mother. O.T. leaned down and placed a gentle kiss on her dark-blonde, snow-covered head. "Let's get back to the truck," he said. "Time's a'wastin'."

Mercifully, the truck started with no trouble, and they were soon back on the road. Ginny seemed in a much better mood, and O.T. was glad she was enjoying their trip; all he felt was nerves. He hoped the weather would hold out long enough to get where they were going, and once there, that they'd be happily received.

Ginny evidently still had Sautee and Nacoochee on her mind. "It's just so sad," she said quietly. "I cain't imagine what that's like, not bein' with the person you love."

Now that he knew she wasn't thinking about Grady Bridges, he was able to smile in agreement. "Yeah, it's real sad," he said. "Back in those days folks picked out their kids' wives an' husbands, and didn't think a thing of it. Still do, sometimes. Heck, for a time I wondered if yer ma's folks would even let her marry me."

"I'm glad they did, Deddy," Ginny said, hugging her arms to her chest. "I want to pick my own husband. And when I want to, too."

"Good," O.T. answered, his eyes clapped on the road. "Glad to hear ya say it. I was worrit for a minute you'd be up and married five minutes after Grady made ya an offer."

Ginny sighed. "Is it terrible that I don't want to marry him? I mean, he's real nice. And he's from a good family and ever'body in town likes him...and he seems to like me so much. He's sweet as pie to me."

"But you don't love him."

"Naw," she answered. "But maybe I would in time. And he could help us around the farm. He'd be a good addition to the family. I could learn to love him, couldn't I?"

"Honest?" O.T. asked. "If it was Maybelle here, or yer aunt, or some other nice lady you were talking to, they might tell you that's true. That you can grow to love just about anybody in this world if you put yer mind to it. You start to get used to yer marrit life and that starts to feel like love. But there's a difference between love and what's familiar."

"What about you and Mama?"

"That was real love," O.T. said. "I loved yer ma since we were little, jes' about. But yer ma was just like *you*—she knew her mind, and she warn't going to accept whatever offer she got, not without some feelin' behind it. She didn't have to, see, because she knew her own worth, and she wasn't goin' to go jumpin' in just because some fool boy asked her. She got plenty of offers before I ever ast her—I didn't know that at the time, but I found out later—and I was the one she said yes to." He shook his head, laughing. "Lord if I ever knew why, but I'm thankful she did." He rubbed at his eyes, which were starting to get gritty with exhaustion. "We had a real happy marriage. All the way up till the end. I want that for you and yer brother and sister. No less than that. 'Cause anything less ain't good enough."

"But—"

"And I can tell you right now—yer ma, my Betty Lou—she would agree with me on this. She would not want yer marryin' when you was fourteen to some boy you don't love."

Ginny was silent. O.T. figured he'd better change the subject, before she got tired of his yammering and decided to marry Grady out of spite.

It was nearly two a.m. according to O.T.'s pocket watch by the time they had inched halfway up Highway 348. The snow was coming down still, but not as heavily as earlier. The air in the cab was so cold their teeth chattered, and O.T. hoped Ginny's hands and feet weren't as numb as his own. "You okay, gal?"

"Fine," Ginny said through gritted teeth. "Just a bit chilly."

"That's the understatement of the century, I reckon," O.T. said with a chuckle. "What I wouldn't give for a mug of hot coffee or some of that cider you had all them hours ago."

"How long affore we're there?"

"Not long," he answered, trying to wipe at the windshield with his shirt sleeve. "Maybe forty minutes."

"You're going to think I'm crazy as a loon," Ginny said suddenly, her breath puffing out in front of her. "But I feel like Uncle Walt's with us."

"Oh yeah?" O.T. wasn't particularly surprised. He felt his brother's presence too.

"Did he love the mountains?"

"He sure did," O.T. said sadly. "But he didn't get up here much after we was grown. I reckon maybe once or twice." Walt had helped Hosey to haul hooch up the mountains, hadn't he? Up here in the snow, so pure and white it seemed to wash things clean. Hosey's transgressions seemed small and O.T. wondered whether he had been too hard on him. He bit the thought off with a grimace. Now wasn't the time to study on that, anyhow.

"Will you tell me a story about Uncle Walt? To pass the time?"

O.T. thought for a moment. "Walt went all the way to City Hall in Atlanta once, did you know that?" he asked, glancing over at Ginny. "He gave Commissioner Eugene Talmadge hell."

"The black-haired feller with glasses?"

"The very one," O.T. said, surprised. "From the Department of Agriculture. How you know him?"

"He writes an article for the *Market Bulletin*. I seen his picture a bunch of times. He's thinkin' about runnin' for governor next year."

"You know more than I do, then."

"That's all I know. Why'd Uncle Walt want to go anyways? I didn't know he was a Democrat."

"He wasn't. Never heard Walt mention one party or the other; he cared more about people," O.T. answered. Walt had been a frequent reader of the *Bulletin*, which had started as an agricultural newspaper, featuring tips and advice on how to run a profitable farm. Eugene Talmadge, before becoming the commissioner of the organization, wrote many articles for the newspaper, and he wasn't shy about expressing his political views.

"This joker," Walt used to bluster, waving the paper high over his head, "ain't got *nothin'* real to say about farming, or about the plight of the farmer in this country. Why, he ought to be talking about the real issues we face—the boll weevil and the cotton gin, and the fact that under the crop lien some folks is gettin' charged 65 percent interest, and colored folks as high as 75 percent!"

Eugene Talmadge was a white supremacist, a fundamentalist Christian, and a segregationist who talked a whole lot about what he called "bootstraps"—teaching young farmers and their families how to rise up in society by showing *true grit*. From what O.T. understood, true grit involved a lot of stepping on the backs of black folks, and a few poor whites, besides. Talmadge, dubbed "The Wild Man of Sugar Creek," had near-cult following, and his essays in the *Market Bulletin* were infamous. To Walt's eternal frustration, Talmadge had many fans in Five Forks. O.T. thought it queer that a little man working for the Department of Agriculture could be so famous.

It came as no surprise to O.T. that this Talmadge scoundrel was running for governor and would probably win by a landslide. When times were hard, people tended to vote for demagogues. Folks liked a scapegoat, liked blaming their lot on folks lower on the totem pole. Men like Eugene Talmadge made it easier for them by loudly giving voice to those feelings folks kept buried for shame.

"So why'd Uncle Walt go to Atlanta?"

"He read a quote in that rag and it got him right fired up. You know how your Uncle Walt was hung up on propriety. He didn't like nobody who used coarse language, or did hurtful things, or acted gleeful about doin' wrong."

"Yeah, he was a saint."

"Not quite. Almost. Anyhow, if I recall, Talmadge was under investigation by the federal government for a while, somethin' about him possibly stealing from the Department of Agriculture. Misappropriation of funds, something like that. I don't know if he were ever convicted or what came of it. But I do know that he wrote an article for the *Bulletin*, justifyin' stealin' funds so long as they went toward furtherin' the white man's cause. Puttin' them above the black man."

"And Uncle Walt got fired up?"

"You bet he did. He heard tell that Talmadge was havin' a town hall, to discuss *farmin' issues*. He welcomed any white member of a rural community who might want to come share ideas. Big ol' mess of propaganda, it was. Little more than a Klan meetin' in disguise." O.T. shook his head in disgust. "Next thing, Walt was hoppin' a train with Hazel and goin' to Atlanta to that meetin'."

"I can't imagine Walt goin' to somethin' like that," Ginny shivered. "Or Hazel lettin' him, much less goin' along. Sounds dangerous."

"You couldna talk him out of it, and Hazel just went to make sure Walt didn't get his head caved in," O.T. replied with a grin. "She didn't want him to go. Said folks need to mind their own affairs, look after their own and not go gettin' in a bunch of mess. But Walt had his mind made up. She complained the whole way, but deep down I think she really wanted to see Atlanta. Anyhow, Hazel told me Walt sat through that whole meetin', quiet as a mouse, just listenin' while everybody talked about how it was black folks to blame for the cotton crop dwindlin' and everythin' going to hell, and the drought, women gettin' the vote, and everything else besides. Then it was time for Mr. Talmadge to have his say, and he got up on the pulpit and pushed back his round-eyed glasses and started in. Gesticulatin' and boomin' around, bellowin' and hollerin'; he had the whole crowd worked up into a lather." O.T. had a sudden memory of Billy Rev in the revival tent on a hot summer day.

"When Talmadge was done with his sermon, he asked the crowd, 'Ain't that right, fellas?' And the whole crowd—mostly white fellers, and a few women—hooped and hollered in agreement. But when they was done, and the room fell silent, Walt stood up. 'No, that ain't right,' he said loud and clear. 'It ain't right atall. You talked a lot about our Lord Jesus here tonight, Mr. Talmadge, and I reckon I can't understand how you can quote the Lord and then talk such hatred. If you ask me, you should spend less time whippin' folks into a frenzy and stealin' money from the State, and more time home at Sugar Creek, readin' yer Bible.'"

Ginny sucked in her breath. "Good Lord, Deddy," she breathed. "And he wasn't beaten to a pulp?"

"Oh, they was callin' for blood awright, but Hazel pulled him out of the place right quick."

"I just cain't picture Uncle Walt doing such." Ginny shook her head. "He was so polite all the time."

"He had a clear sense of right and wrong," O.T. said, near tears, " and he stood up for what he believed." He cleared his throat. "Don't mistake it, gal, any of that goodness you see in me…it come from him. I never cared much about nobody else. I always knew things was unfair, and it bothered me some, but I didn't care like Walt did. Not till he made me understand. He ought to have been a teacher, I reckon."

"Like I want to."

"Yes. Just like you want to."

"I miss him."

"So do I."

"We're here, looks like," Ginny said, pointing to the roadside sign, where Rock Creek Unincorporated was painted on a splintered board.

"Yeah, somehow we made it," O.T. replied. "Now to find these folks."

"Where do they live?" Ginny asked.

"No idear," he admitted.

She let out a small wail. "But, Deddy, it's the middle of the night. Ain't no general store gon' be open for us to ast. We cain't sleep in the car; it's too cold!"

"It'll be awright, gal," O.T. said, ignoring the gnawing ache in his belly. "I got a hunch. Just another ten minutes in the car affore we'll be nice and warm under somebody's covers, let's hope. If they's nice and God wills it."

Chapter Fourteen

"Heard tell of somethin'," said Faye, digging her spoon into her cornmeal mush. "While you was in confinement."

Sivvy picked at her food. She'd lost the taste for mush after they had upped her medicine. Having lost five pounds already, it would be back to Dr. Lowell if she lost any more. Sivvy forced a bite, made herself chew and swallow. "What is it?"

"They're startin' 'em up again," Faye said in a dramatic whisper, pushing her graying hair behind one ear. "The sterilizations."

"Oh." Sivvy went back to her plate. The topic didn't much interest her.

"Ain't you worrit?"

Sivvy shrugged. She'd spent a lot of time in the past worrying about such things, but she found she no longer cared. When she'd first been admitted, she'd been warned in hushed whispers that women were routinely sterilized, especially women who were badly behaved, and those who "got around." With women and men segregated, and the majority of the staff in the women's building being female, there was little opportunity to get up to much, but some folks still found a way. Sivvy supposed a woman would always find a way, if she wanted company bad enough. Sivvy had when she was young, which seemed a million years ago now.

The serious lunatics, patients deranged and out of their wits, were often scheduled for sterilization. Carrying a baby wasn't an easy ride, no sirree. Things could, and did, go horribly wrong all the time. Motherhood may be God's most precious gift to womankind, but it sure had the potential for heartbreak. But to have *the* most important role of a woman's life taken away by force—surely, that was a mortal sin? The women in the asylum had no ownership of their own bodies, Sivvy knew. Not even a little bit. It kept her awake at night, studying the horror of it, the indignity and the shame.

After a time, the asylum wore everyone down, though. Small strippings of rights and dignities here and there, it made a body tired, complacent. Sivvy had no husband, not anymore, and had only briefly been a mother. Most of her dealings with gentlemen had gotten her into trouble and eventually landed her in the asylum. What did it matter if she were sterilized, anyhow? There was precious little chance of ever being with a man again, let alone bearing another child.

Sivvy shrugged again, and Faye gave her a sly look.

"You ain't the only sister who feels thataway," Faye said softly. "Me, I can't stand the thought. Not that it matters to me, my monthlies dried up long ago. But they's women that actually *ast* for it, did you know that?"

"Surely not?" Sivvy replied, in disbelief.

"Naw, it's true. I know one of 'em."

"Why would a woman choose to—?"

"Because they git more freedom, that's why," Faye answered, pushing her spoon around her plate. "Ain't you noticed that they's certain women who get more than their share of free time in the day?"

"Well, yeah," Sivvy answered. "I work in the kitchens, so I get to—"

"No, I ain't talkin' about your little strolls around the pecan trees," Faye said, exasperated. "I mean, there's females in this place that can go where they want, just about. Can see the men. Might even get to town once a month. Can maybe even get an after-hours pass—"

"Naw," Sivvy protested. "Ain't no such thing—"

"Is, too," Faye insisted. "They's things that can be arranged, under cover of darkness. Just 'cause you don't know about it, don't mean it ain't happenin'. Menfolks got needs, and most times a man can get what he wants. And there's freedom for women in that, if they know how to grab a little of it. Only a little pain, and the doctor, he'll protect you."

"You're sayin'—?"

"I ain't sayin' nothin'." Faye stood up. "This mush tastes awful bad, I just cain't eat it. Ain't hungry nohow." She leaned down to Sivvy and whispered, "Just talk to Dr. Lowell. He's the one." Sivvy's face wrinkled in disgust. "Oh, I know, honey. But maybe through him leads the road to salvation," Faye said quietly. "He gon' do what he gon' do, ain't he? Might as well get somethin' out of it. You like bein' out of doors as much as you do, might be worth a thought, is all. Fresh air do a gal like you some good." Faye grabbed her tray and walked off, her legs needle-thin beneath her starched blue shift.

Sivvy brooded into her own cornmeal mush for a little while longer, her teeth working over her bottom lip, her hands moving continuously over her spoon, back and forth, back and forth, subconsciously polishing it to a shine.

જે

O.T. pulled the car up in front of a little wooden shack next to an ancient black Model T whose fender was nearly rusted off. He turned off his lights and stepped out of the car, all the bones in his legs creaking and his hands numb with cold. As Ginny stepped down from the vehicle, O.T. saw a light within the house turn on.

O.T. reckoned luck had been on their side after all.

They'd been eight miles down old Aska Road, with snow coming down so hard he couldn't see more than a foot in front of the car, when he'd spotted the one-lane steel bridge road. Driving over it had felt mad—the steel beams beneath the car creaking—but they's crawled ahead inch by inch, trying not to think about the freezing Toccoa River churning far below. O.T. thanked his lucky stars that Sivvy Hargrove had written about that steel bridge, for otherwise they would surely have been lost in the snow.

Shivering, O.T. and Ginny walked to the front stoop. As O.T. raised his hand to knock, the door opened, and the lamplight illuminated the wrinkled face of an old woman with long gray hair, dark brown eyes, and a welcoming smile.

"Get you inside, out of the cold," the woman said, pulling them both into the house with one arm. "Get you in affore you catch your death."

Inside, the old woman fumbled with the lantern, turning it up until the room filled with a bright amber glow. "Y'all hungry?" she asked. "I got some cold sweet taters and a couple aigs. Ain't much till tomorry mornin' brekkus but its tollible if you hongry."

"Much obliged, ma'am," O.T said, taking off his hat. He couldn't help but smile at the sight of this old, slight woman ambling around the tiny kitchen, preparing food for strangers who had shown up unexpectedly after dark. She busied herself over a little cookstove, hauling a massive iron skillet from under her cupboard.

"Don't you wonder who we is, ma'am?" Ginny asked, grinning with delight.

"Reckon y'all will tell me direckly, but I aim to git a bite in ya affore you do," the little woman said, her gray hair gleaming silver in the lamplight. "Take no offense, but you both look skeerse enough to blow away in a stiff wind. And we's espetin' more'n a stiff wind tonight. Snowstorm is nigh." She gestured for them to pull their chairs toward the kitchen fire. "Y'all git yerselves warmed up. You both half friz."

"That we are," O.T. said ruefully, sitting in front of the fire. "We been drivin' most of the day and the night besides. I was foolheaded and didn't want to stop to stay nowheres. Not till we got to where we was goin'. We're right lucky we found you atall; I almost drove right past yer house, and we woulda been done for then. I swear the temp dropped another ten degrees when I rounded the curve."

"Reckon it probly did," the woman answered, dishing food onto tin plates. "Been livin' on this here ridge my life entire, but folks who ain't from these parts don't rankin on the winter months. Jest a short spell on this hill'll jes' 'bout kill a grown man, if he puny. I seen more than one man start up thisaway and lit a shuck at the firs' sign a'cold. I tol' my husban', just this morn, that the storm was a'brewin'. Didn't even have to leave the shack to tell of it, nairy."

"You could smell it on the wind, I reckon."

"Naw, well, accorse you can, if'n you's outside, but how I could tell was ol' Crackerbox over yonder," the old lady continued, pointing to the hearth in the darkened parlor, where a thin, sinewy black cat stretched out on a threadbare rug. "That's Crackerbox over there. Mangy lil' devil cat, he is. Anyhow, when I got up this morn to fry the bacon and aigs he came over and stretched out in front of the fire with his back to it. The old folks say if a cat lays with his back to a fire, the snow's a'comin'."

O.T. smiled, thinking of how old "old folks" must be to this woman, who looked like she could be anywhere between fifty and two hundred.

"It ain't much," she said as she set plates on their laps. "Just a cold supper, left over from what we had for supper tonight. But it'll do ya fine till you wake tomorry. Y'all stayin' on, I reckon?"

"If you'll be kind enough to have us," O.T. answered.

"Accorse." The woman looked affronted, but her eyes sparkled with mirth. "'t would be a shame on my family name if I turned away half-friz folks from my hearth! Hear tell of it!" She bent to hand them forks, and O.T. could hear her bones creak. "Y'all want a hot cup of somethin'? I ain't got no cawfee, but I got sassafras tea, y'all want some. We always keep sassafras tea."

"Yes'm," O.T. and Ginny said in unison.

The old lady nodded and set about brewing tea. O.T. dug into the cold meal. The sweet potatoes were roasted and smoky. He had two hard-boiled eggs, covered in coarse black pepper, a small piece of trout, and what looked to be bread and butter pickles, piled high. It was the best cold supper he'd ever had, and he finished his entire plate before the old woman had even managed to bring over his cup of tea.

"Tol' you you was hungry. You thin as a poor woman's slip," the old woman muttered, taking his plate.

Ginny hid her grin behind her own cup of tea as she pushed her plate, with half a piece of trout and two pickles, toward O.T. He ate her leftovers hungrily, feeling as if he hadn't eaten in weeks.

The old woman sat across from them, holding her own cup of tea with a hand gnarled and covered with liver spots, but still slim and graceful. A delicate silver wedding band decorated her third finger.

"Now. We've got food and drink, so let's do formality. Pleased to make yer acquaintance. Don't reckon we've met, unless I disremember you, which is accorse possible 'cause I seem to git older ever'day. I'm Julie-Anne Hargrove, of the Rock Creek Hargroves. This is my land; these are my peoples."

There were no other "peoples" in the room, but she spoke for them anyway.

Smiling, O.T. reached out and shook Julie-Anne's hand, and Ginny did the same. "I'm Owen Tolbert Lawrence, but folks call me O.T.," he said, feeling suddenly nervous. "This here's my daughter Genevieve; we call her Ginny. She jes' turned fourteen."

"Please to meet ya both, O.T. and Ginny." Misrus Julie-Anne took a long sip of her tea. The smell of hot sassafras filled the room, reminding O.T. of the root beer syrup they used to sell in the Five Forks diner. "Don't recollect I know any Lawrences, but pleased to meet ya. What brings you to Rock Creek in the middle of the winter, when the wind is blowin' a dang gale?"

"I took a notion to come affer Christmas," O.T. responded. "On account of my brother. My twin brother. He had business with a relative of yers, guess you'd say. And he died. And I reckon I...I wanted to finish that business. For him."

Misrus Julie-Anne looked intrigued but wary, her dark eyes meeting his with a steely stare. "I'm right sorry to hear about yer brother. Cain't imagine to lose a twin." O.T. nodded in thanks and she clasped his hand for a moment. "What was his name?"

"Walt," O.T. replied, feeling a pang in his chest. "Walter Terrell Lawrence."

If Julie-Anne recognized the name she gave no sign. "Awright. And which relative of mine is it he got business with? One of my boys, reckon. They do a little brewin', but they ain't got no debts that I can speak of—"

"Oh, no. No, ma'am," O.T. assured her. "Ain't nothin' like that. When I say business I don't really mean actual *business*. It's more of a personal nature. It's...it's a dilly of a dally, as my late wife used to say."

"Well, I see. You got me mighty interested, young man," Julie-Anne said. "Which relative is it, then? Most of my chilluns is right here on this land, so you won't have a time tryin' to find 'em—"

"No, ma'am," O.T. interrupted. "This one actually ain't here. It's...it's Miss Sivvy. At least *I* know her as Sivvy. I reckon her given name was Savilia, if I remember—"

"Hold on, now." The old woman stood abruptly, confusion crossing her face. "You mean to tell me you know Savilia? You know my Sivvy? You've *seen* Sivvy?"

"Well, not in a long time, years actually, but I had a letter from her just 'fore Christmas."

"You *heard* from her? Recently?" Julie-Anne asked longingly.

"Yes'm, I had a letter. It warn't addressed to me—it was to my brother, Walt. But he had already passed on."

"How'd they know each other?"

"They met a long time ago," O.T. said. "We both met her years ago, when we was still young'uns ourselves. She visited our town— we're from Five Forks. Missy Sivvy was with her uncle, the reverend. We met her at the revival, and became kinda friendly. I reckon, Walt kept up correspondence with her." O.T. omitted the details of their meeting, as there were things that he himself did not know how to explain, things that he'd rather tell her about later, once he'd had a chance to feel her out, and to get his bearings. Once he decided what all to tell and what not to tell.

"I don't understand it," Julie-Anne exclaimed, her eyes a little wild. "I don't understand it atall."

"What is it, ma'am?" Ginny asked softly.

"My daughter, Savilia—Sivvy," Julie-Anne said, bewildered, "lit a shuck outta here with her uncle back when she weren't but fourteen year old, to help him with preachin', and I ain't never clapt eyes on her since. She been gone for fifteen year and I ain't heard one cotton-pickin' thing about whether she was even alive nor dead!"

O.T. felt color creep into his cheeks. "I'm right sorry, ma'am," he said, looking down at his lap. "I didn't mean to give you a shock."

Julie-Anne went on as though she hadn't heard him. "And now you two show up here and say you heared from her! That you got a letter! I ain't been knowin' whether she went off and got marrit and had young'uns or drownded in the ocean! She ain't never sent us one dadgum letter in fifteen year! And neither has her sorry uncle!"

O.T., feeling terrible, remained silent.

"Why wouldn't she write to us? Accorse, it wouldn't amount to never nothin' nohow cause I cain't read, nor can my husban', but just to hear from her, to know she's alive…I ain't never heared of such meanness as this." The old woman sat heavily in her chair, and picked up her cup, her mouth trembling. "Lawd have mercy on me."

"I'm awful sorry," O.T. said again. "If I had known, I wouldn't have dragged up here to give you a shock. We oughter leave, I reckon."

"Hesh yer mouth," Julie-Anne said crossly, looking at them over the rim of her cup. Her gnarled fingers moved absently over the ceramic surface, absorbing the warmth. "Don't be a fool, boy. I ain't mad at you all." Julie-Anne smiled. "And you cain't go nowheres even if you wanted to. Not with this storm." She laughed, a little sadly. "Heck, warn't for y'all showin' up at my door I wouldn't even know what I know now—that my daughter is alive. I always reckoned she must be, 'cause we never heard otherwise, but seemed like she just fell off the earth...."

"Your brother-in-law never told you what had happened to her?"

Julie-Anne looked at O.T. sharply then sighed. "That's a story in itself. The good ol' rev." Her voice held more than a hint of disdain. "He ain't around here no more. Ain't welcome."

Ginny and O.T. finished their tea in silence. Julie-Anne rose to her feet with another sigh. "Seems the both of us have stories to tell and catchin' up to do. Reckon it can keep till tomorry, though," she said, glancing out the window. The snow was blowing sideways, and despite the little fire that blazed in the hearth, the room felt icy. "Y'all ain't goin' nowhere for a while. Yer stuck on the mountain. Might as well get a few winks and we can chaw the fat all the day long tomorry if we aim to. Till the festivities tomorry night, anyhow. Let's get y'all to bed."

O.T. and Ginny followed her dutifully through the little house, the floorboards creaking underfoot. From a back room came the sound of snoring.

"Don't worry 'bout Mr. Nate," the old woman said. "I allus tell him he gon' sleep through his own death. Ain't *nuthin'* gon' wake him. I ain't slept in twenty-five year or more, due to them logs he's a'sawin'."

Julie-Anne led Ginny into a tiny room with a cot in the corner. "Yer young miss can sleep in here. It's cold, but she'll be right cozy with some kivers." She pulled a pile of blankets from under the cot and handed them to Ginny. "Use as many as you want to. That's what they here fer. And just give a call if'n you need somethin'."

Ginny curled up on the cot and was asleep before O.T. and Julie-Anne had left the room.

"The couch is old and rickety, but you'll sleep on it fine, I rankin," she said, producing another fat bundle of blankets. "Get good and kivered up—the wind can howl through those windows to beat the band."

"Thank ya," O.T. said. "These blankets feel mighty warm."

"Well, I'm off to get a few winks. If I can, affer what you done tol' me. Just holler at us should you need anything. I'll be up at the rooster crow to make brekkus."

"Yes, ma'am. Much obliged," O.T. said again.

Julie-Anne padded down the creaky hall to her own bedroom, and O.T. settled on the little couch and kicked off his shoes. His feet felt like ice blocks. He covered himself with every blanket she'd given him and began to drift off to sleep. After that drive, he was plumb tuckered out.

O.T. awoke to the smell of bacon frying and the sounds of a banjo and fiddle. He got up, rubbed at his eyes, put his shoes back on, and went into the kitchen. Julie-Anne stood over the stove in her stiff white apron, frying up side meat and eggs. "Mornin', stranger," she said without turning. "I hope you slept awright. Yer girl is still out like a light."

"I'll let her sleep a bit longer, if y'don't mind. She's wore out, I know," O.T. replied, warming his hands at the hearth. "Need me to git any firewood or do anythin'?"

"No, sirree," Julie-Anne answered, turning the meat with a fork. "My mens is out doin' all that needs to be done. Y'all is guests, you ain't to do nothin'. Leastways not yet. Mayhap I'll put you to work later, after you had a bite of brekkus and tol' yer tale."

"Yes, ma'am."

"Ain't no cawfee, but theys more sassafras tea or, if you like, some hot chicory," she said, cracking eggs into the skillet. "Serve yerself on dranks; I'll have the food out faster'n green grass through a goose."

Smiling, O.T. took a clay cup that was hanging on a peg and poured himself some hot water and chicory. He winced a little at the taste of the stuff, but it was better than nothing. "Am I losing the last of my marbles or did I hear music outside?"

"You heared it," Julie-Anne replied, cracking more eggs into the skillet. How many was she feeding? O.T. wondered. He'd been under the impression that it was only her and her husband, Nate, in the house—though she had mentioned children on the land.

"They's out practicin' in the barn. Like to friz to death out there this early, but you cain't tell 'em a dad-gummed thing, them boys."

"Who is it?" O.T. asked.

"Oh, the boys. You'll meet 'em. DeWitt, Nate Jr., and Adam… reckon Franklin's out there with 'em, too, though he's got a lick or two more sense than the rest. And you can't keep little Nona-Lee out from under 'em," Julie-Anne said, stirring cornmeal mush on the stove. "They practicin' their ditties for the corn shuck."

"Corn shuck?"

"Ayuh. We have us a corn shucking ever' year 'round this time. This year it'll be Becca's house, just down the hill, but I do most a'the cookin' fer it 'cause Becca cain't cook as good as I kin," Julie-Anne stated matter of factly, then cackled. "Ain't you ever been to a corn shuck affore?"

O.T. shook his head. "No, ma'am. I ain't."

"Well, lawdy be. Ain't you a Georgia boy? Shoot. We just git together and shuck corn, git it ready for winter. Stockin' up, like. Usually we do it earlier than this, but there was sickness on the ridge these past few months, and we put it off till folks was well and there wasn't as much chance of passin' it round. The neighbors come, what little they is left, and all pitch in. We all set around in a circle and pull off husks and chaw the fat, and the boys play a ditty or two on they banjos and fiddles, and the girls might git to dancin' if they git a notion. We have a grand ol' time, just a'settin' and a'shuckin'. Five Forks ain't so very far from here. I'm right surprised y'all ain't got nothin' like that of yourn."

"We have dances and revivals." O.T. thought of Sivvy. "Fish fries and barbecues, things like that."

"Well, our mountain ways ain't the same as the rest of y'all folks," Julie-Anne said, poking the potatoes in the fire with a stick. "But still, I cain't believe y'all don't have corn shuckin's. That's the highlight of the year fer some folks up thisaway. Shoot, we even pop corn in the fire! The young'uns stuff theyselves silly, they do!"

"It sounds like a right jolly time," O.T. said, sipping his chicory.

"You'all can see fer yerself! It's tonight, at Becca's house, just down the hill. You and yer lil' gal will be my guests."

"I'm much obliged," O.T. said. "We'll be right happy to join you."

"Accorse you will!" she laughed. "Why wouldn't ya? I reckon you'll be happy to get you a nip of shine with the rest of the gents." O.T. felt his mouth fill with saliva. "And mayhap yer gal will take a passing fancy to one of my boys. All my sons and nephews are the handsomest you ever did see." Julie-Anne beamed proudly, setting a plate in front of him. "Though I got a mind to whip ever' last one of 'em, with all the notions they get in they heads. Ya cain't do *nuthin'* with the young folks these days, 'specially not the young men folks. It ain't a day goes by they don't got some idear or nuther 'bout what they gon' do."

"Yes'm," O.T. laughed. "My gal Ginny's newest notion is to go to college and become a teacher." He watched Julie-Anne pile eggs on his plate, creamy yellow and piping hot. He had no doubt they came from her own hens. This was not a woman who went to the general store to buy many goods. "Last week it was to git marrit."

"Yeah, they change their notions oftener than they change they underclothes," she agreed, placing a piece of cornbread beside his plate, already piled high with eggs, bacon, side meat, a roasted potato wrapped in foil, and what looked to be a persimmon, split in half and drizzled with honey. "Sounds to me like she traded one bad idea for a better one, though, if'n ya don't mind me speaking my piece."

"No'm," O.T. said, biting into the hot cornbread. Shoot, did it have actual *butter* on it? He might never leave this place. "I reckon you got the right of it. She ain't but fourteen. Too young by a lot, I reckon."

"I was marrit at that age," Julie-Anne said, sitting down beside him with her own cup of chicory. He didn't imagine she'd stay sitting for long. "Lots of womens was, and still are…but it's different now, as the years get on. These young'uns have more things to do with theyself now; they can get their studyin', if they want, or go work if they like to. They ain't in sech a screamin' hurry nowadays—well, they are, but not necessa-ly to git marrit and have young'uns. They got more—"

"Opportunity," O.T finished for her.

"Reckon they do. Or did, affore this *business* on Wall Street," she said, wrinkling her nose. "I might be out here in the boonyard, but the young'uns read the paper to me when I get one to hand. And that business is sorry as hell. Pardon language."

"No'm, I agree with you on that, too," O.T. said. "Had bad enough luck back home as it were, what with the sickness and the drought and the damned boll weevil." He took a bite of bacon, then set it back on his plate. "I lost my wife and my brother in the same week, due to sickness. Then, not two days later, Wall Street crashed and it weren't six months affore I lost my farm."

"You don't say!" Julie-Anne exclaimed with a wince. "Shoot fire. That's turrible. You down on yer luck for dern sure."

"Yes'm. Worked on it for a while, the farm I mean, for about a month. Tenancy farmin'. Tryin' to keep my feet on the land long as I could. But then the sharecropper sold my farm right out from under me; they rentin' it to somebody else. We're gonna have to move back to my sister's place, where I grew up. Me and my young'uns havin' to beg her hospitality, and her with a husband of her own and her own problems."

"That's what fambly's for, mind," Julie-Anne said. "Though I can understand, it's mighty hard."

"Six months was all it took," O.T. said bitterly. "I lost my brother, my wife, my land. Then got turned out of my own house. My sister's husband run off. My best friend gone. And I'd already lost both my parents and the folks I knowed as my grandparents affore that. I lost it all, ma'am." O.T. felt his cheeks warm, embarrassed, but once he'd started it had all just tumbled out. "I ain't got a thing in the world but my kids, and they ain't gon' fare too well if I cain't get it together. Folks in my town is like to starve affore long. None of us got two dimes to rub together."

"Lots of folks in that predicament round here. Everywhere," Julie-Anne acknowledged, looking at him over the top of her cup.

"Yes'm."

"I'm right sorry to hear tell of yer wife and yer brother," Julie-Anne said softly, placing a gnarled hand on his arm. There was a frank empathy in her voice, but no pity, which O.T. found surprisingly comforting. She pulled a pinch of snuff out of her apron and put it in her mouth. "We all lose our loved ones, regular as the seasons change, but it don't get no easier."

"No'm, it don't," O.T. replied. "Well, I reckon I cain't feel sorry for myself too much. Somebody out there got it worse, I'm sure."

"Count on that, young fella. And feelin' sorry for yerself don't do nothin' but put you in an early grave yerself," Julie-Anne remarked. "We do well as we can round here," she continued frankly. "'Accorse we pulled out the stops for comp'ny; we don't always eat like this. Don't always have plenty. We been savin' up, puttin' by for the corn shuck, and for the winter storms. We save what we can…and folks in these parts, well, we're all kin, ya see, and we share and share alike. Trade and all."

"We do that at home, too," O.T. said, nodding. He felt suddenly embarrassed, realizing this huge plate of food was for his benefit, and that Julie-Anne had delved into precious rations to make him and Ginny welcome. And here he was gripin' about his lot.

"Although, these days we can't git by on trade. Folks all want the almighty dollar. Things ain't like they used to be."

"No they ain't. Times is a'changin'; they rollin' on, and we got no choice but to roll with 'em or die standin' still," Julie-Anne said sagely.

"Yes'm."

"Well, I aim to hear more of yer story later on. I want to hear all about this twin of yers, yer wife and yer sister, and how you came to have a letter from my Sivvy. But fer now, I got to finish brekkus for the rest of the brood and get to work for the day. I got canning, shelling, and knittin' to do. And then got to git ready for the shuckin' tonight. If you aim to talk some, mebbe you can help with the shellin', and so can yer gal. In about an hour or so."

"Sure thing, ma'am."

"Finish up that brekkus. You eat ever' bite—you too dad-blamed skinny. Skin and bones you is. Then when you done you can head on out to the barn and meet the boys. They'll be glad to make yer acquaintance."

After breakfast, O.T. walked, uncomfortably full, out into the snowy yard. The trees on the ridge were dark and curved, leaning toward the sun that shone dimly through the snow clouds. It had snowed at least three inches overnight, and the yard was blanketed in white, save for a trail of footprints that led to the barn, which together with the house sat atop a large hill. Two houses and a lean-to could be seen at the bottom of the slope, and he imagined that the rest of Julie-Anne's close-knit family lived in these houses.

In the barn O.T. was greeted by warm air from a roaring wood stove, threaded with tobacco smoke. Five men were gathered there, four of them playing a variety of instruments. A little girl in pigtails and a puffy coat played with a dirty, hairless doll in the corner.

"How'do," O.T said, as the men fell silent. The fiddle player—a man with black hair, a sharp nose, and high cheekbones—set down his instrument and came forward, holding out his hand.

"Welcome, man," he said, giving O.T.'s hand a hearty shake. "Mama tol' me yer name, but I'm afraid I disremember it just now. Oliver?"

"Owen," O.T. said agreeably. "But call me O.T. Ever'body does."

"How'do, O.T.," the man replied with a smile. "I'm DeWitt Hargrove, Julie-Anne's son. I live just down the hill. Gesturing to the man with the mouth harp, he said, "That there's my brother Nate Jr., and the banjo player is Franklin, my sister Rebecca's oldest son. He lives in the other house down the hill. That old timer over there in the corner being useless is my pap."

The old man came forward, his face wide and kind beneath his salt-and-pepper hair. He wiped his hand on his overalls before reaching forward to clasp O.T.'s in a warm greeting. "Nathaniel Hargrove's the name," he said. "Julie-Anne is my wife. You're welcome here, so you are."

"Thank ya, sir," O.T. said.

"The little gal over there is Nona-Lee, the baby," Nathaniel said. "Our spring surprise, we like to call her. I got grandbabies older'n her, but she's the baby of the whole fambly." The little girl, absorbed in feeding her baby doll, took no notice of the new arrival.

"We thank ya for havin' us," O.T. repeated. "And I'm looking forward to the corn shuck tonight. Misrus Julie-Anne tells me it's a highlight of the year."

"Of the winter time, anyhow," Nate replied. "Us menfolks look forward to it for the drink and the music, accorse." He nodded to the younger men behind him who had all started picking at their instruments again. "You play atall?"

O.T. hesitated for a moment before answering. "I do; that is, I did. I been playin' the banjo since I was a boy, but I don't no more."

"Fell outta tune?"

"No, sir. I just lost the taste for it, I reckon."

"Well, we got us a banjo player, anyhow. Frank'll play just about anythin' after hearin' it the once't. And he made that banjo hisself. He makes 'em and sells 'em time to time, 'specially around Christmas. Folks travelin' thu like to buy thangs like that, novelty thangs."

"I never seen a banjo like that before," O.T. replied. "Never made one myself. The one I had was a gift from my pa. Heard tell he bought it from a shop in Athens. I don't have it no more, though."

"I'll show you how to make one, if'n you has time," Franklin said quietly. "If you have the interest, that is. Then you kin make one of yourn if you ever take a aim to."

"Much obliged," O.T. said , nodding his head.

"We're gon' get back to it, if'n you want to pop a squat and have a listen," Nate said, bringing an old engraved silver and copper harmonica to his lips. "Or if you change yer mind and wanta join us."

"Thank ya kindly," O.T. said with a smile. "I'm gon' run back in the house and see my gal is up and at 'em. We had a long ride up the mountain last night. But I'm lookin' forward to hearin' y'all tonight."

"Yes'r."

O.T. exited the barn as the strains of the music resumed.

Julie-Anne's house was cozier upon his return than it had been when he'd left, filled with the aroma of toasting pecans and baking bread.

Ginny sat at the tiny kitchen table, drinking a cup of sassafras tea. "Takin' a likin' to this stuff," she said, by way of greeting as O.T. took a seat beside her.

"Uncle Walt used to like it, too," O.T. remarked. "When we was boys."

"Same as the tree, right, Deddy? The old tree on the farm...." Ginny trailed off, her cheeks coloring.

"Yeah, it's one and the same," O.T. said, giving her shoulder a squeeze.

"I'd like to know how to make this. If I can."

"I'm sure somebody around this place would be happy to learn ya," O.T. said with a smile, remembering the afternoon in the motorcar, when he'd shown Betty Lou and Sivvy his favorite sassafras tree. Sivvy mentioned how much she loved sassafras tea, and how the mountain people—her people—drank it all the time. And now O.T.

was with those same people. And his daughter, Ginny, was drinking sassafras tea. Life sure was funny sometimes.

"I cain't remember the last time I had such a big breakfast," Ginny exclaimed.

"Enjoy it," O.T. said. "Once we leave outer the mountains, I cain't guarantee we'll eat half as good."

"We goin' to the corn shucking tonight?" Ginny asked.

"Accorse we will. Cain't make our way down the mountain in this snow, so we'll stay on a day or two, if they'll have us. Misrus Julie-Anne already invited us to go along."

"You should play yer banjo with 'em, Deddy."

"They ast me, but I don't reckon I will," O.T. replied.

"Why not?"

"You know I don't play no more," O.T. said. "I ain't got the feel for it." Banjo playing was for the former Owen Tolbert Lawrence, the O.T. Lawrence who had had a beautiful young wife and a twin brother and a cotton farm and a nice spot of land with a creek and walking trails and pretty trees; not for this broken shell of a man, this alcoholic fast approaching thirty, with three motherless children, no friends, and no future to speak of. And anyway, he'd smashed his banjo. No use in picking up anybody else's.

"Deddy, you sure can be irritatin'," Ginny said with a grin, and went back to her bacon.

"Where's Misrus Julie-Anne?" O.T. asked.

"On the back porch, shellin' peas."

O.T. found the old woman sitting in a rickety rocking chair, shelling what looked to be purple hull peas. It was a wonder her hands weren't frozen to the bone, he mused, sitting out in the winter air.

"When my gal said you was out here shellin' peas, I figured she was tellin' a fib," O.T. said, sitting down in the rocker beside her. "How on earth you got purple hulls in the middle of the winter?"

"They ain't purple hulls," Julie-Anne said, handing him a pea. The skin was purplish, but mottled with gray-green spots, and had a slightly hairy feel to it, almost like okra, but smoother. "They's winter peas."

"Ain't never heard of such," O.T. said, wonderingly.

"I hadn't neither, till I met a man a few years back who was travelin' and wanted to make a trade. He was here on a hikin' trip, if'n you can believe it—wanted to walk the whole of the Appalachian trail. Said it was a life dream a'his. I laughed to beat the band. Can you imagine? Havin' so much time on yer hands you want to do a fool thing like that! Walk from Georgia clear to Maine!" She laughed again.

"Don't sound like a bad way to spend a few months," O.T. answered with a wry smile.

"Heck naw, it ain't, but it just tickled my fancy. Us mountain folks, we's alus trampin' through the mountains, up and down trails, huntin' and fishin' and buildin' and whatnots. It ain't a thing to us. Imagine travelin' half across the world to go trampin' down some mountain trail. Dodgin' the bears and the foxes and gettin' hypothermia in yer delicate places, just to say you done it. Some folks ain't got no sense." Her raspy, cackling laugh was music to O.T.'s ears.

"So he gave you the peas?"

"Ayuh. Traded 'em. I met up with him at Harvey's gen'rul store. He had some seeds and things from his country, stuff he'd brought with him that he wanted to see would it grow here. I warn't too interested in most of it—flowers and thangs—but I took some of the peas. Planted 'em in the fall, like he said to do. I didn't have no hope that they'd grow, cause ain't nothin' stayin' alive in these cold winters, not on this rock, let me tell ya. But then the little thangs grew! And grew *good,* too! I had the biggest crop a'them peas that winter. And let me tell you, they's good eatin'. Sweet and hearty and we live on 'em this time a'year."

"Winter peas." O.T. slid over one of her buckets and started shelling.

"Ayuh. That's what he called 'em. Reckon that man was from Austria, come to remember it," She looked to the side, remembering. "I said something or nuther about that funny man they got over there, the one with that ugly black hair and the mustache that looks like a broom. Their *fur-yer* or whatever they call him. And he din't laugh, no, not one bit. Didn't find it particular funny atall. Said he warn't from the same place, didn't want me to make that mistake."

"Mr. Hitler, I believe," O.T. confirmed.

"Just call the joker Hitler. Ain't no mister about him," Julie-Anne said scornfully. "Hope they'll hang him in town square just as soon as look at 'im. Somethin' ain't right about that man atall. And that mustache. Looks like a dang broom."

"I don't reckon he'll amount to nothin'," O.T. said, though he didn't know much about the man; he didn't read the newspaper anymore. "Sounds to me like he's more a clown than a politician. Folks ain't gonna go for that."

"Don't be so sure, young man. Politickin' ain't nuthin' but a show, and it's right skeery what folks'll do for a bit of entertainment."

"Mayhap you're right," O.T. admitted. "I cain't stand to think about it. I ain't talkin' politics if I can help it. I swear, it just gets to me, the thangs some of these folks say. Don't seem Christian at all, if you don't mind my sayin', ma'am."

"Naw, I don't mind atall, 'cause I agree with ya," Julie-Anne replied, her hands a blur of movement, deftly shelling the peas twice as fast as O.T. "Like that joker, Talmadge. The things he *says* about folks. Good, hardworking folks, just 'cause they colored, he thinks he can make a judgment on 'em. Deny them they livin'. And he don't treat the poor whites no better. Thinks he's gon' cast the lot on poor folks and colored folks, blamin' 'em for ever sin that's happened since the days of Eve," she said, her voice dropping to a conspiratorial whisper. "And folks lap it right up, Mr. O.T. They lap it up like peach ice cream."

"Yes'm," O.T. answered. "Reckon they do where I'm from, and all."

"Blame somebody else, ain't got to look at yerself," Julie-Anne said. "Ain't got to get right, if you figger ever'body else is wrong."

"That, and just plain meanness. Folks like an excuse to hate," O.T. agreed bitterly. "It's like darts, I reckon. Folks need a dartboard to throw 'em at, my brother Walt used to say."

"Interesting way to put it," Julie-Anne remarked with a chuckle. "But it ain't wrong."

"Seems like things just get worse and worse as the years ago by," O.T. remarked, ripping a string from a pea-shell and tossing it into the trash bucket. "The poorer we get, the drier the dirt is, the less cotton we can grow, and somehow we try blamin' the Negroes for it, like it's they fault. They work cheaper for the sharecroppers, and somehow that's they fault, too. Man got to make a livin'. We holdin' out 'cause we too proud to take a penny less, but blamin' them for takin' what they can get. And it goes on and on. One of these days they gon' rise up—" He made an exploding noise and clapped his hands together. "It'll be no less than what we deserve, tell the truth."

"Amen," Julie-Anne replied, looking down at her work. "It's like that ever'where, though. I heared that the further south you git, the worse the colored folks have it."

"I dunno," O.T. replied. "I ain't ever been south of home; aimin' to go after I leave here, though."

"I confess we sheltered up here. We got a fair amount of colored famblies in these parts; most of 'em is related to each other. We git along just fine, most of the time. Mix with each other and trade with each other and generally friendly-like. Them what don't like it know if they start shoutin' too loud, we'll shout right back and run 'em off our rock. The gen'ral store is run by a colored man. He been running it for dern near ten year now, and he does a fine job. Gives folks credit when they need it, charges a fair price, and nice as the dickens. He and his wife got a couple of sweet lil' kids'll come help you any time you need it. Right good folks." She held out her gnarled arm, covered in liver spots and threaded with large, bluish veins. "My skin's damn near brown as a berry, anyhow, ain't it?"

"So it is," O.T. agreed with a smile.

"Tell ya a lil' secret, young fella," Julie-Anne said, leaning close enough that O.T. could smell the raw peas and snuff on her breath. "I ain't what you call solely a white woman, myself."

"Is that right?" O.T. grinned. He was a little in love with this old woman, he reckoned.

"Nawp. My fambly did what they call, uh, assimilated, I reckon's the word…back in the old days, affore the turn of the centry. After that burr-headed bastard Jackson run 'em all out on a rail, sent 'em down the cryin' trail. A lot of folks stayed behind and either hid up in the mountains or tried to blend in. My people did a little a'both. My grandparents on both sides was native folks. Mama's ma was Cherokee, and her deddy was full blooded Creek. They met at one of the schools that aimed to teach native folks English. I say 'teach' but it was more like forcin' 'em at rifle point.

"Then my deddy's folks—his deddy was part Cherokee, too, his folks having hid it out in the mountains for several generations. Deddy spoke the language fluently. And his ma, well, she passed as a white lady and you'd never hear him tell otherwise, but she was part colored—her ma had had relations with a black man who was passin' thu—an escaped slave, heard tell. Never did know who he was. Big family secret, it were, but I know all my fambly's business." She stuck out her thin chest proudly. "So ya see, this skin is Cherokee and Creek and black too, besides. And Lawd, ain't I proud to say so! I'm a mountain mutt lady, yes sirree!"

O.T. burst out laughing. "And a right charmin' one ya are, ma'am," he said, grinning.

"Thank ya kindly. Lawd knows I embarrass the dickens out of my poor chillun'."

"And yer hushand?" O.T. asked. "Nathaniel?"

"Did you catch sight of the man?" Julie-Anne asked with a grin. "Short and fat and round all over, with them rosy cheeks and that grin? Shoot, he ain't got so much as a drop of color in him. He's white all over, ever'where it counts." She chuckled. "His folks came from over the way. Highlander folks, they was. Straight from the isles. Shoot, I like to tell Nate that I half expect him to come walkin' in one day wearin' one of them tartan skirts to bed."

O.T. blushed and glanced down at the peas in his lap, but a laugh escaped his lips.

"Don't act so scandalized. You's a grown man about the world, ain't ye?"

"Yes'm." O.T.'s cheeks burned. Betty Lou would have loved Julie-Anne too, O.T. thought with a pang.

"It's true, though. Nary a thing we got up in the mountains din't come from them Highlander folks, or the Indians besides. Our drink, the way we talk, our love of music and poetry. Shoot, I heared tell that the music we play on our fiddles and mouth harps is the very same that you hear in one of them castles across the water. And the jig-dancin', too. I reckon we'd be right at home in Sir Robert's castle.

"I got me a receipt from one of Nate's old aunts. She was old as the dickens, damn near a hundert when we got marrit, and she lived another twenty year after that. Anyhow, she gave me a receipt for these little cakes she said came from Scotlan'. Good, they are too. If you can git good flour, that is. Tipperarys, they's called. And I got me a receipt for a soup, too; gosh durnit, now I want to make it. Cockaleekie soup. Shore is good."

"Cockaleekie?" O.T, looked at her in disbelief, fighting the urge to laugh. "You a lie."

"I ain't lied a day in my life," Julie-Anne grinned. "'Cept in bed."

O.T. burst out laughing.

They shelled peas for a few moments in silence. Despite the frigid mountain cold, O.T. felt surprisingly comfortable on the little back porch. The tin roof and makeshift tarp curtains shielded most of the wind, and the shelling warmed up the blood in his hands.

"Well, I reckon I should tell you how I came to know Sivvy," O.T. started at last.

Julie-Anne nodded, still shelling, and did not look up from her work. "Ayuh. Reckon so."

O.T. told her of the 1916 tent revival, when he'd first met the girl. He could hear Julie-Anne sniffling beside him as he talked, her hands clenched around a handful of peas. He didn't look at her, just told the story from start to finish. The only part he left out was the fact that he'd been the one to go on the date with Sivvy. He figured no use could come of dredging up that old secret.

"So," he said finally. "Here we are, I reckon. She said she wanted to write to y'all but just couldn't find the courage. She was afraid y'all wouldn't care to know her no more, I think. That you'd be shamed."

"She oughter know better than that," Julie-Anne said sadly, staring out at the snowy woods beyond the porch. "She oughter know that we could never judge her or be shamed of her. She's our gal, my baby girl, ain't she?" Her voice broke, and it hurt O.T.'s heart.

"I reckon she's scared," he said, putting a hand on the old woman's arm. "I would be, were it me. It sounds like she's had a real hard road and ain't knowed who she could trust."

"Shore couldn't trust her Uncle Billy, could she?" the old woman cried, dropping her head in her hands, her long, gray hair streaming around her fingers. "And twas all my fault, and her deddy's. We shoulda kep' her safe and we didn't. We shoulda knowed that scoundrel was up to no good."

O.T. didn't know what to say. None of this was any of his business, and he felt it acutely, but hadn't he come here to tell of Sivvy's plight?

"I suppose you'll be wantin' to know why she left in the firs' place," Julie-Anne said in a pained voice. "I don't know all the reasons why she's locked in that place, but I reckon I can guess at it. I do know why she left here when she warn't but fourteen. I can tell you that much."

"Only if you want to," O.T. said gently.

"I might as well," Julie-Anne replied wearily. "Sivvy reached out to you, or yer brother, I reckon; the least I can do is tell what I know. Ain't much, but you drove all this way."

O.T. waited for her to speak.

Julie-Anne took a ragged breath, set down her bucket of shelled peas, and clasped her hands over her white apron. Then she began to talk.

God, it had been so long since Sivvy had felt the touch of a man.

Sivvy lay on her cot, ignoring the pains in her hips and back, remembering what it had been like to lie in a *real* bed, one with a mattress. Corn shuck mattresses, they had been, when she was a gal. Mama had crocheted an afghan for each of her children. Sivvy's had been butter yellow with coffee-brown and robin's egg blue, and it had cocooned her girlhood years in nighttime warmth and softness—a thing of comfort. Then, later, lying in bed with a man, in a bed you *shared*, seemed a novelty to her now, a memory that wasn't real, couldn't have been real. It had been so many years since she'd opened her eyes to stare at someone's bare back, to count the freckles there; to see the rise and fall of sleeping breath; to hear a little snore; to see a toss of the shoulder, a clutch of the coverlet; to hear the creak of old bones.

Sivvy had loved her husband in the end, as best she could, which made her pain all the more piercing; when you loved people, you *always* suffered for it—Sivvy had learned that much, by God. Still, it had been so long that she couldn't help but yearn a little. What might she do, Sivvy mused, to feel the warm touch of a man's fingers on her skin?

The nurses, pinch-faced and disapproving, told stories of women who had sought the company of men, how even bars on their windows could not stop them; how they'd stand up in the windows, lift their skirts, and push those private, tender parts of themselves between the bars…and wait.

The inmates, for the most part, were skeptical, but Sivvy believed the stories. *A person gets too desperate, too lonely, and propriety goes out the window.* She laughed inwardly at her own joke. And she thought of her earlier conversation with Faye and the possibility of greater freedom. She would have to ask somehow. Find out. But quietly. In secret. To trade one kind of freedom for another—giving up the freedom to bear a child for a little extra time alone outside, and possibly a little contact now and then. Perhaps the procedure would not be so bad.

CHAPTER FIFTEEN

"When Sivvy was born, she come out all regal, like a queen, with an expression of peace on her little red face. I figgered if I wasn't havin' no more young'uns I'd put ever name I never got to use on this lil' gal. I didn't know, see, that Nona-Lee would be comin' after. Savilia Marie Tryphena Hargrove is her Christian name, and even with all those names to go on ever'body still just called her Sivvy. She arrived like royalty and ruled over us all like royalty, so she did. We spoilt the dickens outta her. Ever'body did.

"She was always teeny, skinny as a poor woman's slip, and short. You'd think a lil' gal like that would be sickly, but not my Sivvy. She was sturdy as a horse and a lil' tomboy. Her skirt could be knee-deep in mud and she was still walkin' around like a princess, carryin' on with those shoulders back, and that haughty tilt of her head. I figgered if any of my chillun was gon' get outta this place, it'd be her. Turns out I was right, but not in the way I figgered.

"They's a school near here, the Rock Creek School, and a right jolly teacher named Ella Shunt. She's been teachin' there for over twenty year and taught all my chillun but the oldest two. Anyhow, when Sivvy was six years old she started in to askin' about goin' to school. It was a fair walk to the school for a lil' slip of a gal like her, and me and Nate hesitated 'bout lettin' her go. We had too much work to do around here, you see, to be walkin' her there ever'day. And her brothers could do it sometime, but on the days when they was home helpin' us, she'd have to go it alone. It's just shy of two mile, and that don't sound like much for po' folks who is used to walkin', but it's over the mountain, through a grove of thick pine trees, and back up a steep hill. There's a creek you got to cross over, that leads into the Toccoa River, and for much of the trail the trees is so thick you'd never see a body that got lost. Sivvy knew the way; she were always good with direction and she'd been on that walk a thousand times, but I were nervous about her goin' it alone. Might be bears, or a fox, or some man out in the woods lookin' fer trouble. She was my baby, you see, my youngest, and I doted and worrit on her.

But in the end she won out and we let her go. We spoilt her rotten. Miss Ella Shunt offered to meet Sivvy at the foot of the trail ever' mornin' and she knew if Sivvy were more than five minutes late to go searchin' for her. That gave me peace of mind. Ain't none of us could stand the thought of denyin' lil' Sivvy the right to go to school. It was all she wanted in the world.

"So the summer she was six, she started goin' to her lessons at the Rock Creek School. Loved ever' minute of it. Ever day she'd come home just a'talkin' about what she'd learned that day, would just about talk my blame ear off. Ain't nothin' that child loved more than school. Ever' morning she'd go off faithfully with her lil' lunch pail; I packed her the same lunch ever' day—a baked sweet tater, a little bread or corn pone with honey, and a hard boiled egg—and pulled her knitted cap over her ears. She knew Miss Ella was waitin' for her at the foot of the trail and took care never to be late. She was always the most serious of all my chillun.

"Sivvy had just turned seven and had been in school for about a year when Nate's fambly came to stay. They tol' us they was aimin' to build them a house on some of our land if we was agreeable. This land is mine, but I didn't have no qualm about holpin' out my husband's kin. So we said awright. It was his ma, who had long ago gone blind; his pa, who had the rheumatis bad; and Nate's younger brother, William Brandon Hargrove, who came with his wife. Ever'body called Nate's brother Billy since he was knee-high to a grasshopper. Billy din't look nothin' like Nate or his folks. He was well over six feet tall and skinny as a rail.

"Nate and Billy ain't really brothers, you see. Hear tell that when my Nate was about two, the woman next door died of smallpox and her man up and run off with some harlot, leaving a wee baby behind. That was Billy. Poor wee thing din't have no relations or kin to care fer him and woulda been sent to the orphanage, but Nate's folks took him in and treated him like they own. Never once heard 'em mention that Billy wasn't their own blood relation. Shoot, Nate and I had been marrit for two year at least affore he ever thought to mention it to me. They was just brothers, and close enough when they was young'uns. But Billy changed as he got older. My Nate is just as kind-hearted and hard workin', but Billy ain't so much like that. He's a bitter, resentful man who feels like he's owed thangs he ain't ever got. And lazy, shoot. You never see the like.

"Truth told, I din't care a lick for Billy, though his wife, Nona Leigh, was sweet as can be. My youngest, Nona Lee, is named after her. She helped me that whole summer in the kitchen, that first year they was there; did so much canning, I could scarce believe how fast she could work. I got the idear that she wanted to get out of that house. She did all the carin' for Billy and Nate's folks, which warn't easy, along with keepin' the house, cookin', and helpin' me as much as she could. She was a work horse to beat the band. Bein' around her made me feel right lazy. Us two got real close, and the kids loved her, too.

"All the young'uns went down to Billy and Nona Leigh's cottage all the time, visiting with their grandparents and they uncle and aunt. Nate and I was swarmed with chillun and we was happy to let our kids take up with our fambly much as they want to. Even blind and half bedridden, Nate's folks was both so good to my chillun.

"My daughter Becca lives in that cottage now. She got marrit and went off to Tennessee fer a while, but her husband Jeduthan—Jed— died in a loggin' accident 'bout sixteen years ago. Becca ain't never remarried and turns down ever' offer she gets. And my grandson, Franklin, the young buck with the black hair, ain't never had no papa. We love 'em dearly, but shoot, I wish my Becca could land her another husban' before I'm cold in the grave. She need somebody, we all need somebody, don't we?

"I'm gettin' off the rails again. We're gonna miss the corn shuckin' altogether if'n I can't tighten it up.

"I rankin' Billy and Nona was tryin' to start they own fambly, but warn't havin' no luck with it. Billy didn't never say nothin' bout it, but we all knowed that he wanted a son and he wanted him quick. Nona would tell me in secret, blushin' to beat the band and her face all scrunched up, tryin' to fight the tears, poor dear—all about how it was her fault that she couldn't give him no son. He told her that if he'd knowed she was barren, he never woulda taken her to wife and would've left her to rot in Farmington where she came from. I never did tell Nate about that business, 'cause he woulda tol' me to mind my own, and anyhow, the things women whisper to each other is our own affair, and Nona woulda been shamed. But I ached to say to Billy that it might be *his* fault; maybe he were the one who had all the trouble. And even if he din't, what cause did he have to speak to his wife so harsh, to blame her so? The Good Lord giveth and taketh, and He din't see fit to give them no baby. It were sad to be sure, but they warn't the first marrit couple to have such trebles. And by this time Billy had already started dabblin' in the good book and had aims to be a preacher. He ought have been on his knees prayin', astin' the Good Lord to bless him and his wife with a child. And he oughter be treatin' his wife better, not worse, I reckoned. I kep' my peace, but the more I saw and heard, the more I hated that man. He warn't nothin' like my Nate, who is the kindest soul you ever did meet. And that's how I know he ain't really Nate's blood.

"Sivvy took a real shine to her aunt. Nona Leigh taught her to bake, and Sivvy could turn out the best apple cake you ever saw, and hummingbird cakes and sour cream cola cake and anythin' you could dream up. Them two had a right special bond.

"All that time Billy was still studyin' up to be a preacher. By the summer Sivvy was thirteen, he had started doing sermons down the ridge at the church. Our pastor was real old and goin' soft in the haid, and he din't mind handin' over the reins to Billy now and again. Billy delivered a few sermons and presided over a few weddin's and it seemed like it was to be his callin'. We was right glad because he was durn near forty by the time he'd finally settled down to do somethin'. He went off to do tent revivals all across the state for the next two summers and would stay gone for two months or more. Nona Leigh was never more cheerful than when he was gone.

"Nate's folks caught the flu that fall and both died within a week of each other. The kids was sad, accorse, but Sivvy took it hardest. She quit goin' to school for almost a month and quit goin' down to Nona Leigh and Billy's, too. I reckoned it was too hard for her to be in that house without her grandparents there. Least that's what I thought then.

"Soon after that Billy started comin' up to us. Said he couldn't be in the house with Nona Leigh, said that she was squallin' and carryin' on, that she blamed herself for the death of the old folks. Billy took to eatin' supper with us, and after he'd always preach a sermon, practicin' like. Sivvy would always leave for her bedroom when Billy started in, and it right offended him, but I wasn't aimin' to stop her. Billy was all show and bluster, and I wasn't gon' force Sivvy to sit there and stomach it neither. I couldn't figger out why it bothered Billy so. She wadn't the first teenage girl to glaze over at a sermon and wouldn't be the last.

"One night Billy tol' us how he aimed to make Sivvy a woman of the Lord, an apprentice, like. We laughed to beat the band. Not 'cause she were a girl, mind—reckon a woman kin do whatever she aims to—but 'cause Sivvy din't have a care in her head for no preachin'. Of all my chillun she was the least likely to ever pick up the good book for a sermon. But Billy jes' said the Lord works in mysterious ways and folks kin change. Sivvy could already read and write, he said, and could sing those hymns so purdy. He reckoned it'd be a waste of her talents if she didn't devote 'em to God.

"I wondered then if he had discussed this with Sivvy, and maybe that was why she weren't goin' down for visits no more. He got right teary eyed, talkin' about Nona bein' lonely, and how Sivvy's comp'ny was a balm to her. But Sivvy refused to go. I ast if they'd been a fallin' out or sumpin', and she said naw. I went down myself to see Nona, and she seemed a bit damp aroun' the edges, sad, like. But Nona Leigh always were kinda deflated that way.

"Not long after that Nona Leigh passed on, and Billy played the part of the grievin' widower to a tee, carryin' on, just a snifflin' and a'sobbin, and wringin' his hands. I don't like to stand in judgment of a man a'God, but I tell ya, young fella, Billy was right glad to be rid of his Nona Leigh. He spent the next few weeks at church, getting spiritual guidance, and hittin' up Nate for 'shine. I turned a blind eye to that, 'cause he'd lost his wife and he wasn't the first man to take to drink. I turned so many blind eyes, y'see. So many that I really *was* blind when I shoulda been seein'.

"Then one night Sivvy came to us—lookin' like she'd growed up and become a woman overnight, her baby fat all gone, her eyes tired and sad—and tol' us that she was goin' to leave the ridge with Billy! We thought it was a joke at first. She tol' us that Billy Rev—that's what she called him—couldn't stay in that house no more, that all the memories of his poor dead wife and his parents were gettin' to him. So he decided it was time to start up his travelin' sermons again, jes' as soon as the last frost melted. Sivvy said that she had decided to go with him, that she wanted to honor the memory of her aunt by leadin' folks to the Lord.

"We argued with her all night, tol' her that she din't owe him a thang, that we'd already tol' him no. But Sivvy said she'd always knowed this was her callin', and that schoolin' had prepared her to read the good book and write sermons. I ast her din't she want to grow up and get marrit, and she looked down at her feet and said in a little voice, 'I don't reckon.' We couldn't sway her; her mind made up.

"The next mornin' Billy came for her, so smug he was, and sober for once. He had him a new outfit—a white pressed suit with a black collar-tie, and a wide-brimmed hat that hid half his face. He looked more like a used car salesman than a preacher man, but I held my tongue. Billy said he was givin' up the 'shine, that the Lord had another plan for him. I'd never seen him so happy; shoot, I hadn't seen him smile in years. And then he done tol' us that this is what Nona Leigh woulda wanted, and din't we want to honor her? I could have slapped him silly right then and there, but then I looked over at my Nate, saw the tears on his face. He looked proud and hopeful. And being weak, I let myself be convinced too. I wanted to believe that this plan might be a good thing for Sivvy, and Billy too. I'm a woman of faith, even if'n I don't show it, and part of me was proud at the thought of my baby girl traveling around, spreadin' the good word. It seemed easier, see, to give her our blessin', in the hopes that she'd come back soon. But it din't amount to a hill of beans, because here it is fifteen year later, and she ain't never come back.

"Billy got that house all packed up, gave half of his stuff away, and the other half tucked into that ol' truck he bought. There were barely room for the two of 'em to set in it. Emptied that whole house and left not a sign that he or Nona Leigh or nobody ever lived there. Lookin' back, I shoulda known right then that he wasn't plannin' to return. I was blind as a bat. Sivvy had packed up a little bag, and she got up in the front seat of that truck with her uncle, and they left out one Friday afer'noon. That was the last I seen of her. Sivvy was a good gal, ain't sayin' she wadn't, but she didn't have no head for the gospel. I never could wrap my head around why she went, and I reckon I'll be studyin' on it fer the rest of my life, unless I clap eyes on her again and can ast her. And that don't look likely, do it, young fella?"

"There was one afternoon, after the sermon in Five Forks," O.T. began, with a sudden vision of Betty Lou behind the wheel of the Ford, her hair whipping in the wind, and Walt, all smiles, his gray eyes alight, "when we decided to go for a ride in the motorcar. When Sivvy came runnin' out of the church and ast to join us? She said her uncle gave her leave to come, but I reckon she was tellin' a story. I think she snuck out when he wasn't payin' attention."

"Sounds like her."

"And she done it again, that same night. And she got caught out somehow. I never did find out who, or how. But he *knew* she'd been up to somethin'. I wasn't there, but I heard tell of how he screamed and hollered in the middle of town. He accused my brother of tarnishin' her, and when she came out to plead with the rev, he wrenched her down the road like a mule that got outta the pasture."

Misrus Julie-Anne's mouth pursed in a hard line. "Wanted to remind yer brother of what was his, I reckon. My poor gal. I'd love to git my hands on Billy; I'd wring his neck like a bird for the Sunday table." She laughed joylessly. "You know what the Bible says about accusin'?"

"Not right off, ma'am."

"Long and short of it, the guilty might accuse the innocent of the things theyselves is doin'," she said. "But I don't reckon the good ol' Billy Rev is gon' be pluckin' out his own offensive eye no time soon," she said, brushing pea shells off her apron. "What kinda preacher was he? What kind of things did he say in sermon?"

"Fire and brimstone, mainly," O.T. answered. "Didn't care for it much myself. Didn't as a young man, and still don't now. Ain't nothin' gon' scare me into doin' right. I either do right or I do wrong, but either way, the devil ain't got nothin' to do with it."

"You jes' right," Julie-Anne replied. "But my gal getting' wrapped up into it…well, I jes' hate that so bad." She shook her head sorrowfully. "I don't like to talk about this no more."

O.T. looked down, guilty. "I'm awful sorry, ma'am."

Julie-Anne sighed, putting a hand on his arm. "It's awright, young fella. I ain't tryin' to be angry with ya, no sirree. I'm right grateful yer here, that you've given me news of my gal. I know a sight more than I knew yesterday. And I'm glad to know she's free of 'im, even if she's stuck in that awful place. My poor gal." Then she smiled, her face brightening. "Come on, let's get ourselves washed up and readied for the corn shuckin'. Bad news'll keep. We can chaw the fat some more tomorry when we're good and hungover and feelin' like shit'll be right in keepin'."

"Yes'm." O.T. couldn't help but smile as he followed Julie-Anne into the house. She was a tough old bird.

CHAPTER SIXTEEN

"Right pleased to meet y'all." The woman who shook O.T.'s hand was very tall, with a serene, smooth face and the same eyes as her mother. Her dark brown hair was pulled back in a bun and covered with a bonnet that had gone out of style several decades before, but it became her nonetheless. "I'm Rebecca."

"You kin call 'er Becca, if'n you please," Julie-Anne said, giving her daughter a nudge. "We all do."

"It's very nice to make yer acquaintance, Rebecca—Becca," O.T. said politely.

"All the neighbors ain't arrived yet, but we kin go ahead and start shuckin'," Julie-Anne said, guiding O.T. by the elbow into a small parlor. "By the time everybody is here they ain't gon' be sittin' room fer us all, so might as well pick you out a good spot."

O.T. settled on a chair in the corner, and Ginny sat at his feet. He felt a little on display; folks turned to stare at him, no doubt wondering who these strangers were.

There were at least twelve families from around the ridge who had come to the corn shucking; folks that weren't related to the Hargrove family but obviously knew them well. O.T. tried to remember all the names as folks were introduced—Jean and Gene, a married couple that he found charming, a withered old man simply called "Bug," Eliza, Landron, Melanie, Percy, Hamish, Lillie. And of course all of Julie-Anne's young'uns, save one, some of whom he'd met—Becca, DeWitt, Adam, Nate Jr., Clark, Newton, Isham, and Nona-Lee. Everyone was most welcoming. Packages were pressed into his hand—parched peanuts, dried tobacco, tea leaves, homemade lye soap scented with honeysuckle. O.T. was touched, and he wished he had something to give in return.

"These folks is so—" Ginny began, squeezing O.T.'s calf affectionately, "—so different. They're warm and friendly."

"I like 'em," O.T. said with a smile.

"I do, too."

The little parlor was soon so full of people that there was barely standing room, just as Julie-Anne had promised. Suddenly, Nate was pushing his way through the crowd, a huge shock of corn on his back. He threw it in the middle of the floor, right on the embroidered rug, then returned with more shocks of corn, again and again, until the stack of corn was almost as high as a man was tall. "Let's get us started!" he proclaimed with a grin, pushing his knitted hat off his head.

Folks gathered around, grabbing big shocks of corn, ripping off the papery skins and throwing them in one pile, and tossing the silks in another. There was an art to it, O.T. could see. He'd grown corn on his own farm and shucked aplenty, but watching these folks do it in one fluid motion, working in perfect time with each other, was very interesting. *Crack, shuck, pull, crack, shuck, pull.* Conversations ebbed and flowed around him, people talking about their kids, the weather, and next year's crop. He was content to listen, to bask in the soothing lilt of their mountain accents, to smell the smoke of their pipes and the sharp scent of freshly shucked corn. Ginny was a firm, sweet presence at his feet.

O.T. caught the eye of a man seated by the door, who was himself staring at O.T. with a curious expression. He had a huge shock of corn in his large, muscular arms, and without a glance for his work, he cracked the stalk, then pulled off the entire shuck in one swift motion. O.T. was startled, not just because the man was staring at him so intently but because he was black.

While O.T. had friends who were colored, folks didn't mix like this in Five Forks. It was an unwritten rule that had always bothered him, because he reckoned a man should be able to invite whomever he wanted over for a glass of tea, no matter what color, but it just wasn't done. Even if you did the invitin', they weren't going to turn up, O.T. had always told himself.

O.T. was ashamed at the shock he felt, seeing a colored man sitting in Rebecca Hargrove's little parlor. He was even more shocked when he realized the man's wife and two little children were sitting right behind him, all shucking away. When O.T. looked back up from his pile of corn, the man stared at him still and, raising a hand from his work, made a little gesture with his index finger, tapping at the air. It seemed to suggest, "Later." O.T. wasn't sure what it meant, but he nodded back at the man, who smiled in return, and went back to the corn.

The huge pile of corn had gotten smaller by half, and the piles of silks and shucks were everywhere. One of the men left and returned with several huge burlap bags into which everyone stuffed the shucks and silks. All parts of the corn would be put to some purpose or other, and those that could not be used would be fed to the livestock.

O.T. finished shucking his pile of corn and reached for another, shocked to discover that in a little under an hour the work had been completed.

"Oh, what do ya reckon, I got me a red ear!" Ginny exclaimed at his feet, holding an ear of corn that had burgundy-colored jewels instead of the usual yellow. "I ain't seen one of these in a long spell!" Ginny grinned in delight.

"Ah, that gal got the red 'un!" said a withered old woman by the woodstove, pointing a gnarled finger at Ginny. "And here I was a'hopin' I'd git it!"

"Hesh yer mouth, woman," said an equally withered old man standing beside her. "Ain't nobody gon' waste no kissin' on you. Besides, yer marrit to me, in case you misremember."

"I remember well enough, you ol' coon dog," the woman said with a mock pout. "How long is it now? Forty year goin' on four hunnert?"

"Shush, you'all." Nate stepped over to Ginny and hoisted her up by her elbow. "Good luck'll come to you this year, gal. The red ear is the good luck ear!"

"Suits me fine, mister! Yes, sirree!" Ginny held the ear up proudly, her face flushed with pleasure.

"And now you got to git yer good luck kissin'," Nate boomed, his hand still on her elbow, propelling her forward.

Ginny stopped, turning a little white. "Wait…what? My good luck what?"

"Kissin'," Nate replied, turning to her with a broad, jolly grin. "The fella or gal that gits the red ear has good luck fer the whole year. Everybody gives 'em a kiss to seal the deal, reckon. Otherwise it ain't gon' take."

"I…I…" Ginny's lower lip trembled and she looked like she

might've bolted from the little house, if there weren't ten people between her and the door. "I don't know—"

O.T. had to laugh a little, watching his shy, awkward girl. "Aw, come on, honey, it's just for good luck," he said good-naturedly. "Sure could use all we can get."

"Awright." Ginny's face had gone from flushed pink to white and now back to pink again. She gave Nate a dutiful kiss on the cheek, before leaning down to do the same to O.T. "Awright?" she said again, hopefully.

"And now for the rest," Nate said, with a grin. He pushed her forward, into the wrinkled arms of Misrus Julie-Anne, who gave her a hearty smack on her forehead. Then came the withered old woman and her equally withered husband; then Rebecca, who gave her a dutiful kiss on the cheek with dry lips; then little Nona-Lee, who had what looked to be raspberry preserves all over her. Ginny wiped at her face with the back of her hand, and everybody laughed. She was passed around the room, receiving good-natured kisses from everyone, until only Franklin was left—Becca's only son, and Julie-Anne and Nate's grandson. He stood ramrod straight, all six feet, five of him, looking just as embarrassed as Ginny, his dark brown hair falling into his eyes.

"Oh, shoot, look at that," Becca whispered conspiratorially to O.T. "My boy's just as embarrassed as yer gal is. Ain't it cute."

"They're of an age," O.T. whispered back with a grin. "Cain't be easy, kissin' in front of a bunch of old folks, and yer own parents."

"Cain't blame him," Becca replied, standing up and dusting off her apron. He stood up, too. "Yer gal is right pretty."

"I thank ya," O.T. said politely. "She takes after her mama."

"Naw, she looks like you, I reckon." Becca said. She opened her mouth, seemingly wanting to say more, but then shut it again, giving him a little smile and making her way into the little kitchen.

Franklin leaned down, took Ginny gently by the arm, and gave her a chaste peck on the temple. Ginny's face flamed, as did Franklin's. She smiled up at him for just a moment, then thrust the red ear of corn into his arms. "You keep it," she said quickly, her voice shrill. "Keep it for me!" Then she turned and high-tailed it out to the porch, everyone chuckling behind her.

"Youth is wasted on the young, I tell ya," Julie-Anne said from behind O.T.

"Yes'm. You right," O.T. chuckled.

"Help me clear the floor, would ya? If'n you don't mind."

"Not a bit, ma'am." O.T. helped Julie-Anne clear the floor of stray shucks and silks, tossing them into the bulging burlap sacks, then swept with the corncob broom. Becca set out refreshments as Nate and his sons set up their instruments near the door, which had been opened to let in a blast of chilly winter air. O.T. could see Ginny standing just outside, her face blooming with happiness. Embarrassed or not, this place was doing her good, and for that O.T. was right glad.

"Sure you won't play, young fella? I'd love to hear you pick at the banjo some," Nate said, clapping O.T. on the back.

"I don't reckon, thank ya," O.T. replied with a smile. "I ain't played since my wife died. I lost my love for it when I lost her."

"Reckon I'd feel the same if I lost my wife, too," Nate said, glancing over at Julie-Anne, who was rearranging slices of pound cake that Becca had just arranged moments before. "The ol' goat."

The dance had begun inside, but Sivvy was content to sit in an old rocking chair on the large covered porch. The night was calm and still. She couldn't see the moon, but Sivvy knew it was up there, looming down on them, bright and clear. Through the window Sivvy could see several inmates awkwardly gathered on the dance floor, stiffly attempting to dance a jig to a jaunty tune. The slow dances were awkward too—patients attempted to establish eye and body contact without encroaching on each other's delicate neuroses. After years of being holed up in small rooms, orchestrated extracurricular pursuits no longer came naturally. Physical relationships were discouraged; when they formed, despite the odds, those involved were severely punished. Men and women could dance together, strictly supervised by asylum staff, but that was all. What was the point of making eyes at each other, sneaking a feel of someone's back or thigh, when arousing such feelings—feelings they'd been forced to suppress—would only cause trouble? It was a lot to carry around in your pocket while trying to dance with someone, and Sivvy had no interest in trying to navigate that minefield. At least not yet, she mused, her thoughts drifting to Dr. Lowell's procedure.

The strains of jazz blared from the Victrola, and Sivvy felt her feet start to tap. She longed to dance, and had been asked many a time, but Sivvy always declined. It had been a long time since her days of clogging up on the ridge, and dancing felt like an enjoyment she wasn't sure she deserved. Her Christmas fit had been a doozy, but she'd gotten over it. Sivvy couldn't help but wonder if her "madness" was prompted by her environment, her medication, or her circumstances. She had seen things in this place—people who clawed at their faces, who raved and drooled and thought nothing of doing violence to others; patients who were so far gone they didn't know where or who they were. She wasn't like that, Sivvy knew. She was sick, but she did not believe that she was truly mad.

But Sivvy's opinion, like the many others who had pleaded for release, was irrelevant. Some inmates had families that came to claim them, and others, like Sivvy, who had no family left to plead on their behalf, stayed on, and on, and on....

It was clear that if nobody wanted you on the outside, you weren't going anywhere, unless on a gurney. And your chances were even less likely if you made yourself useful, say, in the kitchens. Sivvy couldn't help but think, from time to time, that her usefulness to the asylum far outweighed her own need of the place. Still, if she got released, Uncle Billy would be notified, and would come, all smug and overbearing, to claim her. And given the choice of living out her days in Milledgeville—a long, seemingly endless prospect; Sivvy wasn't yet thirty years old—or being released into her uncle's clutches, she would choose the asylum every time.

"You want you a nip?" O.T. turned, startled, on the porch where he'd been sitting with his back to the wall, staring out into the snowy night. DeWitt Hargrove was holding out a bottle of something that smelled mighty strong. "White Lightnin'. Came from right here on the ridge. Ain't none better."

"Thank ya, but no," O.T. replied, despite the fact that every fiber of his being yearned to say yes. It had been two days since he'd had a drink of any kind, and his body was beginning to ache something fierce. One little nip would take the pains away and set his nerves on the right course, because Lord knew they were on edge. But he wanted to be on his best behavior, not only for Ginny, but for Misrus Julie-Anne Hargrove and her family, too. In Five Forks he had already begun to take on the appearance of a hard-boiled drunk, with skin like leather, his nose red, his eyes watery. He'd flirted with the idea, since spending time on the ridge, that he might just quit.

"I will take a pinch of that tobacco you got there, if'n ya don't mind, though," O.T. said. "I got me a pipe, but I ain't been able to afford good pipe tobaccy since Christmas, and I gave most of that to my sister."

"Right ya are, man." DeWitt fumbled in his pouch and produced a large pinch of tobacco. "Got yer pipe on ya?"

"Yessir. Right here." O.T. pulled his old pipe out of his pocket, put the plug of tobacco in the bowl, and lit a match. The flame glowed bright in the dark, snowy night, then fizzled as he lit the pipe and tossed the match into the snow. "Much obliged."

"Ain't no problem. So my mama said you was from Five Forks, that right?"

"Yessir. Born and raised."

"I been there before, once or twice't. Not in over a year, though. There's a fella from there who comes up thisaway time to time."

"Don't suppose his name is Hosey Brown?"

"Why, yeah, that's the fella!"

"Seems like I can't stop meetin' folks who know Hosey," O.T. said, gesturing toward the bottle DeWitt held. "That's the stuff brings him up here, reckon."

DeWitt grinned and nodded, tipping up the bottle and taking a long swig. O.T. forced himself to look away.

"Been knowin' Hosey since I was knee-high to a grasshopper," O.T. said, puffing on the pipe, the smoke drifting off into the cold air like a floating cotton ball.

"Rankin' you don't like his chosen profession," DeWitt replied, crouching down beside O.T.

"Why you say that?"

"Soon as you realized who I was talking about, a black cloud came over you."

"I guess I don't."

"Why not? Ain't a fella got a right to make a honest livin'?"

"Honest?" O.T. chuckled.

"Hey now, fella, you forgettin' I just tol' you where this here 'shine comes from? Same folks showin' you hospitality is the same folks brewin' it up, you know." DeWitt's voice was kind, but he meant business. "I met a feller from up north once't. Bought him a whole case of this stuff. I thanked him for the transaction and walked off. As I was leavin', I heard him call me a wool hat. Said we ain't got a lick of sense down in these parts, nor a pot to piss in," DeWitt chuckled. "I went back and tol' him he hadn't give me proper change. That he overpaid me. 'Wouldn't want a fine, educated gentleman like yerself to run out of money on the way back to New Jersey,' I said to 'im."

"I don't mean no disrespect. Hell, I ain't got a leg to stand on nohow. Not to be judgin' folks. It's more about Hosey's private business, involvin' my brother. It's a long story. Personal."

"I see." DeWitt took another long swig. O.T. could smell the 'shine on his breath, strong enough to strip bark off a tree. "Ain't no kind of nasty business than when two friends has a fallin' out. We like to joke about the womenfolks, how they's always gossipin' and fallin' out and carryin' on, but when you get a menfolk with a grudge, ain't seen nuthin' to beat that."

"You right," O.T. agreed.

"Still, I reckon we ain't got too many true friends in this world, not really. When ya think on it. So you find one, best to keep him. Problems or not."

"Maybe so," O.T. said. "Complicated, though."

"Ain't it always." DeWitt stood up and stretched. "I got to help Becca put up refreshments, and get the floor cleared away for the music for the young'uns to dance. She ain't got no husban' to help her, you know. Did you git you anythin' to eat? Becca's spice cake is good as anythin' you'll try. Come on in and hear us play and get you a slice."

"I will," O.T. said. "Hey there, DeWitt? I might have me a swig, after all, if'n it's still on offer. Just one."

DeWitt held the bottle down to O.T. with a smile. "Take the rest of it. I got more. Good stuff."

O.T. looked down at the bottle with a sigh. It seemed as if ghosts were flying all around him, haunting him right out of his skin. Betty Lou, Walt, his parents, Sivvy. He wanted to numb his nerves a little, just so he could go back inside and smile at folks. *Takes a little spirit to boost the spirit,* he said to himself dryly, tipping the bottle up to his mouth, swallowing his self-loathing along with the fiery liquid.

When O.T. returned to the parlor, the crowd erupted into a good-natured cheer, and he felt his cheeks flush, leaning against the doorjamb, and hoped his drunkenness wasn't overly apparent. He'd polished off the rest of DeWitt's shine, and he felt spry, warm, and energetic—better than he had in months.

"Where's my gal?" he asked Julie-Anne, who stood nearby, holding a slice of cake.

"She's in the back bedroom with the other young'uns," she replied. "She's perfectly safe, young feller, don't you worry. I think last I saw they was playin' checkers."

"Yes'm." O.T. lingered in the doorway, a grin on his face, watching the scene that was playing out in the parlor. Though it was a small room, at least eight couples were dancing a jig, their feet flying. Nate Sr., DeWitt, Franklin, and several others were playing their instruments furiously. O.T. had never seen a bow fly over a fiddle so fast and started tapping his feet without realizing he was doing so.

"What's this song called?" O.T. asked Julie-Anne, who had pressed a slice of cake into his hand. He took a bite—it was still warm, and sweetly sticky with cloves and cinnamon.

"It's a ditty my husband made up," Julie-Anne said, laughing as she swiped a crumb from O.T.'s chin. "You been hittin' the sauce out there? You look three sheets gone. Nate calls this the 'Shuckin' Hoedown.' He ain't that original, but he plays a fine fiddle."

"I like it," O.T. replied, his mouth full of cake. "What's the dance?"

"Oh, they's just cloggin'," Julie-Anne replied. "Ain't you ever clogged affore?"

"No'm," O.T. said, watching the dancers. "I kin do the Charleston, and a little square dancin', but I ain't never clogged before."

"It's like y'alls animals down there in Five Forks," Julie-Anne cackled. "Git on in there and dance a jig, son. Do you some good."

"I'm like to fall down if I try, but y'all gon on," O.T. said with a laugh.

He hummed along with the tune, remembering the way his banjo strings had felt beneath his calloused fingers, the sensation of plucking something wound so tightly, so fine.

After some time, Franklin disappeared down the hall and reemerged with Ginny on his arm, laughing and blushing. The two of them danced in the middle of the parlor. His gal was a surprisingly good dancer, and O.T. was struck by how much she looked like her mother. He was right glad, seeing her laugh and dance, that he had whisked her away from Five Forks before she could marry Grady Bridges.

The black man plucked a banjo on a little threadbare couch, playing right alongside the band while two small children played patty cake at his feet.

When the music finally came to an end, and the band began to pack up their instruments, O.T. approached Franklin. "That's a mighty fine instrument. You made it with yer own hands?"

"I did, yessir," Franklin replied with a flush. "Be happy to show you how, tomorry, if you got the time. It's easy as pie."

"I might," O.T. said, the liquor warming his blood. "Reckon my son Owen Jr. might like to have sumpin' like that."

"Yessir."

"Oh, and I seen you dancin' with my Ginny," O.T. said, clapping the boy on the back. "So long as you keep yer hands where I can see 'em at all times, I reckon that's okay."

After an hour of passing the time with folks, O.T. left the party and climbed the hill to Julie-Anne and Nate's cottage. He sat on the woodpile just under the guest bedroom window, staring up at the stars. He could see Venus, shining bright as you please, just in front of him. He knew it was a planet because it did not twinkle. They had spent hours stargazing, he and Walt and their ma. Sometimes Hosey, too. O.T. felt a sudden pang for his friend, wondering why he'd come down so hard on Hosey this past year. O.T. knew the truth of it. There wasn't anybody to be held to account for all his troubles, so he had singled out Hosey. He'd pushed away the best friend he'd ever had, someone who had been a brother to him since he was knee-high to a grasshopper.

O.T. recalled how young Hosey used to cry, furtively, thinkin' about his daddy, lost to suicide, and his poor mama, who was out of her mind, and he felt his own throat close up with tears. Still, he couldn't quite bring himself to forgive the man, not when he thought of Walt, alone in the cold, hard ground.

"Penny fer yer thoughts."

O.T. jumped. "Misrus Julie-Anne! You gave me a start."

"Sorry. Noticed you was gone at the shuckin' and thought you might be sick. Came up to check."

"No'm, I'm fine," he replied. "I was just gittin' a bit of air, I reckon. Lookin' at the stars."

Julie-Anne fished in her pockets and produced something wrapped in cloth. "Here. Snagged that fer ya."

It was a piece of spice cake. O.T. grinned as he unwrapped it. "Much obliged, ma'am. But you didn't have to—"

"I seen you scarf down the last one, so I figgered you musta liked it. You got a cut on there yer forearm, son," Julie-Anne said. "How'd you do that?"

He looked down. "Jee-ma-mee. I don't know, to tell the truth. I don't remember."

"When we git back in the house, I'll mix up a poultice for it. Soot and lard, slap it on, and it'll keep the infection out and help it heal."

"I thank ya."

Julie-Anne was silent for a moment, then spoke again. "You git gone with the drink, do ya?"

"How you mean?" O.T. asked, knowing exactly what she meant.

"You got the affliction," she said matter of factly, peering at him in the dark.

There was no point in lying. "I reckon so."

"How long?"

"Year or so," he admitted with a sigh. "Not long. I started tuckin' into the drink after I lost 'em."

"So it ain't too late to turn it 'round, then."

"I don't know, ma'am," O.T. sighed again. "I was tryin' not to drink while I was here, but DeWitt offered, and after a while it seemed stupid not to have a swig or two—"

"I shoulda tol' them not to offer drink to any ol' body that walks up on the porch," Julie-Anne replied. "It were our fault."

"No, it ain't," O.T. protested. "I coulda had one swig and stopped, or knowed enough to say no altogether. Ain't nobody fault but mine. Y'all didn't know."

"Yer still young yet," she said, reaching into her apron for a plug of snuff. "You got babies at home, don'tcha? Think of them. Think of yer youth. I know you ain't studyin' on it right now, but you might find you a gal you like and git marrit again one day. But you ain't ever gon' get none of that if'n you's a drunkard."

"I know," he said. "I reckon I just need to git up some strength of character, find my way out of this grief, if'n I can."

"Shoot. You can," Julie-Anne said, with a kind smile. "We all of us lose folks. That's just the way it goes. Part of life. We got to keep goin' for the young'uns. That's what it's all about." Her voice wavered. "I don't care what happen to me, long as my young'uns is safe and happy."

"I aim to find Sivvy and meet her, ma'am," O.T. said softly in the darkness. "Just so's you know. That's part of this trip here. Me and my gal is gon' go to Milledgeville and see yer daughter."

"I had wondered," Julie-Anne said in a small voice, wiping at her eyes. "I'm mighty glad to hear that. That she's got friends a'comin' to see her. Yes, mighty glad."

"I'm gon' pay her a visit and see that she's awright. See that she's healthy and happy—as may be, anyhow," O.T. said.

Falling silent, they both looked up at the stars.

O.T. felt the beginnings of a headache form at his temple, the telltale sign of a hangover already starting before he'd even gone to bed.

Then, through the light flurry of snow, he saw a sudden flash of green in the trees. He blinked in astonishment.

"What'd you see?" Julie-Anne asked.

"A flash of green on the ground, a little into the woods. I could have sworn it was glowin' like some kind of green fire," He chuckled. "I'm drunker'n I thought or I'm losin' my marbles."

Julie-Anne grabbed at his arm and pulled him up. "C'mon." Confused, he followed her three yards to the trees, trudging through the ever-deepening snow. Breathless, they stopped before a cluster of pine trees, tall and looming, their spindly branches black against the swirling white snow. Julie-Anne pointed into the woods. Nestled in the underbrush, O.T. saw what could only be described as glowing orbs of green growing on dead pine branches that had fallen, likely from the heavy weight of ice and snow. A gentle, green aura permeated the snow-laden nook.

"How pretty," O.T. murmured, awestruck. "But surely it's one of them optical illusions, ain't it? It can't actually be glowin'."

"No, it's glowin' awright," Julie-Anne replied. "Foxfire, it's called. I can't recollect ever seein' it this deep in winter. Usually only around Indian Summer and on into November."

"Foxfire," O.T. repeated, letting the word roll around on his tongue.

"You see it all around these parts," Julie-Anne said. "Sivvy used to call it fairy lights. When she was little, no more'n seven or so, she'd follow the little clusters of foxfire deep into the woods and half the time she'd get lost and have to call for us to come find her." Her face pinched up. "I thought I was teachin' her a lesson by not comin' for her. I'd make her find her own way back." She put her head in her hands and began to cry.

O.T. wrapped one arm around her shoulders and clumsily led her back toward the house. He glanced over her shoulder at the glowing foxfire, committing the burning emerald embers of its magic to his memory in case he never saw its like again. Fairy lights.

CHAPTER SEVENTEEN

Breakfast the next morning was simple fare—hoecakes, trout, and hot sassafras tea. O.T. nodded his thanks as Julie-Anne placed a dish of honey beside him, ignoring the steady pounding in his head.

The snow had finally let up, but O.T. reckoned they needed to wait one more day before leaving the ridge. He needed to gas up, let the snow melt a little bit, and take stock of things before he took to the road. And he wanted just one more day with these people, who made him feel stronger and less lonely than he had in a long time.

Julie-Anne broke the silence. "The cold just makes my bones ache, I tell ya. They don't ever quit their screamin'. 'Specially in these ol' fingers of mine. How ya feelin' this morn, young feller?"

"Tollible," O.T. replied, feeling ashamed. "Ain't nothin' a few hoecakes and some tea won't fix, I reckon."

"I ain't passin' judgement on you, boy, if'n yous worrit about that," Julie-Anne reassured him. "How could I? Was my own boy offered up the shine, and it's ourn, ain't it? Brew it right here on the ridge, and it makes us a fine profit, it do. We stay fed off that stuff. Ain't gon' try to put on airs."

"Yes'm," O.T. paused, before admitting, "It's good stuff, too. Real good."

"That's why we make a good profit," Julie-Anne laughed hoarsely, then coughed. "Yer young yet, but let me tell you what I know, from bein' old and wise about the world, young feller. They might put on airs up in Washington 'bout how they tryin' to save the young folk from drink, but they don't care a flip about whuther or not a woman's husband lays hands on her, or if'n he comes home at night to see his young'uns, or if'n he blows a whole week's wages on giggle water. No sirree. Don't give a flip. But if'n they make it illegal, see, they know ain't nobody gon' pay the law no mind. And when they git to catchin' folks out, they kin make they revenues. And they's money tied up in ever' single aspect of it, y'see. Ever single one. The fines, the taxes, the jails. Money tied up right to their necks. Profitin' off of *crime*, y'see."

"I see."

"But my husban', he's a Highlander, like I tol' you. Whiskey, scotch, mead, all of that is in his blood They grow up over there drinkin' the stuff like water. And to hear him tell it, ain't no gubbermint or president or lawman or *nobody* gon' tell him he can't make a little shine on his own land. No, sirree. He'd sooner be carrit off to jail. And I reckon I agree with him, 'cause they's a heap worser things folks git up to than a spirit now and agin, I rankin."

O.T. chewed his hoecake. It was buttery, rich and delicious but, feeling queasy he had no appetite. "I know you right, but ain't it the truth that some folks, fellers like me, take it too far? Can't seem to stop; fall right in the hole. Maybe the laws is tryin' to help us poor folks out."

"Yeah, they's always been fellers what got the disease," Julie-Anne replied, taking a long sip of tea. "But what of it? Did prohibition stop you drankin'? Don't look like it. You gon' do what you gon' do, and ain't no lawman up in Washington D.C. gon' stop you."

"'That's true. Yes'm."

"Oh, hesh yer mouth with that 'yes'm' business. Just call me Julie-Anne, or Ma like the rest of 'em do," she said with a smile, fetching snuff from her pocket. "You makin' me feel old. If'n you want to lick it, son," she continued, "you just got to practice sayin' no. It'll be hard; yes, sirree, it will, but half the battle is in not gettin' yer hands on it in the firs' place. Over time you'll find that the cravins' will fade. Won't never go away completely, accorse, but it'll git easier. You got to think of yerself as somethin' other than a drunk."

"It's just hard sometimes," O.T. confessed, "when I get to thinkin' 'bout the rest of my life—I ain't but thirty years old, Julie-Anne. I know you said I'd find me a woman and get marrit again, but I ain't studyin' on that. I loved Betty Lou more'n I loved anybody ever, and I ain't aimin' to replace her. So I jus' get to thinkin' on how many years I got left without her, and it just makes me want to drink till I cain't stand up." He had never confessed as much to anybody. "Don't supposin' you'd understand that."

"I understand a lot more than you might 'spect," Julie-Anne

replied slyly. "Just so happens you ain't the only one of us had a problem with the spirits when grief got too bad. After we lost Nona Leigh and Sivvy run off, I went a little off the rails. I took to drinkin' a lot of the shine affore it ever got out the door. I was still able to keep house and take care of the young'uns and stand up straight, but I was worryin' my husban'." She frowned at the memory. "And I din't like who I was becomin'; din't like the way the young'uns looked at me, how loud my voice got, and the way I felt when I woke up the next morn. Din't seem right, usin' my loss as an excuse to jes' let myself drown in moonshine. So I jes' quit it. I ain't had a drink since, and that was, oh, ten year ago or so."

"You make it sound awful easy."

"Naw, it ain't easy. Wadn't then and ain't now, tell the truth. I got to cravin' a drink last night, just smellin' it on yer breath. Hearin' 'bout my Sivvy gave me a shock, and I was sorely tempted. But I had to get stern with mahself and just say, 'Now, Julie-Anne, you got you ten year sober and think about what you like on the giggle water. Think about how you'd embarrass the young'uns. And you ain't a spring chicken no more, you might have a fall and break a hip or sumpin!' And so I jes' keep convincing myself not to have a drank till the feelin' passes. And it'll come again, sure as the sun'll rise in the morn, but you just got to be strong." Julie-Anne smiled and took another sip of her tea. "Jes' got to."

"I do want to," O.T. said, staring down at his plate.

"Then you'll lick it," Julie-Anne said, rising to her feet. "Them babies will have their sober deddy. Now, is you set on hoecakes, or you need more? Brekkus ain't much this morn, affer we used up all our good store at the shuckin'. But I can fry you a bit of fish—"

"No'm. I'm just fine," O.T. answered, pushing his plate away. "I cain't even finish what I got."

She smiled. "Well, in that case I rankin you'll want to get dressed and git on to the gen'ul store to git you some gas?"

"That's just what I was aimin' to do."

"One of the boys kin ride with you, show you the way," Julie-Anne replied. "You'll like Harvey, the shopkeep. He's a nice feller. He was there last night, but he lef' early. He's got little babies, y'see.

Strict bedtimes. Don't play around none. I ain't never met a stricter mama than his wife, Misrus Lucy Dee."

O.T. wondered what his own babies were doing right now. He had been gone only a couple of days and he didn't know how he was going to manage so long without seeing them. He'd been drunk so often the past year that he really had no right to be missing them at all, he knew, but he did all the same.

"I'll go fetch Ginny," O.T. said, standing. As much as he missed his children, and as much as he was itching to get on down the road toward Sivvy, he was going to be sad to leave the ridge.

Franklin pointed. "Just up here on the right," he said.

"Shoot, it's a good thing you here with us, Franklin," O.T. said as he drove down the narrow drive. "This place is so tucked away I never woulda found it on my own. Run out of gas right there on the mountain, I reckon."

"Yeah, it's a strange spot for a store, it's true," Franklin agreed.

They sat three to the bench seat, with Ginny in between the two men. O.T. was very aware of the fact that the two kids' arms were touching. He supposed he could have told Franklin to sit in the back, but he needed direction as to where to go. And what kind of harm could they get into with her pa right there, after all?

"Harvey and them live in the back of the store, and they built they place first, before they opened the gas station. So I rankin first and foremost it's a home." Franklin smiled at Ginny. "Wait'll you see the view, Miss Ginny. It's a dilly."

Dilly of a dally, O.T. thought, pained. He'd never heard anyone else use that word but Betty Lou. Ginny smiled at Franklin, her face pink. Good thing we're leaving in the morning, else we might have us a heap of trouble, O.T. thought wryly.

O.T. pulled up to a gas pump and turned off the engine. "I'll go on in and pay," he said.

"I'll pump the gas for you, if'n you like, sir," Franklin said. "Jes' tell me how much yer buyin'."

"Much obliged. I reckon two dollars worth oughter do it."

"Yessir."

He and Franklin both got out of the Model T, leaving Ginny sitting primly on the bench, looking mighty pleased with herself. She hadn't said more than two words all morning, but the grin on her face was hard to miss. O.T. shook his head as he walked inside, amused and a little wary. Ginny would put him in an early grave for worrying.

The shop bell tinkled as he opened the door. The inside of the store was dimly lit, a little sparse—the dusty shelves stocked with flour, sugar, cornmeal, and sorghum syrup—but pristine. A tantalizing smell wafted from the back of the store—stewed greens and fatback, smelled like. His appetite had returned, thanks to the fresh mountain air. On the counter sat a glass jar of penny candy and another that held fishing lures.

"How'do," O.T. said as a dark-skinned man appeared, clad in dark overalls and a bright yellow chambray workshirt. "Need a little gas, if'n you please." The man behind the counter was the same one who'd caught his eye over the corn during the shucking.

"Hey there, Mister O.T.," the man said, pulling out a pad and scrawling something on it. "How much gas you be needin'?"

"Just two dollars worth, please."

"You got it." The man wrote down *two dollars* on the pad, and beside it, in impeccable script, *gasoline*. Then, with a deft movement, he ripped the paper off the pad and handed it to O.T. He took the two dollars O.T. gave him and shoved it in the front pocket of his coveralls. "How you feelin' today?"

"Just fine," O.T. muttered, his face hot with embarassment. He reckoned just about the whole ridge had seen him blitzed. "I suppose I had a bit too much spirits last night."

The man chuckled wryly. "Ain't we all had such from time t'time?" He extended a hand, and O.T. shook it. "To meet ya formal, my name is Harvey."

"Pleased to meet ya," O.T. said. Harvey appeared to be about O.T.'s age or a little older. His dark brown skin was smooth and unwrinkled, his eyes almost black, and his teeth impossibly white. Harvey's hair was curly and cropped close to his head, and his large ears stuck out ever so slightly. Something about the man's good-humored smile and almond-shaped eyes struck O.T. as familiar, as if he'd met him before, long ago.

"Well, I 'preciate it," O.T. said, turning to go.

"Wonderin' where ya met me, man?"

O.T. turned back with a smile. "Well, I did think you looked familiar, but figgered it was impolite to ask," he answered. "*Do* I know ya?"

"We met before you was grown," Harvey said with a smile. "I ain't surprised you don't remember me. It were my job to fade into the background."

"I don't understand," O.T. replied, confused. "You knew me when I was a boy?"

"Ayuh. Not a little boy, though. You was on yer way to growin' up."

"I just can't recall." O.T. was perplexed. "I never forget a face, but...shoot, I just cain't remember. I'm awful sorry."

"You remember Billy Rev?"

O.T. stared, unable to speak for a moment.

"You must do, if'n you here visitin' his fambly."

After a moment, O.T. found his voice. "Why, sure I remember Billy Rev," he replied, surprised.

"And Miss Sivvy, then?"

"Well, yeah, accorse I remember her, too," O.T. said. "She's the reason I came—" He stopped abruptly, eyes widening. He'd been so preoccupied with Sivvy and Billy Rev that he'd quite forgotten Harvey. O.T. shook his head in wonder. "Shoot, Julie-Anne tol' me that the man runnin' the store was named Harvey, but I didn't never make the connection! Not till just now!"

"It's me, awright," Harvey replied, making a little "ta-da" gesture with his hands. O.T. chuckled, a little dazzled, because he was certain he'd seen him make that same gesture years before, as a boy, at the tent revival.

When Billy Rev first came to Five Forks, Harvey was by his side at every turn, handing him his notes or fetching him glasses of tea. The year that Sivvy came along, Harvey was at the sermon and the fish fry, but he made himself scarce. O.T. recalled the way the boy's ankles, for he was mighty tall even then, had shown under his coveralls. As a boy, Harvey's hair had been shaved close to his head; now it was longer and naturally curly.

"Ain't no big deal, man," Harvey said, clapping O.T. on the back.

213

"But I would like to talk with ya for a spell, if you can spare me twenty minutes. Why don't you tell yer gal and Mister Franklin to come on in? They kin get 'em a plate—Lucy Dee done made a mess a'greens this morn—and me and you kin take a glass a'tea or a drank if you want."

"Well, awright," O.T. said, confused. "But what you got to talk to me for?"

"It's about Miss Sivvy," Harvey said in a lowered tone, startling O.T. "I rankin you aimin' to go see her, and if'n you are, they's things you oughter know."

"Well…I'd be much obliged. Let me just go fetch my gal." O.T. said curiously.

"Come 'round the back, to the house. I'll be waitin' on ya."

As O.T. approached the car he could see that Franklin had his arm around Ginny, and he started to protest as he opened the driver's side door, but the delighted smile on her face held him back.

"If y'all two is done makin' love," he said dryly, chuckling as they wrenched themselves apart, "we been invited inside to Mister Harvey's for a bite a'lunch. Y'all come on."

Franklin and Ginny scampered out of the car and fell in step behind O.T.

"Y'all is in for a treat," Franklin said as they made their way to the rear of the shop. "Misrus Lucy Dee, she makes the best greens I ever had in my life. Don't tell my granny I said so. I used to sneak off here when I was a lil' boy to get a plate. I'd stay all dang day till somebody came to fetch me back home."

"Sounds like you was a rascal." Ginny giggled.

"I shore was. But Lucy Dee would always send me home with a bag full of biscuits, cookies, or penny candy. She was sweet on me."

"I cain't imagine why," Ginny said with a giggle. O.T. exhaled sharply—she was flirting. Lord help him!

O.T. knocked at the back door. A striking young black woman opened the door and held out a hand, streaked with flour.

"Hey, y'all. I'm Lucy Dee. I saw y'all at the shuckin' last night, but I was wranglin' young'uns and barely had time to take breath, much less talk. The young'uns is inside playin', but don't pay 'em no mind if they ast you a million questions. They's bored. This weather got 'em fit to be tied 'cause they want to play outside, but ever time they go out they come right back in, say it too cold. Soft, both of 'em! Wished I could send 'em on to school, but they got years yet 'fore they kin go. Lord knows I could use a break—might git a bit a'housework done! Haw! Anyhow, I made a mess a'greens, and I got biscuits and a little hog jowl if'n y'all is hungry." Lucy Dee never stopped talking as she ushered the three of them in the house. She pulled Ginny and Franklin along to the kitchen, still talking, and O.T. got the idea that he was to wait for Harvey.

Harvey appeared with a two-year-old boy in blue pajamas, clutching his father's leg with one arm and a wooden toy truck with the other. "This is my son, Grange," Harvey said with a proud smile. "He follows me 'round like a bad smell. Grange, go on now and git you a biscuit. Yer mama's in the kitchen."

"Cute young'un," O.T. said with a smile.

"Cute as the dickens but twice as fresh," Harvey said, giving the boy a playful swat on his diapered bottom as he disappeared into the kitchen. "My girl Lettie is four, and she's even more rurnt than he is. They mind my wife all the livelong day but neither of 'em do a thang I tell 'em."

O.T. laughed. "My young'uns is the same—well, was the same, till my wife passed on. Now they mind me 'cause they have to. They mama ain't around to keep 'em in line with a look."

"Mighty sorry, Mister O.T. Mighty sorry."

"I thank ya."

Harvey gestured to a room situated to the right of the parlor. "My study. It ain't much a'nothin', just a spare room I keep my papers in. It's cold in there, and dusty, but we can talk in private. I can get you some sassafras tea, or a plate if'n you want—?"

"Naw, I thank ya," O.T. said, following Harvey into the study. "I don't need nothin'. Misrus Julie-Anne fed me a hearty breakfast this morn."

"She a right good cook, and a damn good woman," Harvey said, gesturing for O.T. to sit in an old chair with mustard yellow cushions that looked like a relic from the days of Queen Victoria.

Harvey sat across from O.T. and laughed. "That chair looks like somethin' royalty would sit in, don't it?"

"Shore does," O.T. mused. "Like them paintin's you see of the royal fambly off in Europe."

"Suppost to," Harvey said. "Mister Nate's fambly, like half the folks from the ridge, is descended from the Scots an' the Englishmen. Irish, Welsh, all of 'em, so they tell me. Most ever'body can trace their kin back to somewheres over thataway." He shrugged. "I don't go in much for that stuff; my folks came from a whole other continent, and not by choice."

"Yes'r," O.T. said, uncomfortably. He looked at the paintings that hung on the yellow wall, and the long, slender gun that looked to be an antique, centered over Harvey's desk.

"It's from the Civil War," Harvey said, without turning around, accustomed, it seemed, to people admiring the gun. "I inherited that from my daddy when he passed. My most prized possession. Rumor was that it came from a Union soldier what fell in love with my great-grandma and married her. I s'pose you heard all about how mixed everybody is on this ridge." He grinned.

"Yes, Julie-Anne mighta said something about that." O.T. returned his smile. "Beautiful gun."

"Yep, and it'll blow yer damn head off, that I can guarantee," Harvey boasted, with a wink. "Anyhow—Mister Nate gave me that there chair you sittin' on as a weddin' present when I marrit Lucy Dee. He made it. It would've fetched a fair price in Atlanta, but he gave it to me. I reckon it were an apology as much as anythin'."

"What's he got to apologize to you for?"

"I think it was to atone," Harvey replied with a shrug. "For *him* and what he done. Not that they really *know*, accorse, but they know him and that's enough."

"What *who* done?"

"Billy Rev," Harvey said patiently. "You want to hear the tale?"

"For sure I do," O.T. replied, settling into the chair.

"Well, when I came back to the ridge, it were, oh, about 1919 or so...and I was worse for wear, lemme tell ya," Harvey began. "In a right state—not just physically but spiritually. And Nate and Julie-Anne could see that there'd been trebble. They ast me, 'Is Sivvy comin' on back? Is she still with Billy? Is she safe?' I din't have no answer fer 'em. Told 'em I ran off from Billy Rev and hadn't seen him in a long spell. They sensed I din't want to talk 'bout none of that, that there'd been trebble, and they dropped it. I marrit Lucy Dee the very next year. Rankin' they meant the chair kindly, even though they din't have no real idea of what they was sorry for. Beautiful piece of furniture, but I cain't stand to look at it half the time, neither. That's their guilt, their grief, in that chair. You ever had somethin' like that? Somethin' so beautiful you dunno if you want to treasure it all yer days or burn it into kindlin'?"

"My banjo," O.T. said with a rueful smile. "But I smashed it up against a tree in my yard until it was nothin' but splinters."

Harvey winced. "Shoot. That were stupid." He looked upward, remembering. "I reckon you and I played banjo together at the tent revival in yer town. Din't you pick with us a bit after supper?"

"You got a dang good memory," O.T. said. "That were fifteen year ago, and I reckon you musta visited more than a dozen towns."

"I did," Harvey said, "but I remember every face I ever saw. Most of the names, too. When you a black man you got to keep a number on folks if'n you want to keep outta trouble." He smiled. "But I ast you here to talk about Miss Sivvy. In confidence, you understand; don't go tellin' Misrus Julie-Anne."

"I won't."

"Only reason I'm discussin' this with you is on account of my loose lips. That Hosey Brown—got me drinkin' hooch last time he was up thisaway, and before I knew it I done tol' him about Sivvy. I rankin he tol' you, and that's why you're here." Harvey sighed. "I figger least I can do is tell you the whole story. And I ain't ever touchin' that shit again."

O.T. had wondered how Walt had gotten hold of the information about Sivvy. Now he knew. It had been Hosey—of course—who had an ear to the ground at every stop he made.

Harvey continued. "I jus' got the idea that if you was passin' through on to Milledgeville that you might stop off in Farmington."

"Why?"

"That's where Sivvy's husban' is from," Harvey replied. "And still lives there, far as I rankin, unless he dead by now."

"I knew she marrit," O.T. said. "Her husband's last name was Shelnutt. They had a child, a boy, but he died."

"A child," Harvey repeated. "Born *after* she marrit?" he asked.

"Why, I reckon," O.T. replied. "Leastways that's what she implied in the letter."

"I cain't scarce believe it," Harvey muttered, shocked. "All this time I figgered I knowed why she was in that place, but I reckon I mighta been wrong all along."

"You *knew* she was in the asylum?" O.T. asked, stunned.

He nodded. "I knew, and her sister Becca knew, too." He swallowed. "But I din't know 'bout no child."

"How? And why would y'all keep that from—?"

"I'll get to that," Harvey said, his face thoughtful. "Other things to tell first, though. You know, a secret can eat yer heart right out from the inside, Mr. Lawrence."

"That's the gospel," O.T. conceded.

"Amen," Harvey murmured. He sat back, lit his pipe, and began his tale.

Chapter Eighteen

"The first couple years I worked with Billy Rev, I gotta admit, I enjoyed myself. I was just a boy of sixteen and my parents was both dead, I din't have nobody in the world to call a relative, lest you count Misrus Julie-Anne and her young'uns—I reckon she told you we was distant cousins? Real distant, but if we sit down and shuffle our papers, we can trace our relatives back to the same person a few generations ago right here on this ridge.

"Billy Rev came to me when I was 'bout fifteen, said he needed a helper, and ast if I wanted to help spread the word of the Lord. He tol' me I could bring my banjo and my books, and he'd pay me a wage and see that I got three squares a day. What else can a starvin', lonely boy ast for? So Billy Rev and I toured just about all of Georgia, I reckon. All over the Blue Ridge mountains, then on down into Banks County, Hall County, and Oglethorpe County. Cotton ever'where you go. And when we went to Atlanta—Shoot! Ain't seen nuthin' to beat that spot. That city shore moved fast. And you seen folks my color just walkin' around, open as they please. They din't care a lick for Billy Rev's preachin', though, so we din't stay too long. He do better in rural towns, poor towns, with a lotta god fearin'.

"Billy Rev reeked a'shine all the time, and he had that rosy face that drunks git. He'd creep off after sermons and go buy his likker from some shady man in town, then he'd come back to our lil' waggin and drink himself silly, and I'd listen to him yammer on.

"Mostly he talked about his ambition, how he wanted to be a famous preacherman the likes of Billy Sunday or sumpin'. Which struck me as funny, 'cause Billy Sunday preached against the drank, y'know. Billy Rev always were good at shuttin' an eye to thangs. When he weren't talkin' about gettin' famous for the Lord, he talked 'bout how he hated his fambly. Talked ugly about his family, and about his own wife, Nona Leigh, who was the sweetes' lady you ever did meet. It got so bad and ugly I begged him to stop talkin' about it. He din't thank me none for that, lemme tell ya. He reared up and slapped me right in my face, so hard it 'bout knocked me off the wagon. 'I'll thank ya to keep yer uppity fuckin' opinions to yerself, you black ass Negro,' is what he said.

"That's the kinda man Billy Rev was. A hypocrite, like in the Bible. He'd jump off a bridge affore he'd call me the n-word. But he called me 'Negro' all the livelong day, and he'd put a little *tone* in it, you know, so I knew what he were *really* sayin'. And he din't think twice about clapping me in my head. But so long as he didn't use *that* word...well.

"He din't care nuthin' for his kin, but he did talk 'bout Miss Sivvy. He described how she used to come visit 'em and do her homework layin' on a rug by the hearth, her bare legs sprawled behind her. Gave me a chill, the way he described them legs.

"We went back up to the ridge for the winter months, and I busied myself workin' elsewhere for most of that time. When it was real cold, folks was good about giving me work—cuttin' firewood, shovelin' snow, all that kinda stuff—in exchange for a warm place to sleep or a bite of sumthin'. I tol' myself I was done workin' for that lowdown man.

"But when he offered me my job again, you know I took it. Money talks, son. Yes, it do. I already had designs on openin' me a store. Was already lookin' to the future. So that spring I set out with an extra spring in my step, till I seen who was coming with us.

"I ain't never gon' forget the day. I was loadin' the waggin, just gettin' ready to hop in and start it up—Billy Rev liked me to get it good an' warmed up before he'd get in to drive—and here come Miss Sivvy down the hill. I figured she was just comin' to say farewell. The look on her face was jes' pitiful. I threw up a hand to say how'do and she nodded at me, threw a little bag into the waggin and got in. She sat in the middle, with her little hands clasped in front of her, and let out a sigh bigger than she was.

"Wadn't much different, at first. Miss Sivvy din't say much. Billy Rev still drank at night, told his boastin' stories, 'cept now he was bossin' her around, too. As time went on, she got more and more duties while I got less. She was fetchin' his books and singin' the hymns and whatnot while I got to play my banjo. Suited me fine.

"But I couldn't figger on why she'd come with us. She din't care a fig for nuthin' Billy Rev was gettin' up to; it were purdy obvious that he'd wrangled her somehow, forced her to come. But I couldn't say nuthin'. How could I? Even if I'd wanted to talk, she wadn't gon' say nuthin', and we hardly had a chance to be alone. Billy Rev took her with him most nights. He wadn't gon' risk a fourteen-year-old gal settin' alone in the dark of a waggin with a colored boy. Din't matter that he knew me from a baby, din't matter atall. No sirree.

"The next few months we went around the towns, setting up the tents for Billy Rev's sermons. We'd stay two or three days till the welcome started to wear thin, and then we'd make off to the next town. Him and her sharin' the bench seat—though Lord knew how they both fit—him with his legs as long as trees. I'd sleep on the ground, under a tree or in back of the truck on a pallet. We passed mighty fine sights on the road, but neither me nor Miss Sivvy ever ast to stop and look at nuthin' or visit anywheres outside of where Billy Rev had marked on his map. Wadn't no point. Billy Rev wadn't no kind of guy likes to sightsee or vacation. It were all business to him. And that's how our days went. Travel, stop off, tent revivals, then more travel.

"Billy Rev took to drinking more; after supper, he'd have a bottle and then pass out in the waggin, stinkin' to high heaven, snorin' and such. So Sivvy and I would whisper together, when we was feelin' safe about it—we'd keep one ear pressed to the air to make sure Billy Rev wadn't wakin' up. We'd pass the time a little bit, then I'd retreat over to the other side of the waggin' and go to sleep. It got to where I'd look forward to it, and I reckon she did, too.

"One weekend we visited Five Forks—yer homeplace—and I remember Miss Sivvy goin' off with a group of kids to ride in a motorcar. Billy Rev didn't want to refuse her in front of the whole congregation, but what was he gon' do? He let her go, but he was madder'n hell. After the folks cleared outta the church, she still wadn't back. He told me that he'd seen her cuttin' her eyes at the local boys and that she was gettin' to the age where she might be feelin' fresh. Might get herself spoilt. It chilled my blood. Jes' then she came back, lookin' shiny as a new penny with the purdiest smile on her face I'd ever seen. I drove 'em in the waggin' to Misrus Maybelle's house, where they was stayin'—they got offered hospitality, you see, but I had to sleep in the waggin. Wadn't fittin' to offer a room to a colored man.

"Billy Rev got out first, to shoot the breeze with someone out waterin' their yard. Sivvy stayed in the waggin with me for jes' a minute. She inched real close, so I could smell the powder on her face and see the lines in her red lips, and she tol' me she had a date that night. Would I drive her?

"'Lawd no!' I said, shocked. A date? Was she bats? Billy Rev wouldn't let her go on no date, and if I was to drive her I'd get my ass lynched. But Miss Sivvy said she had it all worked out. After her uncle had passed out from drink she'd meet me outside of town. She said if'n I could drive her there, she'd find her own way back. She said she'd be real careful. I can remember our conversation clear as a bell.

"'You takin' a whole lotta risk to meet some fool boy,' I said to her. 'I ain't thinkin' it's worth it, Miss Sivvy.'

"'I got to do somethin' or I'll explode!' she whispered to me. 'It ain't even about the fella. I jus' got to go somewheres, Harvey, or I swear I'll just die.'

"'You comin' back?' I ast her.

"'Got to, I reckon,' she said. 'But just for one night, I want to feel like I got a normal life. Like the other girls.'

"Her eyes were so big and sad. I couldn't say no to her, Mister Lawrence. I knew I was risking my ass and hers too, but I felt so blame sorry for her. I tol' her I'd drive her. I made her promise to behave. 'I will. I just got to get out for the evening,' she said. She put her hand on mine and squeezed. 'Or I'll bust.'

"Miss Sivvy went on in to Misrus Maybelle's house, and I parked the waggin in a grove of trees and tried to take me a nap. I had hours till I had to meet her, and I was madder than a settin' hen, thinkin' about the risk we was both takin'. I decided that when I picked her up later, I was gon' give her what for. I was gon' tell her off for risking my hide to meet some cracker boy not old enough to shave. 'Cause if we got caught out at night without Billy Rev people would assume things and my neck would break for it. Had she even thought of that? Rankin she hadn't. Miss Sivvy was a smart gal but she were young, and she had no life experience atall. She didn't know what she was riskin'. And that made me all the madder. I had a mind to march her tail back to Billy Rev and tell him what his purdy little niece was gettin' up to. For all I knew, she'd a mind to get herself spoilt on purpose, just to spite ever'body, and take me down with her. Oh, I was hot. I was gon' tell her and tell her but good. Darkness fell, and I drove the waggin to the meeting spot, where I waited. But when I saw her I forgot all about the tellin' off I was set to give.

"She was wearin' the same ol' white dress she wore when she sang, and her hair fell around her shoulders like black rain. She jumped in, all smiles, her eyes sparklin' like I'd never seen. I couldn't scarce catch my breath. She was as purdy as any gal I'd ever clapt eyes on, and I realized right then what I was really mad about.

"'Thank ya, Harvey,' she said. Then she shocked me right to death by leaning over and giving me a kiss on my cheek. I didn't say a word. Just drove her to where she wanted to go. It didn't seem safe to me, a young gal her age walkin' off to meet some fella in the dark woods, but I couldn't think of nuthin' else but that kiss on my cheek.

"I spent the next two hours sittin' there just a'sweatin'. She tol' me not to come back fer her, but I wanted to. I was worrit that some boy might take advantage; worrit that she'd get caught and ruin her reputation, worrit that she might get lost out in the woods alone, but most of all worrit that Billy Rev would find out she were gone and tan her hide, or worse. The hold he had on that gal wasn't natural. My feelings was all tore up.

"It was barely gettin' dark and I had started noddin' off when Billy Rev come out o' nowhere. I about fell off the seat, he shook me so hard.

"'Where in tarnation is Sivvy?' he ast me, still shakin' me so hard my bones were a'rattlin'.

"'Lawd, sir, I cain't say,' I told him, wipin' at my eyes. 'I ain't seen her since I dropped y'all off this afternoon.'

"'She ain't at Misrus Maybelle's, you fool Negro,' he spat at me. 'I aim to find out just where she is.' His face was all red; madder than I ever seen him. And drunk, too. Wadn't nobody else around, and no vehicles or nuthin', so he must have walked. That's when I knew he was really in a lather, 'cause that man was so lazy he'd take a car from one house to the house next door. 'Move over, you goddamn burr-headed sonafbitch,' he said to me. 'I'm drivin'. And if I find out you helped her git away, I'll string you up from the goddamn tree myself.'

"We drove around, lookin' for Miss Sivvy till it was full dark. Finally, he parked out in front of some store and we sat there. He was chewin' on the inside of his mouth and fidgeting, tappin' on the steerin' wheel. He cussed up a storm, and I could smell the liquor on his breath.

"'She done run off,' he kep' sayin'. 'She done run off. Don't 'spect she ever gon' come back.'

"'She will,' I said, tryin' to reassure him. 'Why wouldn't she? Why, I bet she jus' went to see a girl friend or sumpin', boss, she'll be back jus' as fast as you please.'

"'You deaf as well as dumb, Negro?' he said. 'I said she ain't comin' back. I got a feelin'.'

"Then, my eyes caught sight of Miss Sivvy creepin' through the dark in the rear view mirror, her white dress gleamin' in the moonlight. *Turn around and run back the way you came*, I thought. *Turn around and go. There ain't nuthin' for you here in this waggin but misery. Run while you can, gal!* But she kept on comin', and then my heart stopped 'cause I seen a young man with her, too. The two of them disappeared behind the post office, and I felt mighty relieved.

"'Let's git on back,' Billy Rev said, suddenly. 'Ain't nuthin' to see here. You take me on back to Maybelle's. I reckon she might come on back after all.' His voice was all soft and casual like, like he ain't had a care in the world, but he'd seen Miss Sivvy, and the boy, too. He was gon' get his revenge and was gon' serve it cold. I dropped Billy Rev at Misrus Maybelle's, but could scarcely drive, my hands shook so bad.

"She'd done gone and messed up but good, Mister Lawrence. I don't know what she did out there; reckon she didn't come back no more spoilt than she was before she went, but that din't make no difference to him. Y'see, she was his and only his, and he din't take kindly to nobody playin' with his thangs. And he was gon' make sure she learned that lesson. I knew it, and she'd know it soon enough. She should have *stayed* gone."

Harvey took a long puff on his pipe.

"I guess you know about what happened the next day?" O.T. said finally, lighting his own pipe and taking a drag. "About the big scene that happened in the middle of town? My late wife and her mama and my brother, gettin' into it with Billy Rev, who accused Walt of meddlin' with Sivvy?"

"Yessir, I was there. Sittin' in the back of the waggin," Harvey replied. "Accorse, none of them had any way of knowin' that Billy Rev had seen the two of 'em, so they was protestin' and carryin' on about their innocence. Shoot, the boy even cried. From them tears you woulda guessed he was as innocent as the angel Gabriel. Accorse Billy Rev didn't believe a word. He knew what he seen. What I seen. He dragged her away from Five Forks, lickety split. We stopped that night at a town called Farmington, where Billy Rev had relatives. We stayed with his father-in-law, who was right sickly. He couldn't even get outta bed to greet us. Tol' Billy Rev to just make hisself at home. I got a room upstairs—first time I got sleep in a real bed since we'd been touring! Miss Sivvy got another. But when it came time to turn in, Billy Rev tol' me to send Sivvy up to *his* room; said he was gon' deal with the situation she got herself in; said it was time to receive punishment from the Lord. I never forgit those words, and the relish with which he said 'em. 'Punishment from the Lord.'"

"Oh—shit," O.T. said, horrified. "You mean he…? The bastard!"

Harvey sighed. "You have to understand, I was just a young black man in the middle of Georgia with a white reverend for a boss, and his niece gettin' up to trouble. What could I have done?"

"There ain't nothin' you coulda done," O.T. said reassuringly.

Harvey sighed, his shoulders slumping. "All I know is two things: one, she din't come out of there the rest of the night; and two, the next day I couldn't stand to look at her. I saw the bruises on her arms, and rankin that was the least of it."

O.T. let his breath out in a long stream. "She was just a *girl*.…" He couldn't bear to finish the thought. "My Ginny's age."

"Yes'r."

"And to call hisself a man of God!"

Harvey laughed dryly. "He ain't that, no he ain't. He's a damn liar and a con man and a pervert. And a bastard, too, I agree with you there."

"What happened after that?" O.T. asked. "I know you got away—how did she?"

"I'm gittin' to it, Mister Lawrence. Might need some nourishment to get through the next part. Lucy Dee!" Harvey hollered. "Hey, baby, bring us some biscuits and a glass of tea, would ya?"

"After we spent the night in Farmington, we went to Madison. Purdy little town with magnolia trees lining the streets, full of big ol' plantation houses, all done up just like affore the war. Some folks still got slave houses on they land. Gave a body a chill just lookin'. Miss Sivvy felt like glass sittin' beside me in the waggin, her breath comin' out in little gasps, her body tense and straight beside mine. I wanted to be away from her, where I din't feel so guilty. Billy Rev sat beside her, chawing on and on 'bout his late wife, of all thangs. He was right conversational, like none of the night before had ever happened.

"Sivvy was quiet for most of the ride, but when he got to the part about Nona Leigh not havin' him no babies, she spoke up in a tremble. 'You just hush about Aunt Nona Leigh,' she said. 'You ain't gon' say nuthin' against her. She were a good woman, good to me and our whole fambly, and she loved you well. May she rest.'

"I thought Billy Rev was like to slap her face, sassin' him like that, but he just grinned at her and let out a hoot: 'Fresh today, Miss Sivvy! You sure is fresh.' That was all he said; then he went on talkin' about the old days when he was courtin'. And Sivvy din't say another word the rest of the drive. It chilled my blood.

"We got to Madison about lunch time, and I got myself busy settin' up the tent and keepin' myself away from the two of 'em. Lord, I felt bad. Miss Sivvy was so pale, tracks on her cheeks from cryin', and the little white dress jes' hanging loose. She looked like a stiff breeze would carry her down the road. She caught me lookin' at her, and her dark eyes were so big and round they almost swallowed me.

"I got to feelin' sick to my stomach; whether it was from the heat or my guilt, I don't know. I ran into the woods and puked my guts out. I was in a field of dandelions behind somebody's house, where nobody could see me. I knew Billy Rev was too lazy to come looking.

I sat against the tree for a spell and, closing my eyes, tried to cool my blood a little. Then outta nowhere, I felt a hand on my cheek, and I jumped up with a jerk. There was Miss Sivvy, sittin' right beside me.

"I yelled at her. 'What you doin', fool girl?' I demanded. 'Ain't you got yourself in enough trouble? You tryin' to get yerself skint? And me besides?'

"'He's gone into town,' Sivvy said. 'Pastor from the local church showed up and took him away in the motorcar. We'll hear it if they come back.'

"'All the same, you best hop on out of here. He ain't gon' leave you by yerself for long. And if somebody see you with me there will be hell to pay.'

"'I know, Harvey,' she said. 'I just aim to say one thing and then I'll go back. He got a new hymn for me to sing tonight. I need to learn it.'

"'So you best go and get to memorizin'.'

"'I *am,*'" she said, 'but first I got to say that I'm sorry for draggin' you into that business in Five Forks. That weren't fair. Like you said, I coulda got you in big trouble. Lucky for us, it was just me that got caught.'

"'Lucky for you?' I couldn't help but snort. 'I wouldn't call whatever happened to you last night lucky.' I shouldn't speak so to her, I knew, but I couldn't help myself. 'Is you all right?'

"She made a noise low in her throat. 'Ain't nuthin',' she said fiercely.

"'But Sivvy—'

"'I might be a little thing,' she said, 'but I know what I can bear up and what I cain't.'

"'But—'

"'Best you don't worry about it none,' she said. 'And look the other way all the time. Just like you been.' I didn't know what to say. I felt ashamed—and relieved. She reached out and took my hand, gave it a squeeze. 'Yer a good fella, Harvey. We just got to pick the battles we can win.'

"Somethin' came over me when she said that; I just felt like butterflies were jes' a'flutterin' in my chest and making me gasp. So much feelin' bubbled up in me that it liked to overflowed. Before

I knew what I done, I had grabbed her up and I was kissin' her. I pulled her close to my body, feelin' how soft and tiny she was, like a little bird, her dark hair flutterin' against my face, light as a feather. The only thing full about that gal was her lips, and they was kissin' me *back*. I could scarce believe it. I had thought of it, accorse—a boy of sixteen travelin' with a purdy girl has *thoughts,* you know—but never woulda believed in a billion years that it could happen. Her arms were around my neck and in my hair, and I thought I'd catch fire and burn right up. I wanted to swoop her up and fly into the sky, away from the world and never come back again. Just protect her and keep her, forever and ever.

"But then the moment was over and we broke apart, and I like to had a heart attack with the realization of what I done. I had kissed a white gal in somebody's backyard. A reverend's niece. From the look on her face, she was having a similar realization. We just stared at each other with wide eyes for what felt like a solid hour, neither of us able to say a word, neither of us knowing what to do next. And then Miss Sivvy jumped up, put a finger to her smilin' lips, and took off sprinting back to the tent. A minute or two later, I heard the sound of a motorcar pulling up on the street. I made my way back, praying like I had never prayed before.

"Somehow luck was on my side and Billy Rev din't seem to notice nuthin'. He was too busy makin' plans, chawing the other pastor's ear off. I dared a quick look at Miss Sivvy while we set up, and her eyes sparkled so, I was afraid he might notice.

"We was in Madison for three nights. Longer than we would usually stay, but Billy Rev had reasons. There was a young widow woman, barely in her twenties, who he took a likin' to. He puffed himself up and made eyes at her ever' time she passed by, and later durin' the supper, all through the baptisin' and all. I rankin that ol' ugly fool was actually tryin' to make Miss Sivvy *jealous.*

"But there were moments over them three days, when Miss Sivvy and I were alone together. Not many, just a couple, and it was a nice time. Her so pretty and sweet. Did we love each other? Naw. Too much weighin' on her, and me too. But I like to think I helped distract her some. Lord, the risks we took—I have to believe it warn't all for nuthin'. I was young. Ain't no woman like my wife—she's the love of my life, for always—but a man can have a sweet memory or two, of the ones that came before.

"Miss Sivvy's liberty was tied up in mine, see. We was both trapped, scairt, and desperate, and more than anything I wanted her to be free. Free of him, and free of me, too, if that's what it took. By the time we left Madison, I was insane with plottin' to try and get Sivvy away, not that it did no good. Every night Billy Rev would slip into the waggin where Sivvy lay, and I'd hear her whimperin' and it started to build a rage in me. I made a vow that if I ever got him back on the ridge, I'd kill him deader than a doornail. It was clear he din't have no plan to go back anytime soon, though—said he was gon' stay out tourin' till Christmas, maybe even beyond. He never did that before, but he had plans that wasn't clear to me and Miss Sivvy yet.

"Eventually, we found our way back to Farmington, where Billy's father-in-law stayed. Billy Rev pulled onto a side street, jes' as we were gettin' into town, and said, calm as you please, 'I know what's been goin' on. Yes, Lord, I know all about the sinnin' you two have done.' We both went straight and still as iron pokers. I could scarcely breathe.

"'You just do as I say,' he tol' us, 'and don't contradict me to nobody. If you both want to get out of this mess alive, you'll keep yer mouths shut and do what I say.'

"Billy Rev's in-law was an old man by the name of Clayton Shelnutt. He was sixty or so, but seemed even older, on account of his pallor. He walked with a cane and had a weathered face full of wrinkles, but his green eyes seemed kind. Sivvy liked him from the start. He was a friendly fella, but he din't like Billy Rev much. He were too polite to say so, but we could see.

"I found out that first night at dinner—Clayton Shelnutt tol' me to sit right at the table with all of them—that Billy Rev hadn't tol' his father-in-law that Sivvy was his niece. Clay seemed to think she was just some hired gal, stayin' on with us 'cause she din't have no folks. Billy Rev sat there, diggin' into his roast beef and smiling jes' as big as you please, me and Sivvy just waitin' to find out why the devil we was even there, what on earth he had up his sleeve.

"Finally, Billy Rev put his napkin in his lap, all delicate like, and cleared his throat. 'Mr. Shelnutt,' he said in a voice smooth as silk, 'Pop. I wonder if you might do me a favor. It was the pride of my life when I married your daughter Nona Leigh, and an honor it was that you was the one who marrit us. I always knowed you was a true man of God, and I owe you for helpin' turn me into the man of God I am today.' Mr. Shelnutt said nothing, just looked at him warily. Billy Rev took a long sip of water and continued, cool as a cucumber: 'Now that Nona Leigh has been gone for over a year, I reckon I should move on, much as my heart breaks to do so. I cain't never replace her, for she was a right good woman and all, but a reverend needs a wife. And I'd like not only your blessin' on the marriage, but for you to do the marryin'.'

"'I haven't performed a marriage in many years,' Mr. Shelnutt said, 'and I've not met this future wife of yours. I heard at church that you were courtin' a widow in Madison, but—'

"'Why, Mr. Shelnutt,' Billy Rev said, his face a picture of innocence. 'Oh no, sir. I can't imagine who you mean. No, I mean to marry Miss Sivvy here.'

"Sivvy dropped her fork on the floor with a clatter that was awful loud in that suddenly silent room. I almost choked on my piece of roast beef. His own niece! And the both of us sitting there like lame ducks, unable to say a word. To raise a word of protest was to get myself killed, and if Sivvy dared to speak up, Billy Rev would punish her something good. My brain was workin' overtime, tryin' to find some way out of this, part of me willin' my tongue to stay shut up, the other part callin' myself a coward, figurin' I should speak the truth and shame the devil.

"Mister Clay, uneasy, ast Sivvy how old she was, and as she opened her mouth to say, Billy Rev interrupted. 'She's seventeen.' He was a lie; Sivvy weren't even fifteen yet.

"Mr. Shelnutt sat there, workin' it over. 'When is you plannin' on marryin'?' he ast.

"'Make hay while the sun shines, I reckon. Tomorry? We need to get her a dress.' Billy Rev smiled across the table at Miss Sivvy, and she looked down at her plate, visibly upset. But that man just smiled and kep' on eatin', like butter wouldn't melt in his mouth.

"'Where?' Mr. Shelnutt asked.

"'Church, I reckon. I know you ain't the pastor there no more but the current pastor will let you perform the service.'

"'I'm sure that won't be no trouble,' Mr. Shelnutt replied, a thin smile crossing his face. He took a long sip of tea, and I noticed his hand tremble.

'Good.' Billy Rev smiled and slammed his hands down on the table in triumph. 'So it's settled.'

"Then this voice came up out of me before I could stop myself. 'But, Boss, Mr. Hargrove,'—I had never called him Mister Hargrove a day in my life—'You cain't do that!'

"The table was deathly silent. I clutched my knife and fork in tremblin' hands, waiting. Sivvy's eyes were wide with horror. Billy Rev took a bite of his roast beef and regarded me with a cold eye. 'Harvey,' he said, icily. 'You dare to speak to me about what I can and cain't do, after what you yerself done?'

"'I…' I stammered. 'I ain't done nuthin', sir. Just work for you and look after you and Miss Sivvy, too. And she don't want to marry you. It ain't fair, to force her—'

"'Ain't done nuthin', is that right? So you mean to say you ain't been meddlin' with Miss Sivvy yourself these days past? You mean to sit here at this table and tell me you ain't had your dirty black hands all over her ever'time my back was turned?' I was shocked that he said all this in front of Mr. Shelnutt.

"'No sir, I—'

"'She done admitted it,' Billy Rev said calmly, leaning back in his chair with a smile. 'So save your lies, you uppity sumbitch. Sivvy is damn lucky that I'm willin' to marry her, after what she done to spoil herself—that I'm able to overlook her dirty sin and save her from the mark you don left on her. She better hope the Lord will overlook it, too. She *does* want to get marrit. This is her callin' and all she wants in the world, ain't that right, Sivvy? You want to get in good with the Lord, don't you? Mend yer ways and marry a man of the cloth?'

"Sivvy gave a slight nod. She did not look at me, or Mr. Shelnutt.

"'I ain't got need of you no more, boy,' Billy Rev said, still smilin'. 'Sivvy and me can make do on our own. I was jus' gon' give you yer papers, and let you mosey on about your business with no trouble. I was gon' follow Jesus' example and turn the other cheek since yous jus' a kid. But since you gone and got all uppity, I reckon I ought to call the po-lice and tell 'em that a no-count black boy been messin' with this here gal. Sivvy will tell 'em you took advantage of her. We'll let 'em sort you out.'

"I didn't need to hear no more. I jumped up from the table and made for the door, but that lazy reverend was faster than me. In the hall, he twisted my arm, and hissed in my ear, 'You meddled with her for the last time, Negro.' And before I knew what had happened, he hauled me into the cellar and locked the door.

"I was there for half the night, just despairin'. I heard Blly Rev leave the house and knew he was going to the police. I'd seen more than one lynching in my time, and knew right well what awaited me. Then Sivvy would be married to that man, and he would have license to hurt her whenever he wanted, however he wanted. The same way he used to hurt Nona Leigh.

"It started to get real dark, but I was afraid to lay down, afraid of lettin' my guard down. My legs were cramping, and my heart was thumping so loud in my chest I was sure it must've echoed through the house. Sometime later, I heard a key scrape in the cellar door, and it swung open. I was sure it was Billy Rev and his friends in blue come to haul me off to jail. I'd heard of sheriffs forgettin' 'bout their prisoners and leaving the cell door open when they went to the john so that townsfolks could deal a little vigilante justice. I wondered what my fate might be. Torn limb from limb? Set on fire or beaten to death? But it wasn't Billy Rev at the door. It was Mr. Shelnutt, with Sivvy behind him.

"'You got five minutes,' Mr. Shelnutt was tellin' Sivvy, 'and that's all. Cain't risk no more.' And then Sivvy was in the cellar with me, alone. She kissed my cheek and explored my face with her hands, like she was trying to memorize me.

"Wrapping her arms around my neck, she said, 'Dance with me.'

"I wadn't in no mood for dancing, for obvious reasons. But I knew I wouldn't see her again after that night, so I put my shakin' arms around her waist. I like to have knocked her down, I was tremblin' and fumbling' so, but she held me fast and put her head on my shoulder.

"'It's gon' be all right, Harvey,' Sivvy said softly. 'I got it all fixed. I'm gonna undo this mess.'

"'You cain't,' I said. 'Ain't nobody can go up against that man. He'll win every round.'

"'Don't you be so sure. I got a trick or two.'

"Then we heard footsteps above and Sivvy pressed her lips to mine real quick and whispered, 'I won't forget you, Harvey. See you don't forget me.' Then the cellar door opened and she bounded up the stairs, and I was alone with Clayton Shelnutt.

"He hurried me upstairs and was pulling off my shirt and throwing another one at me before I could get a word out of my mouth. I tried to ask what was going on, but he put a finger in front of his lips and said, 'Hush, boy. We ain't got time to chaw the fat and the walls might have ears. Just put that shirt on. I got pants for you, too.'

"I changed into the shirt, buttonin' it with tremblin' fingers, and pulled on a pair of dark blue pants, boots, and a dark jacket.

"'Them's my ol' clothes,' Mr. Shelnutt whispered. 'I ain't wore 'em in years. Don't reckon nobody'll recognize 'em. I don't aim for you to be seen till yer outta town nohow. With a little luck, we'll get you to the Oconee before they catch up with us. But we got to hop to it. Let's git.'

"I stumbled down the stairs, Mr. Shelnutt pushing at my shoulder, out through the little kitchen, and into the night. A Model T hummed beside the back door. 'Git in, boy. Hurry up, or the devil take ya.' I ran around to the other side and hopped in.

"'Keep yer head down,' the old man urged, and I scrunched low in the seat. 'The sheriff and Billy Rev will be coming down the main road, so I'll take the cattle roads. Gon' keep the headlights off, so hold on to your behind, it's gon' be a bumpy ride. With a little luck I can cut through the forest and come out on ol' Salem road and hit 441 before they know where we got to.' Mr. Shelnutt smiled grimly. 'Hopin' they don't remember 'bout the cattle roads. Least not till you're long gone.'

"I din' know where we was goin' and I din' ast. I was already thinkin' ahead to how I was gon' haul my ass outta there before the law caught up with me. I knew Billy Rev would've had an old piece of sumthin' with my stank on it, and I was a goner once they unleashed those hounds.

"'Don't fret none about Miss Sivvy,' Mr. Shelnutt said. 'She'll be awright. Woulda been a helluva risk to send a white gal and a black boy out into the night. Y'all wouldn't have made it to the next town before you was in a tree, boy. Sivvy and me got us an arrangement, we do,' he said in a low voice. I didn't ask—better not to know.

"Crouching down low in the seat, my shoulders were on fire, as we drove on in silence for what seemed like days. Finally, the truck slowed. 'We're here. Sit on up and look. Through that clearing a ways you'll meet a grove of trees with rot on 'em. Once you see those trees, oh, about forty yards north, you'll take a sharp left and run like hell, fast as you can. Don't stop till you get outta the woods. Then you'll be right on the outskirts of Bishop. They's a washerwoman in town, marrit to a cook, a nice lady. Look for the sign Stew & Que. She and her husband will help you get further north. Git on back up to the mountains fast as you can. Don't stop, don't try to make friends with nobody, just high-tail it outta here. Me and Miss Sivvy here gon' have us a weddin', and hopefully the goodly Billy Rev will be so mad it'll make him forget all about you.' Mr. Shelnutt took a good long look at me, and smiled a tight smile. 'We'll be prayin' for ya.' The door opened, and I was pushed out into the darkness. I was two miles down the road before it dawned on me what he'd said. *We gon' have us a weddin'....*

"The only reason that ol' man saved my neck was because Sivvy struck a deal with him. Had I not my own hide to save, I mighta gone back.

"But it was too late to help her anyhow, and I'd already distanced myself from Sivvy Hargrove in more ways than one. My feet liked to have flown the whole way to Bishop."

❧

O.T. stared at Harvey for a moment, shocked. "I had no idea..." he began, in disbelief. "You mean to tell me that Sivvy ended up married to Nona Leigh's father?"

"Rankin she did," Harvey replied. "I didn't stick around for no ceremony, but that was they plan."

"Misrus Julie-Anne didn't even know Sivvy was married until I told her," O.T. said.

"No, she don't know," Harvey said, "and there ain't no way to tell her about Sivvy marryin' Clayton Shelnutt without tellin' her the rest, and it would distress her something bad."

"So you got away?"

Harvey nodded. "I followed the old man's directions, half afeared it was a trap, but he told me true. I got to the main road about an hour before the sun rose, and didn't see no law or dogs, but that din't mean they wasn't around. I was too scairt to seek out the washerwoman and her husband. They might well have been good folks—I'm sure they was—but I couldn't chance it. I happened on a group of coal miners what was in Madison for the weekend. Coal miners is all black, no matter what color they is," Harvey laughed. "I seen 'em outside a diner, gettin' ready to load back up in they truck. I ambled up and ast 'em if they needed another hand. Said I was down on my luck, that my wife had just died, and I din't have no reason to stay in town."

O.T. made a whistling noise. "I don't reckon they bought that for a second."

"Naw, only a fool would've. They knowed just lookin' at me," Harvey smiled. "But they tol' me to hop on in. Gave me coveralls and a hat and said they'd put my ass to work. Shoot, when they pulled into Gastonia, North Carolina, I stayed with the crew and worked as a miner for damn near two years. I worked hard. I couldn't bear the thought of goin' back to the ridge to face Sivvy's folks. I stayed with them for a long spell, but I finally came home and met Lucy Dee and started my life." He grinned again.

"You got away by the skin of yer teeth," O.T. said, in wonder.

"I was lucky. You can bet yer ass that if they'd caught me, I'd be deader than a doornail," Harvey said. "Billy Rev was gon' make damn sure of that."

"And you ain't never talked to Sivvy since? You never tried to find her?"

"Naw. Tell the truth, for years I didn't want to see her face. Once I was safe, and could breathe a minute, I got to thinkin' about it all and got to blamin' her. All them risks she took, the sneakin' around, the double dealin'. I was mad at her for goin' with that Clay Shelnutt, too. Girl like her, not but fifteen and him an old man. Don't make no mistake, that ol' feller wasn't puttin' his neck out to save mine. He just brokered that deal for the gal. I just couldn't never wrap my head around the damn fool choices she made time and time again."

"Reckon that might indicate a *lack* of choices, though, don't it?" O.T. asked thoughtfully.

"Ayuh, well, that's true. I know that *now*. But then, I'd just barely escaped bein' murdered in some podunk town by a bunch of Klan and I wasn't feelin' too philosophical." Harvey took another sip of iced tea and sighed. "I didn't hate the gal; I was worrit for her—bitter and scairt. But I never tried to contact her. Not even after I found out where she was. I suppose I ought to be ashamed of that."

O.T. shook his head. "No more'n anybody else, I don't reckon."

"I used to think she was hell-bent on destruction, that gal," Harvey said, "but she was just in a boat with no oars, headed downriver. It all would have amounted to the same, no matter which way she leaned."

"Reckon I know how that feels," O.T. said.

"Rankin a lot of us do," Harvey agreed. "Once I discovered where she ended up, all my bitter feelins' went right out the winder anyhow."

"How did you find out?" O.T. asked.

"Why," Harvey said, with a bright smile, "Billy Rev himself tol' me."

CHAPTER NINETEEN

O.T. and Ginny had been driving down the mountain for over an hour and O.T. still felt like he might cry. He glanced over at Ginny, whose own lip trembled. He reckoned the tall, dark-eyed boy, Franklin, might have something to do with her fretting. For his part, the conversation with Harvey kept replaying in his head, and O.T. couldn't make sense of it. Harvey's grin as he confided that it had been Billy Rev who'd informed him of Sivvy's whereabouts was the least of the things that perplexed him.

O.T. had demanded to know more. "Billy Rev came back to the ridge two years ago and came to see me at the store,' Harvey told him, puffing on his pipe. "He found out I was here and came 'round just outta spite. He tol' me that Sivvy had been committed to the Milledgeville asylum and had been there *ten years*. Took all I had not to bust his teeth out then and there, but I got a business to run and a family to feed so I told him to git out, and he did," Harvey recounted, puffing on his pipe.

"And he didn't go see his folks?" O.T. asked.

"Naw," Harvey answered with a shrug. "Just up and disappeared like a fart in the wind." He grinned again. "I sat on the news about Sivvy awhile…couldn't figger if I should tell her folks. In the end, Lucy Dee an' me decided we'd tell Becca, Sivvy's sister. Her an' Lucy Dee been best friends for years. We figgered if she wanted to tell her folks, she could."

"And she never did.?" O.T. was incredulous.

"Naw, she had her reasons I rankin. But she did write letters to the asylum, askin' 'em to release Sivvy," Harvey said. "She finally heard back after a spell. They said she warn't next of kin so they couldn't release no info."

"And that's it?" O.T. asked in disbelief. "She didn't think to write to Sivvy herself, or tell her folks, or go down there to sort it out? She just sat on it like—"

"It's a tough thang, man," Harvey said firmly. "You don't know everything. Mister Nate's got heart troubles, and Misrus Julie-Anne ain't as strong as she pretends to be. I rankin she was just tryin' to protect her family. Then you come along and we thought you might just be the answer to our prayers."

O.T. couldn't see how that was possible. "Somethin' about this don't sit right. Why do I git the feelin' you ain't tol' me everything?"

Harvey just smiled. "I've tol' you all I can for now. You git Sivvy back to this ridge, and I might add more to the tale one day." With that, O.T. had been given his marching orders.

Now, far removed from the ridge, O.T. could scarcely believe it had all been real—so much of what he'd seen and heard felt like a dream. After losing Betty Lou and Walt, O.T. had been too busy being drunk and grieving to pay attention to the things that used to give him joy—summer nights in Madison County, the humidity thick as a blanket; the creek by the house, its water clear over muddy red banks, loud with the orchestra of full-throated bullfrogs, crickets, and the occasional howl of a coyote; the sassafras tree and the monarch butterflies that reminded him of Walt; the food, friendship, and even secrets of family.

The mountains had forced him to look again, had demanded he pay homage to nature's majesty—it was impossible to step outside into the cold, crisp air without taking a deep breath and letting the eye rest on its craggy majesty. *Nature's stage,* O.T. thought to himself, surprised at his own sentimentality. "All the world's a stage," he murmured, wondering from where he had recalled that line.

"…and all the men are merely players," Ginny finished quietly.

O.T. looked at her, surprised. "You know that poem?"

"It ain't a poem," she replied gloomily, looking out the window. "It's a soliloquy from Shakespeare."

"Oh, yeah. Right," O.T. replied, digging in his pocket for the tobacco DeWitt had given him. "Guess I read it in school or sumpin'."

"Naw," Ginny said. "Don't you remember? Uncle Walt had that book, *The Complete Works of Shakespeare.* He used to read from it sometimes after dinner, in front of the fire. That one is from *As You Like It,* his favorite. Remember?"

"Oh, yeah. Yeah," O.T. felt ashamed that he'd forgotten. "He did like that one a lot. Had the whole dang book memorized."

"He was special," she said, broodingly. "He wasn't like anybody else. I miss him."

"I do, too." O.T. paused for a moment, considering, and then said, "Ginny, I'm sure yer wonderin' why we're taking this trip. What this woman Sivvy and her fambly even have to do with us? Well, I'm doin' this for yer Uncle Walt. This is for him."

"Really? Why?"

O.T. proceeded to recount Sivvy's life story as he understood it to be, and when he was done, Ginny was ashen-faced.

"That poor woman," Ginny breathed in horror. "Franklin was tellin' me about an aunt of his, who he hadn't seen since he was three. Said he used to climb in the bed with her and she'd sing to him softly and rub his head till he fell asleep. I din't make the connection that he was talkin' about *her*, about Sivvy. And she's been in…that place…for all this time?" Ginny looked like she might cry. "Her entire adult life? Deddy, that's awful."

"I know," O.T. agreed. "I keep studyin' on it."

"Are you plannin' to git her out?" Ginny asked. "Are we bringing her back to Five Forks with us?"

"I don't know that I *could*," O.T. replied, weighing the question. "I heard a relative has to sign a person away to the asylum, and I figger you got to have a relative sign you back out. And then you got to git the doctor or superintendent signin' off too. How would I do that?"

"Misrus Maybelle and Mister Nate would sign," Ginny said. "I know they would."

"I'm sure they would, too," O.T. said. "But they ain't with us."

"They'd come," she said firmly. "If you ast 'em. Reckon you thought of that already?"

"Their daughter Becca didn't see fit to tell 'em. Now they know, 'cause of me, but I ain't sure if I got the heart to put more on their shoulders."

"Or mayhap there's a part of you that wants to take care of it yerself," Ginny said. "For Uncle Walt."

O.T. said nothing, and ignored her sidelong smile.

❧

By the time they arrived in Bishop, Georgia, O.T. was so bleary-eyed he almost didn't see the dilapidated storefront with its faded sign announcing the Stew & Que; beneath the sign, a cartoonish pink pig had been painted—long faded into a peachy white, seeping into the red brick beneath—a platter in its hoof, welcoming customers with a toothy grin that was more terrifying than charming.

"Deddy, I hope they're open," Ginny said. "I'm like to starve if we don't eat soon."

"We'll pull in and have a look-see," O.T. said, his own stomach growling in agreement. "But food seems to get scarcer the further we git from the mountains. I swear them ridge folks had magic beans in they yard, all the bounty they had."

"They put it up before times got rough," Ginny said. "Franklin tol' me mountain folks call themselves 'preppers.' Smart."

"Cain't help but agree," O.T. remarked as he pulled into the empty lot.

A rusted old Model T—pulled by a mule and stripped of its engine, windows, and windshield—carried an old man who gave them a friendly wave as he meandered past. O.T. and Ginny watched him as he disappeared down the dusty road.

"That's our old timer, Aladdin Gowe," a jolly voice announced behind them. "He rides the roads all day and all night, but ain't nobody got a clue where he goin'. He don't, neither."

O.T. turned to see a man standing behind him, wearing a white apron streaked with red grease. "I ain't clapt eyes on a Hoover-buggy like that in many a year. I'm O.T. Lawrence. This here's my daughter, Genevieve. This yer establishment?" O.T. asked, extending his hand.

"Yes, sirree, if you can call it that. Pleased to meet y'all. Rob Gum's the name, but most folks round here call me the Singin' Cook." He had a strong, warm handshake.

Rob Gum was stout, but muscular in his camouflage dungaree pants. One beefy arm sported a large tattoo of the same tray-toting pig from the signage wearing lipstick. Rob had piercing blue eyes in a pale face, with ample, rosy cheeks and a cleft in his chin. His hair, so blond it was almost white, was pulled up with a strap, and fell over his forehead in a curly cascade. A pack of Chesterfields protruded from his breast pocket.

"Why the Singin' Cook?" Ginny asked.

"Them's my two favorite things—singin' and cookin'," Rob informed her as he led the two inside, seating them at a wooden table by the window. "Used to run this place with my wife, and she couldn't stand it when I'd sing. When she run off with another fella, I said I'd never stop singin' the rest of my days, just to spite her whorin' behind." Robert unleashed a loud, whoop of a laugh, slapping the table in front of them. Ginny jumped. "Pardon my sayin' 'whore' in your company, little lady," the man said with mock gravity. He cocked his head toward O.T. "Even if she is one."

"We was wonderin' if you had a bite…?" O.T. asked, with a grin of his own.

"Well, yeah, fella, I'd hope so, or I better turn that 'open' sign on the door around." The Singing Cook laughed again, tightening the straps of his white apron over his ample torso. "Tell the truth, I'm just as poor as everybody else in town, but I got enough meat to make y'all a couple hamburgs, if you don't mind 'em without fixins. I know it say Stew & Que out there, but I ain't had pork in a spell. But I got beef, and all the cornbread you could ever eat, and a mess of green beans. Can fry 'em in lard or boil 'em for ya." He winked at Ginny. "Might even have a bowl of banana puddin' for the little lady here, if she cleans her plate."

"I thank ya," O.T. replied, gratefully. "We'll both have a hamburger and some of them green beans. Whichever way you want to fix 'em."

"And a piece of cornbread, please," Ginny said hopefully. "I'm mighty hungry."

Rob gave another booming laugh. "You and ever'body else in the country, gal." He pounded the table with his meaty fist. "I'll go fix you all a glass of tea and get your food a'going. Don't reckon you got all day to shoot the shit; you got the looks of folks passin' on thu."

It was still many more miles to Milledgeville, and O.T. didn't have much money left. He'd been sorely tempted to tell the cook to eighty-six the cornbread, and dessert, too—Lord knew it'd cost a packet. But his Ginny was hungry. O.T. was beginning to wonder what had possessed him to take this fool trip in the first place.

Ginny, as usual, read his thoughts. "You studyin' on Miss Sivvy, Papa?"

241

"I reckon so," O.T. said absently. "Wonderin' what I gone and done now."

"I think it's right nice of you, to do this for Uncle Walt," Ginny said kindly.

Suddenly they both became aware of a bright, raucous tenor coming from the kitchen, among the clatter and clang of pots and pans. O.T. craned his neck to listen, smiling as he heard the familiar refrain of "Ain't Misbehavin'," a song that he and his Betty Lou had danced to more than once in the drafty parlor after the young'uns had gone to bed, but he'd never heard it sung with a southern twang amid the clatter of pots and pans before.

"So, gal," O.T. began brightly, ignoring the dull pain in his heart, "you ain't said nary a word about a certain young man you met in the mountains."

Ginny looked surprised. "What's to say?"

"I seen him with his arm around you. Gettin' fresh. Figgered you'd be talkin' marriage by now."

"Shoot, Papa," she replied indignantly, turning crimson. "I just got out of one marriage, now you pushin' me into another?"

"I ain't pushin' you into nuthin'," O.T. said, looking out the window. The old timer was passing by in his horse-drawn Hoover buggy. Again he waved, even though there was nobody out there to wave to, and kept on going. "I like yer idea of gettin' schoolin'. Like that idear a lot. I jes' wondered if you felt different 'bout him than you did Grady."

"Well…." Ginny trailed off, looking moodily out the window.

The Singing Cook was warbling through the chorus now, his voice husky and dreamlike, if slightly off key; it added a certain ambiance to things, O.T. thought.

"I'm too young to get married, Papa. And I want to go to school. But I reckon it's true that I do like Franklin…."

"I knowed it," O.T. said with a smile.

A loud crash sounded from the kitchen, followed by a stream of cuss words: "Son of a goddamn bitchin' motherfuckin' pans won't stay on the damn pegs!" O.T. bit off his laughter.

"Why does everything have to be decided quick?" Ginny demanded, sitting up straight and looking O.T. in the eye.

"What you talkin' about, gal?"

"I ain't even fifteen. I ain't ready to be decidin' my whole dang life. But all my friends are either engaged or tryin' to catch a man. I just want to have some time to *think*!"

"I can understand that."

"It's like Miss Sivvy," Ginny retorted. "She was younger than me when she went off with her uncle. Then she got to get marrit to some ol' man to save her hide." Her eyes flashed. "She ain't had no choices. Not a one. I can't stand the thought of ending up like that, Deddy. I want to choose my choices by my own self."

"You can, gal," O.T. assured her. "You sure can."

"A woman in this world ain't *got* no choices, from what I figger. Every which way you look there's something or someone standin' in yer way. It's get married and pop out babies or spend the rest of yer life apologizing for not doing it."

"Spoken like a true woman of the world!" Rob Gum pronounced, setting down a huge plate of steaming cornbread and two glasses of sweet tea. "Apologies that I ain't got no butter," he said, wiping his hands on his apron. "My cows are long gone. Sold what didn't go to the butcher." He cocked an eye at Ginny. "So you one of them flapper gals, is you? You go in for all that jazz emancipation and all a'that?" He grinned.

"No," Ginny said glumly. "Wish I was, maybe."

"Shoot, gal," Rob Gum said cheerfully, pulling up a chair and sitting across from them. He rested his chin on his large hands and made doe eyes at Ginny. "I wish you was, too. I sure do love me some jazz." Ginny didn't smile. "What's eatin' you, sugar? Tell the Singin' Cook all about it."

"I'm fine." Ginny picked at her cornbread and O.T. took a sip of tea, sighing. He didn't have the first clue as to how to bring a teenage girl out of a slump.

"Ol' Rob Gum sure knows about a mess of troubles." The Singin' Cook turned to O.T., gesturing at the platter of cornbread. "Get a bite in you, man. You 'bout as skinny as a scarecrow and twice as ugly." He laughed. "The hamburgs got to thaw."

"It's just not fair!" Ginny wailed suddenly, making the two men jump. "What am I supposed to do now? Deddy, you ain't gonna want to hear this, but I'll *bust* if I don't say it out loud," Ginny exclaimed, her face flushing a pretty pink that warmed her cheeks and put a glow to her eyes.

"Go on and tell us, little lady," Rob Gum said, with a twitch to his mouth and a twinkle in his eyes.

"When we got in the truck ready to leave the ridge, you remember how they all crowded round to say goodbye?"

"Yes, course I remember. Wadn't but yesterday," O.T. reminded her, rolling his eyes.

"When we drove off, I turned to look one last time…jus' because. And I saw Franklin walking down the hill, toward his house with his winter cap pulled low and his hair streamin' out behind. He had his hands in his pockets, and he was walkin' real fast, like he had to get where he was goin'. Nothin' special at all. Just a fella walkin' in the snow down a hill. But"—Her voice wavered a little—"it was like a picture in a book, and I jus' felt so much tenderness, I thought I would cry myself to death. Like I was gonna choke on my own heart, it was so—so—" Ginny swallowed, and looked up, embarrassed. "You ever felt that way about somebody, Deddy, or am I crazy?"

"Uh-oh, man," Rob Gum said, looking O.T. dead in the eye, mirth twinkling in his blues. He gave a low whistle. "Yer in for a heap o'trouble."

O.T. felt a hard lump in his throat, and he reached out to grip Ginny's arm. "You ain't crazy, darlin'. Jus' in love," he said softly.

"No." Ginny stared at him, aghast. "I can't.…"

"Hey," said the Singin' Cook in a bright, jolly voice. "Don't you fret about it none, gal! Good thing about bein' in love is the more miserable you are, the better it feels! And purdy as you are, I bet that poor bastard feels about ten times worse than you do right now." He clapped a hand on the table and laughed. "What d'ya reckon, Mr. Lawrence?"

"Prob'ly true," O.T. forced a laugh.

Rob Gum smiled helpfully. "Hey, I gotta pair of handcuffs in the shed, if you want to chain her down. Drastic times, measures, all a'that. Gonna go get them hamburgs and beans. Back in a jiffy." The cook danced his way to the kitchen, slinging his rag behind him as he resumed his raucous rendition of "Ain't Misbehavin'" in a bright falsetto.

O.T. squeezed his daughter's arm again and said softly, "He was just tryin' to make you laugh, gal. He warn't tryin' to make light—"

"No, it's okay, Deddy," she said with a smile. "I like him. I like this place."

"I'm just'a savin' my love for…the Stew & Que!"

A dribbling noise sounded from the kitchen, followed by a loud clatter of pots and pans that could only be a drum solo with utensils. Then: *"Bah ba dooo bah rat a tat a tata tat bee bibbly bop a dum—"* the most pitiful attempt at a scat they had ever heard. He and Ginny laughed until tears streamed down their cheeks.

O.T. pushed back his plate and yawned, covering his mouth with his napkin as Ginny excused herself to go the bathroom. "Sir, that was some good eatin'. You 'bout put me right to sleep, I'm so stuffed."

"You look fit to keel over and die right here," Rob Gum said, stacking their dirty plates in the crook of his arm. "I got a spare bed, if'n y'all want to stay on. Reckon yer gal can have the bed and you can sleep on the floor. Got to charge for the meal, y'see, 'cause a man got to get paid, but the room's free. I wouldn't mind the comp'ny."

"Much obliged," O.T. said, with a sigh of relief. "I reckon I would've had trouble stayin' awake at the wheel and am right happy to sleep on the floor."

"I'll go get that banana puddin'," Rob Gum replied. "My neighbor, widow Beulah Simpson, made it. She feels sorry for me on account of my whorin' wife. She's sweet on me, I think. Wants her some of the Singin' Cook. I was savin' it for my Sunday, but let yer gal have it."

"You're too kind, man."

"Naw, ain't nothin'. Glad to have comp'ny."

"Don't supposin' you'd know where a fella could get a nip?" O.T. hated himself for asking. He fingered the few coins left in his pocket and felt even worse, but he had a bad case of nerves that needed settling.

Rob Gum shook his head. "Cain't say I do. I ain't a drinkin'man, really. And around these parts ain't nobody brewin' nothin', and ain't nobody got extra dime to be buying, neither. Sheriff Jackson lives just down the way, and he wouldn't take kindly if any of his residents was sneakin' illegal drink. But might know where you could get you a pinch of reefer weed, though, if you interested."

"Cain't say I ever tried that," O.T. admitted.

"Dang sight better than alcohol, brother. Nice and mellow. Cures what ails you without givin' you a nasty hangover."

Ginny emerged from the bathroom, stifling her own yawn. "We goin' now, Deddy? I'm so tired. Might sleep a little in the truck."

"I reckon we might bed down here for the night," O.T. said. "I'm awful tired, too, and Mr. Gum offered us a room. Save us a dollar."

"Fine by me."

O.T. settled Ginny in the back room, then, bidding her goodnight, returned to the darkened restaurant. The cook had turned the sign to Closed, and the place was quiet save for the roar of an ancient metal ceiling fan that wobbled to and fro above their heads.

"It ain't gon' fall," Rob Gum reassured O.T., wiping his large hands on a dish towel. "Wife used to worry about it too. Ain't fell in twenty years. Just looks wobbly. Let's go on out back and we can have us a smoke and a chit-chat."

O.T. followed the man through the kitchen—which still held the lingering smells of fried beef and cornbread, and the acrid smell of bleach—and stepped out onto a cement patio, where two spindly-looking chairs were propped up.

"We'll light us one 'o these," Rob Gum said as they settled into the chairs. He retrieved a small bag of something green and a pack of cigarette papers from his pocket. "Awful sorry I ain't got no spirits. I can see you need you one. I quit drinkin' some years ago, used to git slap goofy on the stuff." He grinned. "I'm still the same ol' fat-ass bastard, but at least I ain't drunk. Save a lot of money, too."

"Don't that cost?" O.T. said, gesturing to the little bag.

"Shoot. Now let's just say that I got a right good green thumb and leave it at that."

"I gotcha."

"And if the feds come a'knockin' on my door, I'll know it was you who sent 'em."

"I ain't no nark," O.T. said with a smile. He reached into his own pocket, pulled out his pipe, and lit it up. "Say, I knew the name of yer place, before we even came in. Guy by the name of Harvey tol' me—he came through this way, oh, about fifteen year ago. Thing is, he never did come in here. He passed on by. He was *supposed* to come in, though."

"I ain't even stoned yet, and I sure as heck don't follow," Rob said with a boisterous laugh. "What you mean, he was *supposed* to come in?"

"Well, he was tol' to come here, that you and yer wife would help him. But in the end he got too scairt and took his chances with a travelin' coal miner crew instead. This Harvey was a reverend's apprentice, travelin' around Georgia doin' tent revivals and all...."

O.T. proceeded to tell Rob Harvey and Sivvy's story.

"Next thing happens, Billy Rev has the law ready to lynch Harvey, and the old man—Mr. Clayton Shelnutt, that's his name—helped Harvey get away." O.T. took another puff of his pipe. "Then Sivvy and Clayton was marrit."

Rob Gum leaped up in sudden excitement, the chair collapsing with a clatter. "Shoot, man, why didn't you lead with him? I know Clay Shelnutt! Knowed him all my dang life!"

"You do?" O.T. smiled, surprised.

"Well, hell, accorse I do!"

"Don't supposin' you could introduce me? I'm dyin' to talk to him."

"Well," Rob Gum replied gloomily, righting his chair before settling his girth back into it. "You'd *have* to die to talk to him, I reckon, since Clay's been dead himself these ten years past." He took a puff on the little cigarette he held and let out the smoke in a long stream. "He had some condition. My ex-wife could tell ya more. She was a washerwoman as you know, but she also nursed all over and was right good at it, too. Clay always took a shine to us, Miriam especially. And after his boy died and that funny business with his wife, Clay din't have nobody in that old house to help keep up the fires or get a bite in him, and he just took sick and died. Real quick, too. Miriam was tore up about it."

"That's sad."

"Yes, it was. He was a right good man. Real friendly, smart man, too. Most everybody around here just loved him to death. For some reason he liked *me* a lot, though I couldn't figger why. He was always talkin' about books at me and I ain't ever read more than a girlie pulp or two my whole life."

"What was the funny business with his wife? Do you mean Sivvy?"

"Din't know no Sivvy," Rob Gum replied somberly. "I was talkin' about his second wife. We knew her as Triphy—that's what Clay called her." He shrugged. "I reckon she and this Sivvy got to be one and the same?"

He passed the joint to O.T., who took a small puff, then started coughing. "I think you might be right," he wheezed.

Rob Gum laughed a little, low in his throat. "She and my wife was friends. Not good friends, mind, because Triphy was real shy and quiet. Just liked to keep to herself. Always seemed like she had a lot of thoughts goin' in her head. Clay was besotted with her, though," Rob Gum went on, taking the joint back. "Don't know what their age difference was exactly; I figger he had to have been twenty, maybe even closer to thirty years older'n her; but they got along fine. She kep' his house in tip-top shape and they spent all their time together, holed up in the place, drinkin' tea and readin' books. Neither of 'em had any use for the rest of the town."

"Why?"

"Sheriff's department is half Klan," Rob confided in a conspiratorial whisper, "but you din't hear that from me. Clay, bein' a former preacher, din't hold with violence. and Triphy agreed with 'im, I reckon."

"On account of Harvey, if nothing else," O.T. mumbled, his head feeling fuzzy.

"Still don't know no Harvey," Rob answered. "But Clay told me that Triphy used to be real good friends with a colored boy, when she first got to Farmington. There was some trouble and the boy got lynched—" The cook's eyes widened. "Wait a daggum minute! Din't you just say that fella named Harvey said that he—?"

"Yes'r," O.T. replied, "but he wasn't lynched. He got away, with

Clayton's help, Made his way back up to the mountains, and he's safe and sound, married with kids and everything," O.T. said. "Doin' good."

"Well, I'm right glad to hear. But none of this makes a lick a'sense."

"Amen to that. I can't keep track of who all was in and out of her life."

"I don't envy you. Sounds like you're trying to unknit a blanket." Rob Gum took the spliff back and looked it over. "I reckon Miriam might help you, though. She knew more of Triphy's business than I did."

"Where could I find her?"

"Miriam? She's living in Farmington with that sonofabitch she left me for. She'd talk to ya, I'm sure. I'll drive you there tomorrow, if you want."

"I don't want to cause you no trouble," O.T. protested.

"It'd be awright," Rob said, laughing. "Ain't nobody got nothin' to worry about from the Singin' Cook. She might be a whore, but I ain't mad. Ain't got it in me, I guess."

"Mighty big of ya," O.T. laughed.

"I *am* mighty big, yes sirree," Rob grinned, patting his belly affectionately. "Shit, brother, you look like you 'bout to fall asleep right in that chair. The green man got his hand around your neck. Lemme grab you some blankets and you can get some sleep."

O.T. woke before Ginny and peeled himself off the hard floor, stifling a groan. His back was as stiff as a board, and his mouth felt like it was full of rotting cotton. O.T. felt funny walking into the kitchen and looking for coffee, so he just grabbed himself a cup of water. The dining room was small, with four wooden tables pushed up against the walls—O.T. assumed the open space was for dancing. The Singing Cook had a good spot for fish frys and hoedowns. In easier times, before cotton failed and the stock market crashed, back when the cook was still happily married to his Miriam, they might have made a real go of it. O.T. could almost hear the bluegrass music, smell the smoking barbecue, and see the scores of pretty young girls in fresh-pressed dresses.

The thought brought on a memory of Betty Lou in her pretty homespun dress at Misrus Maybelle's fish fry—her white-blonde hair swept up, a tendril falling over one cheek, her lips of ruby red, with her hands covered in white gloves, those cool blue eyes surveying him with polite interest as he stammered over his words, making a fool of himself. He had forgotten nothing about that night.

He downed his water, placed the cup in the sink, and headed outside, careful to open the door slowly so the bell wouldn't tinkle. The sun was a faint wisp in the corner of the horizon, a handful of faint stars still scattering across the early morning sky. He wondered what Betty Lou would have made of all of this. Would she be pleased that he was driving around Georgia, meeting folks and getting their stories? Would she pity Sivvy, give O.T.'s quest her blessing, or consider his journey a betrayal?

O.T. reckoned she might've felt a bit of both. He'd never have gone on this drive if he hadn't lost her. The truth was he was traveling through Sivvy's life in order to avoid having to live his own.

I'm way too sober for this, O.T. thought bitterly, craving a strong drink. The cook's weed had given him a nice mellow feeling, but it wasn't the same at all. He wished he could find some liquor somewhere. The hurt was coming back, and he'd rather not feel it.

O.T. sat on the front stoop of the Stew & Que, waiting on Ginny to finish showering, listening to Robert Gum the Singin' Cook belt out a gospel tune he didn't recognize, when a car pulled in.

Rob came out to the stoop, wiping his hands on a dish rag. "Well, looks like we ain't gotta go find her," he told O.T. "The jezebel done showed up. I guess her ears was burnin'."

A tall, red-haired woman with wide shoulders and freckled cheeks climbed out from the driver's seat. She was pleasingly curvy and carried herself like she knew it. So this was Miriam. O.T. was relieved to see her—he hadn't been keen on driving out to find her. He was low on gas and eager to get to Milledgeville.

"Hey, Rob," Miriam greeted him, walking past O.T. without a "how-do."

"Miriam," Rob acknowledged solemnly. Then, to O.T.'s surprise, he threw his arm back and wholloped the woman on the backside with his dish towel.

"Rob, cut it out!" Miriam protested, swatting at his arm. "I ain't here to get into the dickens with you!"

"Why you here, then, woman?" Rob asked, his eyes sparkling. "Hope it ain't to get no free lunch outta me. Them days is over, pretty lady. You got to pay like ever'body else."

"Oh, shut up, you dang fool. I had enough of yer stew and barbecue to last me my days. I done et already." Miriam cast a lazy eye at O.T. "I just come by to see if there was any mail. I changed my address at the post office, but I been waitin' on a letter from my sister Louisa these past two months and ain't heard nary a word."

"Yer sister Louisa don't want to talk to you, that's why," Rob said, whacking her with the dish towel again. "She done got tired of your shit."

"Cut it out, Rob," Miriam ordered, stifling laughter. "Well, since I come all this way, don't reckon you got enough Christian kindness to give a woman a glass a'tea? Or you gon' make me pay for that, too?"

"I'll give you a glass a'tea," Rob said, opening the door. "But first you got to say hello to my buddy, here. Walkin' on past him, rude as all get-out. Ain't nobody taught you no manners since you ran outta here?"

She looked at O.T. now, a ghost of a smile on her freckled cheeks. "Oh, well, hey there. I'm Miriam." She made no move to lean down and shake his hand, so O.T. stood up, brushing off his pants.

"O.T. Lawrence."

Miriam nodded, and turned back to her ex-husband. "That tea now, honeybunch?"

"Sure thing, sweetie pie." Rob rolled his eyes at O.T. before disappearing inside.

Miriam lingered on the stoop, staring at the peeling paint on the sign like she wanted to take a paintbrush and fix it.

"Ma'am," O.T. began, "Mr. Gum was tellin' me that you mighta knowed a friend of mine. I wanted to ast you about it."

"Oh yeah? Who's that?" Miriam asked, brightening. "I know a lot of folks round here, on account I was a washerwoman for a long time, and a nurse, too."

"Her name was Sivvy Hargrove," O.T. said, wondering how many names the woman might have collected by the time he finally clapped eyes on her. "But you mighta knowed her as Triphy Shelnutt. She was married to—"

"Clay's wife! Accorse I remember her!" Miriam exclaimed. "I ain't seen her in ten years, but I think about her all the time. And she's a friend of yourn?" O.T. nodded—it was easier than explaining what felt like an increasingly complicated history. "Tell me, is Triphy still in the asylum? That was an awful business, so it was. Not a day goes by I don't think about that poor gal, stuck in that place."

"Last I heard, she was," O.T. answered.

"Thought about visitin' her once or twice," Miriam went on, "but I chickened out. The thought of that place gives me the heebs." She shuddered.

"I wondered if you might tell me yer recollections from when she was marrit to Clay," O.T. said. "I'm tryin' to piece together what happened, how she ended up there."

"Gosh," Miriam said, surprised. "You prob'ly know more than me. I just nursed Clay a little, is all. And most of that business was hushed up. Didn't Rob tell you?"

"He told me some, but I'd like to hear your version."

"All I can tell you is that they got married on the fly, real fast-like, and ever'body in town was shocked because nobody knew the gal, plus he was way older'n her. So much older it woulda been a scandal had it been anybody else but Clay. Folks in town just loved that man. But there was somethin' goin' on with this colored boy, a friend of Triphy's, who had been travelin' with her and the uncle, a real mean fella. I can't remember all the story, but I heard the boy got kilt by the Klan. Sicced their dogs on him, I heard. Triphy was right tore up about that. None of us was allowed to mention it. Them Klan is monsters hidin' in plain sight," she spat, disgusted. "Anyhow, after they was marrit, Triphy took up the nursin' of him, so I was kinda outta a job. But it was awright—he loved that gal. She took good care of him. Cooked for him an' all—gave me the receipt to her angel food cake. To this day, I make the best cake you ever tasted—"

"She a lie." Robert Gum appeared, holding a cold glass of tea. "That cake is dry as a bone."

"Hush yer fat mouth, Robert Gum," Miriam said primly, and O.T. burst out laughing.

"They had a child, a little boy. Sweetest baby you ever saw. You could just tell that Triphy loved bein' a mama, too. They would sit in the front pew at church, all three of 'em just so shiny and pretty like new pennies. But then it all went bad."

"What happened?" O.T. asked.

"Their little boy died. They was a fever goin' around that winter, you remember, Robbo? Most grown folks kicked it off fine, but the little ones didn't do so well. We lost three babies that winter. Their boy already was sickly—his lungs, I reckon—and he just couldn't lick it. It broke ever'body's heart. We all rallied around 'em and tried to help best we could, but Triphy went slap crazy. Clay shut her up in that house and hid her from sight, because she was a risk to herself and others. Those were *his* words—I came with a casserole, tried to see her, and he said I couldn't 'cause she was a risk to herself and others. I heard tell of somethin' goin' down at the church, too, after the service, but I never did hear exactly what."

"So what happened after that?"

Miriam shrugged. "All I know is that one day she was shut up in that house and the next she was gone. Clay came to church by himself that Sunday. Said she'd gone for a long rest to get well. He himself so weak and sick he could barely stand up on his own. I went back to nursin' him after Triphy had gone. He kep' tellin' me that she'd be back, once she was better. But neither of 'em got no better. Clay died just after Christmas.

"I went back to the house once after he died, to clean up and air out the place a little. Thought it was the least I could do for 'em. When I was straightening up his bedroom, I came across the admission papers from Milledgeville in his roll-up desk. I sat down on the floor and cried. Sometimes God can be mean as hell."

PART III

I write her a letter, just a few short lines
And suffer death a thousand times...
For black is the color of my true love's hair,
Her lips are like red roses fair
With the sweetest smile and gentle hands
I love the ground whereon she stands

-SCOTTISH-APPALACHIAN FOLK SONG

Chapter Twenty

"Who?" Sivvy was confused.

"Owen somebody. Lawson?" said Nurse Jenkins. "He's waiting out front. I can give you twenty minutes' leave to go visit him if you promise to stay in the pecan grove. Y'all can sit on the bench."

"No'm." Sivvy shook her head, fretfully. "I don't know him. I ain't had but one fella visit me the whole time I been here, and I don't know that I want to start now."

"But Miss Sivvy," Nurse Jenkins insisted. "He come a long way. He said so."

"Where from?"

"I cain't recall that," Nurse Jenkins said. "But it might do ya some good to see a body."

"I don't want to see him," Sivvy said firmly. "Unless I have to?"

"You don't *have* to, of course," the nurse replied, exasperated. "But why would you refuse—?"

"I better get on to the kitchen," Sivvy said. "If I'm excused?"

"Accorse you are."

Sivvy nervously wiped her hands on her apron and walked into the kitchen, her heart racing. It wasn't until she'd started blending the cornmeal with the big paddle that she realized that Nurse Jenkins had probably meant Owen *Lawrence*. Now *that* was a name she remembered. Oh, well, Sivvy sighed. Too late now.

Sivvy's heart leapt in her chest when the nurse told her that the man had come again. She had written to Walt, though, and couldn't figure out why his brother was here instead. Sivvy couldn't shake the nagging idea that this was some devious trick of Uncle Billy's. Owen Lawrence had a young girl with him, Nurse Burns had said. The presence of a girl made Sivvy feel better about meeting him, so she ventured out to the lobby of the Powell building and over to the heavy desk where visitors were checked in and out. The lobby was grand—adorned with ornate art, comfortable chairs, and spacious, sparkling windows—and gave visitors the impression that the rest of the asylum was equally appealing.

A man stood at the desk, drumming his fingers on the surface. Sivvy hovered uncertainly, shadowed in the hallway, suddenly unsure.

Owen Lawrence was about six feet tall and had sandy-colored hair in need of a cut—he'd at least made the effort to slick it back with a little pomade, though one shock fell over his brow. He wore dark blue jeans that were pressed and clean, and a faded chambray work shirt with rolled-up sleeves. He was gangly and thin, with arms muscular from hard work. His mouth seemed to be working something over, but there was a hint of a smile that Sivvy could see even from the hallway. Her shoulders relaxed ever so slightly.

The girl with him, a shorter version of who Sivvy assumed was her pa, was dressed in a white flour sack dress embroidered with little red cherries. Homespun, clean and pressed, but old. Her sandy-blonde hair was pulled back in plaits, and she had same eyes and easy smile as the man who accompanied her.

Sivvy squared her shoulders, deciding to go on up and say hello. They had come to see her two days in a row, after all. Her hands were shaking badly, and knowing that nothing would stop the trembling, she shoved them into the pockets of her apron. "How d'ya do," Sivvy said as she apparoached them. "I'm Savilia Shelnutt. Hope you ain't been waitin' long."

Owen Lawrence turned and smiled at her, and she could see the gray eyes she remembered so well, which held a great deal of something she could not quite place. Other than the tell-tale signs of drink, which showed in his ruddy cheeks and the soft pouches under his eyes, he looked remarkably healthy. His smile was so wide open and genuine that Sivvy felt her heart catch a little in her throat.

"I wondered which name you'd use," he remarked in a low voice, almost to himself. Then he extended a hand. "Miss Savilia, Sivvy. How-do. I'm Owen Lawrence." Sivvy clasped his hand reluctantly. His touch was feather-light and timid, as though he feared she might break, but there was no mistaking the joy he felt at making her acquaintance. "I'm so pleased to see you, you got no idear. I feel like I spent the last month gettin' to know you."

"We met before," Sivvy said stupidly, after a moment.

"Well, yes, ma'am, we did, but that was so many years ago and I wasn't sure you'd remember." Mr. Lawrence laughed easily. "I know you remember my brother Walt, accorse. On account of yer letter an' all."

"Yes, my letter. Of course." Sivvy teetered a little on her feet.

"This here's my daughter, my eldest, Genevieve. We call her Ginny."

"Right pleased to meet ya, Ginny," Sivvy said, her hands shaking violently in her apron pockets. "Ain't you purdy."

Ginny did not seem to know what to make of this compliment. Her freckled face flushed and she looked down with a smile. "Nice to meet ya," she mumbled.

"She's shy," Mr. Lawrence explained with a wink.

"So am I," Sivvy said to the girl, smiling. "We'll make a fine pair. They gave me leave to sit outside for twenty minutes. In the pecan grove. Y'all want to go out there?"

"Surely." Mr. Lawrence opened the big heavy door and waited for the two women to walk through it. He fell in lock-step beside Sivvy, silent, as she led them to a little bench near a big tree, where she sat, and Ginny beside her. Mr. Lawrence stood, hands clasped behind him, one leg shaking in front of him nervously.

Sivvy waited for him to speak, but it seemed he did not know what to say. "So," she began. "I can't imagine why y'all have come to see me."

He stood there dumbly. "Now that I'm here, I reckon I don't know where to start, is all," he finally admitted.

Ginny made a noise. "For goodness sake, Deddy, fill her in on where all we been." She glanced at Sivvy with a shy smile. "He's impossible sometimes, I swear."

Sivvy looked back at the man, whose face had turned a little red. "Why don't you have a seat, to start with?"

"Awright." Mr. Lawrence hitched up the legs of his pressed trousers and sat down on the grass, pulling his long legs up under him. Sivvy caught a flash of his faded black socks. "As I was sayin'… now that I'm here, I reckon I don't quite know how to start. There's so much to tell you, ma'am, and things I got to ast you, too."

"I only have twenty minutes," Sivvy said warily.

"You sent a letter to my Uncle Walt last year—" Ginny began.

"—and I suppose you was wonderin' why he never wrote you back," Mr. Lawrence finished, his face clouding over. "Well, fact of it is my brother Walt has…passed on."

"Oh." Sivvy pressed her lips together. She did not feel terribly shocked by this, only sad. People died so often. "I'm sorry for your loss. Both of y'all."

"Much obliged." Mr. Lawrence managed, his face stricken. It must be hard, losing a twin, Sivvy thought, feeling herself soften toward him.

"I'm sorry," Sivvy repeated. "Of course, I warn't mad not to receive a reply. Don't know that I expected one."

Mr. Lawrence looked surprised. "But the letter all but begged a reply. You ast about yer fambly…you ast Walt to.…"

"I don't remember," Sivvy said, embarrassed. "I mean, I remember writin' the letter, accorse, but I disremember what all I said in it. I was feelin' poorly then. Maybe I *did* talk about my family."

To Sivvy's horror, Mr. Lawrence reached into his breast pocket and pulled out a faded piece of paper. She recognized her own handwriting. She'd taken pains to make it neat, had written it out several times, taking frequent breaks because her hands shook. Mr. Lawrence unfolded the note and looked at her thoughtfully. "You said you couldn't write to them for shame."

Sivvy's cheeks burned. She felt a cool hand on her arm—Ginny sought to provide comfort, Sivvy knew, but she felt a sudden urge to race back into the Powell building and beg the doctor for a sedative; something to make her sleep, and forget this embarrassment. Her hands twisted and turned in her lap.

"Ma'am," Owen's voice was low and measured, "I don't mean to make you uncomfortable. I didn't come here to remind you of bad times. I just—"

"Why *did* you come, then?"

Mr. Lawrence spoke quietly: "My brother's dying wish was to send you that letter. He died the day I mailed it. Then my wife died. I lost everything." He met her eyes, and Sivvy's heart quickened. His gray eyes reminded her of a thunderstorm on the horizon. They were full of so much pain.

"Scarlet fever took 'em both. Then a few months later, the stock market crashed and I lost my farm." He smiled an angry, sad smile. "I wasn't hangin' on but by a thread. Then yer letter turned up, and I can't explain it, Miss Sivvy, but it was like somebody held a torch out to me, showing me a way through the dark. I thought if I—if I could just find you, I'd be doin' something for my brother. Somethin' that he would have wanted to do himself. That I could—"

"Ease yer sins by helpin' the crazy woman?" Sivvy said.

Spots of color appeared on O.T.'s cheeks. He shook his head. "Don't care to put it that way. It ain't like that. But if I *can* help ya, I'd like to."

"How on earth you reckon you gonna help me anyhow? And what makes you think I *need* help?"

O.T. glanced around the grounds, his gray eyes taking in the look of the place, sweeping over the buildings, the trees, the grave being dug a few yards from them, then looked back at her. "Maybe you don't. But I had to come and see for myself that you were awright. And then at least I could tell yer folks, ease their minds."

"My folks?" she demanded. "You know my folks?"

"That's what I was tryin' to say to you before. Yer letter said that you needed to know that your family was awright. I aimed to find out for you." Sivvy stared at him. "So we went up to the ridge, Ginny and I. We was there not a week past, with the Hargroves."

"How…?" Sivvy fumbled, shocked. "How were you able to find them?"

"I din't have much to go on, actually," O.T. said. "But I remembered enough about you to make a few guesses, and I reckon I got lucky with the rest."

"How are they, then?" she asked finally.

O.T. recounted their snowy drive up to the ridge, how Julie-Anne had greeted them in the night with steaming cups of sassafras tea, and how they'd stayed on for several days, meeting the family and helping at the corn shucking.

"So they know? About me?" Sivvy asked, hating herself for the tremor in her voice.

O.T. looked at her steadily, his gray eyes kind, and said, "They din't. But now they do. I told Misrus Julie-Anne. The way yer ma talked about you, it seemed like to kill her how much she missed you. I had to let her know that you were awright."

"I was always affeared of them knowin'," Sivvy admitted, with a sigh. "That somehow they'd find out. Lord, I don't know what's worse—them knowing that their daughter is a lunatic, or thinking she's dead." Sivvy shuddered, with a sudden chill, and wished she'd brought her cardigan. "I think it might be better to be dead."

"Don't talk thataway, Miss Sivvy," O.T. said gently. "I understand the feelin', but I can tell you it don't do no good. And you ain't a lunatic."

"Yes, I am," Sivvy said, calmly. "Certified and everything." She laughed, but he didn't laugh with her.

"I don't believe it," he said. "You got problems, same as the rest of us. But you look sane enough to me."

"You don't know me," Sivvy said firmly. "Not atall."

"You right, I don't. But Miss Sivvy—"

"I reckon you are a real nice man, real nice. And yer daughter, she's right pretty and nice, too. And I sure do appreciate y'all coming here to check in on me, takin' the time to see my family, too. I rankin that's one of the nicest things anyone ever did for me." Sivvy stood, her arms curled around her torso, her skin prickling with gooseflesh. "But my time is up and I gotta go back in. I rankin y'all oughter just leave and head on back where you from. There ain't nuthin' you can do for me here. And definitely nothin' I could do for you in kind, I'm sorry to say."

O.T. stood as well. "Miss Sivvy, if you please—" he began unhappily.

"Now I know my fambly's well. They know I'm alive. I thank ya kindly for that. I'm sure yer brother would appreciate it and all. You done yer duty, so you can go on home. And don't come back thisaway. This ain't no place for healthy folks."

"Miss Sivvy—"

"Please," she pleaded. "Just go on, now. I druther you just go on."

"Deddy," Ginny whispered, tugging on his arm. "C'mon, let's go."

Sivvy turned away and walked briskly back into the Powell Building, deftly ignoring the look of utter defeat on O.T. Lawrence's face. Her hands shook for a solid hour after she'd taken her leave of them, O.T.'s sad gray eyes and crestfallen face playing over and over in her mind.

☙

However prepared O.T. thought he had been to meet Sivvy, he he hadn't been prepared at all. The woman he'd spent a week getting to know from afar might have been a girl still—she was all angles and lines, tiny and petite, with soft black hair framing a delicate bone-china face. The circles that rimmed her eyes and a few wrinkles around her mouth were the only signs of a life hard-lived. He had expected to find a crone, a wraith, a woman so ravaged by pain that she'd be almost unrecognizable. Instead he found a slip of a girl, a snapshot in time, by which memories of 1916 came rushing back to wallop him in the chest.

Her eyes reminded him of the foxfire he had encountered in the frozen woods—two large emeralds shining huge and wild in the white of her skin, beneath the ink-black of her hair.

O.T. felt as if he were dangling off a precipice, that he was possessed by a moment that could define the rest of his life. Looking into Sivvy's face, he had felt two things simultaneously: that she would surely lead him down a path he wasn't ready for, and that he had no choice but to go down it anyway.

Sitting on the grass in the pecan grove, Sivvy's shins and calves at eye-level, he'd looked up at her, trying not to stare at her legs. She had not been wearing stockings, and the skin of her legs was creamy and white. How long had it been since he'd seen a woman without stockings? he wondered. Since before Betty Lou died, of course. Times were lean and a woman wouldn't waste good stockings around the house, but O.T. didn't think he'd ever seen a bare-legged woman out in public.

It was just legs, so why was his heart beating so hard?

It wasn't just the sight of her legs that had befuddled him; it had been something bigger—*fear*, taking rest behind his eyes, giving a sharp pain to the head. He had come all this way, only to turn yellow at the last. O.T. reckoned he'd scared Sivvy Hargrove, but he'd scared himself, too. Because after seeing her face to face, he knew without a doubt that this woman was not tied to Walt's destiny, but rather to his.

He had stared after her long after she'd fled inside, as though she might come back out, her mind changed, their fates sealed. But she did not return. After a time, he pushed his hands into his pockets, turned to Ginny and smiled a little sheepishly.

"Well, shit," he said, and Ginny's face was full of a sympathy beyond her years. "What do we do now?"

CHAPTER TWENTY-ONE

Ten years. No, *more* than ten years, it had been, since the day Clayton Shelnutt had choked back tears and left her in this place. She had forgotten so many things; she'd lost track of the time. Ten years in the asylum, without much to distinguish one year from another. Until today.

Now, today of all days, after all that time, this man, this gray-eyed farmer who called himself O.T. had come, bringing news of her family and lamenting his poor dead brother, and it had Sivvy tied in knots. Her life had moved onward predictably for all these years, and though she wasn't exactly happy, she was resigned. Listening to O.T. talk of family had lit a small flame inside her that she had thought long extinguished. From the moment he'd mentioned her mother's name, that flame had started to grow, and now it burned inside her chest with such fierceness she thought she might burn right up.

Sivvy felt wracked by guilt. O.T. Lawrence had traveled all the way from Five Forks to the ridge, then back down to Milledgeville, for *her*. Gas, she knew, was very, very dear; he'd likely spent most, if not all of his savings on the trip. He had done her a kindness. And what had she done? Listened greedily until he'd finished talking about her family and then dismissed him. Her rudeness was unforgivable. When she got into a panic, when her hands began to shake, she turned into a person who was terse, fidgeting, rude. Sivvy had sent them away, not out of spite or apathy but out of sheer terror.

I should have tried harder, Sivvy scolded herself, pounding the pillow under her arm. *I behaved shameful. All these years I lamented never having visitors and then one comes, one with news and with real caring for me, and what do I do? I shove him off and tell him not to come back. You're an ungrateful, mean old trollop, Savilia Hargrove.*

The next morning Sivvy felt like one of the ghosts, floating aimlessly through the asylum as she went through the motions of getting ready to go downstairs. Clothes, apron, shoes. Walk to the bathroom. Use the toilet, wash hands, brush teeth. Put the toothbrush on the peg. Fasten cap over head. Nurse Burns wasn't on duty this morning, so Sivvy was accompanied by one of the nurses who usually worked in the Cook building. She was all business, and didn't speak, which was a relief for Sivvy. The strange musings of Nurse Burns unnerved her.

Sivvy didn't dare tell anyone about Nurse Burns and her ghosts, or her bigger secret: that she had finally made an appointment with Dr. Lowell. Thinking of it made her skin crawl—the way his eyes had brightened and worked over her when she'd inquired about the procedure, how eager he had been to aid her in her plan. In two weeks, he would rid her of a burden, and perhaps she might receive some freedom in return. Motherhood was a joy to most, an exquisite pain to others...but the freedom...that was the main thing. Sivvy told herself it was worth it. It *had to be.*

In the kitchen, Sivvy busied herself greasing oven trays with lard and helping May drop the biscuits onto them. Weekends gave the patients something to look forward to—biscuits, side meat, and, every great once in a while, scrambled eggs. They had not had eggs in several months now, but biscuits at least were plentiful today.

Sivvy and May worked quietly in tandem for some time before Sivvy gathered her courage to speak.

"Marm," she began. "Do you still go into town every Saturday afternoon?"

"So I do," May said tersely, her gaze sharp and questioning. "Why do you want to know?"

"I only wondered if...." Sivvy trailed off, her courage failing her. "I thought I might ask...."

"Spit it out, Ms. Shelnutt," May said sternly. "What do you need? You're not the first one to ask me to pick up something from town, though the good Lord knows I've got no money to spare. You'll have to pull it from your own coffers, else you're out of luck. And mind, before you even open your mouth, I won't be buying no prophylactics or instruments of sin, no I won't. I'll buy your feminine products or your aspirin or a book or two, but that's all. And no pantyhose, neither." Her mouth pursed into a grim line. "We've had troubles with them."

"Oh no, marm." Sivvy felt her face turn pink. "Thank you kindly, but I don't have any need for those things." She had squirreled away a meager sum over the years—the odd coin earned for long hours and heavy duties above and beyond the normal chores—but she wasn't about to spend it on sanitary napkins or pulp novels. "Y'see…there's a gentleman come to see me yest'dy afternoon. You mighta heard?"

"Hmph. I don't keep up with you all's social lives. Ain't I got nuthin' better to do?"

"Well, anyhow." Sivvy's face burned. "He and his daughter came to see me and I—I ain't used to comp'ny. I turned 'em away. And I feel right bad about it. Seein' as the dance is this weekend, well, I thought I might make up for my rudeness by askin' 'em if they wanted to come."

"Seems an awright idear," May said, scraping the last bit of dough from the large steel bowl. "But what's it got to do with me?"

"I was hoping you could see them in town and invite them for me. Seein' as I don't got no way to get in touch with them."

"Where they stayin'?"

"I don't know, marm."

"So let me git this right," May said, hands perched on her wide hips. "You're askin' me to take up my afternoon rambling around town, asking if some man and his daughter happen to be stayin'. And then if I find them—*if*, mind—you want me to invite 'em to the asylum for a dance this weekend. And this is after you were rude to him yesterday and all but kicked him off the place?"

"I understand, marm, I just thought maybe…." Sivvy looked down at the biscuit dough, wishing she'd never said anything. "Maybe you could ask at one or two places, and just maybe you might find him. I feel awful bad for being so rude yest'dy. Awful bad."

"Oh, awright, gal. Don't start cryin' into my cat heads." May patted her on the arm, none too gently, but it made Sivvy smile. "I ain't got all day. I got errands of my own to run, you know. But I'll stop by Dick Martin's store and ask if they seen any outside visitors around. He'd probably know where they stayin'. Do you even know they names?"

"Mr. Owen Lawrence, marm. O.T. he goes by. And his daughter is Ginny. They both got sandy-colored hair. And he's got gray eyes, like the sea after a hurricane done come and gone. All stirred up, like.

Almost no color, but then somehow all the colors at the same time," Sivvy said, smiling to herself.

"Oh, heavens' sake, gal," May said in exasperation. "Ain't you a bit old for puppy love?"

Sivvy opened her mouth to tell the cook she'd gotten it wrong, but May was already shuffling off to the pantry.

Sivvy tried to do up her hair a little in the communal bathroom, but Nurse Jennings had only had two pins so the sleek bun would have to do. She wet down her dark strands with a little water from the sink, pushed them back, and hoped for the best. She wished for a bit of rouge or lipstick, then marveled at herself. Careful, Sivvy, she thought, trying to settle the butterflies that fluttered in her belly. *Don't set all your hopes and dreams on these folks. Better yet, don't have any hopes or dreams to begin with.* There was a light knock before the door swung open, and Nurse Burns arrived to escort her to the cafeteria.

"Did you want to dance?" O.T. asked her.

"Oh, laws, no. I ain't danced in…I don't know how long."

"Oh. Well, awright," he said, with an easy smile.

"I mean, unless you really *want* to…?"

"No'm, it's fine." O.T. waved a dismissive hand. "I just wasn't sure why you invited us here."

Sivvy, O.T., and Ginny sat in three folding chairs on the fringe of the dance floor, each cradling a cup of punch. O.T. had drained his and was staring out at the group of people on the floor, some of whom were dancing, others milling around, looking vaguely discomfited. Sivvy supposed to an outsider, a dance like this might seem very odd—all these deranged folks standing around, twitching, nobody looking anybody in the eye. Social graces such as good manners or pleasant conversation were barely expected here, and neither was making friends or flirting. Everyone was a boat in their own ocean, drifting out toward open sea, just trying to stay afloat. One might pass another boat, might even acknowledge it, but they'd keep on drifting all the same. The dances were just a formality, a nice thing for people who didn't get nice things too often.

"I felt right bad about our meetin'," Sivvy said finally. "There weren't no excuse for my rudeness. I thought…here at least, maybe we could get a chance to talk and not worry about me havin' to get back. They keep us busy durin' the days."

"I appreciate it," O.T. said.

"I wasn't sure y'all would even still be in town."

"No'm," O.T. replied. "I was aimin' to leave tomorry or the day after, I reckon. But I was gonna try to come here and see you one more time affore I did."

"You were?" Sivvy asked, surprised.

"Why, sure. I went through all that trouble to meet yer family and all; I wasn't gonna just take off." O.T. smiled, looking suddenly boyish. "And anyhow, I wanted to make sure you were awright." He shrugged. "Shoot, I don't rightly know what I had in mind, other than to just clap eyes on ya. Is that odd?"

"I rankin it is," Sivvy answered. "But odd, I understand. I mean," she said, gesturing around her. "Who am I to judge?" O.T grinned.

A young man approached Ginny, tall and thin in a gray cloth coat. A muscle twitched in his cheek. "Say, ma'am, would you care to dance with me?"

Ginny looked up, surprised, and glanced over at O.T. He shrugged and looked at Sivvy, and she nodded that it was safe. "Go on, if you want to, gal," he said good-naturedly. "Enjoy yourself. We'll be right here."

Ginny reluctantly put down her cup of punch, and took the man's arm. Sivvy had to giggle, watching the two awkward young people dance, both so stiff and nervous.

"He okay?" O.T. asked Sivvy.

"Sure," she said. "The patients that ain't well enough to be around folks don't come to the dances."

"I figured," O.T said, crumbling the paper cup in his hands. "I don't know if you want to talk about yer past, but I'd really like to hear yer story, Miss Sivvy, if you've a mind to tell it."

"My story?" Sivvy asked, surprised.

"Seems like I've heard 'bout yer life from everybody *but* you," O.T. said with an impish smile. "I've met half yer relatives and other folks along the way, but now that I'm here, lookin' you in the face, I'd really like to hear it from you, yerself."

Sivvy considered this. She didn't even like to talk about her life with the therapist, going quiet whenever he tried to bring up her childhood or her time with Uncle Billy. Talking about her previous life, beyond the asylum walls, made her heart ache, her hands shaky, and it filled her stomach with bile. The idea that O.T had talked to others about her was a queer one. Folks talking about *her?* It had taken her a long time to get to a place where she felt solid again; for so many years, her pain had felt like liquid coursing under a thin skin. She was afraid she'd seep out, become a puddle on the floor, then dry up and cease to exist. After all this time, she was afraid to speak, afraid to remember.

But he had come all this way. She sighed.

"Awright," she said. "I'll try. I'll tell you what I can."

CHAPTER TWENTY-TWO

When Sivvy thought back to her childhood, she remembered odd little snatches of time—lying on a thick, green knitted blanket on the grass as her ma hung washing; birthday cake with thick drizzled icing; a white puppy named Sparky. She remembered school, and the joy she had found in books.

Sivvy had been delighted that her uncle, aunt, and grandparents were coming to live on the ridge. She was already part of a big, loving family, and the thought of more kin was a happy one to her. Sivvy was especially eager to meet her Aunt Nona Leigh; her friend, Lisa, had told her that her own aunt snuck her tea cakes and apple cider when her ma wasn't around. Sivvy hoped her Aunt Nona Leigh would be just like that.

Turned out Aunt Nona Leigh was every bit as sweet as she'd hoped. She spoiled Sivvy with tea cakes whenever her neice came to visit and listened attentively to Sivvy's chatter about her lessons and cute boys—things Sivvy could never tell her ma or pa or even Becca. Nona Leigh was on the ridge only a short time before Sivvy loved her best of all.

Nona Leigh was from Farmington. A little town, she said, that wasn't much to speak of—flat and boring and full of cotton. But even while she said it her voice broke with the ache of someone who missed it something dreadful. Nona Leigh talked of her parents a little; her ma who was long dead, and her pa who was a reverend. She had grown up in the church, watching her pa give sermons and officiate over weddings and funerals.

"He was the most giving man you ever did meet, my Daddy," she told Sivvy, proudly. She confided in Sivvy that she'd fallen in love with Billy because he had wanted to become a reverend, too.

Nona Leigh doted on her husband and praised him, but as far as Sivvy could see, the two were like night and day. Nona Leigh was sweet and good-humored with a generous spirit, but Billy scowled and berated all within hearing. Sivvy particularly enjoyed visiting with

Nona Leigh and Sivvy's grandparents, who were both bedridden. They told her stories of what the ridge had been like when they were young, stories of how they had met, and how her own parents had met. They told these stories only when Billy was out of the house, though. He had little patience for people's "recollections" and derided them as vanity.

Other childhood memories were lost to her as the years crept by in the asylum—she could not recall the first boy she'd *really* liked or the first song she'd learned on the fiddlshape. But she remembered everything about Nona Leigh, and there were other memories that burned in her brain like a brand.

When Sivvy turned twelve years old, she realized she was not a child any longer. Nona Leigh, too, was a different woman from the one who had arrived on the ridge four years before. She bit her lips until they bled, and her eyes, once a bright kelly green, became tired and listless. Her hair was yanked back in a messy braid, and her dress was wrinkled and faded where it had once been neatly pressed. When Billy's parents died, Nona Leigh had nobody to care for and there was no longer anyone to check Billy's cruelty. Sivvy still came to visit, but Nona Leigh's stories were few and far between, and if Billy was around, she scarcely said a word. She never mentioned her pa in front of Billy anymore, lest he sneer, "That man never thought I was good enough for the likes of his precious Nona Leigh. Not for the princess, here. The precious reverend's daughter."

"Hush, Billy," Nona Leigh answered back once, her eyelashes fluttering, pretending he was joking to save face, as Sivvy was within earshot. "He liked you fine. He let me marry you, didn't he?"

Billy had focused a steely eye on her and said with a smirk, "He had to, didn't he?"

"Billy!" Nona Leigh cried, her face crimson.

"It was that or lock you away for a ruined spinster."

Sivvy hid her face in her book, pretending not to hear Billy's taunts or Nona Leigh's pitiful sniffling.

Billy's cruelty toward his wife was no secret, and while Nona Leigh had gone from worshipful to resentful to terrified in a matter of years, everyone seemed deaf and dumb. Sivvy couldn't understand how this skinny, sour-faced man could hold such sway over their family. Didn't anyone ever want to stand up and tell him to go the hell or somewhere else? And there was now another matter: the way Billy's eyes had begun to follow her when she visited their cottage. Sivvy felt increasingly uncomfortable in his prescence and took pains to escape his notice, yet she could feel the intensity of his gaze, like steam rising from the road after a summer rain.

Nona Leigh had noticed, too. "You shouldn't come visit no more, Sivvy, baby," she'd said one afternoon when Sivvy sauntered in with her schoolbag. Nona Leigh was furiously scouring the kitchen floor; she'd spilled coffee near the table and there was a stain. Billy would be fit to be tied if he saw it. "I think it's best if you stay at your house."

"But why?"

"I cain't explain, baby. Not in a way you'd understand."

"I'm not stupid, Aunt Nona Leigh."

"Of course you ain't. You're the smartest gal I know. Heck, probably the smartest person on the ridge." Nona Leigh paused, giving Sivvy a kind, sad smile. "But I'm only one person, sweetie. I don't know that I can protect you. And you sure can't protect *me*. You got your own life to live and growing up to do. School to worry about. You just leave us here to our little house and we'll get on just fine."

"Is it because he stares at me?" Sivvy asked, noting the startled expression on Nona Leigh's face. "I don't like it. It gives me the willies."

Nona Leigh swallowed, looking down at the soapy bucket. "It does me, too," she said finally. "A man ought not look at a young girl thataway. He don't know what he does, sweetie. He drinks too much and don't mean no harm. But we ought not tempt the man. Just keep out of his way, and all will be well."

"But I don't want to stop visiting you."

"Maybe I can visit *you* all instead," Nona Leigh said brightly, desperately. But they both knew it would never happen. Even though they lived just up the hill, Nona Leigh had not been farther than her own front stoop in almost a year.

"I ain't gonna let him keep me from you," Sivvy said fiercely, stubbornly, crossing her arms over her chest.

"Sivvy, you listen to me," Nona Leigh said, putting her hands on her neice's shoulders. "My daddy warned me. He said 'that's a boy that'll stop at nothin' to lay hands on what he wants. See that he don't lay his hands on you.' I laughed. I didn't even like Billy thataway. He was a harmless mountain boy; how was a skinny fella like that gon' get one over on me?" She laughed again, a hollow sound. "Next thing I know I'm hitched and he's packing me up to take me to this place. And my Daddy's standing on the porch, holding his Bible, waving goodbye with tears running down his face. I don't even know how it happened."

"What do you mean?" Sivvy was confused.

"Don't worry your head about it, sweetie. Just mind me, hear? You're sweet to look after me, but I'm grown, and I'm tellin' you to stay clear of this place for a spell. He's always got his eye on something or 'nuther. He'll move on to somethin' else before we know it. Till then, though, stay away."

Sivvy wasn't exactly sure what her aunt was talking about, but she was sure enough of the creep that went up her spine. She reluctantly agreed.

The next few weeks were hard. The silence from the little house was deafening. Sivvy longed to go down and check on her aunt; she wanted to talk about all of it with Ma and Pa, but she couldn't do either. Sivvy was certain if she told her parents about Billy's drinking, about the way his eyes wandered over her, about the bruises she'd seen on Nona Leigh, that her pa would take his rifle and march down to the little house. And then what would happen? Sivvy had fearful visions of Daddy going to jail, of Ma all alone with all the young'uns to feed, of Nona Leigh, a destitute widow. Or worse, Billy escaping and coming back in the dead of night to kill them all. Best to just keep clear of him, try not to think of him at all.

But it wasn't that easy, because suddenly Billy was there—all the time, coming to the house for dinner, and dropping by after church.

"Nona Leigh is beside herself," Billy said at the dinner table, winking at Sivvy. "She's mourning Ma and Pop. Without nobody to care for, she's real lonely."

"So you ought to be home with her then," Daddy said, pointedly.

"I'm just in her way," Billy said. "All she does is moan and carry on. She misses you something fearful, Sivvy. Why you don't come visit her no more?"

Sivvy stared silently at her plate, wanting desperately to shout, "Because you gawk at me, you old ugly pervert!" But it would be Nona Leigh that would be punished.

"You ought to go down and see her," Billy pressed.

"You ain't been down there in a while," Ma mused, a question in her voice. But Sivvy still said nothing.

Billy came by several days in a row now, stayed away a time, then would come back again. He'd stay for dinner and a while after, talking of his plans for a traveling church. Like a minstrel show, he said, but spreading the word of the Lord. Tent revivals, he said, were the new thing, and every town wanted to host one. Billy and the colored boy, Harvey, had already toured around twice, and now he was practicing his sermons, writing speeches, and planning another tour. He had even saved money for a better wagon.

Sivvy listened to his bragging impassively, careful not to look up and meet her uncle's eye.

Later, Ma asked Sivvy if there had been some falling out between her and Billy or Nona Leigh. Sivvy denied it, unwilling to betray Nona Leigh's confidence, and worried about what would happen should her pa discover the truth.

Billy appealed to her parents directly. "You ought to make Sivvy go down and see Nona Leigh," he urged. "She went durn near every day for years, and then she just stops. It ain't fair."

"Fair to who?" Daddy asked. "I can't say what kids'll do. I can't force her to go. She says she's busy with school. Why don't you send Nona Leigh up here to visit us? Bring her with you to supper one night? Do her good to get out of the house."

"She ain't gonna do that," Billy said, irritated. "She don't like to leave the house. Her nerves act up, you know."

The next day, Sivvy was walking home from school, pleasantly distracted by the changing colors of the leaves on the trees, the mottled bark that seemed to beg for her touch.

She did not notice Uncle Billy until he was right in front of her, blocking her path. Startled, Sivvy fell back, her rucksack slipping from her shoulder. With a dramatic ceremonial bow, Billy leaned down and swept her bag up out of the dirt, handing it to her with a feral grin. "Afternoon, Miss Sivvy." He tipped his hat.

"Afternoon," Sivvy mumbled, snatching her bag. Billy wore a crisp white preaching suit with wide lapels and a white shirt underneath, oddly paired with his dirty work boots.

"I'm just back from church," Billy told her. "Practicin' my sermon and gettin' ready to travel. Figger I'll ride out in the spring."

"Awright. I better git home. Mama's waitin'." Sivvy nodded and moved to brush past him, but he moved in front of her. She felt her legs start to shake.

"I just wanted to talk to you fer a minute, gal," he said, his voice friendly, but laced with steel. "'Bout yer aunt."

"Okay," Sivvy swallowed.

"Nona Leigh's sad that you don't come to the house no more."

Sivvy clutched at her rucksack, holding it in front of her chest like a shield. "I—I got a lot of schoolwork to do," she said weakly, wondering if she could dash past him, if she could make it home before he caught her. "I'm gonna come down and see her in the next few days—"

"Gal like you ain't got no call to be goin' to school anyhow," Billy said, frowning. "What's schoolin' gon' teach you about bein' a wife and a mother?"

Sivvy bit her lip and stared past him into the woods.

"Unless you have another callin'," he smiled, "which I reckon maybe you do. Maybe you ain't content to be no wife and mother. I always knew you was a queer gal. This place is too small for you, just like it is for me. I can help you—train you myself, get you outta here and into the world, doin' something meaningful, something smart. What do you say to that?"

"I want to be a writer," Sivvy said quietly. She had never voiced this out loud, not to anybody, not even to herself. That Uncle Billy was the first to hear this dream horrified her, and she wished she hadn't opened her mouth.

"That right?" Billy said with a complacent grin. "Well, yer in luck then, gal. Because being a man—or a woman—of the Lord takes a lot of readin' and writin'. You'll be writin' sermons, writin' out your recollections of the word a'God. Why, I do more writin' than anythin' else."

"Thank ya kindly, Uncle Billy, but I better stay in school," Sivvy said, her voice barely a whisper. His body, blocking her way, loomed above her as big as a mountain.

He made a noise in his throat. "Bah."

"Please, I need to git on into the house. Ma will be worrit."

His face turned dark. "Go on, then," he muttered with a scowl. "First, though, you gon' come to the house to see Nona Leigh?"

"I said I would in a few—"

"Come soon," Billy insisted. "Tonight. Or tomorry."

"I'll come tomorry," Sivvy said quickly, ready to agree to anything if he would only let her pass.

"Good, good," Billy said, clapping her on the shoulder and chuckling when she winced. "Good girl. Nona Leigh will be right pleased."

Sivvy pushed past her uncle, aware of his eyes on her back as she trudged down the trail, fighting the urge to break into a run.

And yet, when Sivvy arrived at the cottage the following day, her uncle wasn't home. Nona Leigh answered the door after a long spell, greeting Sivvy with a smile, although her puffy eyes and drawn cheeks suggested she had been weeping.

"Been a while," Nona Leigh said with tearful affection, holding her niece at arm's length so she could look her over. "Lord, it's good to see you, child."

"I'm sorry, aunt," Sivvy said, chagrined. "I should have come to see you—"

"Shush that," Nona Leigh interjected. "I told you not to come, and I'm right glad you minded me. I reckon Billy been on you to come down?"

"Yes'm. He said you were sad."

Nona Leigh coughed but didn't answer. When she finally spoke, her face was grave. "Lots of choices to make in life, Sivvy," she began. "I hope you make the right ones. You got to *fight* for your future, Sivvy. You got to keep your eye on what you want, and see that you get it." Nona Leigh gripped Sivvy's hands and drew her to a bench by the window, her gaze flitting to the door as if she expected to be interrupted. "Billy's got plans for you," she continued. "He wants you to be his apprentice."

"I know," Sivvy replied. "I don't know why. Seems like he druther one of my brothers—"

"They ain't pretty like you," Nona Leigh said bitterly. "Oh, forget I said that. But I'm tellin' ya true, honey. Once my husband gits his sights on something, he does all he can to git it. Now you better get yourself gone, gal, affore he comes back. I'll tell him you paid a visit."

Sivvy allowed herself to be ushered out the door. As she turned to say goodbye, the look on Nona Leigh's face almost broke her heart.

Months passed, and the prospect of Sivvy traveling with her uncle was forgotten for the time being. Billy was rarely at home that fall and gone for much of the winter. But when he *was* home, his eyes followed her like a bobcat lining up a squirrel, and she knew it was just a matter of time before the topic came up again.

As the winter snows began to melt, and the ridge started to warm and blossom in the spring sunshine, Uncle Billy made his final move.

Sivvy was making her way home from school one afternoon, preoccupied with plans to bake a spice cake for Nona Leigh, feeling guilty for not visiting in so long. Tomorrow was St. Valentine's Day, and there were so many boys she liked; she couldn't wait to tell Nona Leigh all about them. She was so distracted by her thoughts that she didn't notice the body in the creek until she started to cross, leaping lightly from one stone to another. The creek was swollen from unseasonable rains, and the stones were thick with algae. Thinking she'd brushed up against a rotting log, Sivvy nudged it absently as she moved past, realization dawning a half-second later. Looking down, her scream filled the silent wooded trail and echoed off the mountain. Sivvy recognized the homespun green dress, and the wet auburn hair, run through with streaks of gray. Nona Leigh.

"Nona Leigh?" Her voice was barely a whisper. Seizing her aunt's shoulders—already cold and rigid—Sivvy tried to turn the body over, but her feet slid in the muddy embankment. She tried again, almost falling into the creek herself. Her eyes blurred with tears, Sivvy staggered down the trail toward the house. Ma would know what to do.

A shape appeared ahead on the path, and Sivvy screamed in fright, but it was only a deer, who started at the sight of her and sprinted back into the woods, its large, curling rack glinting in the afternoon sun. Sivvy was hyperventillating by the time she made it home. Stumbling through the door, she fell into her mother's arms, shaking and crying as she told Ma what she'd seen in the creek. Julie-Anne's face went pale, and she was out the door and racing down the trail in a flash, Sivvy running behind her.

That awful day was burned in Sivvy's memory. The smooth, flat stones that tumbled from the pocket of Nona Leigh's green dress, and the way Mama had clutched at her heart when she'd seen them. The slackness of Nona Leigh's mouth, her open, sightless eyes. At some point, Sivvy's pa and brothers appeared, followed by the police and the coroner, who took the body away. Uncle Billy was fetched, and his brother Nate broke the news.

"To think the wife of a man of God would commit such a mortal sin," Billy muttered, angry rather than distraught. "She done cast off any hope of heaven." Eventually he fell silent, aware of the glares of his family, his face red and splotchy. But he never once cried, not that Sivvy could see.

There was a wake, and people from all over the ridge brought food, flowers, and comforting Bible verses. They cooked for Billy and cleaned his house, and the reverend rose to the occasion with a sermon on mortal sin, hellfire, and damnation. The funeral was somber and small. Nona Leigh was buried in a small plot in the church cemetery, and Ma put purple irises on her grave. Ma sent a letter to Nona Leigh's father, a man by the name of Clayton Shelnutt, informing him of his daughter's death, but he was in poor health and could not make the trip on his own. Uncle Billy made no offer to go and fetch him. So Nona Leigh had none of her own family to see her off, and Sivvy had cried about that.

"*We* are her family," Ma said fiercely, pulling Sivvy close. "You an' me."

"Then why didn't we help her?" Sivvy asked bitterly, but Ma had no answer.

Uncle Billy waited three days.

It was a quiet afternoon, and the residents of the ridge were still in shock. Owing to the oddly flat stones found in Nona Leigh's pockets, and no signs of a struggle, the coroner declared her death a suicide. Sivvy had her doubts, knowing how devout Nona Leigh had been, but there was nothing to be done for it.

Sivvy had washed several loads of white laundry already, adding Ma's homemade blueing agent, and was now hanging the wet clothes on the line. Her hands were wrinkled and pruny, dyed blue, her skin cold. She hung up her brother's pants, a clothespin in her mouth, shivering as her hands worked methodically through the wet clothes.

"Afternoon, Miss Sivvy." Sivvy froze at the sound of her uncle's voice. "How do?"

"Fine, I rankin," she mumbled into the laundry, trying to still the shaking which had overtaken her limbs.

"Been better myself," Billy said, watching her. "But I'll get by. The Lord will provide."

"Amen," Sivvy said dutifully, hating the feel of his eyes on her.

"Shame, them pretty lil' hands of yours all dyed blue like that."

Sivvy ignored him.

"I decided to speed up my trip this year," Billy said conversationally. "Help me get my mind off things. Can't sit in that empty house broodin' all day. Got to get out. Do somethin'."

"That's probably a good idear," Sivvy murmured, trying to hide her relief.

"Yer comin' with me this time, ain't ya?"

"No, I don't rankin so," Sivvy answered calmly. "I've got school. Ma and Pa don't want me to go nohow."

"Still," Billy said, smoothly. "I rankin you can talk 'em into it. You put yer mind to somethin', they ain't gon' stand in yer way for long. You got that way about you. So it was with school, warn't it?"

"Yes," Sivvy declared, finally turning to look at him with a glare. "But I *wanted* to go to school."

"You'll want to do this, too," he said confidently.

"No," Sivvy said firmly. "I've told you before, Uncle Billy, and I'll tell you again. I don't want to go with you on no preachin' trip. Ma and Pa don't want me to go. And I ain't goin'." Then, she added, "I appreciate the offer, an' all, but no."

Billy said nothing, only stared at her with an eerie smile. Sivvy went back to the washing, but her hands were trembling something fierce.

Finally, he spoke, his voice soft behind her back. "You'll go, little lady," he said quietly. "You'll go, awright. I ain't askin' no more, Miss Sivvy. I'm tellin'."

Sivvy picked up her laundry basket and started for the house.

Billy reached out and stopped her with an arm. "Nona Leigh is dead because of *you*."

She wrenched free. "No, she—"

"Shut yer mouth, gal. She's dead because of *you*. You put on airs, thought you was too good to come visit when she was ailin', when she was too sad to get out the bed. You was the only thing what gave her joy and when you stopped comin', she lost all hope."

Sivvy wanted to protest hotly that it wasn't true, that it was he and his iron fists and his black moods that made Nona Leigh miserable. "Nona Leigh ast me to stop comin'," she said instead, looking her uncle in the eye. "I did what she tol' me."

"You a lie," Billy said, his eyes wild. "Look at you, lyin' on the dead. Lyin' on your poor aunt. What a sin!"

"She tol' me to stay away from you," Sivvy said boldly, "and I intend to do it."

Billy reached into his pocket and pulled out a flat, round stone, polished smooth from the water. He twirled it through his fingers and then held it out to her. Her eyes widened.

"Yer a lot like yer aunt, you know," he said idly, studying the stone. "She was a meek woman most of the time, but ever now and then she'd get a wild hair, and she'd test me." Billy grinned at Sivvy and her hands took up their trembling again. "I believe you seen what happens when a woman tests me, ain't ya, gal?" He sucked in on his teeth. "Yes, I reckon you a lot like Nona Leigh—but yer smarter than her, ain't you, honey?"

Sivvy stared at him in mute horror, clutching the laundry basket tightly to her chest. Billy chuckled and tossed the stone into her basket, then strolled, whistling a tune, down the hill toward his cottage. Halfway, he turned and winked at her and said with a dark smile, "You'll come. I rankin you will, at that."

After a while on the road the towns started to melt together. Sivvy could barely remember all the places they went—Jesup, Jonesboro, Statesboro, Talmo, Dahlonega, Columbus. She didn't care a whit for the geography, or about the people she met. One town, one person, was much the same as another. Same kind of folks, the same buildings, the same food, the same "Amens" and "Hallelujahs." But she learned the ropes quickly. She transcribed Billy Rev's notes, helped pack and unpack the little wagon, shook the hands she was supposed to shake, and learned the hymns he wanted her to learn. Billy Rev—who had ceased to be Uncle Billy the moment she left Appalachia—let her pick out the hymns sometimes. She'd select deliberately obscure songs with meanings that Billy Rev never seemed to decipher.

Harvey accompanied them. Sivvy knew him a little; he had been in and out of the schoolhouse and she'd see him around town most of her life. They had never been friends, though, and weren't now, either—at least, not at first. They seldom spoke and only saw each other pinched together in the bench seat of the wagon. Harvey sat with his hands in his lap, staring out the window, with Sivvy sandwiched in the middle, breathing in the stale cigarette and liquor exuded by Billy Rev and the light, grassy sweat of Harvey.

One afternoon, a peculiar incident occurred. Sivvy and Harvey were loading the tent supplies into the wagon in some one-buggy town in South Georgia. It was a blistering hot day, and she was dripping in sweat as she hoisted long poles into the wagon. Harvey stood on the far side of the street, shouldering a heavy package of tarp, staring at her. In a curious flash, Sivvy saw herself through *his* eyes: her white dress, slightly translucent in the sun, her lacy white slip beneath; her legs, short but strong, flexing as she pulled on the heavy pole; her heeled black shoes, hurting her feet but lending a shapeliness to her calves; her black hair, which had grown long, falling past her shoulders and clinging damply to one cheek; her green eyes glittering with exhaustion and exertion; her full red mouth, pursed in a determined line.

Harvey returned to his work, but in that moment, she had seen his appreciative glance and felt that she had been *inside* him for a moment, had seen what he saw through his own eyes. It gave her a fright, and for the rest of the day her hands had a tremble in them.

At the next town, in the middle of Billy Rev's sermon, it happened again. Scanning the townsfolk, fanning themselves in the sweltering heat of the revival tent, Sivvy saw a young man with a shock of black hair and a smattering of stubble on his sharp chin. He was young and handsome and a little wild, and, through his dark blue eyes, she saw herself.

Sivvy began to take note of the men who appreciated her, those who cast a glance her way when their wives or mothers or steadies weren't looking.

Billy Rev, too, noticed the sway Sivvy held over men with her youthful glow, emerald-colored eyes, and inky black hair. He saw the way their eyes lit upon her from under their wide-brimmed hats, how they tried to take liberties in corners and under tables, and he began to scheme.

"Never take 'em *that* far," Billy Rev instructed her. "Never take 'em to the promised land. You understand? Just far enough for some shame, enough that they'll pay for our silence. And that's what we'll eat on." Sivvy had balked at first, but when Billy Rev grabbed her arm, his hot, sour breath in her face, and seethed, "You'll do it awright, gal," she had acquiesced. "And anyhow, what you puttin' on airs for?" he'd said. "It ain't like you got to really *do* nothin'. Just a bit of pretense, it is. Exposin' they sin."

Sivvy didn't like to admit it, but a part of her found a thrill in this newfound power. She was, finally, a woman, one who inspired lust and compelled men to sin.

Billy Rev told her not to tell Harvey. This was one piece of business in which the boy was not to be involved. And so Sivvy started combing through the roving eyes of the menfolk to pick out the ones that might want to do a little sinnin'. Most of the time it worked just the way Billy Rev planned it. Not all men were willing to pay, though, and sometimes they became angry. Sivvy wanted to stop, but Billy Rev reminded her, his eyes flashing and cold, "Remember what happens to gals who test me? Best hush up and bear up." Sivvy remembered those smooth, flat stones. So, in between her hymns, she kept catching eyes.

In the town of Five Forks, the eyes had caught *her*. Gray ones. And she was startled, because there had been four instead of two. Two sets of gray eyes, wild as storm clouds, and she saw herself through them. These boys were *her* age, and she was so tired and so lonely and so very sad. Just one afternoon—that's all she wanted, just a few hours to be young and happy.

Sivvy stole away to spend time with those two gray-eyed boys and their friends—she'd walked among the trees, laughed and joked, and felt like a teenager for the first time. But it only whet her appetite for more, and before the afternoon was over, she'd made a plan with one of the twins. She knew she shouldn't, but she was so lonely, and those gray eyes were so very pretty.

That night, under the stars, in the middle of a beautiful clearing, surrounded by pine and sassafras trees, Sivvy had gotten her first real kiss. She had forgotten many things on her subsequent path to lunacy, but she'd never forgotten that kiss. Rough and soft at the same time, the boy's lips tasting of apples. The way he'd clutched at her almost desperately—he had wanted her, Lord, really *wanted* her; Sivvy no longer simply had the power to enthrall; she suddenly understood it, too. Sivvy felt herself blossom under his hands and, had he not pushed her away, she would have lost herself completely. He had been embarrassed, guilty, so she had pretended to feel the same. She had carried the kiss and those gray eyes with her to bed that night, and every night thereafter, even after her uncle had dragged her out of town and put her on the path to ruin.

As time passed, and the sweetness of that night in Five Forks faded in her memory, Sivvy stopped hoping she'd feel passion like that again, stopped hoping for anything. Billy Rev ceaselessly chipped away at her, possessing her completely, until Sivvy was hollow and dry, and as brittle as a leaf in winter.

Then one afternoon in Farmington, Billy Rev's eye fell briefly upon another, and Sivvy felt a profound relief. She and Harvey unloaded the wagon, not speaking, and she caught him looking her way. Whatever faint blush of interest he might once have felt was long gone. Now, she saw only pity in his eyes, and Sivvy could not bear it.

Later that day, Harvey dashed into the woods, green to the gills, and Sivvy followed. She found him leaning up against a tree, his forehead clammy, his eyes closed. She put a hand to Harvey's cheek, and he jumped about a mile in the air. Then, to her surprise, he kissed her.

Such joy she had felt, but it had been so brief. The risks they had taken, the both of them. Their interlude had been painfully short. Of course Billy Rev caught them out, pulling the entire house of cards down on their heads.

Sivvy paused in her story, dabbing at her eyes. It wouldn't do to cry here in the middle of the dance. One of the nurses might notice and try to make O.T. and Ginny leave. Then they'd force her to go to her room—or worse, to the Jones building for evaluation.

"I didn't know how yer aunt died," O.T. said. "Yer ma didn't elaborate."

"Don't expect she would've," Sivvy answered hoarsely.

"You awright?" he asked.

"Ayuh," she said, "but there's more to tell."

Had O.T. been face to face with Billy Rev at that moment, he could have killed the bastard with his own bare hands, such white-hot hatred he felt. He hid his anger, listening attentively to Sivvy, who had taken herself to some other place—anywhere but a makeshift dance floor in an asylum cafeteria, telling a tale of a broken childhood, as he drank watery punch from a paper cup. She had transported them both solely on the power of her projected voice, which was clear and low, full of an electric gravel that made his blood run fast through his veins.

Chapter Twenty-Three

After depositing Harvey in the clearing, Clayton Shelnutt returned home in a hurry, collected Sivvy and, spinning tires, drove them through back roads to the little brick church at the edge of town. It was full dark, and Sivvy could barely make out the name of the church: *Erastus Methodist Church*. Not Baptist like Billy. Sivvy smiled at that, relieved. There were pink rose bushes in front of the church, and a tall, wooden cross rose in the darkness, draped with a green cloth for the liturgical month of September. Clayton helped her down from the truck and they ran up the church steps.

The preacher sat in the front pew, writing a sermon in handwriting that was sloping and beautiful. He had a leather-bound Bible resting on his lap, open to the book of Luke. Clayton and the preacher, whose name was Mark Shillings, spoke in hushed tones while Sivvy waited in a pew, studying the man who was about to become her husband. Moonlight, streaming through the stained glass window, cast his pale face in an eerie lavender glow. His gray hair was slicked back, and stubble darkened his chin. Wrinkles lined his eyes and mouth, and he was too thin by a measure. But in the flickering light cast by waxy white candles, Sivvy could see her dear Nona Leigh in his face—the steady, calm eyes, the kind smile, the steadfast, gentle demeanor.

"You want to get married, miss?" Preacher Mark inquired in a soft twang.

"I rankin," Sivvy murmured.

"Sivvy, I want you to be sure." Clayton Shelnutt put a gentle hand on her shoulder. She looked back at him, feeling dazed, as if she were watching her own life acted out upon a stage.

"Yes," she said, looking both of them in the eye. "I'm sure."

It was very quick. After a few words, Preacher Mark shut his Bible and looked at them expectantly. "Is that it?" she asked, startled. "Did he say 'man and wife'?"

Clayton Shelnutt chuckled softly. He clasped her small hands in his own, rough and weathered with callouses. "Yes, he did, and it's over."

"Oh."

Her new husband took her by the arm and murmured their thanks to Preacher Mark, who was already retreating back to his Bible and notes.

"Well," Clayton said again, his voice tinged with wonder. "Shall we go home, then? Await his highness?" With a covert, sly wink at her, he added, "Wife?"

Sivvy nodded and let him escort her out of the church, the pink roses clutched against her breast.

Billy Rev turned up at the Shelnutt house less than an hour after the newly married couple arrived home. Sivvy was sitting in the drafty parlor, staring out the window into the night. Her mind was a whirl, and she couldn't get it to slow down, nor could she get her hands to stop trembling. She held them tightly clenched in her lap, nails digging into her palms, but still they trembled; her very lap shook with the ferocity of it. Sivvy took deep breaths, but couldn't stop the panic that raced through her; her gorge rose and she thought she might be sick.

From the window Sivvy saw a sheriff's car pull into the drive, followed by Billy Rev's beat-up wagon. She opened her mouth to cry out for Clayton, to warn him, and found she had no voice. But Clayton was already walking toward the door, putting a finger to his lips. "I'll handle it," he told her calmly. "Just leave it to me."

Sivvy remained in the chair, running her hands over the mustard-colored velvet for comfort. It reminded her of a chair her daddy had made once. Footsteps crunched across the rocks in the drive, and a sharp knock sounded at the door. Clayton, with a reassuring smile at Sivvy, opened it.

"Seems like we rode all over tarnation this evenin', Mr. Shelnutt," Billy Rev said, letting himself in. "We was here not two hours ago and wadn't a soul home."

"I run out for a spell," Clayton answered amiably. "Evenin', Sheriff. Right nice night, ain't it?"

"Mighty fine."

The sheriff—tall and pale, with a bushy brown mustache—sported a sour expression that suggested he'd rather be home relaxing in his housecoat than making a nighttime visit. "How you?"

"Fair to middlin'." Clayton gestured for the men to come into the foyer, shutting the door behind them. Billy Rev surveyed the parlor with narrowed eyes, then, catching sight of Sivvy in the chair, he smiled a slow, cat-caught-the-mouse smile. Turning to Clayton, he said, "We come for the boy. He still in the cellar?"

"I don't know what you mean," Clayton replied. "What boy?"

Billy Rev's face turned a deep shade of red. "What you mean 'what boy'?" he boomed. "Harvey, you ol' fool! He's in the cellar. Gimme the key, I'll go git him."

"Now, Reverend Hargrove, let's not get upset," the sheriff said mildly.

"Cain't imagine who you mean, but be my guest." Clayton handed Billy Rev the key to the cellar and he stalked out of the room.

"The reverend reckons that the colored boy meddled with yon girl over there?" the sheriff said, gesturing toward Sivvy with a nod of his head.

"Sheriff, I have to say, I'm right perplexed. I ain't got a clue who you mean," Clayton answered.

Billy stormed back into the parlor, throwing the keys on the floor, and seized Clayton by his shoulder, shaking him violently. "What'd you do with him, you ol' bastard?" Billy Rev screamed, his cheeks purple with rage. "Where'd you put him? I'll clean yer goddamn clock, swear I will!"

"Reverend, you're gonna have to let go of this man here," the sheriff said, moving to intervene. "He's an old timer, an' sickly. Ain't no call to be treatin' him such—are you sure there was a boy here? Because he says no."

"Of course there fuckin' was," Billy Rev growled. "I put him in the goddamn cellar myself."

"Ain't no call for language such as that," Clayton said mildly. "'Specially from a man of God. Maybe a cool drink of water will help settle some nerves?"

"Stuff that pitcher where the sun don't shine," Billy roared. "Tell me where that boy is, and tell me *now*—"

"Young lady," the sheriff asked Sivvy. "Have you seen a colored boy here this evenin'? You know who I'm talkin' about?"

"*Accorse* she knows him!" Billy screamed. "Ain't a damn body listenin' to me? That negro been meddlin' with her! Straight *ruint* her! And yer wastin' time askin' her if she *knows* him! Where did y'all hide him, gal?" He shook a fist at her, advancing, and she shrank back in horror. "Tell me now or I'll tan yer hide for ya!"

"Billy," Clayton said in a quiet voice, "I'll have to ask you not to make threats against my wife."

Billy whirled. "Your *what?*"

"My wife," Clayton answered placidly.

"Reverend Shelnutt," the sheriff said with startled surprise. "You got married? When? I didn't hear about no weddin'!"

"Didn't have one. I'm an old man, and a poor one at that. Preacher Mark married us just yester'dy."

"Shoot, Reverend Shelnutt, this young lady has got to be young enough to be your granddaughter," the sheriff muttered, bemused.

"Not quite, but nearbout," Clayton answered. "Truth is, I needed me a nurse. Full-time nurse who ain't gotta go home at supper time. I ain't a well man..." he smiled at Sivvy. "And me and her get along fine. She's a good gal, she is."

"How long we gon' carry on this ridiculous farce?" Billy Rev thundered, his hands curling into fists as he glared at Sivvy. "She couldn't have married the ol' fool yesterday, she was with me yesterday. This gal ain't his wife no more than the man in the moon."

"I am, too," Sivvy hadn't realized she'd spoken up until she heard her own voice. "We got married yesterday, like he said." She jutted out her chin defiantly, forcing herself to meet her uncle's eyes.

"You lyin' little harlot—"

"Now, I've had just about enough," Clayton cautioned, producing a piece of paper from his pocket. "If you can't calm yourself, Billy, I'm going to have to ask you to leave. As I said, I ain't a well man, and it don't suit to have my nerves up. And yer upsettin' my wife in the bargain. This here's our marriage certificate, signed by Preacher Mark Shillings. See the date?"

"It appears they were married yesterday," the sheriff confirmed, scanning the paper. "Here's the names—Clayton Shelnutt and Tryphena Hargrove."

"Her name ain't Tryphena," Billy Rev spat. "It's Sivvy."

Preacher Mark, in his rush, had written only *Tryphena* in the county registry. It struck her that Uncle Billy had probably never known her full name.

"My *name* is Tryphena," Sivvy asserted, tucking her hands under her armpits to hide the trembling. "Triphy. And that's Mrs. Clayton Shelnutt to *you*."

"It seems we forgot why we're here," the sheriff interrupted. "Didn't you drag me from my house to find a colored boy you said was molestin' your ward? Well, I don't see no sign of a boy and nobody's ward. All we got here is two newlyweds and we're disturbin' their peace, Billy." The sheriff put a firm hand on Billy's shoulder and guided him toward the door. "If there's a boy out there, we'll find him. I got good trackin' dogs, and his scent's all over your truck. Now let's let these nice folks alone."

Billy Rev stared at Sivvy for a moment, then smiled. Sivvy felt the blood drain from her face. "That's true, Sheriff. His stink is all over that truck. We'll find him, awright. And when we do, his neck'll break. Mayhap from the tree right across the street, so Mrs. Shelnutt here can enjoy the view."

The sheriff pulled the door shut behind them, and Sivvy ran into Clayton Shelnutt's arms and began to sob. "Well, at least Preacher Mark was willin' to back-date that certificate. Saved our bacon," he murmured kindly, his shoulders offering little comfort, but more than what she was accustomed to.

The next morning Sivvy awoke before the sun and crept downstairs into the drafty parlor. The house was silent as a tomb and thickly coated in a film of dust. She could hear Clayton's labored breathing upstairs; he had gone to bed with his door open, telling her that if she was scared or upset to holler for him. She would've died rather than bother the man—the past two days had taken a toll, judging from the haggard look of his face the night before.

Rummaging, she found flour, lard, and a couple of eggs in the pantry, a bit of sweetmilk cooling under an ice block; she had all the makings for a batch of biscuits. So Clayton Shelnutt had enough money to at least do for himself a little, she mused, stirring the dough in a ceramic bowl. It wasn't everyone who could afford ice blocks and lard. When he'd told the sheriff he needed a nurse, he was telling a story, but Sivvy intended to see it through. A proper meal, to start, and then she would do something about the state of his house.

Sivvy rolled out the biscuits, set them on the tray to bake, and set about straightening up the kitchen, discovering a dusty jar of peach preserves on a shelf. By the time Clay ambled downstairs, Sivvy had the biscuits baked, two eggs fried, coffee brewed, and the downstairs rooms dusted. The windows were open, letting in the cool morning breeze, and she was on her knees, scrubbing the floor, a bucket of water, gray with grime, beside her.

"Well, shoot," Clay said, hands on his hips, scrawny white legs visible beneath the white flap of his nightshirt. "I ain't seen a sight like this in years."

"Mornin'," Sivvy said with a smile, dusting off her dress. If it hadn't been ruined before, it surely was now. "You hungry?"

"Not partic'ly, but I reckon you'll make me eat anyhow," Clay acknowledged with a laugh.

"You mighty right," Sivvy replied. "Sit yerself down. I cleaned the table off."

"You din't have to go to all this trouble, Miss Sivvy," Clay said as she put a plate in front of him. "I don't expect no—"

"Triphy," she interrupted, weighing the sound of it on her tongue. "Call me Triphy. I quite like it." Sivvy sat across from him, biting into a warm, buttery biscuit. She hadn't had real food in a coon's age.

Clay took a forkful of eggs and groaned in pleasure. "I ain't had a cooked breakfast in a real long time. This is mighty fine, Triphy. Mighty fine."

Over breakfast, with Sivvy's encouragement, Clayton talked of Nona Leigh. They finished the biscuits, ate half the jar of peach preserves, and drained the coffee. It was as if neither had eaten or spoken to anyone else in years.

"Nona Leigh wanted to sing in the church choir when she was a young'un, but she had stage fright," Clay confided.

"She never told me that," Sivvy said.

"Nona Leigh was real shy, but she did sing in public once't, in the Christmas production at church. She had one line in 'God Rest Ye Merry Gentlemen.'"

Sivvy smiled, imagining a young Nona Leigh in a Christmas play. "She must have been so beautiful."

"She was. All the girls in the choir were wearing white dresses with lace feathers that were all glittery lookin'. They were right pretty, and that was the night that Nona Leigh caught the eye of one particular fella."

"Oh," Sivvy sighed. "That's when she met *him*."

"He couldn't take his eyes off my Nona Leigh. She was singin' just as sweet as a bird, and that Billy was staring a daggum hole through her."

"And the rest is history."

"I din't like him, right off the bat. For one, he was an outsider, and I was nervous about that. But he had a—I dunno, a sanctimoniousness about him. Like he was entitled to her. He came to the house ever night, for two solid weeks. I ast him din't he have nowhere to be, a home to go back to, and he'd just smile and say, 'Naw.' He tol' me he was tourin' around the state of Georgia, studyin' on bein' a preacher. I tol' him that the way to do that was to go to school, that they was divinity schools all over. He said he wanted to do it 'hands on,' whatever that means. Ast if he could shadow me. I said no."

"I bet that got his red up."

"Shore did. After that, he pursued Nona Leigh even more vigorously, just to spite me, I think. She was half in love with him by the end of the month. I told her she couldn't see him no more, and she cried to beat the band. I tol' her that he din't seem like no good boy, and she called me a snob, said it was 'cause he was a poor mountain boy." Clayton shook his head. "That warn't it. I ain't no rich man myself. He just gave me a bad feelin'. The way he looked, like a bobcat about to kill its prey."

"But you can't tell a young'un what they gonna do. The more you try to push 'em to the right thing, the more they gonna do the wrong thing. And I got to figgerin', heck, maybe I was wrong anyhow. I ain't had but one kid livin', and I wasn't gonna risk my relationship with her just because I didn't like the fella she was goin' with. I knew she were a good girl and wouldn't get into no trouble. And I just hoped she'd move on to another fella and stop likin' Billy so good. But it didn't work out that way.

"Wadn't long before she tol' me that Billy had proposed—din't even come to me first—she said yes. I begged her to give it time, but they was in a screamin' hurry. I didn't read betwixt the lines at first." He frowned. "She were frightful ashamed. It was either give in to what she wanted or kill the feller and have a bastard for a grandchild." He ran a finger over his plate. "So I married 'em in my church and gave 'em my blessin'. I was tryin' to keep her, y'see—instead I sent her off with the devil."

"But my ma tol' me that one of the reasons Uncle Billy treated her so bad was because she couldn't give him kids," Sivvy said, perplexed.

"She lost the child," Clay said quietly. "Shortly after the weddin'. Wrote to me an' tol' me. I guess she couldn't never have no others. My poor little girl. I let her marry him for nothin'."

"You couldn't have known." Sivvy reached out and put a hand on his arm.

There was a sudden pounding on the front door. Clay looked somberly at Sivvy, and said, "Speak of the devil. His ears must have been burning." He got up and shuffled to the door, still in his nightshirt.

"No," Sivvy said, feeling protective. "Let me answer it. You're not dressed."

"It's awright, hon," Clay said affectionately, patting her head. "I done dealt with Billy Hargrove plenty in this life. He might like to strong-arm the ladies, but deep down he's a coward who cares too much about his reputation to beat up an old man."

Clay opened the door a crack. "Mornin', Billy. What can I do for ya?"

"Let me in, old man," Billy Rev hollered. "I want to talk to Sivvy."

"*Triphy* is busy," Clay replied. "She don't want to see you nohow. Not now or ever."

"Let me at her!"

"No, sirree. You might as well march your skinny ass back off my porch."

"Sivvy!" Billy Rev bellowed over the old man's shoulder, forcing the door wider with his foot. "You can't hide from me forever! This old man gotta die sometime! Don't you want to hear about your precious Harvey?"

Sivvy's eyes widened, and Clay shook his head at her. *Don't take the bait,* his eyes seemed to say.

"Found him late last night," Billy Rev yelled through the door. "Well, the dogs did, anyhow. Once the hounds catch a scent they ain't gon' let it go. He made it real far, but he wasn't no match for them hounds. Not a chance." Something white fluttered past Clay's shoulder and floated to the floor. Sivvy picked it up, her heartbreat drumming in her ears. It was Harvey's handkerchief, embroidered with a stalk of lavender, and covered in little drops of blood. Sivvy stifled a sob. "Them dogs wouldn't let up long enough for us to get him to the tree. They tore that boy *up,* boy howdy. Wadn't nothin' left but gristle."

"Get off my porch, and the devil take you," Clay seethed, throwing the ruined handkerchief back at Billy Rev and shoving him out the door. "You got three seconds to git before I grab my shotgun and blow your blame head off."

"I'm a'goin, I'm a'goin. Hold your horses, ol' man," Billy Rev laughed. "I'm leavin', Sivvy. But mind, I'll be back for you. Yes, ma'am, I will be back."

Sheriff Denson came by the house later that afternoon, tipping his hat to Sivvy before taking Clay out onto the porch. Sivvy craned her ear at the door, listening to his hushed voice, hoping the sheriff would say it was all a bluff, that Billy had lied, and that they'd never found Harvey. Instead, he confirmed it.

"...I'd gone home for the night, but my deputies were there, and they tol' me wasn't nuthin' left of the boy but the buckles from his overalls."

"State-sanctioned murder," Clay spat furiously. "You sent your men and your dogs out on the word of that charlatan. I'd have thought the sheriff would uphold the rule of law, but—"

"Now, hold on one daggum minute, Reverend Shelnutt," the sheriff protested. "When a white man of the church tells me a colored boy meddled with a white girl, what am I supposed to do? I din't know the boy from a hole in the ground. I got to take these accusations serious."

"You could have conducted an investigation, couldn't you?"

"Well, shoot, Clay," the sheriff answered. "We stood right here in your parlor and the girl didn't deny a thing."

"She sat here and tol' you she din't even know him!"

"If she din't know him, then why you all so upset?" Sivvy could hear the smirk in the sheriff's voice. "It don't matter now, either way, Clay." They had moved further down the porch, and Sivvy had to strain to hear. "Look here, mayhap it's all for the best. Keepin' our town clean, keepin' everybody's noses out of trouble."

"You sat by and let a boy get kilt," Clay said stonily.

"Now, Clay," the sheriff said mildly, "Ain't no sense in getting' upset. It was just a colored boy. One less hooligan out makin' trouble."

"I'll say a prayer for him," Clay replied wearily, heading toward the door. "And I'll say one for you, too."

"Now, Reverend, don't you go gettin' all high an' mighty—"

"Good day, Sheriff Denson." Clay slammed the door and looked over at Sivvy, who was weeping. "I wish you hadn't heard none of that."

"I got him kilt," Sivvy whispered hoarsely.

"There, there, gal," Clayton said, drawing her into a hug. "Like he said—it don't matter now anyhow."

Chapter Twenty-Four

Sivvy took a deep breath, steeling herself to finish the rest of her story, when O.T. interrupted. "Now, wait—Sivvy, you said that Harvey—"

"I don't know no more details," Sivvy replied, her voice wavering. "And if I did, I couldn't say 'em. It was too horrible."

"Did you ever see the body? Go to a service or anything?"

She sniffed. "What service? For one, there wasn't nothin' left of the body, like they said. Anyhow, who would have had a service for a colored boy nobody knew?"

"Oh, damn," he muttered, his voice soft and pained.

"What is it?" she asked him.

"Miss Sivvy, I need to tell you somethin'—" O.T. began.

"Dance is almost over and I ain't got much more time," she interrupted. "Besides, if I don't tell it all now I might never. Can it keep?"

"I reckon," he said softly.

"It was 'bout a week later I got word that Uncle Billy had gone back to Madison and marrit that gal my age he was kinda courtin'. I din't know her from nothin', but I felt right sorry for her. She couldn't have had any idear what she was gettin' into.

"I could scarce believe I was free of Billy Rev, and for the first time in a long spell I felt safe. Clay was mighty kind. I wanted to thank him for rescuin' me, so I cleaned, repaired, dusted, and organized that place, and had it up to snuff in a few days' time. And I kept three squares in that man, or tried to, even though he often protested and said he just wadn't that hungry.

"Clay's health was bad, but I din't know what was really ailin' him because he refused to see a doctor. Said he'd had his fill of 'em, and they couldn't help him no way. There was a gal, Miriam, from Bishop, who came twice a week and taught me about tendin' the sick. I brought Clay broth and tea on the days he couldn't get out of bed, and I'd rub lineament on his joints and read the paper to him while he dozed. His eyes would light up when I'd come in with the mornin' tray. Sometimes, if he felt up to it, he'd tell stories about Nona Leigh, and bout his first wife, his siblings, and his son who had died in the Great War. "It ain't right to outlive your kids," he'd say, and I think he'd have happily gone to join them before I came along.

"I believe my pain mirrored his. We understood each other. The age difference didn't matter a bit. Our hearts were the same. It happened slow, us startin' off as polite strangers, then acquaintances, then nurse and patient, then friends, then good friends....

"One afternoon, I was dustin' his old grandfather clock, shinin' it with some lemon oil. Clay had gone to the church to cut back some rose bushes, helpin' out Preacher Mark. I was runnin' my cloth over the fine old clock, watching the shiny gold hand swoop back and forth, the *tick* so low and quiet that you almost couldn't hear it. I looked out the window and down the drive, to see if Clay was trudgin' on home. Accordin' to the hand on that clock, it was just past four, creepin' from afternoon on into evenin', and it would be time to start his supper. Past time, really, since I had a mess of tough greens to pressure cook. I finished polishing the clock and went into the kitchen to start the greens. Once I had 'em in the pressure cooker, I chopped a few potatoes to boil, and went and looked out the window again, sure I'd see him shufflin' on down the drive. He still weren't comin', and it was goin' on five. Gettin' antsy, I put the potatoes on, fried up the side meat, and got a pan of cornbread on the fire. At ten past five I had it all on the table, knowin' he'd walk in the door just as soon as I set the tea out, because he was a creature of habit and didn't like to eat supper no later than five o'clock. But he still didn't come through the door.

"I went to the window and looked out to the road. I must've stood there for three or four minutes, cranin' my neck, just starin' a hole through the glass, waitin' on him to get home. I chewed the skin off my lip, waitin'. My hands was tremblin' like crazy. I started to get mad. Here he was, keepin' me waitin' and worryin' and his supper done cold. I decided I would walk on down to the church, let him have it, and haul him on home. I threw on my sweater and headed out the door. I was on the last porch step when I saw him round the corner and step onto the driveway.

"'Mighty sorry for bein' late, dear,' he said when he got to the porch. 'I got caught up with the roses and lost all track a'time. I reckon I done let my dinner get cold, ain't I?'

"I nodded, not openin' my mouth because if I did, I'd cuss him good.

"'I reckon you gon' whoop me,' he said with a little grin.

"Suddenly, I knew why I was so mad. Why I'd been so worrit. I loved Clay Shelnutt. I loved my husband. I hadn't planned it so, hadn't even seen or felt it coming, but there it was jes' the same. I was still standing there on the porch step, gawping at him when he reached into his jacket pocket and handed me a little pink rose. 'Hope you'll forgive me, sweet,' he said, with a peck on my cheek. And there's me, just standin' there with my mouth hangin' open. But I knew I loved him before I ever saw that rose come out of his pocket.

"We hadn't been marrit long at all affore I discovered I was with child. I missed the signs at first. I had put on some weight— thicker around the middle than usual, and, beg pardon, my bosom was fuller, too. I was sick every mornin', quietly throwin' up in the basin. The smell of that lemon oil polish I'd loved at first was givin' me headaches. After a week or two, I figgered it out and was right panicked. I din't know what to do—how to tell Clay. He'd already raised two young'uns, and with him not bein' well…it was more than he signed up for, to be sure.

"The morning I tol' him, I stood at the back door, my face clammy with sweat, my nerves shot. I called him in, but he din't hear me and kep' on workin'. Finally I trudged down to the garden and just said it plain, standin' there in the dirt, afraid he'd throw me out on my ear. But Clay was *thrilled*. He just looked me up and down, smiled and said, 'Praise Jesus!' He got to work straightaway on paintin' one of his back rooms. He pulled a crib out of the attic that had been Nona Leigh's and bought cloth and yarn for makin' crib sheets and clothes. All this he did quietly and happily.

"Me, I was happy, but nervous, too. I kept myself busy with knittin' and sewin', cleanin' and cookin'. Anythin' to keep my hands from bein' idle. If my hands sat still in my lap they would begin to shake and tremor so, and the more I worrit on it the worse it got. They'd just tremble and tremble like somebody with the palsy. So I tried to keep busy, secretly prayin' that when it came time to hold a baby, they wouldn't shake no more.

"I shoulda been happy. I was marrit to a good man, sweet as the dickens who took good care of me. I was expectin' a baby, had a big ol' house to call my own, with a pretty garden, and didn't hurt for nothin'. But there was this gnawing at me, like a rat in my belly, just bitin' and bitin', chewin' me up from the inside. I din't deserve any of these things, not with Nona Leigh and Harvey dead, and Billy Rev out there, causin' misery in the world. All the happiness tasted like ashes in my mouth.

"Every day my belly got bigger, and my face started to glow, but underneath, that rat was just a'gnawin'. My hands trembled so bad I started sewin' pockets in my dresses to hide 'em. One mornin', I woke up and I could barely see. The entire left side of my face felt numb and the only thing I saw in my left eye was silver streaks. I thought I'd done gone blind. Slowly my eyesight came back, but my heart was flutterin', and I felt like I might pass clean out on the floor.

I din't tell Clay about the vision loss or feelin' faint, not wantin' for him to be worrit.

"One evenin', I was in the kitchen doin' dinner dishes and I saw Nona Leigh. She was standin' by the pantry, holdin' a jar of preserves. She smiled at me, holding her own belly where a baby should grow, and then she was gone. That Sunday, at church, I saw Harvey sittin' in the back pew with a black fedora on his head. I almost fell down from the shock. The church ladies thought I'd jes' had a dizzy spell.

"By my eighth month, the doctor said I hadn't gained enough weight, my blood pressure was too high, and I'd have to go on bed rest. I din't mind this atall since it meant nobody would be lookin' at me, and I wouldn't have to hide my hands. I went into labor early, and it took four hours for the doctor to come, on account of he was off assisting with another baby in Madison. By the time he got there I was seein' all sorts of folks in the room—Nona Leigh, Harvey, and even my ma—and I was talkin' back to 'em. Clay was gray-faced with panic because he worrit for the baby; that is what I thought then anyhow; now I realize it was because he saw my madness. When the doctor finally arrived—I'll never forget it—Clay said, 'Oh, thank the Lord!'

"The doctor gave me something to make me sleep, and when I awoke I had a baby boy. I held him in my arms and looked at the pretty tone of his skin and his sweet little hands and tiny eyelashes and I knew I'd never love anyone so much as I loved him. For all I had suffered, this was my reward from God. I was a mama."

Sivvy sighed. "It gets hard now."

"You don't have to tell the rest," O.T. said, reaching out to pat her arm.

"I will," she said, after a moment. "But not here, not in the middle of all these people."

"I understand," he said. The question lay unspoken between them. *If not now, when?*

"O.T., I gotta ask you something," she said, after a moment. "I mean, ain't you here to get me out? To take me back home with you?"

"Well," O.T. said, turning a little red. "I dunno, maybe...." He swallowed. "What made you—?"

"Just a feelin'," she answered, looking steadily in his eyes. "But I don't know no man who would come all this way to bust a gal out 'less there was somethin' in it for him."

O.T. looked shamefaced, as though he'd been discovered at a dirty secret.

"You lost yer wife," Sivvy went on, not noticing his discomfort, smoothing out her skirt. "And you need someone, to take care of yer young'uns, right? And you figgered since yer brother was sweet on me...." she trailed off. "You want you another wife."

O.T. went a little pale. "Miss Sivvy, you got me all wrong. I mean, I just—"

"Don't be embarrassed, Mr. Lawrence. I'm right flattered. Yer a handsome fella, truly you are. You could probly have yer pick of any gal in the state. It shows a right kinda honor that you'd come here. But before you go any further, I should warn ya. I marrit before and it turned out real bad. Clayton Shelnutt is six feet under and his namesake with him. And here I am." Sivvy felt tears spring to her eyes and tried to bat them away, fiercely embarrassed that O.T. should see such a thing. "You'd be takin' on a bit more than you could handle, I rankin. But I ain't aimin' to say no. Y'see, I'm ready to get out. I don't want to die here, and if I stay much longer, I will."

O.T. regarded her uneasily.

"I ain't sayin' they treat me awful or nothin'. I got more freedom than some. I get to work in the kitchens an' all. But it gets frightful lonely in this place. Lonely and cold. And I ain't even thirty years old. When I think of spendin' another ten years in this place, I just wish I was dead already. Ain't no life, locked away in a cage. If I was out of my wits, then maybe so, but I ain't." She held her hands in her lap to hide the tremors.

"Miss Sivvy, I…." She smiled at him brightly. "I ain't here to take you to wife," O.T. said finally.

"You're not?"

"No'm." He saw her distress and waved it away with a hand. "But please, don't fret about it none. You wasn't altogether wrong."

"I don't understand."

"'Cause I've done a piss poor job of explainin'. Look," he said, taking her hands in his. "Here's what it is. My brother, Walt—seemed to me, after readin' his letter—aimed to bust you out of here and offer you his hand in marriage. That the long and short of it?"

"Seemed thataway. In his letter," Sivvy said, embarrassed.

O.T. nodded. "I know how my brother's mind works. Worked," he corrected himself. "Tell you true, Sivvy, when first I left on this trip, I think my intention was to come down here and honor my brother by takin' his place. I never said it aloud, but I was studyin' on it. I figgered it was fate—you know, I lost my wife, you lost yer husband. I thought maybe I was meant to come here and spring you from this place and try to give you the life what was stole from you," he said tenderly. "But Sivvy, I can't do that now. I took Walt's place once before, and it—" He shook his head. "Never mind. Now that I've met you, heard you tell yer tale, it don't seem right. Seems to me you have had a life full of men makin' choices for you, and just goin' along, and Lord knows you deserve a chance to make yer own choices now."

Sivvy dropped his hands and pushed her own back into her pockets.

"And there's more. Yer sister Becca already done tried to get you out. She wrote letters. The doctors told her no." Sivvy sucked in a mouthful of air, feeling as if someone had punched her in the stomach. "I swear, though, I *will* try to get you outta this place, if that's what you want. I can't make no guarantees, but…I'm here and I'm gonna try."

"If they wouldn't release me to my own sister, they ain't gonna release me to you. Not without a legal claim." All the tentative hopes Sivvy had built up over the last twenty-four hours came crashing down, and she wanted to crawl under the floorboards and die. He must think her such a *fool*. She had misjudged his reasons and misread his inner turmoil for nerves. Sivvy fervently wished she'd never opened her mouth.

"Listen," O.T. said desperately. "Now that I've seen you, I could write to yer folks and get them here. Maybe between all of us we—"

"No, no, you cain't do that," Sivvy said furiously, wiping at her cheeks. "All these years I ain't wrote to 'em, and I cain't start now. I'm too ashamed."

"Sivvy, they *know* now, and they love you as much as they ever did. Why, shoot, they'd be down here quicker'n lightning. All Julie-Anne talked of was how much she misses you."

"Accorse she did. Don't mean much. We din't part on good terms. She let me leave with that man when I wasn't old enough to make no choice. I been hatin' her all these years, and I reckon she must hate me too."

"Naw, she loves you, Sivvy. I reckon she's full of regret herself. You wasn't but a girl then. Things is different now."

"I don't know," Sivvy sighed.

"She wants you home. She told me so," O.T. said kindly. "They all do. Yer family, and"— he took her hands again—"Harvey, too."

Sivvy blinked at him, her eyebrows furrowing. "What you playin' at, Mr. Lawrence? Harvey is dead and gone, and he and my family ain't clapt eyes on each other since the day I left in the wagon with him and Billy Rev."

"Sivvy." O.T. placed his hand back on her arm, gently, his touch lighter than a feather. Every time he touched her she felt dizzy. "I wanted to tell you before. I'm sorry for just sayin' it like that, but I didn't know how to start. Sivvy, Harvey ain't dead. They didn't get him. I don't know who yer uncle apprehended on the road that night, if anybody, but it wasn't him."

"This some trick?" Furious tears pricked at her eyelids.

"Ain't no trick, I swear. I wouldn't lie to you. I tell you Harvey is alive and well and livin' on the ridge. I saw him not a week ago with my own eyes."

"I don't believe that," Sivvy said in a hot whisper, shaking her head. "You a lie."

"I ain't," O.T. insisted softly. "I saw him. We talked about you for a long spell."

"He died over ten year ago. He was killed in the street near Clay's."

"Sivvy, he wasn't." O.T. looked her in the eyes, and she saw the truth there. "That Billy Rev was lyin' to you out of meanness. Harvey is alive. He runs a shop on the ridge. He has a wife and two young'uns. I sat in a chair in his house that yer own daddy gave him. Yellow, like mustard, with—"

"Brown trim." Sivvy barely got the words out before she collapsed into sobs. Her shaking hands found her face, and she hid herself from O.T.'s gaze.

Harvey alive and well! He whom she'd mourned for ten years. He whose death she blamed herself for. He who now lived a stone's throw from her family; and all of their lives had gone on without her. The bittersweet shock of it was too much to bear.

Sivvy rose unsteadily to her feet, tears pouring down her face, and fled for the door of the auditorium. She heard O.T. shout behind her, "Miss Sivvy, wait!" but she could not. She knew before she reached the door that the nurses would be behind her, and they were. She was escorted directly to the Jones building, through the foyer, into the elevator, and up to her little room with its rectangular window. She was given a shot and sank onto her bed and cried until blackness took her. Sivvy woke before sunrise with an awful pain in her head; by the time the morning light filtered in she was wishing for the strong dress just to stop the shaking in her hands.

O.T. sat in a chair by the window, brooding. Ginny tinkered on the dusty piano in the corner of the parlor. He couldn't make out what tune she was playing and supposed it didn't matter. When Sivvy had run out on him a second time in as many days, he'd decided to just pack up and go home. He was almost out of money, and whatever it was he'd intended to do, he'd failed. No, *failed* was too nice a word—it implied that he'd made a valiant effort. The truth was he'd bungled the entire thing from top to bottom, and all he'd succeeded in doing was further traumatizing an already tortured woman. The worst part was that Sivvy was right. He couldn't do a thing to help her.

Earlier that morning, O.T. had gone to the asylum to visit with the superintendent. He met instead with several doctors and a junior staff member who hadn't even offered his name. They'd listened to O.T.'s story in polite silence then informed him that three letters from blood relatives, delivered and signed in person by at least one of them, were necessary to get Sivvy's case reviewed by the Board. After a study—if they unanimously agreed that she was fit to be released—she could leave, under the care of one such relative. But the process took months at best, and that was *with* all the necessary letters, which he did not possess.

O.T. had neither the money nor the resources for another trip to Rock Creek to fetch a letter from Julie-Anne and Nate. He could—and would—write to them when he returned to Five Forks, but washing his hands of the matter filled him with a queer anxiety.

O.T. was confounded by Sivvy. By her past, her life here, and by his own feelings toward her. Clearly his visit had unnerved her, and that was to be expected; he had come with news of a family she'd not seen in years, and a terrible shock besides. It was a lot for anyone to bear. Still, the girl was a paradox. She'd run from him at first, then had him come back, poured out her life story, and run again. He hadn't expected her to fall at his feet in appreciation, but he had hoped for something more…pleasant. A little humble gratitude, perhaps. Did she think it had been an easy thing, him traveling all this way?

He sighed, knowing he was being unfair. She'd lived a life he couldn't even begin to imagine. So she lacked a little in social graces. What should that matter to a poor, homeless drunk? He hadn't come for flattery or thanks.

So what *had* he come for?

He'd told himself the journey was for Walt; then, it was for Sivvy herself. But the truth, he now knew, was it had been for himself all along. As he sat in the parlor, his head pounding with withdrawals, he could not help but feel the entire enterprise had been a folly. The trip had been nothing more than the aimless wanderings of a lost man, one who'd used his poor dead brother as an excuse. To make matters worse, Sivvy Hargrove had gotten into his head, and he found he could not leave without making it right for her. But how?

Ms. Dawkins, the help, entered the room with a platter of cake and coffee. *Lord, was that real coffee?* O.T. inhaled for a moment, savoring the deep, roasted smell of real beans. *Christ, was that lemon cake on the platter?* His mouth watered.

"Lil' afternoon bite for y'all," the woman said with a smile as Ginny left to wash her hands.

"Miss?" O.T. called, hesitantly, and the woman turned.

"Yes'r."

"What was your name again?"

"Ms. Dawkins. But y'all can call me Thelma."

"Thank ya kindly for this, Thelma. It looks delicious. I did have a question for you, if'n you din't mind."

The owner of the bed and breakfast, Mrs. Atworth, a pinch-faced woman with a severe bun and stern voice, had told O.T. that her kitchen help had been "boarded out" from the asylum.

"I don't worry none about Ms. Dawkins' state of mind," Mrs. Atworth had said conspiratorially, "because the asylum done diagnosed her as 'improved.' She works hard, don't ask for much of a wage, and it keeps me from runnin' myself ragged tryin' to look after my boarders."

From what O.T. had seen, Mrs. Dawkins—a young, fresh-faced black woman who couldn't be a day over twenty-two—was the one being run ragged, but she had a sweet smile and, judging from the smell wafting from the platter, could bake a mighty delicious lemon cake.

"I wondered if you might've known a patient at Milledgeville?" O.T. said.

"You here to visit somebody?" Thelma asked.

"Yes, matter of fact, I am. I just thought you might know her, is all."

"White or black?" she asked. "You know they separate us colored folks from the white folks. Different buildin' an all."

"Yes," O.T. replied. "I had heard that, but this woman works in the kitchens, so I thought you might have seen her anyhow." He took a sip of coffee. It was strong, bitter, and delicious. "She's a white woman—well, white-passin', anyhow. Name of Sivvy Shelnutt."

"Don't know her," Thelma answered.

"Oh." O.T. was surprised by his own disappointment.

"You worrit about this woman?" Thelma said kindly.

"Mayhap so." He thought for a moment, then said confidingly, "I was tryin' to get her out, but it ain't going so good."

"Naw, it wouldn't, would it?" Thelma said sagely. "Her workin' in the kitchens an' all."

"I don't follow." His brow furrowed.

Thelma gave a low chuckle. "Kitchen help don't come easy. Don't come cheap, neither. The wages they pay the hired staff in that place is peanuts. Janitors, seamstresses, laundresses, and cooks—most of 'em come from the patient wards. Naw, they ain't gon' let your gal out if she's a good worker in the kitchens. No, sirree. They'll keep her in long as they can, 'cause they want that free labor, y'see. My daddy tol' me once, and I ain't never forgot it, that half the world's money is made on the backs of the incarcerated. And don't you doubt for one minute, sir, that Milledgeville is a prison just like any other."

O.T. regarded her. "So you're sayin' it's a hopeless business?"

"Prob'ly so," she answered, meeting his eye. "Lest you willin' to go some other route." She brushed off her apron and started back for the doorway, then turned and said in a low murmur, "You look like a man could use a drink. My mistress don't know it, but I found me a key to her liquor cabinet. Stowed away in her dead husband's rollaway. You want you a gimlet? I could make you up one real fast."

O.T. could taste the gin and lime in the back of his throat before she'd finished speaking. He'd had a gimlet once, a sip of his ma's at Hazel's wedding, and he could still recall the bitter freshness. "I 'preciate it," he said, his heart thudding in his ears, and she turned toward the kitchen. Watching her retreat, his entire body buzzing with the sweet promise of alcohol, he swallowed hard, then called out again, "No'm…nevermind. I reckon I'll be awright with this here coffee and cake. I ain't had a slice of cake in a coon's age."

Thelma looked surprised but said no more, retreating into the kitchen.

O.T. swallowed painfully, for his mouth was full of saliva, and dug his fingernails into his hand, drawing blood.

CHAPTER TWENTY-FIVE

Sivvy assumed O.T. Lawrence and his daughter had left for good. Of course they would've, given her behavior at the dance, running out without so much as a goodbye. That was two times, now, that she'd run out on him. Any goodwill or generosity he might've felt for her was surely now gone, and she deserved it. It was just as well, Sivvy supposed. Following O.T.'s visit, she found that all she could seem to think on was Harvey. *Alive.* Sivvy's memories of the ridge often included the boy, who had grown up a stone's throw from her house. She liked to think had Billy Rev not meddled in both their lives, they might've grown up to be friends.

Sivvy's ma had always told her children that everyone was the same, and all were loved by God. She'd told Sivvy, when she came of age, that their family weren't strictly white, anyhow. All that was fine with Sivvy; she didn't think much of it, never had. Life on the ridge had its own set of privileges, away from the rigid, bigoted hate that flowed freely in other towns like a broken faucet. Sivvy had been ignorant of what life was really like for a person of color; it hadn't seemed her concern.

It was only when Sivvy left the ridge that she'd begun to understand. She'd seen the way people looked at Harvey, the way they stepped to the other side of the street when he passed, the way they always made sure to tell Billy Rev in low tones that he and Sivvy could have a room in so-and-so's house, but that there was no room for colored boys. Had Harvey not been with a man of the Lord who commanded best behavior, it would have been a lot worse. Billy Rev's position provided Harvey with some protection, but not enough goodwill to keep him regularly fed or to avoid the late-night slurs hurled at him by rough men staggering home from the juke joint. Sivvy had heard the "N-word" in a variety of different Georgia dialects. As far as she was concerned back then, this was just Harvey's lot, and there wasn't anything she could do about it. She was worried about her own self, and life was rough and hard all over.

Her attitude had been sinful, Sivvy now knew. Her actions had made his life so much more complicated. She had pulled Harvey into all manner of trouble and then absolved herself of it. He had suffered for her immature selfishness. Now, knowing that he lived, she thought some of the guilt might dissipate, but it lay heavier on her breast; for now she knew he was alive and could remember all that she had done.

Somehow, despite her melancholy, Sivvy had made it through her check-up with Dr. Lowell without screaming herself into a fit, though she shuddered still at the memory. He'd reminded her of her upcoming procedure, and as much as it terrified her, Sivvy felt reconciled to the idea. Perhaps putting an end to her tainted bloodline might be for the best, she thought, as people she loved didn't seem to fare well. She had left his office feeling bereft, but resigned.

Telling O.T. her story had let loose something in Sivvy, something long buried. It had been a long while since she'd allowed herself to think of Harvey and Clayton, of Clay Jr. and Nona Leigh, and of her ma and pa living on the ridge. Usually thoughts of family triggered her fits. The tremors, she knew, would get worse and worse until she broke apart entirely, and they would put her in a strong dress and serve her broth and water until she was right again—until her screaming subsided and she stopped trying to claw at her own skin.

But somehow, Sivvy was not breaking, not this time. Over the course of the next few days, Sivvy began to realize that the tremors in her hands were *lessening*. She no longer had to grip the metal bowl so tight when she mixed the biscuit dough, and she managed to tie her apron behind her without assistance. Nurse Jennings said her improved condition was due to the medication, but Sivvy thought not. Something lifted in her, and it wasn't just Harvey's miraculous rising from the dead. It was a pair of gray eyes.

"Miss Sivvy, wake up!"

Sivvy rolled over with a groan, cracked one eye open and saw that it wasn't yet dawn. The room was dark, and Nurse Burns was standing over her, holding a flickering candle, shadows dancing on her face.

"I'm sorry, ma'rm. Did I oversleep?"

"No, Sivvy. But you need to get up. You're needed downstairs."

Sivvy sat up, confused. "Extra work in the kitchen this morning?" she asked groggily.

"No." Nurse Burns took Sivvy by the arm. "Something else. But we need to get downstairs, before morning breaks."

"I don't understand." Sivvy shuffled toward the door, pulling her dress over her shift, and slipping into her shoes.

Nurse Burns pulled the door behind them until it clicked gently into the frame. Tugging on Sivvy's arm, the nurse led her down the hall, a finger to her lips to indicate silence. Sivvy could see that Nurse Burns was carrying a burlap sack, cinched tight and bundled under her arm like a sack full of stolen money.

Something wasn't right, Sivvy worried, alarm bells clanging in her head. She headed toward the bathroom to brush her teeth and use the toilet, but the nurse seized her shoulder. "No, there's not time."

"But—"

"Let's *go*, Sivvy."

"But I don't understand," Sivvy said, pulling her dress over her shift.

Nurse Burns didn't answer, only put a hand to Sivvy's back and pushed her toward the door. Sivvy, wide-eyed, was shuffled down the long, cold corridor, which, in the eerie first light of dawn, was as quiet as the grave. The chill climbed further up her back as they stepped inside the elevator. Was she being taken to the Powell building? The doctors and nurses had kept a watchful eye on her since her flight from the dance. Sivvy clapped a hand to her mouth to fight the wave of nausea that rose in her throat. Had they decided to do the sterilization procedure early? She thought she had resigned herself to the surgery, so why did she suddenly feel struck with terror?

The elevator doors opened and Sivvy stepped reluctantly out and peered into the foyer, which was dark and quiet as a tomb. Nurse Burns, holding Sivvy tightly by the hand, led her through the large front door and down the steps, into the pecan grove, and through the trees. The moon was hidden by the dark silhouette of the buildings, but the gray light of morning already had hints of pink. They walked silently through the grove of trees, to the other side of the complex. Sivvy began to cry as she saw Powell building loom ahead and attempted to tug away from the nurse's grip.

Nurse Burns stopped and looked at her, exasperated. "Oh, for heavens' sake, Sivvy."

"I don't want to go to the Powell Building," Sivvy croaked through her tears. "I know I said I would do the operation, but I changed my mind. Please—"

"Hush up your sniveling, gal. We ain't goin' into the Powell building. Calm yourself down. Here, wipe your face." The nurse produced a handkerchief from the pocket of her white gown. "Where we *are* goin', it won't do to have a mess of tears all over you."

"Where *are* we goin', then?" Sivvy dabbed at her eyes and nose and handed the handkerchief back to the nurse.

"C'mon and I'll show you." Nurse Burns tugged her forward again.

Sivvy's momentary relief subsided as she began to wonder if Nurse Burns was working with Billy Rev. This sneaking early-morning furtiveness seemed like something he might have a hand in. Fear crept low in her belly.

They stopped in front of the chapel. "I've delivered you and now I've got to go back before I'm missed," Nurse Burns said. "I told 'im that's all I'd do. Go on in. He's waitin'."

Sivvy stared. "Who?"

Nurse Burns deposited the burlap bag in Sivvy's arms. "That there's your things, what I could grab quick. Go on, now, there's no time to spare." The nurse disappeared into the trees as Sivvy pulled open the heavy wooden door. Stepping into the dark chapel, she let the door boom shut behind her. Moving tentatively up the aisle, she made out a figure in the darkness, standing before the first pew.

To her surprise, it was O.T. Lawrence. He stepped out of the shadows, holding a hand out to her. "Sorry to have to drag ya out of bed at this time of mornin'. There wasn't no other way around it," he said, his face cloaked in shadow.

"What am I doing here, O.T?" Sivvy asked, her frazzled nerves killing what was left of politeness. He stared at her with bright eyes.

"Last I saw you, you tol' me I was tryin' to find me a wife, to replace the one I lost," O.T. said, taking her arm. "I *did* consider it, for Walt's sake more than mine, or even yours." He cleared his throat, looking suddenly nervous. "But I just cain't see that a shotgun weddin' would be fair to either one of us, 'specially considerin' what you told me about yer last marriage. And it don't honor Walt or none of the rest of 'em, if it's a sham.

"But I cain't shake the feelin' that I was *meant* to come here. My feet brung me like they was outside of me; like it was fate. Does that make sense at all?" He shook his head. "I guess it don't, but now I've seen you, I'm sure of it. I've looked in those green eyes of yers, and you ain't unwell, Sivvy Hargrove, no more than the rest of us. We all got problems. If I can stagger around in the world a no-good drunk, what business has they got keepin' you in this place on account of some hard luck? I been studyin' on getting you out of this place—I went to see the superintendent the other mornin', and I asked them to release you to me. But they said no."

Sivvy was unable to hide her dissapointment. "Well, that's what we expected." she said finally.

"I tried everything. I told 'em I was actin' on behalf of yer family, and friends, too. I argued all of that and then some, but they's a mountain of red tape we gotta go through to get you out. And we ain't related, so the chances of me succeedin' are slim to none. Even if we *was* married." He laughed hollowly. "They want to keep you on in the kitchens, is what I think. From what I hear, they don't like to let good help go."

"Oh." Sivvy thought of all the time she'd spent bent over a stove and sighed.

"They said things about you, to discourage me. Said you had visions, that you been seein' ghosts all these years. Called 'em delusions—said you was a danger to yerself and others." He snorted. "Little man, pressed into a suit too small for him with an ugly-ass bowtie, couldn't even look up from his dad-blamed papers long enough to meet my eyes while he spouted off that nonsense. Me and Ginny were right upset; we was stormin' out of Dr. Swint's office, when this little bitty nurse stopped me. She said she'd help, that she had access to you in the early morn. I threw a little change her way, and here you are."

"I don't understand."

"Well, you got a choice, I reckon," O.T. said, moving closer until his breath brushed her cheek, and his eyes glimmered close in the dark. "We can leave things how they are; you can stay on here, and I'll go on home and write a letter to your folks, telling 'em that I saw you and leave it to them. Or, you can come with me now and leave this place behind. Ginny's waitin' in the truck."

"What do you mean, 'leave this place behind'?"

"I'm bustin' you out, Sivvy," O.T. said gruffly. "If you want me to, that is."

"And I'd just go with you…?"

"Yes'm," he said. She hesitated, and O.T. continued. "I know it's hard to trust a body, after all you been through," he said. "But it ain't no trick. I just want to see you out of this place. Once we're clear of Milledgeville, where you go and what you do is yer own affair."

Sivvy considered this, her heart pounding so hard she felt faint.

"It's just, Miss Sivvy, well, it seems like every day you're in this place you get smaller," O.T. said softly. "I barely know ya and I can see that. So I'm just…offerin'."

"It's got to be illegal, what you're doin'," Sivvy cautioned. "You could go to jail."

"Mayhap," he shrugged. "I doubt they're gonna waste precious resources to go after somebody like me, or you, an escaped mental patient." He smiled. "Beggin' yer pardon. And anyhow, if I get caught, it's worth it to me."

Sivvy swallowed. Could she really ask O.T. to risk his neck and the wrath of Dr. Swint and the board to get her out of here? If O.T. wrote to her family, maybe they could come for her, and she could get out of here without putting O.T. and Ginny in danger. But in her heart Sivvy knew the truth—there would never be enough letters or relatives.

"I hate to rush you," O.T. said, his eyes glowing like gray pools in the dark room. "But if we're gonna do this we got to hurry. If not, I'll see you back to yer building."

"What are you…will I have to—" Sivvy struggled for words, heat flooding her cheeks.

"You don't owe me nothin," O.T. reassured her quickly. "I'm just tryin' to get you out of this godforsaken place."

"What would Walt think of this plan, O.T.?" she asked quietly.

"My brother was a stickler for fairness and goodness," O.T. said, with a wistful smile. "But there was one thing he set a store by more than anything else, and that was family. Rules and laws are important, but helpin' folks is more so. He taught me that. He's smilin' down on us right now, I bet." O.T.'s eyes shone with tears. "But, Sivvy, I ain't doin' this for Walt. For the first time, I'm makin' this choice because it's what *I* wanna do. Will you come?"

There was nothing else to consider. "Yes," Sivvy said.

"Will you bear up?" he asked, delight evident in his voice and in the sudden grin that crossed his lips.

"I'm a lot tougher than I look, Mr. Lawrence," Sivvy said, taking his arm.

"I reckon you are, at that."

The truck rumbled down the road out of Milledgeville, the three occupants within as silent as ghosts, each lost in their own thoughts.

Sivvy held her embroidery in her lap, stabbing the needle in and out, working on a yellow rose that was already crooked and uneven. She was barely aware of what she was doing, but she had to occupy herself somehow; she was a mess of nerves, bright-hot and firing with relentless intensity.

Within the burlap bag, Nurse Burns had put her embroidery and Bible, her toothbrush from the peg, and the little bit of money she'd saved over the years. Folded up in the bottom, Sivvy found her letter from Walt. Seeing that, she'd been struck by a sudden affection for the odd nurse.

Sivvy had always assumed she'd live out her days in Milledgeville, and now she had no idea what to do or where to go, or how she might live with a freedom she hadn't tasted for over a decade. She'd just looked into O.T.'s gray eyes and jumped off the ledge, with only his hand to cling to. She didn't know O.T. Lawrence from diddly squat, but she trusted him. She believed him when he said he wanted nothing from her. Everything had been taken from her anyway; what was left for O.T. Lawrence to take?

Sivvy poked the needle into the fabric, and drew it out again. She had finished a second rose easily, then stopped, holding her hands out in front of her, waiting. They did not shake, not even a little bit.

"Everything awright?" O.T. asked, looking over at her.

"It is, ayuh," Sivvy replied, realizing that finally, it was true.

They had been driving for about an hour when it occurred to Sivvy that if she were caught, the doctors would drag her back and throw her into solitary in a strong dress she'd never get out of. The police with their dogs might already be in pursuit with Dr. Swint, Dr. Powell, and their legion of nurses not far behind. How far and how long would they search? Perhaps even now Dr. Lowell was preparing electric shock treatments. Still, all of that was preferable to being given over to Billy Rev.

As if he read her thoughts, O.T. said, "Don't fret none, Sivvy. We ain't gonna let nobody take you back."

"You cain't stop them," Sivvy said. Despite this, she felt surprisingly upbeat. She was *out*. She was free! She didn't know what it was— maybe the lush forest around her, the birds singing, or maybe it was O.T. and his friendly daughter—but suddenly she no longer quaked at the prospect of her uncle.

"That Billy Rev won't come on my property, lest he wants to see the business end of my shotgun," O.T. said forcefully. "And I reckon yer kin would feel the same."

"What about the asylum? You rankin they sent the police out to find me?"

"Naw, doubt it," O.T. answered. "Like I said, they ain't gonna waste no police on one lone woman. Wouldn't be worth the scandal, I don't reckon. And if they do catch up with us, I'll just lie and say you my wife. So don't fret about it none."

"I ain't frettin'," Sivvy said happily, leaning back in her seat. "Not with the sun shinin' like it is today. I feel like I ain't breathed in ten years. The air sure does taste nice. Are we going straight to Five Forks?" she asked, a little wary at the prospect of meeting O.T.'s children and sister. She couldn't imagine what they would think of the situation; she wasn't sure what *she* thought of it yet. O.T. had told her she was welcome at his house as long as she wanted to stay, but

Sivvy was wary of overstaying her welcome. O.T. had a big family to take care of, a family that might not take kindly to a woman fresh out of the asylum taking up space and eating their food.

"I figgered we'd stop off in Bishop, grab a bite of lunch and stretch our legs," O.T. said.

"Bishop?" Sivvy looked out the window, her stomach twisting with emotion. "We'll pass right through—"

"I know," O.T. said, eyes on the road. "If you want to stop, we will."

Ginny put a loving hand on her arm, and Sivvy felt her eyes brim with tears.

"Yes," she said finally, after a long silence. "Yes, I'd like to stop. If you please."

"Your wish is my command, ma'am."

ॐ

O.T. kept sneaking side glances at Sivvy, and Ginny seemed to notice every one of them, damn her. O.T. just couldn't get a line on how Sivvy was feeling and wanted to make sure she was all right. She had been preoccupied for most of the drive, staring out the window, hands clutched in her lap, forehead resting against the glass. Likely she was taking in sights and smells she hadn't had the pleasure of in the past ten years, he reckoned, noticing how her shift dress had slipped a little off one shoulder.

She's purdy as a picture, O.T. thought to himself, but she could do with a little more meat on her bones. *She ain't had it so easy. If she was rounded out just a little more she'd be about the purdiest woman I'd ever seen.*

O.T. guiltily forced his eyes back to the road. He hoped Ginny couldn't see the way his thoughts had been going. It was a betrayal of her ma, to be looking at another woman. Sivvy was pretty, but he was a married man. Dead or no, Betty Lou was his wife. And what about Walt? Why, Sivvy was *his* girl, as much as he ever would have had any girl.

O.T fixed his eyes on the road, trying to ignore the gentle, low thrumming that had begun in his blood. It was a pleasant, heady sort of feeling that made him feel slightly high, like when he'd taken a puff of Rob Gum's funny cigarette. Aside from the creamy shoulders, shining black hair, and shapely legs he'd admired, was Sivvy herself. There was something about her that struck him as wholly new, a quiet mixture of vulnerability and strength. She was like a bird, just out of the nest, with sharp claws but not yet able to fly.

A wave of tenderness rushed over him, and he couldn't help but glance over at Sivvy one more time. With her pale forehead pressed against the glass, her dark hair falling behind her ears, and her long neck, she seemed both damaged and exquisite. He would do whatever he had to do to protect her.

Ginny smirked in the seat beside him, and he ignored her.

An hour later, O.T. pulled the truck into a parking space in front of a dilapidated diner. "Lordamercy," Sivvy exclaimed. "I'd forgotten all about this place. Is it still run by—"

"The Singing Cook?" Ginny said with a laugh. "None other. He's a sight, ain't he?"

"He always was," Sivvy said with amusement, climbing from the truck. "Is Miriam here too?"

"I don't reckon she is," O.T. said as they walked to the door. "I guess when you knew 'em they was marrit, but when Ginny and I came back last week, he said that Miriam'd run off—"

The diner door swung open and the stocky figure of Rob the Singing Cook appeared, his apron stained with grease and his white blonde hair piled haphazardly under a hairnet.

"Triphy Shelnutt, if you ain't a sight for sore eyes!" he exclaimed in delight, his blue eyes shining. "I never believed he'd bust you out. Shoot fire."

Sivvy ran to Rob and was immediately enveloped in a warm hug.

"How're you, little girl?" Rob asked, holding her at arm's length. "You look the same as the last day I saw you. Tiny enough to fit in a teacup."

Sivvy smiled. "I'm good. I feel real good."

"Get you on inside then and have a bite." Rob whipped his dishrag at her and grinned. "All of y'all. Ain't got nothin' but brunswick stew and cornbread, but y'all gon' eat."

"Don't have to twist my arm," O.T. said, following them inside.

Sivvy sat at the little wooden table, half expecting Clay to come shuffling out from the back. Her stomach hurt at the thought. O.T. kept casting glances her way, trying to gauge how she was holding up; she hoped they wouldn't do that the entire way to Five Forks—it made her feel like glass set to break any time.

"Where's Miriam?" Sivvy asked as Rob reappeared with bowls of steaming hash.

"Run off with some bootlegger," Rob replied. "This here stew is thinned down, and got too many potatoes, but got to make do."

"We're much obliged for food, however we can get it," Ginny said with a warm smile.

"Too bad there ain't call for women lawyers round these parts," Rob remarked with a wink and a smile to O.T. "Yer gal can lie with the best of 'em. As for Miriam, she got sick of my shit—er, beg pardon. I get poorer and uglier and fatter ever' year, and I reckon she just got fed up." He made a scoffing noise at Ginny's expression of pity. "She was just here last week, though. She shore din't believe Mr. O.T. here would be able to bust you out. I cain't wait to crow over her when I tell her he done it."

"I'm sorry she left," Sivvy said. "She'll be back, though, don't ya rankin'?"

"Don't know if she will this time," Rob said. "And even if she does, I might have to turn her away. Can barely afford to keep food in my own mouth."

"And here we are taking advantage of yer hospitality," O.T. said.

"Naw. I don't mind. Nice to have a bit of company, 'specially this gal here," Rob replied, beaming. "I'd be glad to take a quarter or two off of y'all in payment, though, so don't feel shy."

O.T. dug into his pocket, but Sivvy stopped him. "No, let me. I'm glad to pay."

"All due respect, Sivvy, but you surely don't have money to—"

"I do, actually," Sivvy said, reaching into her pocket. "Clay sent me a little bit, and I held on to it. And they paid me some wages for kitchen work. Not much, mind—just a few cents—but I saved it all."

"Well, you ain't payin' for our meal," O.T. said decisively. "No, ma'am, you ain't. You keep that. Put it by. But you ain't giving it to me."

"But—"

"No, ma'am. I won't take one red cent."

Sivvy's cheeks burned with emotion and she looked down at her stew, overwhelmed.

"We all need some pie, I reckon," Rob sang out. "Some good, hot-out-of-the-oven apple pie with crumbs on top. Or banana cream with meringue so thick you could sit on it."

"They both sound like heaven," O.T. said, patting his stomach. "I ain't had pie in a coon's age. I'll take a piece."

"Me too," Ginny agreed.

"That's too bad," the cook said with a grin, "'cause I ain't got none."

"Then why did you offer?" Ginny asked, her expression so downcast that Sivvy had to laugh.

"I din't," Rob said, lumbering up from the table and whipping his dishrag at them. "I was just sayin' we needed some." He sauntered back into the kitchen, singing loudly and out of tune.

"He ain't changed one bit," Sivvy said, looking after him fondly.

Sivvy stepped gingerly into the graveyard, pushing past the moss-covered fence and trying to keep her feet from sinking into the rain-soaked ground.

O.T. held her arm and led her through the rows of headstones until she got to the one where her loved ones rested. Ginny had remained at the diner with Rob, who had set his sights on making a pie after all. "Don't know how I will, since I ain't got nuthin' in the cabinets but mothballs," he had said with a laugh. "But we'll eat them and call it mothpie."

"I'll go see if I can find me a service station, get a dollar or two of gas," O.T. said. "And I'll be back for ya."

"I wish you'd let me give you some money," Sivvy said a little desperately. "For all you've done. Just a little to help—"

"Stop that, Sivvy. I ain't gonna hear it." O.T. shook his head firmly. "You just go on and visit with yer fambly and don't mind me. I'll be back for you just as soon as—"

"O.T.?" she interrupted, haltingly.

"Yes'm?" He was still holding her arm, and she was afraid if he let go her trembling legs might not hold her upright.

"I hate to ask but—but could you stay? I thought I was ready to do this, but now that I'm here—" she bit her lip, hard. "I ain't so very sure I got the strength. Maybe I ought to just leave."

"No, don't do that. You'll regret if you do," O.T. said firmly, pulling her closer to him. "I know a little something about that. I'll stay. I'll go wait in the truck or go sit a spell in the grass, whatever you want. You jus' take yer time. I'll be right here, when you got need of me."

"Thank you."

"You welcome."

Still clutching his arm, Sivvy stepped forward, the ground squelching under her feet, and sighed. "I don't know which one is his, exactly," she said quietly, her voice quavering.

"I'll help you. We'll find 'em." O.T.'s voice, strong and calm, steadied her as they stepped lightly down the row, stopping at each gravestone to read it and move on. The inscriptions on a number of graves were so faded that she could not decipher them. The few flowers that adorned the graves were dry and brittle, flaking off in the wind.

"I forgot to bring them flowers," Sivvy said despairingly.

"Just don't you worry on that, Sivvy," O.T. said, guiding her slightly to the left. "Just here, see, there's the name." He pointed downward, his voice gentle. "Here they are."

Sivvy put a hand to her heart, and with a deep breath, knelt to get a better look at the headstone of her husband. The stone was sparse, with only his name and the date of his birth and death recorded. He was flanked by his two sons—Gerald, who had died in the war, and her baby, Clayton Shelnutt Jr., who would have been nearly thirteen if he had lived.

O.T. momentarily forgotten, Sivvy leaned her head against the tombstone, the granite cold beneath her skin. She placed a hand on the grassy grave of her son.

"Hey," Sivvy whisperered hoarsely. "Hey, Clay. Hey, baby. I'm so sorry," Her voice broke. "So, so sorry."

Clayton Shelnutt, Jr. beloved son. Rests with Angels. Clay had chosen the words, organized the gravestone, and presided over the funeral. Sivvy remembered the little coffin being lowered into the ground; she recalled screaming like a banshee, and someone's wife throwing a shawl over her head, trying to calm her, whispering in hushed tones, "There, there. Please, you *must* try to be calm, Mrs. Shelnutt—" Three days later she'd been sent to Milledgeville.

Sivvy ran her fingers over the engraved letters on her son's headstone, whispering his name into the wind. She had seen his face every night before sleeping—his delicate eyelashes, his light brown skin, his perfect tiny fingers. She felt the wind lifting her hair and settling it softly across her back; she heard trilling birdsong, and the rustle of leaves falling from the trees. She could smell smoke on the breeze and feel the dampness of the wet ground seeping through her skirt. But she was far removed from those things, because it had been thirteen years, and she was finally reunited with her men. She let the tears stream down her cheeks and drop to the ground.

After a long while, Sivvy became aware of herself and stood on shaky legs, wiping her eyes and smoothing her hair.

O.T. sat on the ground two rows behind her, leaned up against a headstone, a small, ragged bouquet of blossoms resting in his lap, his hat pulled over his eyes. Sivvy cleared her throat, and he sat up and looked at her. "Awright?"

"Yes," she said. "I think so. Were you asleep?"

"No," he answered. "Just giving you privacy." He stood up, brushed off his pants, and handed her the blossoms. "There was a mimosa tree just over thataway," he said, "and I found a few dandelions. Best I could do. But I thought you might want 'em to put on their—"

"Yes. Yes, I would," she murmured gratefully, fresh tears welling up in her eyes. "Thank you, O.T."

He looked embarrassed. "Why sure, Sivvy."

"Just give me a—a moment."

"Accorse."

Sivvy returned to the graves, dividing the sweet-smelling bouquet in two. The mimosa blossoms looked like little pink and yellow puffballs, so soft and sweet smelling, like something that might decorate a baby's cap. Sivvy swallowed a sob and placed them gently on the little grave.

"I love you all," she murmured. "And I'll come back, I promise I will. Until then, y'all will be in here." She touched her hand to her heart, and turned to go.

O.T. stood behind her, ready, and offered her his arm. Sivvy did not take it; instead, she threw her own arms around his neck and clutched him tightly. "Thank you," she said fiercely in his ear. "Thank you so much."

"What for?" His arms went around her waist and held her tight. He smelled like fresh-cut grass, and his cheek was scratchy with stubble.

"For my life," Sivvy said. "For helping me get it back."

When O.T. and Sivvy pulled in at the Stew & Que, Rob and Ginny were outside riding rusty bicycles. A grin lit up O.T.'s face. "Look at them beauts!" he exclaimed. "I'm surprised Ginny remembers how to ride! Their bikes are all broke," he confessed quietly to Sivvy. "And I was too drunk to fix 'em."

"Come take over," Rob said, hoisting his hefty frame off his bike. "I'm slap wore out. Tire's in need of a little air, but it still rides okay."

"Naw, I'm happy to just watch y'all," O.T. said, sitting down in the dirt for the second time that day and pulling his hat down over his eyes. "I want to soak up as much sun and dirt as I can into these old bones."

Rob held a bike out to Sivvy, a smile curling his lips. "You ever rode one?"

"You jokin'?" Sivvy laughed. "Accorse I have. I ran my bike all up and down the mountains when I was a young'un." She seized the bike and threw a leg over, not minding about her slip. "But it's been years."

Ginny was riding around the parking area of the Stew & Que, her braids trailing behind her, her laughter like music. "Come on, Sivvy, let's go down the road!"

"I ain't going in no road with traffic," Sivvy protested, fixing her wheel toward the back lawn. She sped downhill, gaining speed, feeling her skirts and hair flapping in the wind behind her. Her front wheel hit a rock, and her bike flew into the air, before it landed back on the damp grass, propelling downward toward the stream at the bottom of the rise.

"Watch for the stream!" Sivvy heard the bellow behind her but paid it no mind. She had no intention of stopping now. Just before the stream embankment, she hit another rock and this time went flying, landing with a splash in the icy creek water.

Rob, Ginny, and O.T. bounded down the hill to find Sivvy standing, drenched and bent over with laughter.

"Good Lord, woman, are you okay?"

"I'm fine," Sivvy managed through her giggles. "Lucky I got a fat bottom and landed in a pile of mud. Shoot, this water's cold!"

"You're gonna catch yer death," O.T. said sternly, but he was laughing too. "And you look a real fright."

"My clothes was rurnt anyway," Sivvy declared, taking O.T.'s offered arm. She was beginning to like the way it felt, her arm linked with his. "Rob, say, is them bikes for sale?"

"Gal, you know just about anythin' I got on my property is for sale," Rob said with a booming laugh. "But I ain't so sure you need to be buyin' no rusty bikes. From the looks of it you don't know how to ride no more."

"Come off it, Singing Cook," Sivvy said smartly, wringing out her skirt. "I just felt like a dip, is all. How many bikes you got?"

"Five, I reckon," Rob said. "Well, six, but one of 'em got a broken chain."

"I'll take the five best ones. What's yer price?"

O.T. spoke up. "Miss Sivvy, what you doin'—?"

"One for me, one for you, and one for each of yer kids," Sivvy answered.

"Naw, Miss Sivvy, I cain't accept such a thing. You need to hang on to yer money, and I don't need no bike nohow. Besides, the kids' bikes I can fix—"

"Shush up, O.T. Lawrence," Sivvy said, hands on her wet hips. "I intend to pay you back for all you done for me somehow, and this here's a start. Young'uns need bikes, don't they? I'm willin' to bet you told 'em you'd bring 'em back a souvenir, didn't ya?" He looked down at his feet. "Thought so. Now, Rob, what you want for 'em?"

"I'd ast a dollar a piece for anybody else, Triphy—" he grinned. "I mean, er, Sivvy. But since it's *you*, and you a pal an' all, I reckon I could let all five of 'em go for three dollars."

"You got room for 'em in the back?" Sivvy asked O.T.

"I reckon so, but Sivvy—"

"Then it's a deal." She started to wheel her bike up the hill. "My money's inside. Glad of it, too, because Lord, my clothes are drenched. You might have to start a fire in the hearth so I can dry out, Rob."

As she walked ahead of them, she heard the Singin' Cook chuckle to O.T., "Hope you like handfuls, my man."

Rob Gum sat in his rocking chair out on the stoop, lighting a match. He inhaled swiftly, pulling in the sweet, skunky smoke and letting it back out in a long stream. From where he sat he could see inside the house, to the figures inside, sitting on the floor in front of the wood-burning stove. They were lost in a little world that contained only the two of them, their bodies leaning in to each other, shoulders almost touching, their heads mirrors of one another. Sivvy's hair shone in the dim light of the room, and O.T. Lawrence looked half drunk, though if he was to be believed, he hadn't touched a drop in days.

Rob Gum was happy. This happiness was low and sweet in his belly, finer than any wine or home-cooked dessert. He had a houseful of folks with full stomachs, a warm fire in his stove, and a puff of reefer to cap it off. He was a simple man, and he couldn't ask much more than this. Except for maybe Miriam, but…hell. This little slice of home here was his proudest achievement, even if he had to shut the whole shebang down inside the year, which seemed likely if things continued on. Just having a little spot to rest your head, folks to cook for, a song or two, was all one really needed in life, he mused.

Rob leaned back in the chair and sighed contentedly. He never thought he'd see that black-haired gal again. His heart surged with warmth. Sometimes, folks surprised you. Yes, sometimes they did. He decided to go in and say goodnight before he started blubbin' and embarrassed all three of them. Tomorrow he might pay Miriam a call. Bring her some pie.

Sivvy's clothes were very nearly dry, but she felt so toasty sitting in front of the wood-burning stove that she didn't want to get up. They were leaving at first light for Five Forks. O.T. had wanted to get on the road directly, but he seemed to understand that Sivvy needed a little time to gather herself before meeting the rest of his family. She knew he must be itching to see his kids, though.

He was crouched beside her, also enjoying the warmth. His long-fingered hands were spread in front of the fire, and he moved them back and forth, massaging his knuckles, his mouth curved in a worried line. Ginny had long since gone to bed, and Rob was out on the back porch, having a smoke.

"Are you awright?" Sivvy asked. "Are yer hands painin' you?"

O.T. held his hands out before him, as if noticing them for the first time. "Oh. No, they're fine," he said, with a small smile. "I'm a little jittered up, that's all. I'm fine."

"Jittered about what?" she pressed. "All this business with me?"

"Don't fret," he said, though he seemed to be the one who was fretting. "Naw, it ain't about you, Sivvy. Truth is, I'm hurtin' for a drink."

"Oh." She should have realized. Sivvy had seen inmates suffering the effects of withdrawl in the asylum, and he'd told her more than once that he was a drunk. While she hadn't seen him have a drink the entire time she'd known him, now that she was looking, she could see the signs. His limbs had a slight tremor to them; his face was pale; at times he seemed irritable and other times exhausted.

"When was the last?" she asked.

"Back on the ridge. With yer family." He flushed a little, embarrassed.

"Oh, honey, don't think I'm ignorant to the gettin's on they do up there," Sivvy said with a laugh. "I had my first drink in my bottle, prob'ly. So that's been a week or more?"

"Yeah," he said. "My hands won't stop shakin', and I ain't got no dang pockets in these pants, and I don't know what to do with 'em."

"Can I show you a trick I know?" Sivvy asked, taking his hands in her own and laying them flat on the floor. She applied gentle pressure with her own hands for a few seconds, then stopped. "If they get to shakin', just press 'em flat like that, palms down, against a hard surface. Press for ten seconds, let up. Breathe in deep while you do it. I dunno if it's the breathin' or the pressin', but it helps me some."

"Thank you," O.T. said. "How'd you know to do that?"

"I been plagued with shaking hands for years and tried different things till I found somethin' that worked," she replied, keeping silent about the fact that her hands hadn't shaken once since she'd met him.

"I do believe it has helped some," O.T. said. She picked his hands up, cradled them in hers, and let the weight of them rest there. They were still trembling, but not as badly. She ran her fingers over his knuckles, applying gentle pressure, squeezing each one until she felt his hands relax.

"What made you decide to quit drinkin'?" she asked.

"Up until a few days ago," he answered, looking into the flames of the wood stove, "it was just that I couldn't get no booze. Warn't nowhere to buy it, and I'm dern near broke anyhow. But now I find that I don't really want it no more." The firelight lit the planes of his face, casting his gray eyes aglow. "I don't know if it's gettin' out of my system, or if it's meetin' *you* that did it, or...." He trailed off, suddenly embarrassed. "I guess I just woke up one day and realized that I got to start takin' care of the people in my life, and that means me, an' all. There was a time when I wanted to die. I couldn't see past my own grief, I reckon. Since then I've met so many folks, folks who've had it worse than me, who are still walkin' around to kick another rock." He smiled. "Like you."

Sivvy laughed. "Well, I'm much obliged for the compliment, O.T., but I think yer givin' me a tad too much credit."

"No, I ain't," he said seriously. "If I'd lived through all you lived through and still had life enough in me to go ridin' my bike down a hill into a creek and come out laughin', why, I'd consider myself a happy man."

"Gosh." She didn't know what to say.

"You seem so...so *well*, to have been in that place."

"Not really," she said softly. " I have...things that I was being treated for. Things that haunt me. I hope I can do okay, now that I'm on the outside."

"I ain't no doctor," O.T. remarked, "but I wonder if half of what was ailin' you was caused by that place, rather than the other way around."

"Maybe so," she said thoughtfully.

"I like you, Miss Sivvy. Though I already knew I would, after meetin' yer kin." He smiled at her. "I wish I'd known Clayton Shelnutt. I think I would have liked him, too. I like that crazy Rob Gum." His eyes danced. "I like yer people. I really do."

"Though they're all scattered to the wind now, and often it feels like it's just me," she answered softly.

"It ain't just you," he said quietly. "You got me."

"I've hurt a lot of people," she said.

"So have I," he replied steadily.

They stared at each other in the shadowed room for a time, the only sound the popping of the kindling in the wood stove. The room smelled sweet and smoky, and Sivvy felt pleasantly drowsy. But she had a story to tell before they slept, and it had to be told here, and left in this place, before she could move forward somewhere else.

"So…about my boy," she began, taking a deep breath.

He put a hand on hers. "You don't have to tell me—" he began, but she cut him off.

"It's now or never," she said. "Just keep holdin' my hand, and I'll tell it fast."

"There ain't no easy way to say it, no way that don't hurt. He died. We got shy of two years with our boy, and then he was gone. I don't remember much about my delivery, other than Clayton bein' there, holdin' my hands. I remember them layin' the baby in my arms and wonderin' at his little fingernails and eyelashes, thinking what a beautiful color his skin was. Takin' a peek at his eyes when they finally opened and seein' how sparkling blue and purdy they were. He had the most beautiful full-throated cry. I almost din't want to start nursing him 'cause I wanted to keep hearin' that cry.

"The night after he was born I was in a kind of twilight, dozing in and out. Clayton was there, and the doctor, and other people, too. Miriam brought clean linens; others had brought casseroles and pies for Clay. I jest remember holdin' my baby and feelin' so lightheaded I thought I'd fallen right off the earth and was just floatin' on up to the stars. I din't care if I lived or died. I was just *out*. Other than my boy, I din't care 'bout a thing.

"It was deep in the night that I suddenly came around enough to realize that somethin' was wrong. I reckon I cried out, but it may have just been a whisper. Clay tol' me that the baby couldn't git his breath good; his lil' face was gettin' blue. He was having trouble cryin' and wouldn't take my milk.

"'But he's fine,' I managed to croak out. 'I heard him cry loud as the dickens.'

"'He ain't cried none since that first time,' Clay said gently. 'Doctor is doing all he can. Let's just pray, Triphy. Pray hard as we can and maybe the Good Lord will bless our little son.'

"I weren't afeared. Not then. I was still too sleepy to understand. I held Clay's hand while he prayed, but fell asleep affore he finished.

"I dreamed. I usually din't remember my dreams, but this one I'll never forget. There was a man in that dream, one I'd never seen affore. Tall, handsome, with light brown skin and bright blue eyes. He was leaning up 'gainst a church pew with his hands in his pockets; he had on the smartest black suit I'd ever seen. I was holdin' a bouquet of pink carnations. I stared at the young man as his beautiful lips curved into a smile, his eyes locked on mine, and that smile jest grew deeper, and I could hear my heart beatin' in my chest. I felt a sharp pain in my hand, and looked down—a thorn had cut my finger. But I was confused, since carnations haven't thorns. When I looked up again, the young man was gone, 'cept for his shoes, which were still there on the church floor. Shiny and black and brand-new, never-worn shoes.

"Then I woke and opened my eyes and saw the sun streamin' through the window, so bright and purdy it hurt my eyes, and I started in a'cryin'. I just knew my baby was gon'. But through the goodly work of the doctor and with the blessin's of the Lord, my boy had pulled through. He was weak, but alive. I buried the dream and told mahself that everythin' would be awright.

"Clay had ladies in and out for a long while, tendin' to me and the baby; we was both weak. They took up collections for us at church. Clay wanted to write to my fambly and tell 'em 'bout their grandyoung'un, but I din't want to burden 'em. I was happy, bein' a little family of three. We named him Clayton Shelnutt, Jr.

"I took to motherhood easy. I loved holdin' his little body in my arms and tendin' his needs. Changin' diapers, feeding him, bathing him—it all felt as natural as anything. But I knew my boy weren't well, and truth is, I weren't neither. I was havin' bad thoughts;

sometimes I felt like hurtin' myself, but I never breathed a word to anyone. I remember sittin' up in the night, cradling his little body 'gainst my chest, listening to the rattle of his breath, feelin' the sweat that covered his little back, fightin' the urge to claw at my skin, and prayin', just prayin' to God to take me instead.

"We got a couple years with him, always knowin' it was borrowed time. Lil' Clay was already sickly and then that fever hit, and…all I can say is my prayers weren't answered. I cain't say no more; it's too hard. I thought I knew pain, but losing my child was worse than anything I'd faced affore.

"Clay read a Bible verse at the funeral, or so they tol' me later; I cain't remember a word of it. I was thinkin' 'bout Clay Jr.'s first haircut. The lil' fella had sat perfectly still all the way up till the last snip, when he'd moved his head suddenly and Clay had nicked his ear. The boy screamed to beat the band, cryin' and carryin' on. There was scarcely a drop of blood, but he'd just cried and cried. "Daddy cut me!" he wailed, his big blue eyes puddlin' with tears, fixed on my husband like he was the worst kinda scoundrel. I laughed into my handkerchief during the service, thinkin' 'bout this, and several women looked at me in horror.

"I held mahself together for the rest o' the service, grittin' my teeth to keep from cryin' out. My brain felt like it was unravelin', and my hands begin to shake. By the time the readin's were done, my fingernails dug blood from my palms. When twas time to see the body, I couldn't move. For two days I'd begged to see my boy, but now that I had the chance, I couldn't. I let mahself be led outta the church while Clay saw our boy buried.

"I took to my bed. I begged for my son. I knew he was dead and cold and in the ground, but I wanted him anyway. I screamed mahself hoarse. I knew the toll all this was takin' on Clay, who was shrunken and haunted, but in that moment I din't care none. I was overcome by my own grief. I finally understood why my Clay had died. I was covered with sin because of Uncle Billy, and Harvey, and the men I'd dallied with from town to town. My baby had been smothered by my sin.

"That night, I staggered out of bed and dressed, though my hands shook somethin' fierce. I crept out of the house and down the footpath toward the church. 'Twas silent as a tomb inside, and the flowers from my baby's service still decorated the foyer, huge sprays of flowers, all fragrant and velvety. Among them was a huge cluster of pink carnations with a pink rose in the middle, and I felt a chill; what Ma used to call "a ghost walkin' over my grave." At the pulpit, I found the silver jug of holy water and washed my hands before going to the cemetary.

"Clay found me an hour later, scrabblin' frantically in the dirt, diggin' with my raw, bare hands. Desecratin' my own child's grave—Lord! I fought him when he tried to pull me out. I hollered about my sin, 'bout how I had cleansed mahself, and how I needed to be with our boy, but I couldn't make him understand; he just sat beside me in the truck and cried. I slapped myself. I bashed my head up 'gainst the window. But I ain't never hit him. I couldn't hit Clay.

"Clay told me to sleep, refusin' to leave me. After he fell asleep, I pulled out a kitchen knife hidden under the mattress—I din't even remember puttin' it there. I wanted to die, truly, but that would be one more sin. So I just sat there, holdin' it. Clay woke with a start and seized the knife from my hand. He held me on the bed, rockin' back and forth, and cried, tellin' me he was sorry. I din't yet know what he was sorry for, but I soon found out.

"The next morning he drove me to Milledgeville. I remember that drive like it were yesterday. Nona Leigh sat beside us, with her kind and gentle smile. We passed Harvey, standing by the road, watchin' us pass. I saw the young man from my dream with the shiny unworn shoes, leaning against a tree, a grown man I now knew was Clay Jr. And all the while, Clay tellin' me that I would get well and come home again, that it weren't forever, that we'd have another baby. He talked on and on in a quiet murmur, real peaceful, as was his way.

"Clay lied to make me feel better, you see. He wanted to write to my folks, to tell 'em what had happened, but I made him promise not to. Once I got out, we agreed, when I was well, we'd make the trip to Rock Creek together and tell my fambly ever'thing.

"'Something for us to look forward to,' Clay said with a sad smile, and I knew then that our life together was over. I never blamed the man for what he did; what choice did he have?

"I sat in the foyer of the Powell Building while he signed me away. The orderlies led me up to a room where I was given a pill that made me sleep for a long time. And then I was jest there. I was jes' there for over ten years. Because, you understand, Clay never came back for me. He died less than a month after I was admitted to the asylum. The sheriff found him one afternoon, out in his garden, a hoe in his hand, lyin' sideways on a row of cherry tomatoes. They buried him between his two sons.

"It was Billy Rev came to Milledgeville to tell me the news. I don't know how he found me, though it din't surprise me that he had. He was smug, like a cat who'd got into the cream. He tol' me that my husband was dead and that I'd never be released from the asylum. Not unless *he* decided, because he was now my closest living relative. He knew, accorse, that I'd never try to get in touch with my fambly, that my shame was too great.

"'I'll come back for you,' he tol' me. 'If you ever want me to. Until then, you'll stay.'

"I swore that I'd never, ever ask him to release me. I'd druther stay in the asylum till the day I died, if I had to. He visited me regular for a long time, but I never ast him to release me. By the time you showed up, he'd stopped comin'—rankin he knew I meant that vow.

"Everyone I love is dead, O.T. Nona Leigh, Clay, my little boy. And I'm sittin' here now, looking at this fire, and wondering who will die on me next. I'm scared to go back home to the ridge, to see my ma and pa and my fambly, 'cause ever'thing and ever'one I touch is cursed. Even yer brother wasn't immune to my bad luck," Sivvy whispered, her eyes shining like luminous emeralds in the firelight.

"My brother got sick and died," O.T. said after a time, staring into the fire. "Same as my wife, and my ma years before that. I lost my deddy as a boy, too. If you're cursed, then so am I."

"Y'all still up?" Rob startled them, and O.T. realized he was still holding Sivvy's hands in his own. He dropped them, his face burning, and Rob chuckled. "Don't let me disturb y'all. I got me a good buzzin' in my head, so I'm gonna go catch a few winks before it's up and at 'em. Just don't leave the door open on the stove. You burn my house down and I might have to get mad."

Rob sauntered toward the back, humming an off-key rendition of "Boll Weevil."

"I reckon I've kept you up half the night," Sivvy said, embarrassed.

"I didn't mind," O.T. said softly. "I don't sleep so good these days nohow."

"I guess I'll turn in," she said reluctantly. "Big day tomorry. Are you gon' be awright...?"

"Oh, sure, sure," he said quickly. "Don't worry. I ain't got a pint of whiskey stowed away in the truck."

"If you did *I* might drink it." Sivvy laughed, her eyes sparkling.

O.T. briefly considered escorting her to the room, then dismissed it as improper. The way her hands had felt in his had set him alight in some way, reopened a part of him he had thought forever closed. He hadn't realized how lonely he was.

"Foxfire," he said, a little dreamily. "Anybody ever tell you that before?"

"What?"

"Yer eyes," he murmured, staring at her. "They're the same shade, and they glow just like the foxfire I saw on the ridge, with yer ma."

"I forgot all about the foxfire," she said, looking at him. "Gosh, I can't believe that. It was so pretty, too. I used to love it as a child. I called it—"

"Fairy lights," O.T. interrupted as her face lit up with pleasure. He was sorely tempted to brush away her dark hair where it fell across her forehead, but he was afraid to touch her, afraid he would lose control.

"O.T., thanks for hearin' all of that. It weren't easy to tell, but I feel some lighter now."

"Thank *you* for tellin' me," he replied. "You can tell me anything. And that's the truth."

"Goodnight."

"Night, Miss Sivvy."

O.T. stood, watching Sivvy as she disappeared down the hall. He waited until he heard the door gently shut and the creak of the bedsprings as she settled into her cot. He stared a little longer into the fire, rubbing his hands, thinking of all they'd lost, the two of them, and wondering how on earth either of them was still standing.

CHAPTER TWENTY-SIX

The three of them pulled into Five Forks at noon and would have arrived sooner if they hadn't had a flat tire just outside of Athens. They'd broken down near Finley Street, near to the Tree That Owns Itself, a famous local novelty. Ginny had insisted the two walk there while O.T. changed the tire, and Sivvy had obliged, though she couldn't quite believe that a man might up and die and grant a tree ownership over itself in his will. It seemed a mockery, given where Sivvy had spent the past ten years; she was a *person* and had had no such ownership over her own self. When they returned, O.T. had the tire changed, but he was covered in sweat and grease and cussing up a storm. Sivvy was grateful they'd be on their way.

"I remember this place a little," Sivvy remarked quietly as they drove down Main Street, arriving in Five Forks. "I remember how the stores were all lined up like little matchbox cars, each one painted a different color."

"Yeah, has its charm, I reckon," O.T. said finally, clearing his throat. "Used to be a lot nicer place to live, affore things went to hell."

"Things is bad ever'where, so I hear," Sivvy offered.

"That's true," he said, "but it hurts more when it's yer own home."

"Was things bad on the ridge?" she asked.

"I reckon so, since things is bad ever'place," O.T. responded. "But they sure didn't show it. They knew how to roll out the welcome wagon for comp'ny. I never ate so good in my life."

"Did Mama make you her yellowjacket soup?"

"No, cain't say she did," O.T. said with a grimace. "Though she did talk about some soup…cocka-jee-me or somethin'. That the same thing?"

"Cocka-leekie," Sivvy said with a laugh. "And no, they ain't a bit the same."

"I'm too simple and country for such oddities," he replied, with a sideways grin.

She giggled. "Maybe you are, O.T. Lawrence."

"They're good folks, your people. I liked 'em a lot, Sivvy."

She looked down at her hands that no longer trembled. "They are," she said softly.

"I hope you'll think as well of my family as I did of yers."

"I'm sure I will, O.T."

"Well, we'll see in about thirty seconds," he replied, pulling into a long, dusty driveway. "We're here."

O.T.'s home was a small wooden house with a lean-to porch, tilting beneath gray shingles. A barn and run-down toolshed stood to one side of the house, and the fields in between were strewn with a glorious array of azaleas, hydrangeas, marigolds, tulips, and roses.

"Gin." O.T. shook his daughter, who woke with a start. "Hop to, hon. We're home."

"Oh!" Ginny was up and scrambling out the door in a heartbeat. Sivvy couldn't help but laugh as she watched the girl scamper into the house, a cloud of red dust in her wake. Sivvy opened the door and stepped down from the truck, taking O.T.'s offered arm as he came around to meet her. Down the porch steps streamed O.T.'s folks, all with wide grins on their faces. Two little ones bounded ahead in a frenzy of happy hysteria.

"Deddy! Deddy! We ain't seen you in forty forevers!"

The little girl—barefoot and wearing a blue sack dress—had dark blonde hair, pulled back in a messy braid, her face streaked with dirt. O.T. scooped her up with one arm and covered her face with kisses.

The little boy hung back, but couldn't hide his grin. He put a finger in his mouth and drew it out with a loud *pop*. "Hey, Deddy," he said, trying to sound casual. O.T scooped him up with the other arm.

Both children convulsed with giggles, arms clinging around their father's neck. For all he'd done to convince Sivvy that he was a no-good drunk who had failed his children, they sure seemed to love him. A man and woman waited on the porch. The man was handsome with short brown hair, a bemused mouth and a babyish face that wasn't fully hidden by his closely cropped beard. The woman was clearly O.T.'s sister, with the family's signature dark blonde locks. Her face, though tired and thin, had delicate, pretty features and eyes that sparkled.

The woman came down the steps, shielding her eyes from the sun with a delicate grace. She smiled, watching O.T. swing the kids around, all of them whooping and hollering with delight. Eventually O.T. managed to extract himself from his children, though they still clung to his legs. His face full of joy and pride, O.T. took Sivvy's arm. "Hazel is my sister," he said, by way of introduction. "In case you don't see the resemblance."

"Pleased to meet ya," Hazel said with a smile.

"These here is my kids, Belle and Owen Jr.," O.T. said, gesturing to the two dirt-streaked, grinning children clinging to his legs. "My two youngest—" his gaze fell on the man in the doorway and he scowled. "Hosey Brown. What in the dickens are you doing here?"

"Now, O.T., this is *my* house, so don't you start that mess—" Hazel began.

"You got a nerve comin' here when I'm away. What the devil—" O.T. interrupted angrily.

"Now ain't the time," Hazel said firmly, putting one hand on her brother's arm. O.T. immediately stilled, and Sivvy smiled. This was a woman who'd had a hand in his raising. "Who's your friend?"

"Sorry," O.T. mumbled, removing his hat and putting a gentlemanly hand on the small of Sivvy's back. "This here is Savilia Hargrove. Sivvy."

"I'm pleased to meet you, Sivvy," Hazel said politely. Sivvy extended her hand, but Hazel pulled her into a sweet hug.

"Looks to me we both got things to explain," O.T. said, forcing a laugh, despite his scowl. "For right now, though, I'm dog tired and starvin'. I need me a chair and a plate if you got anythin' to put on it."

"Y'all come on in then," Hazel said. The next thing Sivvy knew she was inside the kitchen, sitting at a table with a bowl of cornmeal mush as Hazel fretted about her.

"It ain't much," Hazel apologized. "I ran out of everythin' while O.T. was gone."

Sivvy dipped into her bowl as Belle and Owen Jr. crowded round, peppering O.T. and Ginny with questions. They wanted to know what they'd brought them, all they'd seen. Sivvy smiled, watching them.

Later that evening, after the day had turned dark, Hazel took her brother by the hand and led him out onto the porch where they could talk. Hosey pulled up a chair and sat down across from Sivvy. The children were out riding their new bikes up and down the dusty dirt driveway.

"I'm Hosey Brown," he said, extending his hand. "You and me wasn't properly introduced. I'm an old family friend. Fact, I remember you, though I'm not sure you remember me."

"Oh my lands, I do remember you!" Sivvy exclaimed. "You was with us that day we went for the joyride. You was the smilin' boy in the coveralls who hung like a monkey from the big branch and teased everybody." She laughed. "And covered in dirt an inch deep, if'n I recall correctly."

"Yes'm," Hosey admitted with a wide grin. "That was me. Me, O.T., and Walt been like brothers since we was small," he said, his grin fading. "Ain't nothin' been the same since Walt passed."

"He was a sweet boy."

The room was silent for a moment and the two could hear the joyful sounds of the children riding their new bikes. "O.T. and me, we fell out," Hosey confided. "He don't like me bein' here, with his sister. I reckon he'll ast me to go."

"Why would he?"

"Hazel married a no-count sumbitch. Mean as a snake. He finally up and left her after years of runnin' around. I stepped in to help." His face flushed and took on a happy glow. "I've loved her since I was a boy. Turns out she loved me too."

"Well," Sivvy said warmly, "that's real sweet."

"We're gon' get marrit, just as soon as she's free and we can get a license," Hosey said. "O.T. ain't gonna like it, though. Well, if you'll excuse me now, ma'am." He pushed his chair back and stood up. "I'm gonna head to bed. I'll see ya in the mornin'. Nice meetin ya—again."

"Thank you, Hosey," Sivvy said with a smile. Hosey disappeared down the hall and Sivvy was left alone at the kitchen table. She could hear the rise and fall of Hazel and O.T.'s voices outside and didn't want to disturb them, so she washed the dishes and put everything away in the cabinet, then set herself to sweeping the floor. She was looking for a dustpan when Hazel and O.T. finally came back in.

"Why, Sivvy," Hazel exclaimed, "you didn't have to clean my kitchen!"

"It was no trouble, marm."

"Lord, gal, don't call me marm. I feel old enough as it is." Hazel patted Sivvy's shoulder. "I 'preciate you doin' that. I made you up the bed in the kids' room. The little ones can sleep in the living room for now. My fool brother can sleep with 'em."

"Miss Hazel, I put a little something by for you, in that little frog tin you keep on the windowsill," Sivvy said, suddenly shy. "Ain't much. Just a little something for a thank you."

"Now, Sivvy, I done tol' you—" O.T. began.

"And I told *you*," Sivvy said, scowling at O.T. "I want to help. Now just hush and let me do it."

"I sure do thank you, Sivvy," Hazel said with a dip of her head. "She sure learned how to handle you quick," she declared over her shoulder to O.T. as she left for her bed. He hid his smile in his hand.

"I reckon she knows where I came from?" Sivvy asked tentatively, when she was gone.

"She already kinda knew, on account of Walt," O.T. answered. "I just filled in a few details. You ain't got to worry. My sister is stern, but she ain't the judgin' type. And she's happy to have you."

"I don't want to be in anybody's hair."

"Yer not. We're glad you're here," he insisted. "All of us."

"You remind me of Clayton," Sivvy replied. "Just as kind and selfless."

"I ain't selfless. No, ma'am," O.T. protested with a laugh. "I been selfish all my life. Hazel, Betty Lou, Walt, and even Hosey done more for me than I ever did for myself. I made some mistakes, and I want to get right, is all. I want to help you the way folks is always helped me. I feel like we understand each other."

"I rankin we do," Sivvy agreed softly.

"I'm gonna go tuck my young'uns in," O.T. said. "I missed the little hooligans. I'll sleep on the floor with them. Fact is I could sleep outside in the field with no trouble, I'm so tired."

"Goodnight, O.T.," she said softly, touching him lightly on the arm. Her heart felt like to burst, so she didn't wait for his reply, only turned and padded off to the spare bedroom, where Hazel had made up the double bed with a beautiful rainbow-colored afghan that lay atop a fluffy white quilt. Sivvy thought, as she undressed, that this warm, love-filled home reminded her of her parents' house on the ridge. The moment her head hit the pillow, she fell into a sound and restful sleep.

When she woke the next morning, she rolled over and smiled. O.T. had let himself into the room, and now slept stretched out on the floor next to her bed.

Sivvy held Belle on her hip, watching O.T. and Hosey plow. The two men worked silently, rapidly turning over the earth in long dark mounds. Tom had left the garden in a shambles, and Hazel had been too run off her feet to tend to it. If she didn't have a crop come harvest time, she might get turned out, and all of them along with her. So she'd enlisted O.T. and Hosey to help her prepare the fields for planting. Sivvy knew nothing about cotton farming, so she'd offered to help with the children instead.

Hazel had left for Misrus Maybelle's to get her hair curled, and Ginny had gone with her. Apparently there was a boy in town whom Ginny needed to "break it off with." Sivvy felt sorry for the poor boy, whoever he was, because Ginny had the makings of a fine young lady. Whoever failed to win her hand would be all the sorrier for it. Hazel had initially refused the outing, protesting that there was too much to do around the house, but Sivvy had insisted, whispering in Hazel's ear, "Just think how pretty you'll look for your fella." The pink that appeared in Hazel's cheeks said it all.

Sivvy just didn't understand O.T. Lawrence. He referred to himself as a drunk and a scoundrel, but since they'd arrived in Five Forks he'd been working his fingers to the bone, staying in the fields till well after dark, clearing the garden, chopping firewood, and fixing boards and shingles around the house. Every night he collapsed onto the floor of their makeshift bedroom and was asleep before he even shut his eyes, but only after taking the time to read his children a bedtime story. As for what had transpired between O.T. and Hosey, Sivvy knew very little, but despite the silence there was love there, too; plain as the nose on his face. Sivvy reckoned for all his talking, O.T. Lawrence was something else altogether from what he claimed.

Sivvy's cheeks flushed when she thought of how she yearned to have just a spot of time alone with O.T., and how disappointed she felt every night when he immediately fell asleep, curled on the floor. She recalled the warm tenderness of that night at the Stew & Que, in front of the wood burning stove, and felt a fierce pang of missing him even when he was right here.

He ain't yer husband, she reminded herself, shifting Belle on her hip. *He ain't even yer beau. You ain't got to be in love with the man, and he ain't got to love you. Remember, get yer heart wrapped up in things, and you'll suffer for it.*

"Can I go play in the sandbox with Owen Jr., Miss Silvy?" Belle asked.

"You sure can. Just see that you don't get your dress dirty. When you done playin', shake the sand out of it affore you come into the house."

"Yes'm."

"And don't run off. Stay just there at the sandbox where I can see you."

"Yes'm," the girl shouted again, running toward her brother.

Belle and Owen Jr. were dear children. They reminded her of her own childhood, when she'd been doted on as the baby in the family, just as Belle was now. When O.T. had told her, to her shock and surprise, that she had a younger sister by the name of Nona-Lee, her heart had soared. Mama must have been near to fifty when Nona-Lee was born.

Sivvy found that her mama was a constant presence in her mind. Ten years or more she'd spent polishing that stone of hate toward her family, but that was done now. The blame lay squarely with Billy Hargrove, and she vowed that his spectre would haunt her no more. Now that Sivvy had relinquished her bitterness, she found herself curious as to how her home had gone on without her. She yearned to see her parents, the little sister she'd never known, her nephew now grown up, and dear Harvey.

Sivvy sat on the porch steps and picked up her embroidery. Belle had mentioned that her mother, Betty Lou, had been a talented seamstress who made neat sack dresses, pretty curtains, and all sorts of things. Sivvy remembered her a little—her light blonde hair, blue eyes, and creamy skin. Betty Lou had possessed the smooth sort of confidence that Sivvy had never had, a way of coolly looking at folks and seeing right into them. The type of woman who was good at everything, did for all, and who was deeply loved by those who meant the most to her. But she had died all the same. She had died, and O.T. would always love her.

Sivvy stabbed a needle into the cloth and set to work on little orange leaves. She hoped she had enough thread—the orange and red were both almost gone, but she had plenty of brown, borrowed from Hazel. After half an hour, Sivvy stretched and looked up from her work. O.T. and Hosey were coming in from the field, both coated in sweat and red dirt. Belle and Owen Jr. were still playing in the sandbox and pouring water from a bucket into the pit to make sand castles. Their clothes, stained red with Georgia clay, were ruined, and Sivvy hoped Hazel wouldn't be angry. Rising to her feet, Sivvy shoved her embroidery into her apron pocket.

"Get you boys a cold drink?" she asked as O.T. and Hosey approached.

"Much obliged, Miss Sivvy," Hosey said wearily.

"Both of y'all wash up affore you come in," Sivvy replied with a smile. "You're head to toe in filth and I'll have to answer to Hazel if you dirty up her floors." With a swish of her skirts, she went inside to fetch some tea, but not before catching a queer, stunned look on O.T.'s face.

By the time she had returned, O.T. and Hosey had washed their hands and were stripping off their coveralls. Sivvy averted her gaze, to give them both privacy, though she doubted if either of them cared whether or not she saw them in their shorts. Folks all wore the same thin white shorts under their clothes, and everybody was too skinny in them, since nobody had anything to eat anymore.

Hosey held out a plug of chew to O.T., who hesitated before taking it. "I ain't had a plug since I left, practically," he said by way of explanation, to himself more than anyone else. "Hey, Sivvy. I reckon one day this week I'm gon' go have a look-see at my ol' place next door. You wanna come?"

"Ain't somebody livin' there?" she asked.

"Naw," O.T. said, shaking his head. "The bank's got new tenants, but Hazel said they ain't moved in yet. Thought I'd see it one more time before they do."

"Okay," she said, "If'n you rankin it's awright."

"They ain't nobody out there," he assured her. "And anyway, I know the best places to hide." He grinned, and Sivvy couldn't help but grin back.

Two days later, Sivvy and O.T stood together at the edge of the woods. Sivvy wore a flannel coat of Hazel's but O.T. had waved off the coat she had brought for him to wear against the pre-dawn chill that suggested rain.

"It ain't gonna rain. It's just the early mornin' light trickin' you," he'd said. "I ain't cold, nohow."

He was the stubbornest man she'd ever met, Sivvy was sure of that. She looked at him expectantly, and he put out his hand-rolled cigarette, grinding it into the dewy grass, and smiled at her. "Awright then, Miss Impatient. Let's go."

O.T. led her down a path carpeted with fragrant needles and fringed by thick pines. Breathing deeply of the damp, woodsy smell, Sivvy sighed with happiness. O.T. led the way, silent now as he cut at overhanging branches with his hoe.

"They're buried there, you know," Hazel had told Sivvy. "Walt and Betty Lou. They're both buried on the property. He ain't been back to see 'em since it happened."

"You awright, O.T.?" Sivvy called to the back of his head.

"Fine," he said shortly, without turning.

Sivvy had not told O.T., but the day before, she'd written home to her ma and pa. She couldn't stay in Five Forks forever, resting on the hospitality of O.T. and his family. Living on scraps of charity was no life at all, and besides, O.T. had his own life to live. It was time to go home. Staring at the back of O.T.'s head as he led her through the wet woods, Sivvy memorized the way his dark blond hair tangled beneath his threadbare cap, knowing that before long she'd have to say goodbye.

They passed a dilapidated woodshed, filled with rotting logs, and a gnarled tree with a split trunk. From the woods a rocky riverbed emerged where a narrow thread of clay-red water formed a stagnant puddle.

"This used to be much wider," O.T. explained. "There were falls and everythin', not half a mile thataway. Now it's all just dirt."

Sivvy glanced around the property, noting the sturdy barn, the patchy front yard, and the green expanse of empty cowfields. Her eyes fell on a large tree with beautiful leaves to the right of the house.

"O.T.!" Sivvy exclaimed, "Is that the tree where—"

"Yeah, that's the one." His voice was flat and joyless, and Sivvy cursed herself for momentarily forgetting what Hazel had told her.

"Did you want to pay yer respects?" Sivvy asked tentatively, wishing she could melt into the ground.

"I might sit a spell." O.T. settled himself on a large rock, staring out at what had once been the water.

"Are you awright?"

"I'm fine," he snapped, before drawing a sharp breath, "Sorry, Sivvy. I didn't mean it."

"No, I'm sorry, O.T.," she replied, a lump in her throat.

"It ain't yer fault. I asked you to come out here. I just cain't go near it. Why don't you go on, have a look-see? I know you loved that tree." He smiled at her. "I don't mind."

Instead, she sat down beside him, placing a hand lightly on his arm. She noticed a monarch butterfly flitting around on the breeze. She hadn't seen one in so long she'd almost forgotten the beautiful rusty-orange color, the intricate black marks. It flitted by once more and was gone, no doubt off to shelter from the oncoming rain.

"I druther stay with you," she said. "Unless you want a bit of privacy."

"No," he said. "I like having you here."

"I'm awful sorry," she said, giving his arm a squeeze. "I know how hard this is."

He leaned close to her, his voice quiet. "Want to know the worst thing?"

"What's that, hon?" Sivvy immediately blushed, but O.T. didn't seem to notice the endearment.

"I'm right glad I lost this place. I don't think I could continue to live here without 'em. Couldn't stand to look at that goddamn tree or this damn dried-up creek. I'm glad it ain't mine no more. That's terrible, ain't it?"

"No," she said. "I wouldn't want it, either."

O.T. let out a ragged sigh of relief and looked down at the ground. Then he looked at her. "I reckon you're wanting to hear my story, since I forced yours out of you." He gave her a wary smile, and his eyes were full of sudden tears.

"Not if you don't want to tell it," she said.

"If I start blubberin', are you gonna call me yaller?"

"I'll pretend I don't even see," she said with a smile.

"Then I reckon I'll tell it." He took a deep breath and began to speak, his voice so low she had to crane toward him to hear. "But I hope this'll be the first and last time."

CHAPTER TWENTY-SEVEN

To O.T.'s surprise, he got through most of his story all right. Sivvy sat beside him silently, giving him strength with her quiet grace. He'd thought he could get through it without crying, but when he started in about smashing his banjo against the tree, he dropped his head in his hands, openly weeping.

He felt Sivvy's arms encircle his waist, her sweater soft, her skin sweet-smelling, and his heart swelled with something unidentifiable.

"The truth is I'm scared all the time," he admitted. "Scared of what's going to happen, of who or what I'm gonna lose next. I'll never see my brother again, and my young'uns will never get another hug from their mama. And I don't know what to do with all that, Sivvy. I'm supposed to be a man, ain't I? So why cain't I bear up?"

Sivvy, not knowing how best to comfort him, gave his arm another squeeze.

"Why cain't I be strong like you?" he demanded. "Why can't I get *over* it?"

"Hush up," she said in a soft, scolding voice, low in his ear. "I won't hear none of that talk." He felt her lips, gentle on his temple. "Grief ain't a hurdle to jump over the once't, and you punishing yerself ain't gonna bring 'em back neither. It's awright to be scared and to feel pain. You gotta allow yerself that, and then you can start to heal."

"You's a smart woman," he said hoarsely. "You know that?"

"You just go on and finish yer story." Her voice was a sweet whisper. "I'll hold you tight."

So he told her the rest. He told her all of it until he got to the parts he could not remember, the parts that had been clouded by drink. Then he stopped and took a deep breath.

"Sivvy, I...." He wiped at his eyes, at his nose. "There's one more thing. I shouldn't say this to you, but I just got to say it somewhere. I feel so guilty, and it's been eatin' me alive. I keep studyin' on it."

"What is it, O.T.?"

343

"I made love to Betty Lou the morning before she died. Not even twenty-four hours before." He shook his head. "What you said to me, about how you thought the sin was on you? How yer sin killed yer boy? I feel like that. My brother was out there dyin' and I was busy doin'—" he broke off, gathered himself, and then continued. "My lust killed 'em both, Sivvy."

"Don't go soundin' like my sorry-ass uncle," Sivvy said softly, turning his face toward hers. "Betty Lou was your *wife*, hon. It's not as though you knew she'd take sick. Y'all was comfortin' one another. Why, that's natural. Ain't no sin." Her eyes, bright and sure, steadied him. "Anyhow, I think that's a nice thing. You know…one last time."

"I just feel like…."

"I know what you feel," Sivvy said. "I been up and down that road. But O.T., I just don't believe that love could ever be a sin. I don't guess I never did, though I tried to convince myself it was."

"After I'd found out Betty Lou had passed, I just got drunk, and laid on our bed. I could smell her on me still, Sivvy. She had this real distinct smell, of sweet powder and roses. I couldn't bear to wash it off 'cause I knew I would never smell it again," O.T. finished hoarsely, tears streaming down his cheeks.

"It's awright." Sivvy held him tight. "You ain't to blame, not a bit."

"Ain't that disgusting, though, and sinful?"

"No, it ain't."

O.T. wiped at his cheeks, embarrassed. "How do we go on with so much pain, Sivvy?"

"I wish I could tell you, O.T.," she answered, her hand resting on the back of his neck. "All this time I was hopin' you could teach *me* that."

O.T. laughed. "You're done for then, if you're bankin' on me. I ain't got nothin' to offer no damn body, least of all advice."

"That ain't true," Sivvy said softly.

O.T. stared into her foxfire-green eyes, flooded with the sensation that he'd finally stopped spinning wildly and had somehow clicked into place again. He forced himself to look away. "Christ," O.T. muttered, his face wet with tears. "I could use a fuckin' drink."

Sivvy looked alarmed, and he quickly added, "I won't. I done good so far, Sivvy. I swanny I have." He realized he'd used a mountain word, and they both smiled at each other. "I coulda got some white lightnin' any day of the week, and I ain't got none."

"Who from?" she asked curiously.

"Hosey," he said, surprised. "You ain't figgered him out yet? He's a bootlegger, an' all."

"That right?"

"Yeah," he replied. "Trades with yer kin, in fact, or did."

"You mean to tell me that Hosey is running my own family's white lightnin' and I been living in the same house these weeks and never knowed it?"

"It appears thataway."

"He offered me some," she said, "but I said no."

"Keep sayin' no," he advised her. "Family business or not, that stuff is the devil. Ain't nothin' but trouble."

"I know," Sivvy said softly. "But surely that can't be why you hate Hosey so much?"

"I don't hate him," O.T. said quietly. "Just disappointed. His deddy was a drunk who killed himself and here is Hosey, sellin' shine, followin' in those same footsteps. And now he's shackin' up with my sister, livin' in sin. It ain't gonna be long before tongues are waggin' about that." He sighed. "I jus' wish he woulda done somethin' more worthwhile, other than runnin' hooch to drunkards. Chrissake, he had my own *brother* out there helpin' him—"

Sivvy fixed him with an odd smile. "You're a hypocrite, O.T."

He was startled. "How's that?"

"You judgin' on Hosey, fallin' out with him because he's sellin' hooch, tryin' to make a livin'. Lord knows we got to make one somehow or we'll all starve to death. You gonna sit there and judge him for sellin' the very stuff you been drinkin'? And tellin' me what a low profession it is, knowin' my own family—"

"Hey, Sivvy, I din't mean no disrespect—"

"You keep sayin' that you just want to get right, be a good man. You think quittin' drinkin' will do the trick. Well, okay, that's a start. But here's what I rankin: you already a good man, O.T., where it counts, but you don't believe it. You wanna start believin' it, you need to start in here." She put a hand on his chest, over his heart, then tapped his temple with a finger. "And in *here*. Quit judgin'. Yer brother was helpin' to make money to give *you* and your fambly. Hosey, too. Anybody can see how much he cares for all y'all."

O.T. wanted to argue, but he found he had no words. Her face was hot and flushed and irritatingly pretty.

"I rankin the truth is it's easier to be mad at him than to be mad at yerself. You cut him out, you ain't gotta look no deeper. But your anger ain't got nothin' to do with Hosey, not really. I rankin you already forgave him, but you just bein' stubborn. You ain't mad that *he*'s not a better man, you mad 'cause you think *you* ain't."

O.T.'s mouth dropped open. "Shoot, Sivvy," he said. "Is my ass smokin'? You burned my damn house *down*. Shoot, take it easy!"

Sivvy smiled wanly, a little astounded at her own gall. "It just seemed like—"

"I get you very well, thank you, miss." He threw up his hands in mock surrender. "I ain't never gon' say another word against Hosey Brown in *yer* hearin', no sirree. Damn." He shook his head, feeling as though a bucket of icy water had been tipped over him. O.T. seized her hand and gave it a squeeze, then pulled her to her feet. "Reckon you want to go have a look around now? Now that I'm done feelin' sorry for myself?"

"I s'pose," she sighed in mock weariness, but her eyes danced. O.T. let her walk ahead of him, and as he watched her jaunty shoulders lead the way, black hair streaming in the wind, it occurred to him that he would be heartbroken when she finally left. He almost hoped, maybe, that she wouldn't.

They were halfway across the yard when a large drop of rain fell, followed by another. "Hell," O.T. cursed. "I guess you was right. Here comes the rain."

"You want to run for the house?" she asked.

He shook his head. "I wish we could, 'cause I'd like to show it to you, but it's boarded up. We'd just be stuck on the porch." As he spoke, the drizzle gave way to sheets of pelting, cold rain. "Let's just head on back!" O.T. yelled, pulling her along. They ran into the woods, where the thick pines offered some shelter. Water streamed off the back of O.T.'s hat, and Sivvy's clothes stuck to her body, her drenched skirt making running hard. She held tightly to O.T.'s hand but still managed to trip and fall into the dirt, pulling him down with her. He fell to one knee, slipping and sliding in the mud.

"You clumsy woman!" he yelled, laughing. "Let's take shelter in the woodshed till this lets up. It's half a mile back to Hazel's and we're already soaked."

In the woodshed, Sivvy found a seat on a thick log and took off her cardigan, which was now soggy with rain, and set it to the side. The rain hit the little sagging tin roof over the shed, tinkling like the high notes of a piano, and she tucked her knees into her arms, trying to get warm. "I told you it was gonna rain, you rascal," she said with a laugh.

"I don't listen so good," he said, grinning.

"You're tellin' me."

"You recognized the tree back there in the yard," he said with a sudden mischievousness. "Do you recognize that one over there?" Through the rain, he gestured toward the tree with the split trunk. She stared at it for a moment before blushing to the roots of her hair.

"Oh, Lord," she said in mock despair. "My days of teenage sinnin', when the world was a simpler place." She remembered all too well the kiss she'd shared under that tree. Lord, she'd only been fourteen then! It seemed like a lifetime ago. Someone else's lifetime.

"I got a confession to make," O.T. admitted. "I reckon I ought to come clean."

"I'm listenin'."

"That night, by that tree...yer date with my brother..." His Adam's apple bobbed nervously in his throat, and Sivvy waited patiently, trying not to smile.

"Yeah?"

"That weren't my brother," he said. "Walt had a fit of nerves right before and sent me on the date instead. It was me that met you out here. It was me that kissed you."

Sivvy stared at him for a moment, looking into his gray eyes, fringed by dark lashes, enjoying the way his hair fell in a shock over his forehead. She drew it out a little, savoring the delicious look of him sitting there vulnerable, looking so much like the boy he had been. "Why, O.T.," she said finally, leaning a little toward him, so he could see the smile that lit up her own face. "I do believe I already knew that."

His mouth fell open for the second time that morning. "What? You knew? How?"

"You have a birthmark," she leaned forward, touching a mark just below his right ear, "right here." She smiled. "Walt didn't have one. I noticed it when we was in the car. I was sittin' behind you. Y'all was totally identical, 'cept for that one thing."

"Shoot fire, woman, ain't nobody ever been able to tell us apart, and you know us *one day....*" O.T. trailed off, surprised.

"I got good at memorizing faces, at noticin' things about folks," she said. "It was a skill I had once upon a time."

"So you knew. You knew it was me all along, and you kissed me anyway."

"So I did," she said softly.

He shook his head. "Shoot, woman. I...shoot."

"I reckon that was *why* I kissed you," Sivvy said archly, shooting him a devilish look. "I liked Walt; he was a real sweet boy. But you had an edge to ya. I had an edge myself, so I guess that spoke to me. And yer eyes was a little more wild. They still are, right there, lookin' at me now." She stared into them. "I always was a sucker for a boy with nice eyes."

O.T. reached over and grabbed a handful of her hair, caressing it between his fingers, rivulets of water running down his arm. "So much rain," he said softly. "You're soaked through."

Then he was running his wet, calloused hands down the length of her arms, rough and slippery. She shivered, her eyes locked on his, suddenly unable to breathe. His hands went from her shoulders all the way down to her lap, where they found her hands, and her fingers locked with his, clammy and fumbling, his eyes never leaving hers.

And he kissed her.

His lips met hers and she was instantly filled with a sense of something *familiar*. Tentative, hungry, sweet. His lips were softer than they looked, and his stubble brushed like sandpaper against her chin. Even as she kissed him back, her lips melting into his, her tongue darting, tasting him, she was screaming inside her head—*Don't do this! It always ends in ashes!*— but her body was not listening, her heart was not listening.

She pulled him to her, and he gave way, his body falling into her, pulling her down onto the ground, which was wet and red with mud. *My clothes will never be clean, so long as he's around, but who cares about such things?* His hands were on her face, still wet from the rain, stroking her cheeks, down her neck, and threading through her hair, making her sigh with pleasure.

"I been tryin' so hard not to do this," he murmured into her ear, his hot breath making her entire body erupt with sensation. She leaned into him, wanting to feel his lips on her skin. "I tried everything I could. I slept on the floor, I stayed out in the fields, I tried to keep my distance—"

"I'm no good at this," Sivvy confessed, pulling at his shirt so she could feel his bare skin beneath her hands. "Everyone I love—"

"And everyone I love," he finished for her, kissing her collarbone. "We shouldn't do it."

"No," she agreed, her voice melting into a whisper. "We shouldn't."

But neither of them stopped. It seemed to go on forever, the kiss, and Sivvy let herself sink into the dirt, and into O.T., his mouth delicious, his hands wet with rain, yet so warm. His hands made their way up her bare legs now, and trailed across as she gave a low moan, her eyes squeezed tightly shut. He tickled her unexpectedly, lips still locked to hers, making her giggle, and he bit off her laugh with his teeth, tugging gently at her lips. She felt the nearness of him against her, trying to hold back, and she wanted him something fierce. His voice was a low growl in his throat, his breathing heavy and fast in her ear.

Then O.T. stilled, his head buried in her neck. Sivvy put her arms around him, trying to hold him in place, but he pulled himself up and looked down at her, dazed. "The rain stopped," he said hoarsely.

"Yes."

O.T. stared at her, breathing heavily, his gray eyes boring into hers. "I guess I...lost control there," he said finally.

"Yes," she repeated, sitting up in the puddled dirt, not sure what else to say.

"We shouldn't do this," he said again. "It was my fault. I apologize for bein' improper."

Sivvy laughed, though she was near tears. "O.T., save yer apologies. Ain't either of us kids no more. We're grown."

He smiled a little. "So we are." He offered her a hand and helped her up, then swept his wet hair back, before it promptly fell again across his brow. He placed a chaste kiss on her cheek and smiled. "Let's get ourselves out of the rain then, Miss Sivvy."

A few days later, the letter came. Sivvy recognized the paper—powder blue with pink roses—which had sat in the same parlor bureau drawer her whole life. Excusing herself, Sivvy slit the envelope open with eager fingers, imagining she could smell home, wafting from the envelope.

My precious Savilia—Sivvy—

Well, I guess he gone and done it. I knew when I met that young man that he would bring you back to me somehow. God bless his sweet heart. Yes, yes, of course we want you to come back home, fast as your little legs can carry you. Franklin—who is writing this letter for me— will drive the truck down to fetch you, so expect him sometime around the first of the month. I cannot wait to hold my daughter in my arms after all these years. I'll save all the rest of talking for later, but you be sure to give O.T. a kiss from me. You're the answer to all my prayers these fifteen years, and he's the blessing on them.

Your mama,

Julie-Anne Hargrove

Sivvy wiped at the tears in her eyes, joy and sadness filling her in equal measure.

O.T. had avoided her since their rain-drenched kiss in the woods and had taken up a pallet on the floor with his children, without so much as a word. He couldn't avoid her completely, though, not in such a little house. She saw him at the breakfast table, passed him a dozen times throughout the day, sat with him and the others at supper. He was sweet enough to her that nobody took notice of his coolness, but detached enough that she noticed the distance. She didn't know if he regretted the kiss, or if he was just trying to make things easy, but it hardly mattered. Clearly he did not love her. She tried to swallow the pain she felt, to forget her own feelings. Perhaps it was for the best—they both seemed to be doomed, after all. She just wished it didn't hurt so bad to look at the man.

She folded up her letter and stuck it into her apron pocket, calculating the date in her head. She had just over a week before Franklin arrived to collect her. She'd need to tell O.T. soon and preferred to do so alone. Tomorrow was Sunday church, and Sivvy decided she would skip the service and ask O.T. to stay behind. She would tell him of her plans to leave and thank him for all that he had done for her. She owed her life to him, and for that, she'd always be thankful for O.T. Lawrence, even if he didn't love her. And that was the truth.

Chapter Twenty-Eight

By Sunday morning, Sivvy had managed to tell everyone she was leaving, everyone except for O.T. She'd whispered the news to Ginny and Hazel while washing dinner dishes the night before, had confided in Hosey on the porch when she'd been out stargazing, unable to sleep, and had told the children just before they'd left for Sunday school. Sivvy was both heartened and upset when everyone had protested.

Hazel had said, "But you're part of our family now. Why on earth would you go back?"

"I have family there who I miss," Sivvy had explained. "And it's my home."

"But this is your home, too," Hazel had protested. "Are you saying you'll never come back?"

"O.T. needs shut of me. He disrupted his whole life to help me, bring me here. We always said I'd go on back eventually. I've already overstayed."

"I don't think he sees it that way—" Ginny had interjected, but Sivvy insisted. The two women exchanged a look, but neither protested again.

"We'll miss you," Ginny had said finally, downcast.

Hosey—who had reached a tentative peace with O.T. in a private meeting in the barn days before—had wished her well, clapped her on the back and told her she was a fool to go.

Sivvy hadn't been prepared for the children's reception of the news. She'd expected little fanfare and was shocked when both Belle and Owen Jr. had started to cry. "Please don't go, Miss Silvy," Belle had wailed, clutching her leg, while Owen Jr. stuck out his lower lip and wiped at the tears welling in his eyes. Sivvy hadn't counted on how much she would miss O.T.'s children.

She couldn't study on that now, though. As she sat in the kitchen, a cup of chicory in front of her, her stomach rumbling with hunger—she'd skipped breakfast, along with the other adults—watching the sunlight stream through the window, she pushed away the pain in her heart. O.T. had a life to get on with, and they were *his* kids, not hers. She was just getting in the way, and it was far beyond time to move on.

She wished he'd hurry up and come in, though. When she'd asked him the night before to skip church, he'd agreed easily enough, but looked wary. He probably thought she was going to make some kind of move on him, and was figuring on how to turn her down. Well, she wasn't planning to do that. *Sivvy Hargrove might be a lot of things—a harlot, a trollop, even, but she ain't about to put her hands on a man that don't want her,* she thought to herself, bringing the steaming cup to her mouth. *Even if I want him so bad I can taste it.*

As if on cue, O.T. entered the kitchen, rubbing his eyes. He was dressed, but only just. His shirt was untucked, his hair stuck up in tufts, and he wore socks on his feet. "Any more of that?" he asked, gesturing to the chicory.

"Yeah. I'll pour you a cup."

"Much obliged." He sat at the table, yawning. "It's just as well you asked me to stay in today. I overslept and would've missed church anyhow."

Sivvy placed a hot cup in front of him and sat back down at the table.

"You hungry?" she asked. "There ain't much left, but the children left a bite or two...."

"Naw," he said. "I'm awright for now."

They both spoke at the same time.

She: "I wanted to see you alone so I could tell you—"

He: "So what did you ask me to stay for—"

Sivvy laughed nervously and gestured for him to go on. He shook his head, and she realized he was just as nervous as she. This was a silly business. Two grown folks and they couldn't even have a conversation between them.

"I have a gift for you, O.T.," Sivvy said, standing up and going to the porch. She brought back a tall package, wrapped in furniture paper and tied with a thick blue bow.

"What's this?"

"Open it and see for yourself."

Frowning, O.T. pushed his chair back, set the object on his lap, and began to gingerly unwrap it. When he'd pulled the paper off, he sat for a moment, stunned.

"You made this?" he asked.

"I did," she answered, beaming. "My pa taught me how when I was small. Our whole family knows how to make 'em."

"I knew that," he said, without looking up. The corner of his mouth twitched as he touched the banjo lightly with his right hand.

"I found some pretty yellow gourds hanging in the shed, and I ast Hosey if I could have one. I've been working steady on it for a few days." Sivvy smiled. "Those there strings are made of horsehair. I had to ask all around town to find some. What you said, O.T., 'bout destroyin' yer banjo—well, it broke my heart. It's time you played again, but with a new banjo. I hope you like it."

O.T. stared at the banjo in his lap, his mouth set in a hard line. Sivvy began to feel nervous. When he'd told her about bashing his banjo against the sassafras tree, she'd immediately thought to make him another. Had she overstepped? Swallowing hard, Sivvy pulled a small packet from her apron pocket and unfolded it in her hands. Too late to back out now. "If you're going to play the banjo, you need a strap." She held out a narrow cut of fabric and waited. He looked at the object in her extended hands, seeing, then recognizing. Sivvy had embroidered the guitar strap with tiny sassafras trees, the leaves the signature orange-red of autumn, which had been painstaking work, mixing two colors and overlapping stitches. It had been almost beyond her skill, and she'd stayed up late nights, trying to get it perfect. She had bound it to the back of a piece of soft brown leather with braided ends.

O.T. looked up at her, his expression unreadable, his eyes flashing.

"This way…no matter where you go, yer tree, it's always with you. Do you like it?' Sivvy waited for him to speak, to say anything at all, but the drawn-out silence in the kitchen was a gulf that yawned between them. "I thought it would be a nice gift," she added helplessly. "I'm sorry if I…if I did wrong. Oh, please, O.T., don't be angry. I'm sorry."

O.T. glanced down at the banjo again and back at her. His voice was soft in the morning light. "Angry…no, Sivvy. I'm not angry." He took the guitar strap from her hand and she realized his voice was choked with tears. "It's only…this is the nicest thing anyone has ever given me. And…well, I ain't been too nice to you these past few days."

"That's awright," Sivvy whispered, choking back her own tears. "The banjo is a parting gift. I had a letter from my mama. She wants me to come home to the ridge, and she's sending Franklin to fetch me."

O.T. blinked, staring at her. "When?"

"In 'bout two days, I rankin."

O.T. placed the strap on the table. "Well. Well, then."

"I'm ever so grateful for all you done for me, O.T.," Sivvy rushed to say. "I'll never be able to repay all you done. But it is time. Time to get outta yer hair and let you get back to yer life. And I need to see my family. It's been so long."

"Yes." O.T. nodded. "Yeah. Accorse. I understand, Sivvy."

She fell silent, and so did he. She wasn't sure why she had been so nervous before. Or why she was still so nervous now. Or why her heart had fallen a little when he hadn't protested her departure. A tear rolled down her cheek, and she stood up, wiping it away hastily. "Does yer sister's Victrola work?"

"I dunno," he said, looking up from the banjo strap, as if waking from a dream. "I reckon it does. It used to. Why?"

"I wanted to hear a little music, is all," she said, walking into the parlor to switch it on. It took a few moments to power up, and the sound that came out was tinny and full of static, but she could hear the unmistakable ditty "Little Log Cabin on the Lane." Fiddlin' John Carson, it was, if she knew her pickers right. She hadn't heard a true mountain fiddle in years.

Retrieving the fiddle that had been Walt's from the corner stand, she settled on a chair by the window, wondering if she still knew how to play. She hadn't touched a fiddle since she was a girl, and she had refused to do so for Uncle Billy, despite his urging. Too much of her soul was wrapped up in fiddling to allow for trivial display. Sivvy liked singing well enough, but the fiddle was her lifeblood. She bent her chin to the instrument, held her bow gently to the strings, and began to play. She knew the song by heart; everybody in the mountains, shoot, everybody in Georgia knew it. She played it fast and frenzied, the way her pa and brothers and everyone back home played, like a spinning top that had just been let loose on the floor.

She wasn't even aware that O.T. had sat down beside her and was strumming his new banjo until she hit the third verse, when she glanced up and saw him singing along, his hands caressing the instrument like a lover, his fingers plucking the strings as though they had been made for him, which indeed they had. Sivvy sang along with him, hitting the high notes as he hit the low ones, their instruments drowning out the radio, like their own little Sunday morning bluegrass band.

When they finished, Sivvy stood up, sweating and breathing hard, and put the fiddle back on the corner stand where it belonged. Seeing the banjo in his lap made her heart swell. "You play so well," she said sincerely.

"Me? What about you!" He smiled. "What a secret to keep, Sivvy. Between the fiddle and that voice, you ought to be making recordin's."

"Oh, shush up," she said, embarrassed.

"It's true," he said. "I ain't never heard something so beautiful."

Sivvy flushed with pleasure. The song that came on next was a Louis Armstrong number that she'd once heard Rob Gum, the Singin' Cook, belt out over pans of barbecue, on some long-ago evening.

"Care to dance with an ol' farmer? Since you wouldn't back in Milledgeville?"

She looked at him, surprised. "Right here in the living room?"

"Hate to waste a good song," he said.

Sivvy stepped into his arms, and he tightened them around her, his mouth near her ear. She rested her head on his shoulder. Louis's gruff voice sang of a love departed, of regrets and missed chances, and Sivvy felt her eyes well up with tears as she swayed in O.T.'s warm embrace, an embrace that felt so much like home. She realized after a time that O.T. had stopped dancing and, pulling back, was shocked to see tears streaming down his cheeks.

"O.T., what on earth's wrong?"

"Sivvy," he said desperately. "Don't you know?"

"I don't reckon so." She was confused and alarmed.

"I ain't never been a very good liar. My whole life people saw right through me. And you see through me even more than most folks." He looked into her eyes, his expression desperate. "Can't you see it? Sivvy, I'm in love with you."

Sivvy thought her knees might buckle. "But you said...out in the woodshed...you said that—"

"I know what I said." He took her hands in his own. "I was trying to convince myself I didn't love you, because I felt like I was betrayin' my wife. And I din't want to take away yer choices by bein' the selfish man I've always been. I thought it would be better to let you go, better for us all. But now I can't bear the thought.

"I can't pretend no more. I can't keep tiptoein' around, tryin' to pretend I don't see you. Tryin' to pretend I don't love you. Do you want to know something crazy? The truth is I been in love with you since before I ever stepped foot in Milledgeville. How could I not be, hearin' tell of you through the eyes of so many? There's no other woman as strong or as brave as you. Then, once I'd seen you, I knew there were none so pretty, either. But I was affeared." He cupped her face in his hand. "I thought there was no way, after all you been through, that you want to be saddled down with some poor drunk farmer, without a pot to piss in. But when I saw that banjo—"

Sivvy didn't let him finish, but pulled his face down to her own and pressed her lips against his, her limbs turning to liquid. He picked her up effortlessly and carried her down the hall, into the bedroom, and over to the bed.

He took his time, slowly undressing her there. He pulled her light cotton shift over her head, laughing as it caught in her long black hair. He ran his hands over the curves of her body, feeling her heartbeat, tracing the warmth of her skin through the thin fabric of her shift. His eyes were closed, and Sivvy smiled to herself, enjoying his expression as he used his hands to see. O.T. Lawrence, her dirty-blond cotton farmer who kissed with his eyes closed. She thought she would burst from the sweetness.

He moved so achingly slowly, she almost couldn't stand it. Impatient, she unbuttoned his cotton shirt and moved to his belt buckle, savoring the groan he emitted when her hands grazed his navel. His mouth met hers again, and she pulled him closer, wanting to feel his entire weight on her body, as close as two people could be. Her hands ran through his hair, reveling in its thick softness, memorizing every part of him, learning his language.

Finally her shift was off, and so were his clothes, and they lay together, skin to skin, both breathing fast. Sivvy leaned into him, gently biting his bottom lip with her teeth. He groaned and pulled her on top of him.

"You did that once before," he said, finally opening his eyes to look at her, his hands moving up her body like electric fire.

"I did? When?"

"At the butterfly spot," he whispered. She moved her hips against his in a rhythmic circle, smiling at the blissful expression on his face. "All those years ago. You bit my lip then, too."

"Did you like it?" she asked teasingly.

"I was scandalized," he answered, his hands locked on her hips. "I wasn't but a boy then, and you just about gave me a stroke." He chuckled. "Yes, I liked it."

"You ain't seen scandal, my handsome man, till you've skipped Sunday morning service to do *this.*" She lowered herself upon him, feeling his delicious warmth inside her, and began to move with agonizing slowness.

"I always was a sinner, deep down in my heart." He kissed her again, and her world exploded into joyful lightness.

"So what do you say?" he asked as they lay in bed, lazy and naked, watching the sun stream through the windows. "Can I share yer bed now?"

"I never said you couldn't before," she murmured drowsily as she nestled contentedly into his shoulder.

"I just want to spend every minute with you." His hands caressed her back as his lips found her mouth. "Till you leave. I just want to soak up every bit of you that I can. I'm so damn angry at myself for wastin' all this time."

"You weren't ready," she answered. "You needed time. We both did. But let's not waste any more worryin' and frettin'."

"You got yerself a deal, darlin'." O.T. kissed her long and hard, pressing his body against hers.

She laughed into his mouth, her limbs quivering, her blood rushing. "We don't have time."

"We can be fast."

She giggled. "O.T., *no*. The kids—"

"Oh, awright." He sat up in bed, stretched, and threw his legs over. "But I'll be walking around all day, aching for you, woman."

Sivvy felt herself blush. Nobody had ever said anything like that to her before. "O.T.?" She asked hesitantly as she stepped into her shift. "Do you want me to stay?"

O.T., pulling up his trousers, turned to look at her. "What?"

"If you want me to stay, I will."

O.T. crossed the room and scooped her up into his arms again. He planted a kiss on her lips, another on her nose, and one on each of her eyes. "Oh, darlin'. Sweet, wonderful Sivvy. I want you to stay more than anything in the world." He smiled down at her. "You do what yer heart tells you to do," he said. "You've lived enough of yer life for other people. Now it's yer turn. Me, well, I'll keep."

After supper, Sivvy and O.T. sat on the back porch and played their instruments. At first she didn't want to sing, not in front of everybody, but his begging charmed her.

As they played "Little Log Cabin on the Lane," and "Amazing Grace," Belle and Owen Jr. danced a feverish jig that reminded Sivvy of a Scottish dance her pa had taught her years ago. She laughed, finding it hard to concentrate on playing while their little bare feet joyously stamped the dirt. Hazel sat on Hosey's lap in the rocking chair, her head resting on his shoulder, her expression one of delirious happiness.

It was going to be hard to leave them all. Sivvy had been mulling it over in her head all day, considering staying on, now that she knew O.T. loved her. But something was calling her home to the ridge. She felt a powerful need to join her breath with the mountain air and return once again to the place of her birth.

They finished their last song, and O.T. told the children it was time for bed. They protested and wailed, but he held up a hand. "Right now, young'uns. Go brush yer teeth and wash up."

Hazel rose to assist them, but he stopped her. "I got it, sister," he said with a smile. "You and Hosey stay out here and enjoy the evenin'. Just look at all them stars."

Hazel settled back with Hosey, beaming at her brother. "It's nice to see you lookin' well again, O.T." Hosey nodded in agreement. "Nice to have you back."

"Nice to be back." O.T. went into the house, and Sivvy moved to follow.

"You take that fiddle with you, Sivvy," Hazel called.

"Beg pardon?" Sivvy stopped in the doorway.

"When you go back to the mountains. Take that fiddle with you. You play it so well, and it deserves to be played."

"I couldn't!" she exclaimed. "It was Walt's. I know O.T. would want to keep it."

"Walt would have wanted you to have it," Hazel insisted. "He would have loved the thought. I reckon O.T. will agree. The look on his face when you was playin'…I ain't ever seen a man so smitten."

"Not since we was boys," Hosey agreed, and Sivvy flushed.

"I…thank you," Sivvy murmured, touched.

Joining O.T. in the living room, she plopped herself down on one of the sleeping pallets next to Belle, Owen Jr, and Ginny. A fire burned in the grate and O.T. was telling a tall tale about a fairy princess, a warthog, and a cotton gin haunted by the ghost of a crazy old man. All the children had fallen asleep long before O.T.'s story was over, but he and Sivvy remained there for a long time, warm and cozy, staring into each other's eyes over the sleeping bodies of his children.

CHAPTER TWENTY-NINE

Sivvy sleepily threw out an arm, expecting to pull O.T. close for warmth, but his side of the bed was empty. Opening her eyes, she smiled at the open window, breathing in the chilly morning breeze that wafted in. She'd told O.T. how trapped she'd felt in Milledgeville, how the tiny windows could not be opened, and he'd made sure to open them for her every morning since.

Pulling on her dressing gown and house slippers, Sivvy made her way to the kitchen, which smelled of frying meat and cornbread. Her stomach rumbled sadly as she saw nothing but empty plates beside the sink. Hosey had traded a case of white lightning for a couple of rations of side meat, and the children had been eagerly awaiting meat with breakfast for a full twenty-four hours. She did not begrudge them that they hadn't saved her any. There was no sign of life in the house; everyone had gone outside, it seemed. Most likely getting a start on field work, or doing washing, or other chores. She felt lazy and slatternly, that she'd been allowed to sleep in.

"Mornin', sunshine," Hazel said brightly from behind. Sivvy turned to see her decked out in her washing apron, her hair pulled back in a bun and covered by a scarf. "Sleep well?"

"I did," Sivvy answered, "but I wish y'all would've woke me. I like to pull my weight."

"Oh, bah." Hazel waved a hand. "You need yer sleep. We got plenty of hands to do work around here. Besides," she said, with a twinkle in her eye. "We don't want to get used to you."

"Oh. Awright," Sivvy said with a sigh.

"Oh, don't get yer shift in a knot, I was just teasin'." Hazel held out a cloth-covered parcel. "The kids tore up that meat affore I even had it out of the skillet, but I sopped up a piece of cornbread in the grease. Sit you down and have a bite, and I'll make you a cup o' tea."

"You didn't have to save me none."

"Gotta eat, don't you?" Hazel set to making tea. "You and my brother both too skinny by a measure."

"Where is O.T.?"

"I don't rightly know, hon. Hosey's out in the fields. Owen Jr. and Ginny's with him. Belle is helpin' me pound the washin'. You should see her out there, tryin' to whack out the stains. That paddle is bigger'n her." She grinned as she sat at the table, passing Sivvy a steaming cup of tea. "O.T. took off about an hour or so ago, but don't fret about it. I'm sure he'll be back before you've et up the crumbs. He's fine."

Sivvy ate the cornbread and drank her tea while Hazel watched her quietly. Finally, she said, "He loves you, you know." She gave Sivvy's hand a squeeze.

"I know," Sivvy said. "I don't know why he does, but I know it."

"I thought he'd never…not after…." Hazel wiped at her own eyes. "My heart like to broke for him. I prayed he'd find happiness again. Somebody to talk to, to hold in the night. To give him a little hope. We all need that."

"Yes," Sivvy agreed, with a wobbly smile. "We do."

"You're the answer to my prayers." Her eyes misted and she stood. "Well, I better git my hind-end out to help Belle before she pushes all them clothes into a mudhole." She gave Sivvy's hand another squeeze and left the kitchen, before either of them could see the other cry.

Sivvy was still sitting at the table, running the last dregs of cold tea through her teeth, when she heard the crunch of tires on the gravel drive. Rinsing her cup in the sink, Sivvy made her way toward the bedroom to get dressed when, glancing out the window, she stopped in her tracks. She knew that face. She was out the door, down the porch steps, and in her mama's embrace in seconds. Julie-Anne's arms held tight around Sivvy's waist, her gray hair soft on Sivvy's cheek.

"Mama, mama." Sivvy buried her face in her mama's shoulder, tears pouring from her eyes, wetting her ma's shirt, breathing deeply of her familiar scent of wood smoke and sassafras.

"My Savilia. My baby." Julie-Anne's voice was full of tears, too. "I didn't know that I'd ever see you again."

Pulling away, Sivvy took a good long look at her mother's face, twenty years older, but still kind, smiling, and framed by wrinkles.

"And how is my gal?" Julie-Anne asked her, her voice thick.

"I'm awright, Mama," Sivvy said. "I'm awright now."

"I just cain't believe it's you," Ma said. "When I got yer letter I...I didn't dare to hope."

"Here I am," Sivvy said with a smile. "It's me." Then, aware of the presence of another beside her, she turned and exclaimed, "Why, is that you, little Frank?"

Her nephew, Franklin Hargrove, Rebecca's youngest, had grown into a strapping young man who was at least six foot five if he was anything. Taller than any man she'd ever clapped eyes on, he had gleaming dark brown hair, almost black, and ice blue eyes. He barely resembled the shy little boy who had crept into bed with her all those years ago, afraid of thunderstorms.

"Yes'm,' he said shyly. "It's mighty good to see you, aunt. I'm glad you remember me."

"Remember you! Shoot. Of course I remember you!" Standing on tiptoe, Sivvy pulled Franklin into a stiff hug, and he laughed. She had to stand on tiptoe to wrap her arms around his neck. "Franklin Hargrove, as I live and breathe. You wasn't but a little thing toddlin' around when I left."

"Yes'm, that's right."

"Don't you dare call me ma'am again."

"Awright, Aunt Sivvy."

Wanting to share her happiness with O.T., Sivvy looked around the yard, but there was still no sign of him. Hazel and Hosey stood behind her, though, and Belle and Owen Jr. studiously looked at their feet, curious but trying not to be overtly nosy. Ginny stood on the porch, her eyes wide and excited. Sivvy could see the blush on her cheeks from the driveway. Her gaze went from Ginny to Franklin and back. Then she smiled.

"Mama, Frank...these here are Hazel—that's Mr. O.T.'s sister—and her enfianced, Mr. Hosey Brown." Hazel's face went pink with pleasure. "And here is Mr. O.T.,'s children, Belle and Owen Jr. And there on the porch is Miss Genevieve, though I understand y'all met already?"

"We sure did," Franklin answered with a grin. Ginny was making her way down the porch steps to him, and his eyes never left her.

"The young will do what the young do," Hazel said with a spirited laugh, coming forward and taking hold of Julie-Anne's arm. "Let's us go inside and get a glass of somethin' cold. Y'all been out early this mornin' to make the journey. I ain't got much to offer but what's ours is yours."

"So long as I got me a little snuff and a cup o' tea, I'm happy as a lark," Julie-Anne said, still unable to tear her gaze away from her daughter.

Sivvy followed them into the kitchen, shaking her head in disbelief. Mama was here to take her home. She could scarce believe it.

But where in the Devil was O.T.?

O.T. was running the risk of being caught on the property, but he didn't care. What were they going to do, slap cuffs on him and throw him in the county jail? They wouldn't waste time on him, probably just set him on the path back to Hazel's with a warning. The house loomed over his shoulder, and as he sat on his usual rock with his fishing pole he tried to avoid the sight of it. The fish weren't biting, and he figured he'd best be getting back soon. He was very aware of everything around him, the spirits working in tandem to speak: the flutter of the wind in the trees, the gentle lapping of the creek, the trilling birdsong from the woods, and the fluttering monarch butterflies dancing on the breeze. Today they were orange, but he knew he would see a blue one soon enough. He no longer thought of his poor mama when he saw them, no longer pictured a scaly red rash on her tender face; no, when he saw the butterflies he thought of Walt, and that soggy green piece of grass he used to keep between his teeth—green like the slick algae on the creek rocks, like the foxfire up on the ridge. And when he thought of Mama, he remembered her dishwater blonde hair, braided and cascading down her back, and the sweet smile she always had for her boys.

For so long, remembering those he had lost brought him physical pain. He had numbed the pain with alcohol, which had worked for a time, but he knew now that he had grown beyond such folly. His recollections of his lost loved ones still *hurt,* but he found he could breathe again. He could think of Betty Lou's ice-blue eyes and sassy expression, as he did now, without wanting to plunge a knife into his chest. He could remember rubbing Walt's back, easing his brother to sleep, without needing to wail in anguish. He could remember Ma and Pop, solid and alive, loving and protective, and feel more comfort than pain. Remembering them all was bittersweet, but he understood now that he had passed some threshold, and for the first time, it was more sweet than it was bitter.

O.T. sat on his rock, thinking, remembering, until the sun had crept down into the corner of the sky. Finally he stood up, brushed off his pants and started back toward his sister's house. He stopped for a moment, looking a final time at his house, the place where he'd begun his life, had brought his new wife and raised his children. The house where he'd lost it all. It was perfect to him, standing there in the looming dusk, a small shack built with two-by-fours and shingle, a modest place, a beginning place. It seemed fitting to him that he'd begin again under the shadow of this house. It seemed to groan in the darkening sky, to speak to him, and give him permission.

He walked quickly up to the yard and paused under the tree. They were there. He felt them. He spoke a few words, low and soft, and put his hand on the tree, feeling the deep grooves his ax had made. He was sorry for it, but it didn't matter. The tree would keep on, long after he had ceased to be, nourished by the bones of those he had loved the most. He picked an orange leaf from the branch over his head, closed his eyes, and popped it into his mouth. He chewed it to a messy pulp as he walked back to Hazel's house.

O.T. climbed the porch steps just as supper was being laid out on the table. He was overjoyed to see Julie-Anne, enveloping her in a hug as she squeezed him right back. When he shook hands with Franklin, Sivvy could see the genuine affection there, too. After they had eaten, they gathered on the porch to play a little bluegrass before bed, Franklin and O.T. on the banjo and Sivvy on the fiddle. After all had been bedded down, weary with the excitement of the day, Sivvy and O.T. were finally alone.

"You mad at me, darlin'?" he asked as he undressed. "You scarce said two words all evenin'."

"Where were you all day, O.T.?" she asked, frustrated. "I didn't see you till dinnertime, and I was worrit."

He looked surprised. "Why, Sivvy, I didn't mean to disappear on you all day, I just lost track of time."

"Well, as it turns out this is our last day together, and you was gone," she retorted. "I didn't know if you was dead in a ditch, or run off and left me or off with some other woman or what." She pouted. "Scared the dickens out of me."

He burst out laughing. "Aw, hell, Sivvy. I ain't got the energy for no other woman. You done ruint me. Truth is I was next door." He kissed her forehead. "I wanted to go and see the place one more time. Just sit awhile and be there…with them."

"Oh," she said softly. "I can understand that…it's only…our last day…."

"Speakin' of which," he started. "I been studyin' on that." He guided her over to the bed, and sat down, looking into her eyes. "That's why I was gone so long. I had to think, sit with it all, and come to a decision."

Sivvy was confused. "About what?"

"I know what I aim to do. If you…if you'll have me, Savilia Hargrove, I reckon I'd like to go with you to Rock Creek."

Her mouth fell open. "You want to go with me? You mean to live?"

"Yes."

"But…" She was shocked. "This is yer home…Yer sister is here, Hosey, the land—"

"It ain't my land no more," he said. "Got to get that in my head, don't I? Black Tuesday mighta been the start of it all, but I really lost it when Walt and Betty Lou died and I picked up that bottle." He took her hands in his. "I can live here with my sister, watching her raise my kids, or I can go live my life. Start over. Be with the woman I love." His gray eyes were solemn. "If you'll have me."

"What about the kids?"

"They'll come too. New start for all of us." He smiled at her. "A family. If you want one."

Her breath came out in a whoosh.

"If I want one, he asks. Shoot!" Her eyes filled with tears. "Of course, I'll have you, you son of a gun."

He kissed her, his lips soft and warm. She pulled him on top of her, and they fumbled with their clothes, the exhaustion of the day forgotten.

Breathless, she whispered in his ear, "What kind of woman would I be if I said no?"

He laughed. "A smart one, I reckon."

He leaned over her, her arms around his neck, hands entwined in his hair, and blew out the candle. In the darkness, as their lips met again, neither noticed the pretty blue butterfly alight on the windowsill. It lingered for a moment, then flew away on a breeze into the night.

EPILOGUE

Lunch break between classes was only a half hour, so Ginny raced down the steps, her satchel bouncing behind her. She nearly twisted her ankle leaping from the last step, she was in such a hurry. One of the headmistresses, Missus Playmaker, called out sternly, "You mustn't run on the lawn, Miss Lawrence."

"Yes'm, sorry, Mistress Playmaker," Ginny called, slowing to a fast walk. Having crossed the courtyard, she paused a moment to smooth her wind-whipped hair. Franklin was leaning up against the fence by the university entrance, as usual, his dark, thick hair gleaming in the sun. He held his brown trilby hat in one hand and turned as she approached, holding out a bouquet of magnolias with a smile. The newspaper under his arm caught her eye. '*GUBERNATORIAL RACE HEATS UP FOR WILD MAN OF SUGAR CREEK.*' She made a face. Uncle Walt would have been mad as a setting hen over that. That blasted Talmadge.

"Hey, Ginny-Lou," he said with a grin.

She took the flowers, leaning up to give him a kiss on the cheek. "Hey, Franky," she said, butterflies aflutter in her belly.

Frank had proposed to Ginny the moment she'd turned sixteen, and she figured he'd move on to some other girl if she didn't act quick. After all, he was a fine-looking man from a respected family, and any girl with a lick of sense would appreciate such a man. But to her surprise and delight, when she'd told Frank of her plans to attend college first, he'd been proud.

"I'll wait for you," he'd said. He came down to Athens whenever he had time, despite the two-hour drive and the cost of gas. Ginny was counting the days until graduation, when she'd be a real teacher, and would become Franklin's wife.

It struck her as funny that she would be joining Franklin's kin, and Sivvy had joined hers. Switching families, as it were. Their two families had become one sizeable happy family. Hazel and Hosey, married the previous year, had recently moved to Rock Creek. Hosey and O.T. were opening open a juke joint around the corner from Harvey's store. The Butterfly Spot would serve a little food, a little spirits, and a lot of music. There was already a buzz, with folks waiting all over the Blue Ridge mountains to come to hear a ditty and do some clogging. Ginny was very proud.

"Sorry I'm late," she said breathlessly. "Class ran over."

"Ain't no trouble. I was almost late myself. Harvey had me run into Farmer's Hardware for him, since I was out thisaway."

"Where did you get the magnolias?" she asked, inhaling them deeply.

"Big ol' tree, passed it on my way," he said. "I couldn't help myself."

"Magnolias are my favorite," she breathed.

"Rankin you told me that once," he said. "You gonna have 'em at our weddin'?"

"Accorse." She grinned at him. "If I decide to marry you, that is."

"You meet some handsomer boy here at school?"

"All these city boys," she said dismissively. "No thanks to that. They all got corncobs rammed up their backsides."

"Lucky for me," he said with a hoot of laughter. "Though I 'spect I do need to tell yer deddy about the way you talk nowadays. It ain't proper atall."

She gave him a mock slap, and he leered at her. "Hey, Ginny-Lou. Can you get a weekend pass from your dorm mistress, darlin'?"

"What for?"

"I'm supposed to fetch you back to the ridge. The juke joint is openin' tonight, and there's some folks be put out as all hell if Ginny-Lou ain't there. There's a gal, fresh from Milledgeville, set to sing a ditty and play the fiddle."

"Already?" she squealed with delight. "Oh, Frank, that's swell! Are you gonna play, too?"

"I aim to, but only if my gal is there in the audience." He gave her a flirty smile and she dissolved like sugar in coffee.

"What reason will I give? Tellin' her my boyfriend's playin' a juke joint might not fly."

"I ain't sure," he replied, tipping his hat conspiratorially. "But I reckon me and you can figger it out under that magnolia tree, if you're agreeable to come sit with a feller for a spell."

"Oh, yes." She took his arm as they walked toward the courtyard. "I'm very agreeable, hadn't you noticed?"

O.T. sat in the back of the room, his fingers drumming the little wooden table beside his bottle of Nehi Grape, staring at the vision on the stage he'd built. She was a tiny thing, petite and bird-like, with feathery black hair that came down to the middle of her back. It was pushed back from her forehead and behind her ears, revealing her bright green eyes as she cradled the fiddle under her chin. She began to play. The fiddle sang, quietly at first, then swelling into a wail that was both cheerful and sad, light and dark. Time seemed to stop as she played. She finished her solo, then pulled the microphone to herself with shaking hands; she had not sung in public in a long time. She had practiced every night in bed for two solid weeks. O.T.'s heart swelled with love as he watched her, his eyes damp.

A chair was pulled back and Harvey sat down beside O.T., clutching a beer in his hand. "Congrats, O.T. This place is mighty fine."

Sivvy finished her song and exited the stage in a flurry before the crowd had a chance to start clapping. O.T. knew she wouldn't want all that fanfare; it embarrassed her. Ginny was sitting in the corner opposite him, her eyes on Franklin, who was set to go on next. O.T. himself would play his banjo later with Nate and the boys for the finale.

O.T. turned to Harvey. "Cain't believe it still," he said ruefully. "That we pulled this off."

"To realizin' dreams." Harvey held out his glass. O.T. picked up his bottle and clinked it.

"To realizin' dreams," he agreed. "Of all kinds."

Sivvy joined them, her cheeks flushed, her face dewy with sweat. She looked pleased. "I'm surprised I didn't pass out cold, I was so nervous," she muttered. "Did I sound awright?"

"Sounded just like an angel," O.T. answered, leaning in to kiss her on the lips. "I'm real proud of you, honey."

"It'll get easier," she said, with a shy smile, "once I get used to it. And once I can get that Billy Rev out of my head. I can't help but think of him when I sing, you know."

"Aww, just forget him, Sivvy," Harvey said easily.

Sivvy grabbed O.T.'s bottle and took a swig. "Easier said than done." She shivered, hugging her shawl around her thin shoulders. "Despite how perfect everythin' has been, I can't help but worry he's gonna creep up behind one evenin' and drag me off into the night." She leaned into O.T. for comfort. "He might just come back here one day."

"And he might not, at that," Harvey said, draining his beer. He looked at O.T. and grinned. "Y'all don't snitch to Lucy Dee that I had two of these." He got up from the table and walked to the bar.

"Say, darlin'—" O.T. murmured into his wife's hair, "Speakin' of the old bastard, when was the last time you saw him, the last time he visited?"

Her voice was dreamy. "Oh, dern, I can scarce remember. He came real regular for the longest time, every couple of months. But by the time you busted me out, O.T., I hadn't seen him in a year or more. I kept thinkin' he'd show up any day, but he never did."

O.T. wondered why that was. The Billy Rev he had known would never have lost interest in plaguing Sivvy. He glanced over to the bar, where Harvey was paying for his beer. As he pulled his worn leather wallet from his pocket, O.T. caught sight of a faded white handkerchief, embellished with purple. Harvey felt O.T.'s gaze on him and turned around, lifting his bottle with another self-effacing grin.

Bring Sivvy back to the ridge, O.T., and I might add more to the tale one day, Harvey had told him when O.T. had shown up on the ridge long ago, asking questions. At their table O.T. and Sivvy sat with their heads turned into each other, a picture of cozy intimacy, filling Harvey with warmth. He might be riding the wave of love and pride tonight, but Harvey had come to know his friend well, and O.T., like a coon dog who had the scent, would not stop till he followed that trail to the end.

It was time to tell the two of them, and soon.

Harvey sat his empty mug on the bar, waving the bartender away when he offered another. Lucy Dee griped like the dickens when he came home with booze on his breath, and he aimed to put a little lovin' on her tonight.

He snuck out into the cooling night for a cigarette, the crisp, cold mountain air cradling him like a lover. Building the store had been his dream, but he'd also spent years cultivating the land, planting his garden, and clearing out trails throughout the woods, thick with skinny pines and sassafras. Harvey liked nothing better than to take off for walks among those trees in the moonlight, whenever the mood struck him. Those trails, those trees, were a place he could go to disappear, fly into the night, deposit his pain, and come home whole again.

The woods held his secrets, so they did.

He took a drag on the home-rolled cigarette, allowing his mind to wander to one patch of woods in particular, two miles away from the house, deep in a gully, the ground damp and musty, untouched by the sun. Below the rotting logs and moist leaves, a man slept, in what Harvey hoped was an uneasy sleep.

The night Billy Rev came to Harvey, crowing over poor Sivvy's fate, he'd given Harvey quite a shock. After the man had taken his leave, Harvey had gone out into the night, into his woods, to walk the trails and clear his head. He'd taken his shotgun with him—you never went into the woods at dark without protection; you might run into a rabid bobcat or wolf mama protecting her cubs—furiously wiping tears from his cheeks. Poor, poor Sivvy, he'd thought. What that man had done to that gal. It just wasn't right.

He'd walked for a long time, crying, before he began to tire. He sat down on the damp ground and leaned against a tree, reminded of the last time he'd sat, weary and heartsick, against a similar tree—a moment that had ended with a kiss. He heard the snap of a twig behind him and jumped to his feet, cocking his shotgun and scanning the darkness for the critter that had interrupted his reverie. He had no cause to shoot an innocent animal, and he hoped it'd leave him in peace and be on its way. But his heart almost stopped when a man emerged from behind the trees; outfitted in a white suit and shiny black shoes, now caked with dirt from the long walk, was Billy Rev. For the first time, Harvey saw him without his hat, the moonlight gleaming on his nearly bald scalp, a wisp of whitish hair plastered to his temple.

"You followed me, you rascal," Harvey seethed, raising the gun. "How dare you set foot on my property."

"Wanted to see where you was goin'," Billy Rev said easily, taking a step closer. "Why don't you put that thing down, son?"

"I ain't yer son." Harvey stayed where he was. "What in the devil do you want?"

"I wanted to say before—preachin' ain't what it used to be," Billy Rev answered conversationally, "'specially without you an' Sivvy. Folks ain't hospitable no more, ain't so interested in the word of the Lord. They's too hungry." He took another step closer. "Been studyin' on retirement. I got remarried some time ago, did you hear? Got a fambly to take care of now." He smiled. "You know all about that, huh? You done good for yourself, boy, real good. I can see that with my own eyes."

"What do you *want*, Billy?" Harvey's hand rested on the trigger.

"Seems a man doing so good for himself don't want to mess that up. Wouldn't want Lucy Dee and the young'uns, and yer cousins the Hargroves besides, knowin' about all that business what happened with Sivvy," Billy Rev said, brushing his hand on his lapel. "I thought you might be feelin' generous toward an ol' man, might be willin' to pay for my continuin' silence. In the spirit of appreciation, for old time's sake...."

"Appreciation? For all you *done* for me?" Harvey spat, the gun heavy in his arms. "You tryin' to bribe me, there, *Reverend?*"

"Ain't no bribe, no sirree," Billy Rev said, unruffled. "Let's call it a business deal. A few bucks and I'm gone. You'll never see my face again, that I can guarantee."

"That's a mighty fine prospect, Billy Rev," Harvey said, his smile hidden in shadow. "Only thing is that's a guarantee I can get without paying one thin dime."

Billy Rev didn't have time to register his meaning before the gun went off. The force of it threw Harvey backward, the bullet blasting a large hole in Billy Rev's forehead, knocking him off his feet, where he landed in the damp dirt with his hand over his heart—theatrical to the last.

"That was for Sivvy, you no-count piece of shit," Harvey said, lowering his gun. "Take *that* to the bank."

O.T. couldn't stop his feet tapping; the frenzied music swirling around the little juke joint filled him with joy. He caught Hosey's eye from across the room and grinned. The jagged pieces of his life were coming back together, finally, and he was almost whole.

Harvey reappeared at their table, pushing his smokes in his pocket. "I know I'm gonna miss the finale, but I got to go. Next time we'll get someone to watch the young'uns and me and Lucy Dee'll stay till the end," he promised. "Say, y'all busy tomorry?"

"Not that I can think," O.T. answered. "Why?"

"Come on to the house, both of y'all. Bring the kids. Lucy Dee's cookin' a mess of ribs. We ain't had y'all to dinner proper since you been back on the ridge." Harvey smiled, his teeth bright and white. "After supper, I might take y'all for a turn around my land. I got a right pretty piece I wanna show you an' Sivvy. Much as you love trees and all, you just gotta see it."

"Why sure, Harvey. Reckon we'd like that."

"Oh, you will, Mr. Lawrence. You will." Harvey slapped him on the back and, with an enigmatic smile, was gone.

O.T. stared after him for a moment, puzzled, then pulled his wife closer to him, kissing her hair. "I love you, Savilia Hargrove Lawrence."

"I love you, too, Owen Terrell Lawrence."

As his beloved rested the weight of her head on his shoulder, O.T. found that all other weights had lifted away.

ACKNOWLEDGMENTS

My deepest appreciation goes to:

Jennifer Babineau, Alice Hayes, Lauren Emily Whalen and Elizabeth Tankard, who read, blurbed, edited, and supported me throughout the drafts of this book. It has been a joy reading and writing with you over the years, and I'm lucky to have your insight, feedback, and best of all, friendship.

My editor, Jaynie Royal, and the Regal House team, for guiding me through the process, answering my millions of questions, and for forcing me to cut words when I just couldn't bear to. Working with you has been a pleasure.

Claire Campbell and Hope For Agoldensummer, R.E.M. and Kevin O'Neil, for your words and your music; the wonderful staff at Harold S. Swindle Library, without whom this book would not exist; Melanie Cossey; Meghan O'Keefe; Cate Short; The Northeast Georgia History Center; the staff at Central State Hospital; Sautee-Nacoochee Center and Museum; The Foxfire Museum & Heritage Center; Tallulah Gorge Museum; NaNoWriMo; Ellen Burke; Ginger Stickney; Crystal Zerbe; Melanie Stodghill; my parents, John and Teresa, for encouraging my dream; my grandparents Clark and Julia Ann (who inspired this book), John, aka "Zach" (from the hymn of Zacchaeus) and Anita; Jon, Chris, Robbie, Dot, and the rest of my wonderful family; finally, Blake and Cal, who I couldn't have done this, or anything, without.

Last, to "Dolly", my ancestor, one of many who fuel my constant quest to find out who and where I came from: of the many ways in which I've imagined your mysterious life, the image I like best is of you, walking among the lush pecan trees at Milledgeville Asylum, a breeze in your hair, finally at peace.